ANNIE GROVES

The District Nurses Make a Wish

HarperCollins*Publishers*

HarperCollins*Publishers* Ltd
The News Building
1 London Bridge Street
London SE1 9GF

www.harpercollins.co.uk

HarperCollinsPublishers
1st Floor, Watermarque Building, Ringsend Road
Dublin 4, Ireland

This paperback edition 2021
1

ISBN: 978-0-00-840242-6

Set in Sabon LT Std by Palimpsest Book Production Limited,
Falkirk, Stirlingshire

Printed and Bound in the UK using 100% Renewable Electricity
at CPI Group (UK) Ltd

MIX
Paper from
responsible sources
FSC™ C007454

District Nurses Make a Wish

About the author

Annie Groves is the pen name of Jenny Shaw. For many years she lived in the East End, and is fascinated by its history.

Annie Groves was originally created by the much-loved writer Penny Halsall, who died in 2011. The stories drew on her own family's history, picked up from listening to her grandmother's stories when she was a child. Jenny Shaw has been a big fan of the wonderful novels by Annie Groves for many years and feels privileged to have been asked to continue her legacy.

To Kate and Teresa, without whom the story
of the nurses would never have been told. And to the
staff of the Queen's Nursing Institute,
for being so welcoming.

CHAPTER ONE

June 1944

It was not often that Superintendent Fiona Dewar opened the front door – someone else usually got there first, because the head of the nurses' home had her office on the first floor of the big double-fronted house, but it just so happened she was at the bottom of the stairs when there was a loud rap.

She took a moment to glance around at the high-ceilinged hallway. Everything was in its place, the brass door handles gleaming, the post tidily stacked on its special shelf so that the many nurses who lived here could easily find any letters. The long, wood-panelled corridor stretched back to the lower ground floor, the door to the canteen standing ajar so that a low buzz of conversation reached her, from nurses between shifts, grabbing the chance of a cup of tea or cocoa.

She knew that each and every one of them deserved it. She was proud of them, her team who had kept

1

going through all the privations that the war had flung at them. Fiona liked to think that she balanced strictness with tolerance when it came to running the place – it was no small thing to ask so many young women to stick to their posts when bombs were dropping – and none had disappointed her.

Wondering who would knock so sharply, she patted her neat auburn hair and went to open up. A young policeman stood on the step and she idly thought he must be new to Dalston, because she knew everyone in the service, as well as every ARP warden and most of the firefighters. Then her common sense returned and it hit her: this could not be good news. For a wild moment she wanted to rewind time, to pretend this hadn't happened, that this young man, almost a boy with his pale face showing signs of spots, was not standing there, waiting to deliver a dreadful message. Then she squared her shoulders, forcing her diminutive frame into readiness to deal with whatever was coming.

'Are . . . are you Superintendent Dewar?' The boy was clearly consumed with nerves and hesitated to say any more.

Fiona knew she must take charge of the situation and asked the question to which she did not want to know the answer. 'Yes,' she said steadily. 'You'd better come in. But first – just tell me who it is.'

The day had started with a telephone call.

Fiona had been reassuring but once she had replaced the receiver she had tutted in frustration. The regular midwife due to attend the woman about to give birth was unavailable because it was all happening two weeks too soon, but babies weren't inclined to fit into nurses' schedules and this child was set on arriving today.

Frowning, she made her way into the big room on the lower ground floor which served as a combined common room and canteen. 'Has anyone seen Bridget?' she asked, glancing around to see which of the nurses were still finishing their breakfasts.

'You've just missed her.' A tall nurse with dark blonde hair in a bun stood up from her table, balancing an empty plate and tea cup in one hand. 'She's only now left for her morning rounds. Can I help?'

Fiona tried not to let her frustration show, realising her accent grew more Scottish the more irritated she became. 'Thank you, Alice, but no. I need someone with specialist midwife training. I know you've delivered babies but I'd prefer to send somebody who has completed the official course.'

The young woman who had been sitting with Alice now looked up. 'Well, I'm trained. I did the course with Bridget, after all. What do you need?'

Fiona smiled but shook her head. 'I know you did. You've been invaluable ever since, Ellen, but if I'm not mistaken it's your day off, as you did extra rounds last weekend. It's important to get your rest. Take advantage of it while you can.'

'Yes, you never know when we're all going to have to pitch in and work around the clock,' said the third nurse at the table. 'What if more of those horrid new bombs fall? You heard about that one near Bethnal Green, didn't you? They say they make a noise and then the sound just disappears and that's how you know it's going to fall on you. Ugh, imagine.' She shuddered, causing waves of her chestnut hair to swing around her face.

'Yes, thank you, Mary, we all heard about that incident,' said Fiona crisply, to put an end to the conversation. 'It doesn't help to speculate. Our job is to deal with whatever situation we are faced with, and this morning that includes finding a replacement for the unavailable midwife down at Victoria Park. What a shame I missed Bridget. Perhaps I can telephone the Tottenham nurses' home – didn't some of them go on the same course as you, Ellen?'

Ellen grinned and her dark hair bounced a little. 'They did, but there's no need, really there isn't.' Her voice still had strong traces of her Dublin background, despite several years of living and nursing in London. 'I don't mind in the slightest. I'll swap today for an extra Friday off, that would be grand. So tell me where this baby's being born and I'll hop on my bike.'

'If you're sure . . .?' Fiona pursed her lips. Despite Ellen's enthusiasm, she had no wish to overtire her charges. They all worked hard enough as it was.

'Think no more of it. I'll go. Let me check my bag's all refilled and then I'll be away.' Ellen stood and brushed the toast crumbs from her skirt. 'Oh, I'd better get changed. But I'll not be a minute.'

Fiona nodded, giving way to the inevitable. 'Ellen Devlin, you are a life saver in more ways than one.

Very well. Here's the address. It's a second child for the lady in question and we don't anticipate any complications, other than it coming earlier than expected.'

Ellen smiled in acknowledgement. 'Then I'll be back here in no time. See you later, Alice, Mary. You're to come to the cinema with me and Bridget this evening, don't forget. *Meet Me in St Louis* is on at the Odeon, you'll not want to miss that.' She gave them a quick wave and was off through the big door to the corridor. It had been propped open to let in a breeze as already the day was warm.

'Excellent, that's one less thing to worry about,' said Fiona, relieved now the decision had been made. 'Enjoy your film if I don't see you beforehand, girls.'

Ellen groaned as her bike chain came loose. It was the third time this week, although she'd tried to mend it after every shift. Sighing, she admitted to herself that she just didn't have the knack. She hopped off the old bike and gave in, pushing it along in the gutter while she walked along the edge of the white-painted kerb. The clanking noise was horrible but she gritted her teeth, knowing she couldn't abandon it. Bikes were valuable, even ones as decrepit as this. There simply weren't the materials available to make many new ones.

She remembered Mary's comments from breakfast as she passed the narrow terraced houses. Some of them had their windows open in the June warmth and she could hear wireless programmes blaring out.

Trust Mary to voice the fear they'd all felt when they'd heard the news about the new sort of bomb down at Bethnal Green. Ellen preferred not to worry about what she couldn't change, and besides, there were all manner of rumours flying about. Mary might have got it wrong. It wouldn't be the first time. Ellen was very fond of her colleague but Mary did have a tendency to speak whatever was on her mind and think about it afterwards. Perhaps it was coming from a more privileged background that did it.

Ellen shook her head to dismiss the idea. She'd be better off planning ahead for their evening out. Bridget had chosen the film, starring Judy Garland, and it sounded as if it would cheer them all up. If they left early they could go to the fish and chip shop first. She could wear her new pale green bolero – that was smart, and warm enough if the evening turned cool later on. She had a green polka dot scarf some-where, if only she could find it.

Through a gap in the row of houses, she caught sight of the big trees marking the edge of Victoria Park. Not far to go now, then. Ellen turned her bike at the next corner, vaguely wondering what wireless show could be playing such a strange noise. She was distracted, though, by the memory of lending the scarf to one of the other nurses. Not Bridget, her best friend, who always immediately handed back whatever she borrowed. Mary? No, she had plenty of her own. What could that noise be? She'd never heard anything like it. But then, just as she began to consider it seri-ously, it stopped, and she caught the familiar sounds of the Glenn Miller Orchestra drifting from the next house along. In fact, that must be the start of the street she was looking for. She idly tapped her fingers on the handlebars in time to the music, humming along a little as she searched for the right number on the front doors with their faded paint. Good job that awful noise had gone.

Ellen had just propped the battered bike against her patient's doorpost when the realisation hit her. A dreadful noise that came to a sudden end. She turned cold, the hairs on her arms bristling. It wasn't something on the wireless. It must be what they'd meant . . . But she never finished the thought.

Now the young policeman hesitated on the topmost of the wide stone steps which led up to the immaculate navy front door. He nervously cleared his throat. 'It's – it's about Nurse Devlin,' he said.

Fiona just managed to stop herself from crying out.

'You'd better tell me everything,' she said after a moment in which she summoned every ounce of self-control that she possessed. 'Come up to my office.'

Meekly the policeman followed her up the broad stairs with their polished wooden banister, all the woodwork gleaming and smelling slightly of beeswax. Wartime or not, standards were never allowed to slip at Victory Walk. Fiona and her deputy firmly believed that a sense of cleanliness and order was good for morale, as well as enforcing the level of hygiene that every nurse had to rigorously adhere to.

The office was equally well-ordered, even if every

shelf was laden with files and medical textbooks. Fiona slipped behind the big wooden desk and clasped her hands as she sat. 'Well, then. Sit yourself down, that's right. Spell it out to me with as much detail as you have.'

The young man gulped and pulled at the sleeves of his over-large uniform jacket before replying, 'It was one of those new bombs, what they're calling doodle-bugs. It was a direct hit so they couldn't have got out even if there had been a proper warning.'

Fiona shut her eyes briefly and nodded. 'So the mother and baby . . .'

'Nobody survived. They couldn't have,' the policeman said succinctly. 'I believe there was an older child and he was with his granny, so at least someone from the family made it. We'll have to let you know about arrangements and all that.'

'I see.' Fiona knew that Ellen had family back in Ireland and that she was a practising Catholic. No doubt they would want a full funeral. Perhaps Bridget would know; the two nurses had trained together and come to England together, had shared the little flat next door that served as an annexe to the big house and they were as thick as thieves. Bridget would have to be told before anyone else . . .

Rising, Fiona thanked the policeman and showed him out. As he left, she intercepted one of the younger nurses who was climbing the stairs.

'Ruby, could you find Bridget and send her to my office? And please, don't tell anybody what you're doing or speak about it afterwards. I'll explain later.'

Ruby's dark eyes widened but she didn't argue. 'Of course. I'll go right away.'

Fiona went back upstairs, thankful that Ruby was known to be extremely discreet and there would be no gossip until she could break the dreadful news to Ellen's best friend. Of all the tough jobs she had to perform as superintendent, this was the worst. The lamps shone brightly on the worn carpet and there was a hum of chatter from the bedrooms upstairs as well as the canteen below, as if it was just another day in the busy home. Yet they had now suffered the saddest loss, one of their close-knit team in the line of duty.

But it wouldn't do to become upset. Fiona could not allow herself that luxury.

Even while she gathered herself for the distressing conversation, she registered that she had another pressing problem: Victory Walk was now a nurse short – and a highly experienced one, trained in midwifery. They would need a replacement, as soon as they could possibly find one.

CHAPTER TWO

Iris Hawke hesitated as she opened her battered leather suitcase. It had once belonged to her father, who had used it when he had had to travel for his work; that now seemed like a lifetime ago. Iris had never had cause to pack it before. She had rarely gone far from her home town – while she was younger there had never been the need. Then, when she had become an independent woman, practising her chosen career of nursing, the war had come along and put paid to any ideas she might have had of glamorous foreign holidays. Not that anybody she knew ever went on such things. She'd seen them in the cinema – that was as close as she had come.

She sat down on her creaking bed, with its sagging mattress and scratchy quilt, wondering for the hundredth time if she was doing the right thing. It was such a big leap – from rural Devon to the East End of London. She was accustomed to the green hills, the open moorland, the wild weather, the sound of the birds; all of these had been a welcome balm in the past few years. Then there was the fact that everybody knew everyone else. To go where nobody could pick her out in a crowd was at once a terrifying prospect and a relief.

As a district nurse, she had her own tiny bungalow, nestled behind a stone wall for protection from the westerly gales, with a view over the moors, and a bike that she could safely leave outside without anyone threatening to steal it.

'It won't be like that where you're going,' Mrs Bassett, the local shopkeeper, had warned her. 'My nephew went up there – didn't last more than six weeks. Robbers got into his lodgings, took everything but the clothes he stood up in. Horrible place. You'll be back before you know it.'

'Maybe,' Iris had said politely, wondering how much truth there was in the woman's words. She had been known to exaggerate and loved a good gossip.

Well, that was one more reason to go. Iris would never live it down if she backed out now; Mrs Bassett and her cronies would never shut up about it. How they would love to point out her failures as she cycled past them. They wouldn't say anything to her face if she called on them on her rounds, but they would raise their eyebrows and that would be enough. She'd know what was on their minds.

Pushing herself off the old mattress, she returned to the task in hand. It wasn't as if she had much to pack. Most of her clothes were sturdy and serviceable, many of them darned over and over again, and there was little that would count as fancy. It didn't matter.

She wasn't going away to live the high life. She was more likely to need a warm woollen vest than a lacy camisole.

Nursing was nursing, after all. People still had accidents, grew sick, suffered injuries, the same in London as they did in Devon. Babies were born in the same way and mothers needed her help. Iris would never have got the position of district nurse in such a cut-off rural area if she hadn't been able to prove her midwifery skills.

She bit her lip as she folded the one item in her wardrobe that could be described as frivolous. It was a delicate cream frock, its front decorated with piping and pale rosebuds embroidered in silk thread around the neckline and cuffs. She packed it lovingly in old tissue paper, which had faded and grown frayed at the edges.

It had belonged to her mother, but her mother wouldn't be wearing it any more, not after her final stroke. Iris sighed, but knew that deep down it had come as a blessing. Her doughty, strong-minded mother, who had thought nothing of walking on the moors in all weathers, would never have borne the indignity of a long-drawn-out death. All the same, Iris could not bear the idea of remaining here without her. While in some ways they had been too similar, Iris had drawn upon her mother's strength for comfort when she'd needed it most and had never begrudged the time she had spent nursing her when she'd become ill, even though it had been in addition to her actual nursing duties. Now she was left only with memories and they were altogether too painful, every street corner, every outcrop of rocks bringing them flooding back.

It wasn't as if she'd never lived elsewhere. It felt like a long time ago now, when she'd been younger and more optimistic, waving her parents goodbye as she set off for Plymouth, thrilled to be moving into the big hospital after being accepted for training. The world had been at her feet, back then, but the war had changed everything, delivering exhausting hardship but also adventure – before it plunged her into heartbreak. She had turned her back on the bombed-out shell of the city centre and set her sights on becoming the best district nurse this village near her home town had ever known, a demanding role to absorb her and blot out what had happened. When the painful memories plagued her, she could always turn to her mother. However, that comfort had now gone and she could not stand to stay here without her.

It was time to fly the nest again. Here she was, the wrong side of thirty, and with no reason to stay. The new position might have been designed exactly for her: experienced district nurse, trained as a midwife, must be available for immediate start. The notice in the nursing magazine had caught her eye at once. 'Are you ready to take on a new challenge?' It was exactly what she wanted: a total and complete change. Besides, Iris had never shirked a challenge in her life. The transfer had been a formality. They had an urgent vacancy, and she was willing to go, her replacement, a widow whose children had both left home, eager to take up the reins of her former career.

Iris carefully rolled her once-peach dressing gown and fitted it down the side of the case. She'd grown used to having her own bathroom and kitchen; she hoped she would be able to adapt to sharing again. Well, she'd have to.

Victory Walk in Dalston needed her. The question she refused to consider, however, was: did she need them even more?

Alice stared out of her attic window, trying to be calm. She hated being in limbo like this. If there was a problem she liked to work out a way to solve it and then act upon it. That wasn't possible now though.

She had known Joe Banham from the summer before war broke out. To begin with she had found him infuriating, but for most of the time since then she had called him a very special friend. She had been determined it would not be anything more than that – she'd had her heart broken once before when she first trained as a nurse back home in Liverpool, and had had no intention of ever allowing that to happen again. She wouldn't even come close.

Yet, bit by bit, Joe had got under her skin. He knew her better than anybody, shared the same tastes and ideas, didn't laugh at her for always having her head in a book or a newspaper, didn't blame her for not going out dancing like the other nurses and she could tell him anything. Gradually he'd confided in her too – or as much as he could. She knew he was no run-of-the-mill engineer on his ship. Before enlisting in the navy he'd been a post office engineer and he'd become a vital part of the ship's communications team, handling top-secret messages. At least, that was as much as he'd allowed her to piece together.

Alice could work out that the D-day landings must have had clear instructions relayed from naval vessels just offshore, taking messages to and from the command centres back in mainland Britain and the forces on the ground. The trouble was, she didn't know which ship he was on and if it was safe. If *he* was safe.

Just before he'd been summoned back, cutting his brief leave short, they had confessed what had been obvious for a long time, if only they could have admitted it: that they loved each other. Alice knew that what she felt for Joe was of a different order to that which she had known with the young doctor who'd claimed he loved her years ago. This was a full and adult love and Joe had felt the same. He'd asked her to wait for him, knowing that the big onslaught was imminent, and she had promised to let him know the next day. But by then he had been ordered back on duty and had had to set off at once. She had missed him by a few short hours.

Alice had no way of knowing if the letter she had written would have reached him in time. In it, she had told him what she should have said long before: she loved him beyond doubt, she was his, heart and soul. Did he realise that she was on tenterhooks, desperately needing to hear back? She had faith that he wouldn't change his mind, would reply as soon as he was able – as long as he received the letter. Yet in the chaos of D-day, one little envelope could have gone anywhere.

She had no choice but to sit it out. During the daytime there was more than enough to occupy her mind, with so many patients to see to. It was in the evenings that the thoughts assailed her. She told herself not to imagine what might have happened to him, but it was useless. Earlier in the war he'd been on a ship that was attacked and, even though he had tried to downplay the danger, the details that he'd let slip kept flashing into her mind. The screams, the cold water, the injuries . . . No, stop that right now, she told herself, gripping onto the window frame, as the sun set behind the rooftops of East London.

Normally Alice would have confided everything to her best friend Edith but these days, since the birth of her new daughter, Edith had other concerns. Edith had been Alice's constant companion ever since they'd taken their specialist district nurse training together and they'd even met the Banham brothers on the same day. Edith was now married to Harry, the younger one, and had finally hung up her nurse's cloak when she was too heavily pregnant to manage the cumbersome old bikes they all rode on their rounds. Little Teresa had arrived right before D-day and for a while had driven every other worry from their minds, as it had been touch and go whether mother and baby would survive. Survive they did – but Alice felt she couldn't really burden Edie with her anxieties. The

Banham household would be worried enough for their eldest son's safety.

Alice turned away from the little window and began to lay out the clothes she would wear the next day. The uniform dress, in strict utility design, was already showing signs of wear and tear. Still, Alice thought wryly, her patients weren't expecting a fashion show. Just as well.

She could go downstairs and make herself a last cup of something hot, cocoa or that coffee substitute they all did their best to pretend they liked. Then again, the mood was often sombre after Ellen's death. They were still trying to come to terms with it, to accept they'd never hear her merry laugh echoing down the corridor or her gentle teasing for not agreeing about a popular film. It didn't seem possible. The two Irish nurses had become part of the framework, fitting into the home so easily that it beggared belief. Now, everyone was extremely careful what they said in front of Bridget, who had kept working but whose face frequently bore the signs of deep grief. Yet to say nothing did not feel right either.

Alice decided she'd finish her rounds tomorrow and then go and see Edith. No matter what else was happening in the world, that was something to look forward to.

CHAPTER THREE

Oh no, thought Iris. This couldn't be right. She'd only been in London for a couple of hours and already her fingernails were dirty. Her neatly starched cuffs, kept pristine white with Reckitt's Blue, were smudged with soot and her sensible brogues were smeared with dust. This was *not* how she had wished to arrive at her new posting. She'd forgotten what it was like to be in a city, breathing in the smoky air, specks and smuts everywhere, that sensation at the back of your throat of needing to cough all the time, and what a palaver it was to maintain standards of hygiene with all that going on.

She had fortified herself with a pot of tea on arrival at Paddington Station, feeling that she deserved it after such a long journey. The noise there had been over-whelming, everything echoing under the grand ceiling: shouting porters, screaming children, hellos and good-byes from big groups of friends. Uniforms of every service and nationality swarmed before her as she drew back into the shelter of the café wall, away from the concourse. She was used to Plymouth and Exeter stations – it wasn't as if she'd been confined to the tiny rural ones – but this was on an altogether bigger scale.

She could hear her mother's voice in her head: *you should have packed a nice Thermos, then you wouldn't have had to waste your money, or been thirsty on the journey. Only yourself to blame, my girl.*

Still, Iris thought now, as she surveyed her new home, chin up. Another of her mother's favourite phrases. They couldn't expect her to arrive fresh as a daisy after a long and tiring trip. She'd get changed as soon as she was able and she walked with determination up the short path to the wide steps.

Before she could knock at the navy-painted door of the big double-fronted house, a window flew up from the first floor of next door. 'Hello! Are you Iris?' A young woman with very fair skin poked her head out. 'Wait there, I'll be down.' The accent was Irish. Iris had just a moment to register this when the window slammed shut again.

Iris dropped her hand and turned on the spot. A moment later, the neighbouring door flew open and the young woman reappeared. Iris noticed she had a sprinkling of freckles across her nose and her cheeks were rosy from being in the sun.

'Welcome to Victory Walk.' She smiled broadly. 'I'm Bridget. Bridget O'Doyle.' She held out her hand.

'Iris Hawke.' Iris shook hands, wishing hers wasn't so warm from gripping the handrail on the bus that had brought her here.

'Come away in.' Bridget swung open the big door. 'It's awful bright out, isn't it? You'll be wanting to freshen up, no doubt.'

'Oh, yes please!' said Iris fervently. She picked up her suitcase and followed the younger woman into the relative dimness inside, and then upstairs.

'Sorry, it's two flights, into the attics.' Bridget had no difficulty talking and racing up at a swift pace, and Iris was grateful that cycling around the hills of her old patch had kept her fit. She didn't want to appear short of breath, but she couldn't have gone much further at such speed.

'Here you are.' Bridget opened a narrow dark wood door with a flourish. 'This is where you'll be staying. Bathroom's down at the end there. Everyone's out on their afternoon rounds at the moment, but it's my half-day so I said I'd watch out for you. Fiona, she's in charge, said she'd see you in her office before the evening meal – that's next floor down, directly under here.'

'But you came from the house next door?' said Iris, confused. Her eyes were still adjusting to the contrast between the sharp sunlight outside and the shadows inside, and she couldn't make out what the room was like.

'I did,' Bridget agreed. 'My room is there, in the first-floor flat. It's like an overflow to the main place here.' Her smile grew a little strained and her eyes were not as bright as the tone of her voice. 'Well, I'll not keep you. You settle in and I'll be downstairs – the lower ground floor, that's the canteen. Come down for a cup of tea. Or we might push the boat out and find some lemonade, cool you down.' While the young woman was very friendly on the surface, Iris thought that she seemed in a hurry to be off, now that she'd done her duty. Perhaps she had work to catch up on. Reports could build up; heaven knows she was familiar enough with that.

'Right you are. I'll see you down there.' Iris nodded politely and Bridget made off, almost as quickly as she'd appeared.

Well, no time to think about it now, Iris decided as she kicked off her brogues and subsided onto the bed – narrow but perfectly comfortable and not remotely creaky. She would just take a minute to stretch out and then she would find that bathroom. She couldn't stand feeling this grimy any longer . . . but with the warmth of the day and the golden sunlight pouring through the dormer window, within moments Iris was asleep . . .

Noisy chatter drifted through the corridor leading back to the short flight of steps to what must be the canteen. Iris gave herself a shake, mortified at dozing off, but she couldn't deny that she felt the better for it. Now, having had a thorough wash in cold water and with a new, clean frock on, she felt ready to face the world again. She just hoped she hadn't kept Bridget waiting.

'. . . asked about next door,' came the voice with the Irish accent, from the canteen.

'Did you tell her?' asked another voice.

'Well, no. Isn't it enough that she's only just got

here? I thought that it could keep for another day.' Bridget sighed and the sadness in her tone was evident, even from this distance.

Iris paused. There was something she didn't know, something about the flat next door, something that made Bridget upset. What could it be? Had she stumbled into a problem, or a mystery, or what? For a moment she would have liked to run away, turn back up the stairs, not face whatever was troubling her new colleague. Yet that would not do. She'd only have to come back again. Chin up, she told herself once more, and stepped through the open door to the big room with huge windows on the opposite wall.

Bridget caught sight of her and visibly altered her expression to one of welcome. 'Iris! I was just after telling the others you'd arrived. Come and join your new colleagues in some lemonade.'

'Go on then, show me my goddaughter.' Alice leant over the big pram, which had been wheeled into the shade in a corner of the area at the back of the Banhams' house. The generous-sized terrace stood on Jeeves Street, a short walk from the nurses' home, just the other side of the big main road that ran north to south through Dalston. Where they were now wasn't quite a yard nor quite a garden, with a chunk of it given over to an Anderson shelter. Still, the family had managed to grow fruit and vegetables in every conceivable free space, with the roof of the shelter put to use as well. A row of radish leaves waved in the gentle breeze.

Edith tucked her dark hair into a scarf tied around her head. She'd let her curls grow now that she no longer had to keep them tidy for her patients. Also, she no longer had time for a haircut – her new daughter demanded round-the-clock attention and she wouldn't have had it any other way. 'She's sleeping, mind.'

Alice gently folded back the light sheet to see the baby's face. She was indeed fast asleep, her mouth a little open, the oak-brown hair that she'd inherited from her father already growing across what was visible of her head. Edith had dressed her in a pale lilac cotton top, with a bib tied under her chin. Alice recognised it. 'That's the one Ruby got her, isn't it? That funny cartoon of the fox.'

Edith nodded. 'It was kind of her, and you can't have enough of them. Now I know why Mattie was always washing clothes. You wouldn't think someone so small could get through so many things a day but she does.'

Mattie, Edith's sister-in-law, chose that moment to step through the open back door, bearing a tray with a jug and glasses. 'Thought we could do with a treat,' she beamed. 'I've got some fruit cordial. We made it last year, from those blackberries that grew down by the canal. Much cooler than tea.'

Alice straightened up. 'Here, let me help. I won't say no – I can't remember the last time I had black-berry cordial.'

Mattie set down the tray on a low picnic table next to the pram and her perpetually uncontrollable hair fell loose as she did so. 'It's pretty watered-down but I reckoned you wouldn't mind.' She wiped her hands on her faded dirndl and then attempted to reassemble her ponytail.

'Too true, I don't.' Alice handed a glass to Edith and then accepted one from Mattie. She glanced through the door for Mattie's mother. 'Where's Flo? Won't she want one?'

Mattie sat down beside the pram, on a small stool that usually stood in the back kitchen. 'She'll be back soon, after her WVS meeting. They're busier than ever since D-day, collecting things to send to all the troops in France.' She took a long swig of the cordial. 'Ah, that's better.'

Edith did the same. 'That's nectar, that is. Mattie, you're a genius when it comes to plants – whether it's growing spuds in old dustbins or finding berries out in the open. You should go in for it properly, you know, when the war's over and all that.'

Mattie raised her eyebrows. 'Fat chance. Alan's not three yet. It's hard enough working the shifts down the gas-mask factory and keeping him out of trouble. Takes straight after his sister.' She rarely complained, knowing she was lucky to have her sister-in-law and mother on hand to help raise her two children. Nobody knew when or if their father would ever reappear; Lennie had been a prisoner of war ever since Dunkirk and, like so many other young women, she lived each day hoping for the best while steeling herself against the worst.

'At least she's at school now,' Alice said consolingly,

pulling up another stout three-legged stool. She picked up her glass once more, noting how neither of them had argued with Edith when she mentioned the end of the war. Now that the Normandy landings had happened and the allied forces were beginning to make their way through France, they had begun to dare to imagine the end might be in sight. A long way off, maybe – but not as unlikely as it once had been.

Mattie nodded and her untidy hair fell out of its ponytail once more. She batted it out of her eyes. 'Yes, she came home and said Miss Phipps had told her off for running in the corridor. That's your friend, isn't it, Alice?'

Alice laughed. 'That's right. Janet's been a big help with our hygiene campaigns over the years. Well, if *she* can't stop Gillian misbehaving then I don't know who can.'

'I wish her good luck.' Mattie smiled mischievously. 'So, Alice, I know there's not much point in me asking, as you'd have said if you had heard anything, but no word of Joe yet?'

Alice's face fell and she hastily forced a smile back onto it. No point in worrying Joe's family. 'No, not yet,' she said. 'It could take ages, we know that.'

'Of course,' said Mattie staunchly. 'It doesn't mean anything; he could be out to sea or anywhere.'

As if to take her friend's mind off the subject, Edith turned to Alice. 'How's your new recruit?' she asked. 'Has she arrived?'

'Well, she was due today, but I came over here straight after afternoon rounds and so I haven't met her yet if she has.' Alice shrugged. 'Someone said she was coming up from Devon so that could take ages. Remember when Joe was based at Plymouth's Devonport Docks? He could hardly ever get enough leave to cover the journey here and back.'

Edith winced, recalling how Alice had worried at that time, making do with the occasional letter for most of it. 'That's a marathon, all right. Is she going to have Ellen's room?' She took a hasty gulp of cordial, to cover her sadness at mentioning her late friend.

Alice shook her head, squinting as the angle of the sun began to dip. 'No, she'll be in the main house.' She cleared her throat. 'It's so strange, without Ellen. We're all trying to come to terms with the fact that she's gone. It could have been any one of us.'

Edith nodded grimly. 'It's horrible. And nobody knows what to think about those new bombs. There's not much in the papers, is there, Alice?'

Alice shook her head.

'When you think about it, we've all come close, one way or another,' Edith went on. 'There's no rhyme nor reason to it. Why somebody gets hit and others don't.'

Mattie closed her eyes briefly. 'I used to think about it all the time but it drove me mad and didn't help at all. Then, after I had Alan, I suppose I reckoned if I could survive that, then I'd survive anything.'

Edith smiled despite herself. Mattie had gone into labour during a heavy raid in the Blitz and all her careful plans for giving birth had had to be ditched. Alan had arrived in his own sweet time while his mother was stuck in the Anderson shelter, with Edith and Alice on hand as makeshift midwives, bombs falling all the while. It was something none of them would ever forget.

Now Alice smiled as well, acknowledging the truth of her friend's comment. 'Yes, if you think about it all too much you just end up being unable to do anything.'

'And that won't do at all,' said another, slightly deeper voice, and Flo Banham stepped into the back yard. 'You've all got important work to do.' The matriarch of the Banham household had aged a little since the start of the war but she still bristled with infectious energy as she put down her big shopping bag and rolled up her sleeves. 'I heard you were all out here, and yes, I don't mind if I do have a glass of that cordial.' Mattie jumped up at once to fetch another glass. 'Alice, I'm so sorry to hear about your friend. I only met her once or twice but I know how valued she was from the way you all talked about her.' Her kind eyes crinkled in concern. 'How've you been?'

'We're managing.' Alice swallowed hard. It was painful to think about and yet it got slightly easier every time. 'I was just saying to Edie and Mattie that the new nurse is arriving today. We'll never forget Ellen but we have to carry on.' She shrugged. 'Not much else we can do.'

Mattie set down another battered stool and her mother sank gratefully down, stretching her feet out before her, ankles swollen in the heat of the day from

27

being on her feet too long. She accepted a glass of cordial. 'Well, that's only right,' she proclaimed. 'You keep your friend's memory in your heart, of course you do, but you carry on. That's what she would have wanted.'

Edith and Alice met one another's glance and both dipped their heads in agreement.

'When I think about how far all of you have come, these past few years . . .' Flo breathed out. 'You two only just arriving and then the blessed war breaks out. You've been tested under pressure, all right. We couldn't have asked for a better set of nurses, though – and I couldn't have asked for better for my boys.' Her face broke into an expansive smile.

'And now there's Teresa to show for it,' Mattie grinned.

As if on cue, a wail came from the pram and Edith sprang to her feet.

Alice watched as her friend rocked the pram, her figure almost as slight and birdlike as before she'd had the baby. The wails started to die down at the comforting movement, and Alice wondered if the new nurse knew what she had come to. It was never easy taking up a new position, but to turn up as a replacement for someone who had been so well thought of and loved by her colleagues and patients alike – that would be doubly difficult. Well, no doubt Fiona would have explained. She was good at things like that, being straightforward.

'Godmother, would you care to hold your goddaughter?' Edith's dark eyes flashed with humour as she reached into the pram. 'This is what you've signed up for, you know.'

'Of course.' Alice rose at once, eager to help. Any worries about the new nurse would have to wait; Teresa was more important. As she hugged her goddaughter, Alice did her best not to think of anything else other than breathing in that special scent from her tiny head.

CHAPTER FOUR

'Ah, excuse me – what time is breakfast served at the weekend?' Iris had survived her first day in harness but kept forgetting details she must have been told in her first interview after arriving. As it turned out, the head of the home had been unavailable for that, and the deputy superintendent had spoken to Iris instead. The woman, who informed her that her name was Gwen, had a dour countenance but Iris had found her reassuring, even though their meeting had been very short. Gwen had apologised and promised to fill her in with any remaining details at a later date. Iris was certain they would work well together. It helped that she was older; plenty of the Victory Walk nurses were younger than Iris, one or two markedly so. Such as this young woman in the attic corridor now, who was most likely getting ready to go to bed after a tough day working on the district.

'Oh, yes – Iris, isn't it?' The nurse had an angular face, dark hair and pale skin despite the recent sunny weather, but her eyes were bright with interest. 'I'm Ruby. I've got this room here, opposite yours.'

'Ah, of course.' Iris remembered that they had been introduced, but there were so many of them to keep track of.

'So, well, Gladys gets in the same time as always on a Saturday. She's Cook's help, and does all sorts of work around the place – when she's not on duty at the first-aid post. So you can go down whenever you like, 'cos there's always someone doing Saturday rounds, as we take it in turns. If you fancy a lie-in, they leave out bread and oats so you can make your own toast or porridge later on. And we can always have tea.' Ruby paused to draw breath.

'A lie-in!' Iris couldn't help smiling. 'It's been a long while since I had one of those.'

Ruby looked dubious. 'What, did you always have to do the weekend shift? That don't seem fair.'

It was just one more detail that underlined the difference between working solo in a rural district to being part of a big team. Iris shrugged. 'There wasn't anyone else to do it. It was just me. So I had to be up and waiting, ready for whatever might come my way, weekend or not.'

Ruby's eyes widened. 'Oh my goodness. That would be terrible. I love the nursing and everything, but I don't half look forward to my lie-ins.'

'Well, don't let me keep you from your bed,' Iris said hurriedly, sure that Ruby must be exhausted.

Ruby shook her head. 'No, no, I'm glad you asked me. Would you like to come in to my room and tell

31

me what it was like where you were before? I never met nobody who had to do it all on their own. I've even got some biscuits, if you're peckish. My ma sent them.'

Iris surreptitiously glanced at her watch. She didn't want to be late to bed – but it would be rude to refuse the hand of friendship. Even if Ruby was only in her early twenties, they would still have their profession in common. 'That's very kind, thank you,' she said.

Ruby pushed open her door and Iris saw the room was much like her own: not large by any stretch of the imagination, but with everything a nurse might need: bed, somewhere to hang uniforms and other clothes, a desk and chair to write up notes. Ruby had added a rag rug in cheerful colours and some framed photographs. She noticed Iris looking at them and grinned, as she fetched a biscuit tin from a shelf next to the desk.

'Here you are. The biscuits are in here. Ma even found some dried fruit to add to them. Hope you like sultanas.'

Iris's eyes widened. 'I love them and haven't been able to find any for ages.' She took one, and sat down on the wooden chair. 'Oh, these are good! Your mother's clever.'

Ruby beamed. 'She is, only she don't get no credit for it usually. That's her there, in that picture.' It showed a woman with the same-shaped face as her daughter. 'That's me brother, and me sister, and her husband. She's still home but Colin's in the navy and Terry, well, he's in the army somewhere and we aren't rightly sure where. Italy, probably.'

Iris nodded. That made sense; and it was inevitable that young men of that age would be in the services, somewhere.

'And who's that?' she asked, pointing to a black-and-white shot of a young man in civilian clothes, with a pleasant face, glasses perched on his freckled nose.

Ruby blushed a little. 'That's Kenny. We're . . . we're walking out. He's ever so nice.'

'Is he away too?' Iris wondered.

Ruby shook her head. 'No, his eyes aren't good enough. He tried, back when it all started, but nobody would have him, said he'd be a liability. Which I don't think is fair.' She sighed. 'He works down the docks. So like he says, he might as well have gone round with a target painted on his back anyway. They didn't half cop it in the Blitz.'

'Yes, I know,' said Iris shortly, then covered her abruptness by taking another bite of biscuit.

'And now he's going to do even more,' Ruby went on, pressing her hands together as she sat on the bed, its deep green counterpane shining in the lamplight. 'He ain't told his family yet 'cos they'll be anxious that he's working too hard, but we're an ARP warden short round here 'cos one got caught in a fire just before D-day and he hurt his lungs. Now he's got to take it easy, no more all-night shifts. So Kenny said he'd do it. I'm ever so proud.' She paused. 'And worried to bits, to tell you the truth. But I can't say that to him, can I?' Suddenly she looked stricken.

Iris cleared her throat. She hadn't expected the young nurse to pour out her heart like this, but it was clear she had been bursting to tell somebody. What could she say? She didn't want to think about danger in the dockyard; that was too raw, too personal, and wouldn't help here anyway. She was trying to leave Plymouth behind.

'Well, you can tell him how proud you are,' she said instead. 'He must be a hard worker, to do a dock shift and then go out on patrol at night. Doesn't he need any sleep?'

Ruby gave a small smile, evidently feeling relieved to have got her concern off her chest. 'He's only doing the training at the moment. They won't set him loose till he knows what he's doing.'

'Quite right,' said Iris. Then inspiration hit her. 'Ruby, what did your mother say when you told her you were coming to the East End to work? Wasn't she upset?'

Ruby hesitated. 'Well, I only came from Hammersmith, so it wasn't far,' she confessed. 'We had bombs over there too. But she thought it was out of the frying pan into the fire.'

'And was it?'

'It was, a bit,' Ruby admitted, rubbing her hands again at the memory of the first proper bombing raid she had endured in the refuge room downstairs. 'But somehow, when you're in the middle of it, it ain't so bad. It's the worrying about someone else that's worse.'

'There you are, then. You're bound to be worried,

but he's probably worried about you too. It's what it's like these days.' Iris shut her eyes briefly. 'Let's hope it's not for too much longer.'

Ruby nodded fervently. 'I do hope not, Iris. I couldn't bear it, just meeting Kenny and then for something to happen. But I'd hate it if he backed out of it because of me. That would be worse.'

'Yes indeed; if he's set his heart on it, then you've got to give him all the encouragement you can, and then enjoy whatever time together you can manage.'

'Won't be much of that,' Ruby predicted. 'Still, it'll make it extra special, won't it? When we go to the cinema and all that.'

'Exactly,' said Iris, recognising the look in Ruby's eyes. The young nurse was in the first throes of love – maybe her first-ever proper boyfriend. Somewhere deep inside Iris felt a stab of pain, even after all this time.

'You've been ever so helpful,' said Ruby. 'And I haven't even asked about your previous job – that was the whole reason you came in. I'm a terrible host.'

'Not at all.' Iris cast another glance at her watch, and Ruby noticed.

'Next time, then. Have another biscuit. No? Well, take one with you. You listened to me going on and being silly, and I feel tons better for it.'

Iris rose and gave in to temptation, accepting one more biscuit. 'It wasn't silly. It's only human to worry about such things. We live in worrying times,' she said ruefully. 'I'll see you tomorrow, Ruby.'

'Goodnight, then.' Ruby smiled warmly before shutting the door.

Iris crossed the corridor to her own room, pleased to have helped the young nurse but with her own memories threatening to break to the surface. She bit her lip, willing the thoughts to recede. They were never far away but she tried not to let them swamp her. Somehow she had to carry on, no matter what lay in her past. Chin up, she told herself. It's all over and done with.

Gladys was up with the lark as usual, singing to herself in the kitchen. She loved her job helping at Victory Walk, even on a Saturday, despite having been on duty until late evening the day before. Friday nights at the first-aid post were always busy, as some people still worked a five-day week and wanted to celebrate the end of it. No matter that pubs found it more and more difficult to fill their cellars and often resorted to watering down their drinks; if people were determined enough, they would get hold of the strong stuff. Then, like as not, a fight would break out and injuries would follow. That was on top of the usual casualties from the blackout, from bomb damage, and from everyday accidents.

Far from being depressed by it, Gladys enjoyed it. She had spent so long believing she could never be a nurse that she had been close to giving up hope, but here she was, trained as a member of the Civil Nursing Reserve and relishing every moment. She wasn't squeamish – she'd coped with enough nonsense from her younger siblings that she took none from difficult patients – and she wasn't afraid of hard work. Never mind that she was permanently tired. It was a small price to pay.

'Morning, Gladys.' It was Belinda, the nurse whose turn it was to work the Saturday morning rounds tending to the most urgent patients or those who needed daily care. She yawned. 'I don't know how you manage to be so sprightly at this time of day.'

Gladys gave the tallest nurse a sympathetic glance. 'Didn't you sleep well?'

Belinda shrugged as she helped herself to the porridge, which was only just ready. 'Oh, I slept all right. I went out with some of the ambulance drivers to see a George Formby film at the Savoy and we got back a bit later than I thought we would. I'd seen it before but that didn't matter.' She sighed. 'It was a nice way to end the week, even though half of us are on shift today as well.'

Gladys busied herself setting out cutlery for the rest of the nurses. 'Is it your brother?' she asked sympathetically. She knew how Belinda worried about him. David was a pilot in the RAF and had spent much of the war flying daring raids into enemy territory. As they were Jewish, they were all too aware of what fate would befall him should he end up in the wrong hands.

Belinda shrugged, looking down at her feet in their flat black shoes, tightly laced. 'It's always my brother,' she confessed. 'I haven't seen him for ages and they say that the RAF are joining the effort to retake

France . . . he'll be over there again.' She met Gladys's gaze. 'There's nothing I can do, but I worry anyway. It's just how it is.'

'I know,' said Gladys seriously. 'You got to keep your strength up all the same. Have some extra marmalade. That always helps.'

Belinda grinned despite herself, knowing that Gladys kept it in reserve for special occasions. 'You spoil me – but I won't say no.' She moved back to the tables in the canteen, a plate of toast smeared with the precious marmalade in one hand, her porridge in the other.

Iris came into the bright, wide room, taking in the fact that there was only one other nurse down at this early hour, along with whoever was singing in the kitchen – the notes of 'Oh What a Beautiful Morning' drifting through the open doorway. Iris didn't know if she'd go that far, but the sun was out and she'd been unable to sleep in, despite having the day off.

She nodded to Belinda, who had looked up. 'Iris, isn't it? Do you want to come and join me?' she offered, indicating the empty chair beside her.

'Oh, well, yes, if you don't mind,' said Iris hurriedly, still unsure of how to cope with all her new colleagues. 'I'll just get a cup of tea and something to eat.'

She had just returned bearing her own plate of toast when Gwen came quickly through the door from the hallway. The deputy superintendent would never countenance actually running, as that was strictly against the rules, but she walked very speedily when the circumstances dictated. 'Ah, Belinda, good. I hoped I'd catch you.' She stopped, realising that a second senior nurse was also already up.

Belinda recognised Gwen's urgent tone. 'What's happened?' she asked at once. Gwen wouldn't interrupt anyone's breakfast without good reason.

'Bus crash,' said Gwen brusquely. 'Full of factory workers on their way to the early shift. It got diverted and nobody reminded the driver that there's a big hole in the road from a recent bomb. We don't know how many injured there are. First aid and the ambulances are alerted but the ARP just rang to ask if we had anyone available.'

'Oh no.' Belinda put down her last corner of toast. 'Shall I go?'

Gwen paused. 'That's what I was going to ask. But, now you're here, Iris . . . Look, I'm sorry to say this as I know how precious a day off is, but can you assist us? Belinda's rounds still need doing, and I am sure you would be capable of that but you don't know all the back streets and short cuts. This crash is at just one location, easy to find. I'm sure you've dealt with worse in your time.'

Iris took a deep breath. 'Yes, unfortunately I have.' She remembered the flames, Plymouth on fire. The Devonport dockyards. She swallowed hard. 'Yes, of course I'll help. Let me finish this quickly and then tell me where it is. My uniform's still clean, and my bag is ready.'

Gwen beamed. Here was a reliable professional in whom she could have complete confidence. She'd known it from the first moment of the welcome interview. What a relief.

'That's the spirit, Nurse Hawke,' she said. 'You must have your breakfast and then come to the office, by which time I hope to have more details. Belinda, you complete your rounds, and then if there are any further developments we may require your help afterwards.'

Belinda nodded sombrely. 'Yes, I'll be as quick as I can.' She stood, brushing the crumbs from her uniform dress. 'Good luck, Iris. See you later.'

Gwen watched her go and then turned back to their newest recruit. 'Best to prepare yourself,' she warned. 'This sounds as if it could be very serious.'

Three hours later, Iris sat back on her heels and took a breath. Her once-pristine uniform was covered in blood and all manner of other bodily fluids it didn't do to dwell upon. Her eyes ached from squinting in concentration as she methodically treated patient after patient, those who weren't so badly hurt as to need a trip to hospital. All the while, the sun blazed down. It was indeed a beautiful morning, if she had had time to appreciate such a thing.

She looked up to the skyline to give her eyes a much-needed rest. The rooftops were uneven; several had buckled under the force from the nearby bomb attack, and nearly all had tiles missing. All the same, pigeons still cooed from the guttering and a flock of sparrows had taken up residence in a nearby patch of privet hedging. Their chirping had formed the background to the morning, as ambulance drivers shouted out how much room they had or police called to passersby to stay away and keep their distance.

She took a deep breath and turned to the next patient, a woman maybe ten years older than herself, with a cut to her arm and grazing on her face and neck. She anxiously rubbed her chin and Iris had to gently take her hand away to dissuade her. 'Try not to touch it, or you might get an infection,' she said firmly. 'Why don't you sit down on this wall and we'll get you cleaned up? I know it's not the most comfortable seat but you'll be at the right height for me to see what I'm doing.' She smiled brightly, knowing that her own confidence would help to lessen the woman's worries. Her patient didn't need to know that she found the scene of the crash distressing and had to hide it. 'There, that's better. Now, this will probably sting a little but it won't last long.'

The woman grimaced. 'Smells like the stuff I used to put on my boy when he fell over in the playground,' she said, wincing as Iris carefully wiped her forehead.

'It most likely is,' she agreed. 'It's disinfectant. There, that's not too bad – it isn't deep, so you should heal nicely. Whatever you do, try not to scratch it. Now let's check your arm. Hmmm . . .'

An ambulance driver approached. 'Everything all right? Will this patient need stitches?' She looked at the woman's biggest injury with concern.

Iris had been a little surprised when she first arrived on the scene to find that every one of the drivers was female, but then berated herself. There were women drivers in Plymouth, she knew. It turned out that there was an all-female ambulance station not far from the accident, and some of them had American accents. This one was British, though. She was tall, with short fair hair, and looked as if she could lift a heavy stretcher with no trouble at all. Iris found her presence comforting; if something went wrong then this driver would be able to cope, she felt sure. It made her feel less alone, in the face of all the injuries and pain.

Iris shook her head slowly. 'I don't think so. See, I've disinfected it and the wound is very neat. If I bind it carefully, then we should be able to avoid stitches. That's if you can avoid using it very much,' she said sternly, turning back to her patient. 'Will you have to do any heavy lifting?' She assessed the woman's age again; she was unlikely to have young children, she thought, but it was always possible – living through the Blitz could age a person, and she might have elderly relatives to care for besides. There weren't many women who didn't have somebody relying on them.

The woman sniffed sadly. 'No, not really. There's only me at home these days. My old man got caught in a raid two years ago, and my boy's gone into the army, so heaven knows where he is right now.'

'Do you have anyone else nearby who could help with your shopping, just until your arm begins to mend?' Iris asked, partly because the professional side of her needed to know, but also to keep the woman talking, to calm her.

The patient nodded slightly. 'Me sister. She's only down in Shoreditch. I could ask her, or see if I could stay with her for a bit. She's got room – her boys have joined the navy. I think I'll do that, she won't turf me out.' She smiled wryly.

'Excellent. That sounds like a sensible solution,' Iris said encouragingly as she bandaged the arm, taking care to position the sides of the wound in such a way as to ensure they would meet at the correct angle. 'You make sure to contact the district nurses where you're staying and have one come out to check this. They'll understand.'

The woman nodded, distracted from what was happening to her arm by the nurse's idea. 'I'll do that, Nurse. I never had much to do with district nurses before but if they're like you then I shan't mind. We're all so scared, what with all these newfangled bombs and that, but you've made me feel much better. Thank you.'

Iris helped her to her feet and patted her gently on her shoulder. 'You take it steady, but I don't think you'll have too much trouble.' She watched as the woman made her way to the main road, from where she could catch a bus south to Shoreditch. She hadn't wanted to say anything about the new bombs. She didn't know much – but the injuries were the same, no matter what the cause.

The ambulance driver grinned in appreciation. 'You did well there, Nurse . . . Nurse . . .? I don't think we've met, have we? I know nearly all the nurses around here, the district ones and the ones from the hospitals. It's a small world. You must be new.'

Iris was a little flustered. 'Well, yes. I've only just got here, as it were. I'm at Victory Walk.'

The driver smiled and relaxed. 'Ah, then you'll know my friend Belinda. She said they had someone coming to join them. This is a bit of a baptism of fire.'

Iris smiled a little, not wanting to admit to a stranger how close to the truth that was. 'The sad thing is, I've seen worse. But yes, as a matter of fact Belinda and I had breakfast together this morning – and then of course we got word of this accident. It was meant to be my day off,' she added ruefully, 'but someone was needed here and yet the morning rounds needed doing too. Belinda said she'd come here if she could finish in time, so we might see her yet.'

The driver held out her hand. 'I'm Geraldine. Pleased to meet you. Always a pleasure to find someone else who doesn't mind losing their leisure time.' She grinned ironically. 'We get that all the time as well. We'll just be getting ready to hit the town when the siren goes and it's everyone to action stations.'

'Have you been doing this for long?' Iris wondered.

'Oh, from the moment I could,' said Geraldine at once. 'I love driving. I'm not bad at mending the ambulances either – we've all had to learn, because if one breaks down in an emergency there isn't the time to wait for someone else to turn up and fix it. I learnt to drive as soon as I was allowed to and I've got a motorbike as well. Not that I can get the petrol to run it,' she added sadly. 'Still, the minute all that changes, I shall be first in the queue.'

'Gosh,' said Iris, not sure if she was full of admiration or alarm. It was almost enough to divert her senses from the horrific scene all around. 'I've never ridden one. Not sure I'd want to. A pedal bike is different, I wouldn't be without mine.'

'You want to try the speed of a motorbike,' said Geraldine at once. 'There's nothing like it. Being in a fast car doesn't come close – you're still shut away from the elements. On a bike you can feel them all.'

'Exactly why I don't think I'd like it,' replied Iris, who had had ample experience of howling gales bearing heavy rain on the Devon moors. She was saved from further awkwardness by a blue-cloaked figure calling to her and waving. Belinda had found them.

She hurried over from where she had propped her own push bike, carrying her nurse's bag. 'Am I too late?' she asked, glancing around to where the last ambulances were leaving and the walking wounded were heading home. 'I came as fast as I could but there were problems with two of the diabetic patients and they couldn't be rushed. I see you two have got to know each other.'

Geraldine gave a broad grin as Belinda picked her way across the final few yards, wobbling on the broken kerbstone, stepping around shattered glass. The wreck of the bus was behind her, looming sadly over the potholed road. 'Better late than never. Seriously, you couldn't help it – you couldn't dump your regular patients when they needed you. Anyway, you've got an impressive new colleague – you never said how good she was.'

Belinda grinned back. 'I didn't know – we haven't worked together yet. That's good news but I'm not surprised. You've been nursing for ages, haven't you, Iris?'

Iris blushed furiously, being unaccustomed to taking compliments – or indeed any kind of comments from professional colleagues. That was the trouble about working on your own; it had been too long since she had been compared to others in the field. She knew, deep down, she was good, or she would never have lasted in her previous position, but to have it proclaimed in the open like this . . . no, she was embarrassed. 'Really, it was nothing,' she muttered.

'I'm sure that last patient didn't think it was nothing,' Geraldine insisted. 'You should have seen the woman's arm, Belinda – even you might have thought it needed stitches, but your colleague here did such a neat dressing that they weren't necessary. And I don't even know your name.'

'Iris. Iris Hawke.'

'Well, Iris, you did a damn fine job there!' Geraldine tugged at the cuffs of her uniform. 'I'd best be off – got to get the ambulance back to the station. We might have more callouts this afternoon. Shall I see you later, Belinda?'

Belinda nodded. 'Yes, like we planned. Corner of Dalston Lane, six o'clock, unless there's another incident.' She waved as Geraldine made her way back to her vehicle. 'Don't worry,' she said, turning to Iris, 'I know she can be a bit over-enthusiastic, but she knows what she's talking about. If she says you did a fine

46

job then it will be because it's true. She's a good person to have on your side.'

Iris nodded, not wanting to offend someone who seemed friendly – but her ears were still burning as they left the forlorn street, where the only sounds of joy came from the cooing and chirping of the birds.

CHAPTER FIVE

Why was it, Alice wondered, that everything became busier just when you needed a few minutes to yourself? It wasn't any one particular incident. Throughout July the raids had continued, not in such numbers or severity as in the Blitz, but enough to cause plenty of damage and to shred everyone's nerves. It was this new sort of bomb – the V-1, as they were formally known. But everybody called them buzz bombs or doodlebugs, and their horrible noise, followed by the ominous silence, was fast becoming the stuff of nightmares.

To begin with, any official information about them had been hard to come by and the rumours had grown. Thanks to the nurses' links to the ARP, particularly to Joe's father, Stan Banham, they had learnt more than most. Stan was a senior figure in the area and sat on several committees with Fiona. While not wishing to feed the rumours, he had told the doughty superintendent what he'd gathered so far, in the hope that she could reassure her nurses, and they in turn could do the same for their patients. None of it made much difference to the outcome though.

It added to Alice's workload, as every visit meant extra time spent calming the patient. It didn't matter if they were young or old, desperately sick or recovering from a minor injury. They were all shaken by the new weapons, which seemed to be aimed straight at East London. Alice knew they weren't; she'd heard that the major towns on the south coast were in the line of fire as well. That would mean that all service personnel based there would be targets yet again and she couldn't help worrying about the doctors she knew there. There was Mark, for a start, who had broken her heart back when they'd trained at the same hospital in Liverpool. Then there was his best friend, her former colleague Dermot, who was never far from her thoughts. She'd bet he was once again working flat out.

Now that she was finally sure where her heart lay, she had waited and waited for news from Joe, to learn if he had received her letter, or even that he was still alive. The not-knowing was gnawing away at her, preventing her going to sleep, or waking her in the small hours when everything was silent. It was no good giving herself a talking to; what had happened between them was too momentous and she could not rest until she knew.

Then this morning, just as she was setting out, an envelope arrived with her name on it. She had gasped aloud at the handwriting – no mistaking that it was

Joe's. It was a small envelope and felt miserably thin but she didn't care.

There was no time to stop and open it though.

The first patient of the day was tubercular, which meant she had to attend as early as possible. Mr McCafferty lived in one of the houses along St Mark's Rise which had once been grand, but was now divided into separate flats although they all shared one front door. He was lucky; his main room had a bay window, which still retained its glass, unlike some of the neighbouring buildings which had lost panes in the raids. As Alice checked his pulse, temperature and respiration, she could see the big, imposing church of St Mark's over his shoulder.

'What do you make of these new bombs they're all talking about?' he'd asked, his voice querulous. He seemed even older than the seventy-two years Alice knew him to be. His hand shook a little as she set his wrist back down on his lap.

She went about her regular routine, trying to allay his fears by being vague, but he was having none of it. 'They say that when one's got yer name on, there ain't nothing you can do, just got to say yer last prayers,' he said, his grey face growing red with the effort of speech.

Alice's heart sank. She didn't want to think about it, didn't want to imagine what Ellen had gone through in those final few moments. 'Now, do try not to over-exert yourself,' she said as calmly as she could.

'But we don't know what to do,' he complained.

'It's all very well for you young folk, you can take to yer heels and make a run for it. Not much chance of that for me, not with my chest being what it is.'

Alice sighed. 'I'm not sure running would do much good,' she said. She rearranged his bobbled cardigan over his shoulders and made sure he had a blanket nearby in case his legs grew cold, despite the morning showing promise of another warm day. 'I can't say I know much more about it than you do, but what I do know is that getting yourself worked up won't help. That's the best advice I'm qualified to give.'

The old man coughed. 'So you're telling me that me chest is more likely to see me off than those blasted bombs?' he groaned.

Alice gathered her equipment together. 'Not at all,' she replied steadily, although she thought he might well be right. 'Just that we can do something to help your chest. I'll see you soon,' she added, hastily fastening her bag, knowing that their conversation had made her late for the next patient on the list.

It just got busier from there. Extra patients were added at the last minute, and every single one wanted to know what she thought about the buzz bombs and who had been hit so far and what were the chances of one landing on their street, their house?

By the time she had seen the last patient, Alice's own nerves were shredded. She seriously doubted if any of her reassurances would have done much good. She couldn't be expected to predict what would happen and yet that was exactly what her patients asked of her. When it came to medical matters, she had no hesitation in recommending what they should do, but this new threat was way beyond her.

As she eventually turned her heavy bike for home, she felt again the rustle of the poor-quality paper in her pocket and considered leaning against a wall and opening the message. Yet she wanted to be somewhere more private when she did so; it could contain anything. She didn't want the world to see her reaction if it was bad news. Not that she thought it would be – but there was so much at stake. She had taken the irreversible step by putting her heart on the line and had risked it being broken again. The idea was unbearable.

'Miss! Nurse!' Alice was jolted out of her thoughts by a high voice nearby. She looked up and focused on the young girl of about eleven who stood before her in the street. She was thin, wearing a patched pinafore that was several inches too short for her, but she was grinning widely. 'Ain't seen you for ages, miss. I thought one of them doodlebugs had got yer.'

Despite her inner turmoil, Alice smiled back. She shouldn't be surprised that this child was up to date about the new bombs. 'Not yet they haven't. How are you, Pauline? Have you grown since we last met or am I imagining it?'

Pauline shrugged. 'I might have. I don't have no time to notice such things. I got me hands full, looking after Gran and me brother.'

Alice knew that Pauline was the mainstay of her small household, as her mother had died of blood poisoning earlier in the year. Admittedly the woman hadn't been around much, but she had at least brought in some money – mainly from her work as a prostitute, though Alice was never entirely sure just how much Pauline had known about her mother's activities.

'How is Larry?' she asked instead. Pauline's little brother had never been robust and she'd had to intervene several times in the past, bringing the pair back to the nurses' home for a decent wash more than once.

Pauline kicked her feet and little specks of gravel blew along the dusty pavement. 'He's all right, miss. Well, some days. Truth to tell, he misses our mum. So do I, sometimes, though I says to him, she weren't never there, how can he miss her? But he does.'

'I'm sure he does,' Alice said sadly, 'and you as well. It's not even that long since she died. It's only natural to miss her.'

Pauline gave a deep sigh. 'I know that really. It don't help, though. He keeps thinking she's coming back, even though I tell him over and over that she ain't. I mean, he knows it deep down, but sometimes he wakes up at night and calls out for her. Gran don't hear him, so it's up to me. I'm fair bushed, miss, I don't mind admitting.'

'I'm sorry to hear that.' Alice could believe it all too readily. For years Gran's main source of sustenance had been gin, and that was by far the most important thing in her life. The grandchildren were well down her list of priorities. 'Are you keeping up your schooling? Shouldn't you be there now?'

'It's dinner time, miss.' Pauline nodded towards Alice's nurse's watch.

'But you get your dinners at the canteen,' Alice pointed out. It was a quiet relief to know that the worst-off children had this means of having at least one decent meal a day.

'Yes, but I got to do my errands,' Pauline replied. 'There ain't time for both. I got to nip to the shops, see what I can get for later. Miss Phipps knows, and she'll keep me a sandwich or something.'

'You need more than a sandwich.' Alice frowned.

'Can't be helped, miss. I can't be in two places at once.' Pauline drew out a list from her pocket. 'I best be getting on. I'll probably have to try several places to find what I want.'

Alice nodded resignedly, acknowledging that the girl was in an impossible position. 'I'll see you soon,' she said. 'Try not to miss too many canteen dinners.' She knew that this girl was one of many with unreasonable burdens resting on them – the 'little mothers' who dealt with troubles at far too young an age. It put some of her other patients' complaints into bleak perspective.

'Easier said than done, miss. Ta-ta for now.' Pauline sped past, waving her list in the warm midday air.

Alice pushed her bike along the last street before the turn for Victory Walk, worried for the girl and her brother. Still, that was nothing new. Ever since she'd met the family she'd been torn between horror at the adults' neglect and admiration for the way Pauline somehow kept things going. The girl was rarely downhearted and put up with hardships most people would find unendurable. Alice made a mental note to talk to Janet Phipps, to see if they could come up with anything to improve matters, although she didn't hold out much hope.

Finally she could park her bike in the rack at the back of the home and sprint inside. 'Alice! You're late. You could have missed the bread-and-butter pudding,' Mary admonished her in the hallway.

Alice waved her off. 'I'll be down in a minute.'

Mary did not take offence. 'I'll save you some,' she offered – missing food was one of the worst things she could imagine.

'Thanks.' Alice was already halfway up the stairs to the first floor.

Shutting her bedroom door behind her, she threw down her bag and reached at last for the envelope. Despite her urgency, she could not resist tracing her finger along the lines of the address. Joe had written the words – he was alive! Or, he had been when he wrote this. Nothing could be taken for granted.

Carefully slitting open the envelope with her special little knife, she edged out the single piece of paper. The message it contained was very short.

Dear Alice,

I hope that you are well. I expect you've been wondering about me, so this is to let you know I'm alive and safe, though of course I can't tell you where I am or what I'm doing. You won't be surprised to learn I am very busy, after all the

events you'll have heard about in the news. I'll
write to Ma so she won't need to worry any
more either. That's all I can really say for now.
    Love from Joe.

That was it. No mention of heading for a home base,
or upcoming leave. No personal details. Not a hint
of what had passed between them on that fateful
evening before D-day or if he had received her letter
with its message of undying love.

Alice felt as if someone had thrown a bucket of
cold water over her. After waiting for all this time,
what she had just read was a terrible disappointment.
She had dreamed of a fulsome declaration of everything he had said on that last visit, something that
she could read and reread when she wanted to think
of him, to hold on to her belief that they had a future
together. This was an anticlimax, to say the least.

For a moment fear swirled through her, that she
had misunderstood him, that she had committed to
someone who didn't feel as deeply as she did – the
old horror, after Mark had trampled on her love so
freely given. She had put her heart on the line, telling
Joe how she loved him, how she'd wait for him. Then
good sense reasserted itself. Joe was not like that. He
had been as genuine as she had. She had nothing to
worry about on that score.

Realisation dawned that this was a letter he had
expected someone else to read. It was obviously done
in a hurry – his normally meticulous writing was at
an angle, some of the dots over the Is missing their

56

mark, the Ts sloppily crossed. It was not a love letter between the two of them; it was rather a public note that he was alive and safe. She had to have faith that a proper letter would follow, in which she would garner at least some idea of what he had been through in the past weeks, and how he truly felt about her. The pain of absence was never far away and for a moment she shut her eyes, wishing beyond anything that he was here in person, where she needed him so badly.

And through all of that, Alice still had no idea if he had received her precious letter, sent with such hope and love. It could be anywhere. She just had to keep her fingers crossed that somehow, by a miracle, it was still winging its way to him – wherever he was now.

CHAPTER SIX

'Oooh, don't you look smart, Kenny!'

Kenny went beetroot-red to the tips of his ears. He'd made an effort, as much as he could in his ARP warden's outfit, because he wanted to look good for Ruby when he called for her at Victory Walk. Now her best friend was teasing him. Self-consciously he took off his glasses and polished them with his handkerchief. 'It's only the uniform,' he muttered shyly.

Ruby's great friend Lily stepped forward and patted him on the lapel of his blue serge battledress overalls. 'That colour suits you, you know.'

If Kenny could have gone any redder then he would have. Lily was extremely pretty by anyone's standards, and made the most of it. It made him nervous, even though he privately thought she couldn't hold a candle to Ruby.

'Stop teasing him, Lil.' Ruby came down the front steps of the nurses' home and tucked her arm through Kenny's. 'He does, though. Not that you didn't before,' she added loyally.

It was a Sunday afternoon and several of the nurses were on their way either in or out, making the most of yet another sunny day and a temporary absence of emergency callouts. Ruby had changed into a light cotton frock, happy to be out of the restrictions of the nursing uniform with its many stiff pockets, and she'd added a jaunty bright scarf at her neck which set off her dark hair.

Even so, she couldn't compete with Lily. The blonde nurse had gone through her extensive wardrobe to pull out a pale blue blouse edged in white piping, which she'd teamed with a deep blue skirt cut on the bias, and red sandals. She'd aimed for casual but patriotic and reckoned she had succeeded.

'Are you coming down the Duke's Arms with us, Kenny?' she asked. 'Are you allowed to, dressed up like that?'

Kenny shook his head, knowing that the teasing was well-meant. 'No, I'm taking Ruby for a walk before I start my shift,' he said proudly. 'It don't do to turn up half-cut. That wouldn't go down well at all, not now I've finished my training and everything.'

'I should think not,' Lily replied, mock-severe. 'You could have a lemonade though. Even if you'd really prefer a pint.'

'I've had plenty of those and I'm sure there'll be plenty more to come,' he said cheerfully, pressing Ruby's arm close to his side. 'I'd rather have a wander by the Downs for a bit. It'll be cooler there under the trees, for a start.'

Lily nodded. 'Yes, and that uniform does look as if it's a bit warm.'

Kenny ran his free hand around his collar. 'It's not too bad. It won't be as bad as in some of the warehouses down the docks. They heat up something dreadful this time of year.'

Lily pursed her lips in acknowledgement; having grown up near the Liverpool docks herself, she was well-aware of the tough conditions many of the workers put up with.

'You'll never guess where his sector is,' laughed Ruby. 'He's only gone and bagged the one next to the Boatman's. You'll have your work cut out there, Kenny.'

'Don't I know it!' For a moment his smile wavered. The Boatman's was a pub of dubious repute down by the canal, which hadn't stopped him frequenting it in the days before he began walking out with Ruby. The beer was cheaper than at the Duke's Arms, but there was no chance of taking the likes of Ruby and Lily to such a place. The Duke's was respectable, with a garden out the back, and its interior polished to gleaming perfection. The Boatman's was its exact opposite.

'He'll lay down the law with them, no doubt about it,' said Ruby happily, and Kenny hoped it was true. Ruby hadn't been there on the evenings when fights broke out – and worse. He wasn't looking forward to any of that.

'I'll see you later, then,' Lily said, and strolled off towards the bus stop, managing to make her narrow skirt swing around her hips as she did so.

Ruby and Kenny wandered in the opposite direction, along the side street of tall, terraced houses that led to Hackney Downs. The broad green space was still bordered by old trees, now in full leaf, as well as train tracks, but much of the area had been taken over for growing fruit and vegetables. As they approached there were plenty of people out, determinedly digging for victory as they tended the plots.

'Tell you what,' Kenny said as they approached the cool avenue of trees, 'all that first aid I had to do made me appreciate you nurses even more. It took me ages to get the hang of it. We had to practise on old butcher's bones and they all laughed at me to begin with. Said the way I splinted a leg would mean the patient would never have walked again.'

'Oh, we've all been told that,' Ruby assured him, even though she never had. 'What was the worst bit, would you say? 'Cos you've been in all sorts of tight corners down the docks – it must have been familiar.'

Kenny came to a halt under a grand old sycamore. 'The fires,' he said. 'It was horrible. They got this sort of concrete bunker in the corner of the yard; they set light to old furniture in it and you have to crawl in to pretend to rescue someone. I been in the odd fire down the docks and they was horrible, but at least they was in a big space. This is all crowded and on top of you and there's nowhere for the smoke to go but down your lungs. I passed that bit, but to this day I don't know how.'

Ruby hugged his arm more tightly. 'I know. It's horrible. I only done it once but that was enough.' She and Lily had helped rescue a former ARP warden. 'You're very brave, Kenny, 'cos you knew what it would be like and you did it anyway. Me and Lily didn't really know – we just went ahead and went in the house, but if we'd thought about it then maybe we wouldn't have.'

Kenny cleared his throat. 'Just as well you did.' He looked away, weighed down with the knowledge and in full realisation that he might well have to go into more burning buildings, perhaps even tonight if there was another raid. 'Anyway, Ruby, I been getting some right old comments with the first aid. They reckon I got better at it because I was getting extra tutoring after hours.'

'Oh, did they?' Ruby turned to face him and arched an eyebrow.

'They did. They reckoned a certain nurse was giving me private lessons.'

'Cheeky so-and-sos! As if. That wouldn't be fair, would it?' she protested, but she was laughing.

'Course, I wouldn't say no if you offered.' Kenny's eyes grew bright behind his glasses.

'Not if you start bringing round butcher's bones. I'm not touching those old things.'

'I won't if you don't want me to. But you could improve my bandaging skills.'

'Maybe I could.' Ruby giggled in delight as he drew her closer and further into the shade of the trees, out of sight of the Sunday afternoon gardeners.

She held him tight and breathed into his neck, not caring about the starchy blue serge which rubbed against her face. She was proud of him, the way he'd put himself forward for a dangerous job on top of what was already a perilous position at the dockyards. She was lucky to have him and she knew it.

'Well, I think she's standoffish.' Mary was in her usual early morning bad temper, polishing off a second round of toast. 'Maybe I'm being mean but there it is. I speak as I find.' She took another bite and Bridget took this moment to get a word in edgeways.

'She's not so bad. It takes a while to get used to the place. I remember it well – you lot had nearly all been here for ages when we arrived.'

Alice nodded, recalling the first few weeks of the Irish nurses settling in, and knowing this must bring up the loss of Ellen afresh. 'But it didn't seem like that to us, as you were very easy to get along with – you fitted straight in.'

Bridget shrugged. 'All the same, it wasn't easy. Being in a different country, even if you speak the same language . . .'

'Or almost,' Mary chipped in.

'Almost, then. Well, the food's different, the wireless is different. All these little things take a bit of adjusting to. That and there was a war on and Hitler kept trying to kill us every night.'

Alice dipped her head in acknowledgement of the

truth in that but Mary used it as ammunition for her argument.

'Exactly, that's my point. Iris doesn't have any of those problems – she's only come from Devon, where I'm assured they do have food and the BBC on the wireless. Has she even spoken to you about Ellen, Bridget?'

Alice winced. Sometimes Mary could be as subtle as a brick.

'Well, no. But why should she?' Bridget stirred her tea, more out of habit than because there was any sugar to put in it.

'I'd have thought it would be polite. You know, to show that she knows she's stepping into a heroine's role here.' Mary raised her eyebrows and picked up her last corner of toast.

'Maybe she doesn't know,' Alice suggested reasonably.

'Doesn't know? How can she not know?' Mary was outraged. 'Surely it will have been the first thing Fiona would have told her. Anyway, wouldn't you want to know why there was the sudden vacancy? I would.'

'Perhaps she thinks it's none of her business,' Alice observed. 'The job's the same however she got it, isn't it? Besides, I gather it was Gwen who did her welcome interview, not Fiona. It might have been overlooked. Is everything all right, Mary? Only you seem a little . . . on edge.'

Mary looked as if she was going to throw her cutlery down but then she sighed and her shoulders

64

sagged. 'Sorry,' she said. 'Am I being horrid? I suppose I am. I'm just worried, that's all.'

'What, about Iris?' Bridget looked surprised.

'Yes. Or, well, not really. Only a bit.' Mary fiddled with her empty plate, pushing her finger through the crumbs. 'No, all right, it's mainly Charles. It was bad enough in the run-up to D-day but now he's working flat out and wearing himself out. I thought everything would be better now all that's over and done with, but no, if anything it's worse.' She looked so woebegone that Alice almost smiled. Captain Charles Paynter had been courting Mary since the beginning of the war, but even though he obviously adored her, he was increasingly tied up with matters at Army HQ. That meant their time together had been limited no matter how much they wished it otherwise.

'Except it's not over and done with, is it,' Alice asked gently. 'Perhaps the top brass thought we'd progress through France more quickly, but it's been a hard slog in some places by the sounds of it. Anyone involved in the planning of all that must be tearing their hair out.'

Mary nodded, all the fight drained out of her. 'He is, he is. And I'm worried that his lovely hair is thinning with the pressure of it all. It's so unfair. Sometimes I think we're never ever going to have a chance to be together properly and all our best years will be behind us even if we do.' She blinked rapidly and Alice could tell that her friend was near to tears.

'Come on, Mary, this isn't like you,' she pointed

out. 'You've waited this long, you'll have your reward at the end of it.'

Mary shook her head and her own hair, thick and glossy and the envy of many of the others, swayed about her shoulders. 'I know some say he's been lucky, working at a desk for most of the war, away from the fighting.' She sighed again. 'Well, now I think he's going to be sent abroad. After all this time. And I don't know if it's better or worse, but he wants to go. He says he'll be useful. He can speak French, for a start. So off he'll go and I won't know where he is or how he is . . .'

'Shh, Mary, don't upset yourself,' Alice urged. 'Perhaps he feels bad about not being in the thick of things. This is his chance to use all those ideas he's been coming up with for years. Maybe he can bring you back a present from France? You'd like that.'

'And we all know you can just as easily get killed in London as on the front lines.' Bridget pointed out the obvious. They didn't need to be reminded who she was thinking of.

Mary gave one more almighty sigh and heaved herself to her feet. 'You're right, of course. Look at me, wittering on when all of us have someone who's away, out of contact and all we can do is miss them. I shall make a list of all the things he can bring back for me.' She brightened. 'A bottle of perfume from Paris, that would be nice. I don't suppose there will be much in the way of elegant clothes.' She regarded her old shoes, polished carefully but showing their age.

'There, you're better already,' Alice told her. 'Just keep thinking of that favourite scent. I'm sure if there's any to be had then Charles is the man to find it.'

CHAPTER SEVEN

Iris was uncertain exactly where she was as she pushed her bike along the canal path. Her previous patient had assured her that this was a shortcut to the next household, but perhaps that had been a mistake. She looked around uneasily, the absence of any kind of signs making her even more unsure. Then, to her relief, she realised the path ran around one of the big parks and that she could work it out from there. Victoria Park, that was it.

The other nurses had so far been very friendly and at pains to show her around the area during her time off. And she hadn't wanted to appear rude, but honestly! Some of them had plainly never been to the countryside, as they made a point of showing off Hackney Downs and yes, Victoria Park. 'Look at all this lovely green space!' the young one with dark hair called Ruby had said. 'You'll never be short of somewhere to walk to unwind. We're very lucky to be near to such lovely places.'

Iris had nodded and smiled, but she couldn't think

of it as lovely. True, there was green grass, but it was all so small and flat. Everything stretched away on the same level, barely a curve to be seen. She had been used to the big sweeps of land rising and falling all around her tiny village, the steep inclines and the great, pitching declines, with the clouds changing the patterns of light all the while. No day was ever the same. She hadn't realised how much she relied on those rhythms until she left.

Now she pushed her bike up the next exit ramp and took a moment to orient herself. There was the corner shop she'd been told to look out for – she was in the right spot after all. So, two streets along and to the left. She berated herself for doubting the old lady who'd told her the shortcut. She would thank her on the next visit.

Her destination was one of a row of neat terraced houses, mostly undamaged by bombing, where the residents took a pride in their street's appearance. Windows shone, and across the road one woman was polishing her downstairs ones with newspaper. No doubt she was applying vinegar for an extra sparkle. Iris paused at number eight and carefully propped her bike against the low wall separating the house from the pavement; you couldn't call it a garden, more like a narrow strip barely big enough for a dustbin. She shook away memories of the abundant gardens in her village, the flowers spilling from pots and borders.

Iris knocked firmly and the door was answered by a woman of maybe forty-five, her face pale and drawn, stooping as she clutched at her stomach. 'Oh, nurse, I'm glad to see you. Do come in.' Iris followed the woman into a respectably tidy front room, most likely kept for best. Sunlight filtered through stiff net curtains. The woman indicated an armchair with a lace cushion and matching antimacassar and sank onto a similar one opposite.

'Now, why don't you tell me what's troubling you?' Iris had the doctor's notes but wanted to hear the woman describe her problem.

Her patient shook a little. 'I don't like to say,' she said. 'It's . . . it's around here.' She wrapped her arms around her abdomen, bending forward.

'Your stomach?' Iris queried.

The woman nodded mutely.

'Is it painful?'

Another mute nod.

'All the time?'

The woman shifted a little in her seat and would not look up to meet Iris's gaze. She stared instead at the brass coal scuttle, polished as a mirror, no coal to be seen. 'Worse after I've eaten,' she whispered.

Iris tipped her head thoughtfully. 'Does it hurt anywhere else?'

The woman straightened a little and tapped her chest. 'Maybe here, like it's burning.'

'I see.' Iris thought it sounded like nothing more than indigestion but the woman seemed agitated. 'So you have a touch of heartburn. That's not very nice, I know.'

'No, it's not.' The woman finally looked up. 'I get

it all the time, something awful. I don't know what to do. It brings me down, it does.'

'I'm sure,' said Iris, opening her bag and using the diversion to run her practised eye around the rest of the room. Everything was in order – more than in order: there was *nothing* out of place. Ornaments were at right angles to the edge of their shelves and there was not a speck of dust anywhere. Not a room used by children or pets, that was for certain. And definitely no cause for her to have any hygiene concerns.

'I'll just check your temperature, pulse and respiration,' Iris said cheerfully. 'We do this for every patient, so there's nothing to worry about.' This basic precaution was instilled into every district nurse from day one: always, always take the TPR readings. Iris performed the movements smoothly, but not automatically; you never knew when a little fluctuation might indicate an underlying problem. If anything, the pulse was a touch fast. Then again, it was the first time she'd met the woman and it might be her normal resting rate, or simply having a nurse tending to her causing the pulse to speed up. Iris wrote down the measurements in her neat hand and made a mental note to mention it when she saw the doctor.

'Thank you, nurse.' The woman still looked uneasy, as if afraid to speak. 'Is it . . . is there anything wrong with me? Have I got something terrible?'

Iris hesitated. Nurses were not meant to diagnose – that was the doctor's business. Then again, in her rural community, it had not always been easy to get hold of the doctor and she had been accustomed to stepping in. Dr Forrest had never minded; he knew how experienced she was and trusted her implicitly. In London, however, nobody knew her, and she had better stick to the rules. It need not stop her giving advice, though.

'I shouldn't think so,' she said reassuringly. 'Sometimes we find it more difficult to digest our food. I expect that's all it is. So you need to be sure to have plenty of rest and to avoid rich or spicy food.'

'Rest!' the woman burst out. 'I would love to have some rest, nurse, but how can we sleep easy in our beds with those new bombs? I lie awake waiting to be next on the list, I don't mind telling you.'

Iris blinked at the sudden outburst, more pieces falling into place. The woman might or might not have actual indigestion, but here was a different root of her problem. Her nerves were worn out by the constant uncertainty and threat of danger.

'Your street looks as if it's come through everything,' she began, but it was the wrong thing to say.

'So far! That's all – so far! Plenty of our nearby streets have copped it in the bomb blasts. We're bound to be next, it stands to reason.' Now the woman had started there was no stopping her. 'I've got a shelter but it won't be any good in a direct hit like what they had in my sister's road. Didn't stand a chance. How are we expected to sleep a wink? I just lie there, tossing and turning.'

Iris nodded. 'Yes, it's very hard sometimes. What about your husband – can he sleep?' She had noted the wedding ring and knew that the woman's title was Mrs, so thought it safe to guess there was a husband on the scene.

'Oh, he's never here. He's a warden, an ARP warden, and he's always at work.' The woman sniffed, almost dismissively. Then she glanced at her watch, which hung loosely on her thin wrist and gave a little start. 'He'll still want his dinner, though. I'd better check the stew. Not that I can eat it. He does love a bit of fatty meat if I can get it.'

Iris rose, sensing her time here was done. 'You might try regular smaller meals of plain food,' she suggested. 'Milk, eggs if you can get them, bread and butter, some fish if there is any. That kind of thing.'

The woman nodded dubiously. 'We don't see much of that.'

'Or even offal. How about tripe?'

'Oh, my husband won't eat that,' the woman said immediately. 'He says it fair turns his stomach. No, a bit of fatty pork is what he likes best. And I don't like to think of him out there hungry when he's keeping us safe at night.'

Iris pursed her mouth. 'Yes, I see.' She turned at the sound of a door opening.

'It'll be him now, he's early.' The woman was jumpy. 'I'll see you out, nurse, thank you so much for taking the trouble.'

'Think nothing of it—' Iris was interrupted by the parlour door swinging open and a short, upright man with a razor-sharp parting in his greying hair stepped in.

73

'Where's my dinner, Agnes? You know I don't have time to waste.' He stared at Iris, caught out by the sight of her uniform.

'Iris Hawke, pleased to meet you.' Iris held out her hand, refusing to be put off her stride by the unpleasant little man. Good manners dictated he had to shake it but he dropped her hand as soon as he could.

'Delighted, I'm sure.' He raised his eyebrows. 'Don't you go listening to my wife's nonsense.' His words could have been said in jest but there was an unpleasant undertone.

'I would not say it is nonsense,' Iris replied, her voice clipped. 'Far from it. We must pay attention to any symptoms, however slight, so that we can ensure they aren't the first signs of anything more serious.'

This made no impression on the man. 'There's nothing wrong with her. Don't let her waste your time.' He was completely dismissive.

The woman seemed to shrink even further into her cardigan, which hung off her. It was almost as if she was afraid.

Iris picked up her bag. 'Well, you'll have to allow me to be the judge of that,' she said brightly but firmly. 'I'll ask the chemist to put aside a bottle of milk of magnesia for you – and don't forget what I told you about meals.' She pasted on her best professional smile as she reached the front door. 'Good day to you both.' She slung her bag into the wire basket on the front of the bike and pedalled away, trying not to let the husband's hostility rattle her.

How dare he belittle his wife like that! No wonder she was nervous. The poor woman got it on both fronts – the constant worry about the air raids, which they all shared, and then the lack of appreciation from the pint-sized bully she was married to. He should be grateful to have a hot meal at midday, Iris fumed as she turned towards Dalston. Wouldn't touch tripe, indeed. She'd bet he had no idea how hard it was to put any kind of food on the table with all the rationing in force. He was simply typical of someone who expected it all to be done for him. She wouldn't put it past him to use this against his wife from here on. Truly, Iris thought, these bombs were managing to hurt people in umpteen different ways, apart from the raids themselves.

It wasn't quite the way Alice had expected to hear from Joe, nor the way she had hoped for deep in her heart. Stan Banham, Joe's father and also the well-respected senior ARP warden of the area, had stopped by Victory Walk late one evening, being a gentleman and making sure Fiona got back safely after a late-running committee meeting they had both attended.

'I'll be perfectly all right,' Fiona had insisted when the discussion finally broke up.

'Yes, but I'll make sure you don't hurt anybody on your way home,' Stan had grinned. He was at least a foot taller than the superintendent but pitied anybody who tried to pick on her. Yet it was blackout and accidents happened – besides, he had a message to deliver.

Alice was still up when the pair arrived back at the nurses' home, poring over the day's newspapers in an attempt to allay Mary's anxiety. Charles had whisked her off for a surprise evening meal but had broken the news to her right at the end that it was the last one for a while as he would be leaving for a tour of duty the next day. Very wise, Alice had thought when Mary told her but didn't say; telling Mary at the start of the night out would have ruined her fun. Mary had come back and cried on her shoulder but had now disappeared upstairs to prepare for bed, resigned to her lonely fate.

So Alice was turning the pages, trying to read between the lines, when Fiona exclaimed from the canteen doorway, 'The very person! Mr Banham, she's in here. Why don't you come through? I shall leave you as I now have a mountain of minutes to decipher.'

Alice stood up, her heart suddenly hammering. It brought back the evening four years ago when Stan had come to Victory Walk to break the terrible news that they believed Harry was lost at Dunkirk. Surely this couldn't be a repeat of that unforgettably harrowing night? No, she'd had that short note. Joe could not have died. It had been his writing. Hadn't it?

Then Stan smiled and she felt her spirits lift. 'Let me get you a cup of t—' she began, but he cut her off.

'Alice! No, thank you, I won't stay, Flo will be sitting up and waiting, but I wanted to bring you this.' He drew out an envelope from his warden's uniform. 'Now don't take on, but he could only send one letter, and so he put one inside ours for you. Don't worry,' as she sent him an anxious glance, 'he's all right now. This will explain it.' Even in her agitation Alice noticed that Stan didn't even mention his son's name; he knew that there would be only one person on her mind. Some things were so important they didn't need to be said out loud.

'What happened?' She reached for the envelope.

'A bit of a do after the Normandy landings,' he said succinctly. 'It was too much to expect that they'd all get through it unscathed – his ship attracted a bit of enemy attention.' Typical Stan, to understate everything. 'That's why we haven't heard much these last weeks. Anyway, it'll all be in there, I'm sure. You have a read and then why don't you come over when you have a few hours off and we can compare our news? I know Edith wants to see you.'

Alice remembered her manners. 'And how's baby Teresa?'

'Probably still wide awake.' Stan's kind face broke into a broad smile at the thought of his youngest grandchild. 'So I had best be away, in case my expertise is called upon to rock her to sleep. Got us all wound around her little finger, she has.'

'Quite right too.' Alice followed him to the door. 'I'll see you soon – and thanks.'

He nodded and said no more as he turned and left

for home, fully aware of how important this letter would be for her and how she'd waited.

Alice took her lukewarm cup of tea across to one of the battered old sofas by the big windows, where a standard lamp cast a welcome glow. She took a deep breath and then ran her finger under the envelope's flap, careful not to tear anything inside. There was more than just a brief scribble this time – even from a cursory glance she could tell the handwriting was steadier, back to normal.

He'd received her letter at last. That much was plain from the first line. He'd never called her 'my dearest Alice' before. This was a letter for her eyes only, the one that told her everything she'd hoped he would have said when she ran to his house that morning – only to find he had already left. She read it as fast as she could, knowing she would go back to it again and again to savour every word.

I can't even begin to explain how I felt that morning, knowing you were only a few streets away. There was no choice. I had to leave that very moment, but my heart was in my boots. I wanted only to see you, to hear your answer. I'm so sorry you've had to wait so long for my reply. Your letter reached my ship after all the action of D-day. Alice, my love, I was hoping and hoping you'd say yes. I want nothing more than for us to be together when all this is over. You have my heart, you know that. There is nothing in this world as important as knowing

*for certain that you feel the way I do. I can't
tell you just how relieved I was when your letter
finally reached me. You've been waiting all this
time . . .*

She shut her eyes and breathed in deeply, hugging the
letter to her. It was all true, it was real. She and Joe
would have a future together. Quite what sort of
future it would be was as yet impossible to tell – but
it didn't matter, the main thing was they would face
whatever came together.

Then she read on. Biting her lip, she learned how
he had suffered a head injury – *not much more than
a scratch, honestly, it wasn't worth worrying you
about* – and had been out of action for a while. Not
out of action enough to be transported back to base
or even to be given leave, she thought instantly.
Clearly enough to prevent him writing home, either
to her or to his parents. That was more than a
scratch.

Yet she had to admit he sounded more like his
old self, as he went on with his descriptions of
his messmates and the life on board ship, along with
the very few books he'd managed to read. She could
imagine him, as he had the knack of writing just
how he spoke. He'd be telling her about the
Glaswegian in the bunk opposite, the Yorkshireman
in the one underneath, the miserable former foot-
baller who had nowhere to practise. She planned
how she would write back, with news of Mary's
tempers, Teresa's progress, their new team member.

Then she remembered their final moments together, the intensity of that evening, and she longed for him more than ever.

If only she could tell him all of this in person. How she wished he was coming home.

CHAPTER EIGHT

'Am I the only nurse around here to have noticed more stomach complaints?' Ruby wondered at breakfast on Tuesday morning.

'Are you really going to talk about that while we're eating?' Lily asked, raising her eyebrows. 'Oh, no, thanks, I'll have my toast plain. Got to watch my figure.'

Ruby tssked loudly at her friend. 'Oh yes, we're all in danger of putting on weight, seeing as we spend all day sitting around doing nothing!'

Lily smiled easily. 'Doesn't hurt to take precautions.'

Gladys, on duty helping in the kitchen, caught their conversation as she passed by with a tray of salt and pepper pots. Once they had all matched but now they were drawn from several sets and most were chipped, thanks to the many shakings they'd received in the various raids. 'Does that mean you'd like to help out more down at the victory garden?' she asked, always keen to drum up recruits to help grow their own fruit and veg. 'It always needs weeding, you know.'

Lily had been inspecting her nails but now she looked up. 'I don't mind. After all, I planted some of it – it would be a shame if it didn't make it back onto our plates.'

'And it needs regular watering,' said Gladys, warming to her theme. 'My Ron got us some big old dustbins to catch rainwater, that what they had down at the docks. Him and Kenny brought them up last weekend and they'll have filled up a bit from those showers in the week, but somebody's got to get that onto the veg beds. Everyone welcome.'

'All right,' said Lily. 'I've got hygiene classes at the school later today but I can come along tomorrow.'

Gladys set down the tray on the table next to where the young nurses were sitting. 'Did I hear you mention stomach complaints, Ruby?' she asked. 'It sounds daft but we've had people come with those.'

'You'd think they'd know the first-aid post was for emergencies,' Lily protested.

Gladys pulled a face. 'The thing is, some really do think it is an emergency,' she said. 'There's not much I can do for them though. They have to see their doctor – I can't tell if it's something serious like a peptic ulcer or just eating the wrong food for their dinner. They're frightened, if you ask me. They just want someone to talk to, and they often live on their own. So they come down to the church hall.'

Ruby leant forward. 'What do you do then?'

'I give them some tea, with extra milk if we can spare it, and maybe a biscuit if anyone's brought some in,' Gladys said. 'That's as good as anything, I reckon.'

Ruby nodded dubiously. 'Maybe that's best. I sort of do the same. It's not like broken bones or something definite, is it? It could be anything, serious or not. We just don't know, but I swear I'm seeing more and more patients who complain of it. Could be coincidence, I suppose.'

Gladys frowned. 'I dunno. I wasn't nursing at the start of the Blitz, but I remember there was talk about it then. A bit during the really bad times of bombing but lots just after. Maybe this is the same, now we've got those blasted doodlebugs. You all right, Ruby?'

Ruby blushed, annoyed that she'd been spotted shuddering. 'I am, Gladys, sorry. You caught me out. It's just that Kenny got called to an incident a couple of nights back, a bit out of his sector but it was a bad one. Not that far from the nice cinema up near Clapton Pond. It was his least favourite sort of call out – a building partly collapsed, some of it on fire, and he had to check inside.'

'Ugh!' Gladys voiced her distaste. 'Not surprised you shuddered, Ruby. Anyone would. That's like a nightmare. Well, you two would know.'

Lily blinked hastily, to disperse the picture that immediately came into her mind: the burning house, the smoke, not being able to see where they were going once inside but knowing the warden was in there somewhere. She didn't like to admit just how disturbed she had been by it. She wouldn't like to have to do it again.

'Anyway, he made it out all right,' Ruby went on. 'Got an old man to safety, he did, my Kenny! So he's learning the ropes and his seniors are pleased with him. I can't come down the garden tonight, though, Gladys, 'cos I'm seeing him as he's not on shift till tomorrow but I could come then.'

Gladys nodded. 'I'll keep you both to it, in that case. The beetroot might be ready if we're lucky. See you later.' She picked up her tray and took it back into the kitchen so that she could refill the cruets.

Ruby watched her go and Lily watched Ruby. 'Are you really all right?' she asked. 'You don't seem quite yourself.' She pulled her chair a little closer to her friend's.

Ruby exhaled forcefully. 'I'm being silly, Lily. I am all right, honestly. This is how things are going to be for a while, isn't it? I'm proud of Kenny and he's doing what's right. It's only that I can't help worrying for him and I can't say that to him, can I? I want him to feel better when we see each other, not worse. He can't do anything about my worrying, so I bottle it up.' She didn't add that this was one of only several things she was worried about: her brother off fighting in Italy somewhere, her widowed mother trying to be staunch in the face of uncertainty but sometimes too anxious to venture to meet halfway, in the West End. Everyone had worries. That was taken as read.

Lily gave her a pat on the shoulder. 'But you can tell me, Ruby,' she said. 'That's what friends are for, isn't it?'

Ruby had more cause to be worried as the week went on, with more doodlebugs falling, and everyone

84

dreading the distinctive sound they made, which then cut out just before they exploded. She and Lily had to run for cover at the end of their stint in the victory garden and had to divert into Dr Patcham's surgery, which was nearer than the nurses' home. He had a basement room he used for some clinics and which doubled as a secure refuge. As a thank-you, they felt obliged to give him half the beetroot.

They arrived back after the all-clear had sounded, still muddy from the gardening, to an anxious welcome from the rest of the nurses, emerging from their own refuge room.

'Good to see you made it back in one piece,' Fiona said briskly. 'I take it that the good doctor's surgery has survived intact? Was it at all evident where the explosions happened this time?'

'Not really. To be honest, we just picked up the trugs and ran,' admitted Ruby. 'We'll have to go back at first light tomorrow and check we didn't leave any tools out. I don't want to have to tell Gladys that her trowels are missing.'

'Better that than either of you getting hurt,' said Fiona firmly. She didn't have to add what they were all thinking: they couldn't bear to lose any other members of the team, especially not so soon after Ellen's death.

It was very late and some of the nurses were drowsy, having started to drop off while sheltering in the refuge room. 'Glad you're back safe,' Bridget muttered sleepily. 'Come on, Belinda, let's get back to the annexe.' She followed the tallest nurse, who had moved into Ellen's room to make space for Iris, along the downstairs corridor to the front door.

'Yes, it's good to see you back in one piece,' Iris added. She had become fond of Ruby, despite their age difference, and she could tell the two young women were more frightened than they wanted to let on. 'You'd better have a good wash and then head off to bed at once.'

Iris turned to the canteen and made for the service room just off it, where each nurse had her own small cupboard to keep drinks and food, in case they were hungry between the three meals provided each day. Mary was right behind her.

'I don't know about you, but I could do with a cup of cocoa before turning in,' Iris confessed, craving the sweet comfort of the warm drink. She paused, troubled by the atmosphere she'd detected once it had become apparent that the two nurses were absent when the alarm sounded. She was missing something, but could not put her finger on what. It brought back that sensation she'd had just after she'd joined the home. Despite her hatred of gossip, she decided to take the plunge.

'Perhaps you'd like some of the cocoa I brought with me?' she offered. 'It's not really any different to the sort you can buy here but I didn't want to leave it behind.'

Mary looked a little surprised but accepted the generous suggestion. 'You must try some of mine next time,' she replied, tucking a chestnut lock behind one ear. 'My godmother used to buy it for me in

Fortnum's . . .' She trailed off, not wanting to rub in her good fortune.

'Then it must be very special,' said Iris briskly. She had placed Mary immediately from her cut-glass accent, realising her background set her apart from the rest of them. 'I'll look forward to it.' She busied herself heating water in the kettle and making the drink. 'Here you are – give it another stir.' She paused, wondering how to broach the subject. Leaning back against the narrow counter, she cautiously felt her way forward in the conversation.

'I might be wrong, and I realise I'm still very new here but everyone is always so friendly and I—I don't think it's deliberate but it feels as if there's something I don't know.'

Mary took a sip of cocoa as if to delay her answer. She squinted a little in the dim light cast by the over-head bulb. 'Do you mean about this evening? As in, once the siren went and we couldn't find Ruby and Lily? Well, that's probably because the last time it happened, Ellen didn't come back. We thought she was held up at a difficult birth, but no, she'd got caught up in one of the early raids.' She stopped. 'But you must know all this.'

Iris stared. 'No, no, I don't, Mary. Who is Ellen?'

Mary swallowed hard. 'More like who was Ellen. She was one of us. She died just after D-day.' She stopped, took a breath and then went on. 'She wasn't even on duty but she went anyway.'

Iris blinked. 'I had no idea. How awful.'

Mary ploughed on. 'She was Irish; she and Bridget

came over together ages ago, when there was a shortage of nurses here. They were best friends, had trained together in Dublin. Then they both did the midwifery course, that was why she was on that call . . . Bridget still can't get used to it and that's why Belinda moved into Ellen's old room, so she wouldn't have to share the annexe with a stranger. You've got Belinda's old room.'

Iris nodded slowly. Things were beginning to make sense. 'I didn't know any of that,' she said sadly.

Mary cocked her head. 'What, nobody told you?'

'No,' said Iris. 'Well, obviously I knew there was a vacancy but it didn't say why, and it could have been for any number of reasons. The notice mentioned taking on a challenge – I suppose I thought it would mean they wanted an extra level of experience. I honestly had not imagined this. Poor Bridget! Yet she carries on.'

'Of course,' said Mary shortly, then, realising that sounded ungenerous, continued, 'she would, and Ellen would have done the same had it been the other way round.'

Iris nodded again, taking in what it meant. She had inadvertently stepped into a heroine's shoes. That placed a whole new weight on her shoulders and it made her feel uneasy. That explained why there was such urgency to find an experienced nurse who could handle midwifery as an everyday part of the job; there would have been no time to train anybody up. It was reassuring to know that she had been picked for her skills, but she wondered if the others resented her for arriving so blithely ignorant of the circumstances.

'It must have been a shock,' she said.

'It was terrible. We all know people who've been killed in the war, at home or abroad on duty, but it had never happened to one of us before. I mean, we all knew it could, and we've all had close shaves, but for it to actually happen . . . it was horrible.' Mary looked away, the events of June still too close.

'I see.' Iris found it hard to say any more. What was there to say? It was a long time since she had worked closely with colleagues and already she had seen for herself the depth of the bonds between the team of nurses. She was not a part of that, or not yet, and she couldn't share their grief. Once again she was the outsider. It made her even more awkward.

'I'm very sorry to hear it,' she said quietly.

'She was always such good fun, from the moment she got here,' Mary went on. 'Both of them had come over to help us in our time of need, and they needn't have. They could have stayed safe back in Dublin. It was sheer good-heartedness and we'll never forget it.'

'Well, no.' Iris knew that nobody would ever describe her like that. She couldn't remember the last time she had had what she could describe as fun. She worked hard and then she slept, then she worked hard again. That had been the pattern for years. Not that the other nurses didn't work hard, they very plainly did, but as for having fun . . . no, that was not for Iris. Maybe if she had been younger – but she felt as old as the hills most days.

'Ellen was always so lively.' Mary could not stop, now she had begun to talk about her friend. 'And kind – she and Bridget would ask their families to send over things we can't get here. Once they sent ingredients to make a cake, that sort of thing. They didn't have to do that, and yet they did. Ellen would always put herself out to help anyone. I can't believe she's dead.' Mary suddenly ran out of steam and dashed her hand across her eyes. 'Listen to me, going on. It won't bring her back. It must be the shock of tonight's air raid. You think you're getting used to them all over again, but deep down it's always a surprise, an unwelcome surprise.'

'I suppose it must be.' Iris sensed that this was not a fulsome reply but words failed her. What could she possibly add when Mary had lost a friend and such a valued colleague? No words were adequate.

'Yes. Goodness, look at the time.' Mary had noticed the little clock that Gladys had positioned on a high shelf alongside a pile of saucers. 'I'd best be going to bed. Thanks for the cocoa, Iris. I'll make you some of mine soon.' She quickly swilled her mug clean and left it to drain overnight.

'Yes, that would be nice.' Iris found she still had a lump in her throat. Mary was in a hurry to go, but it had been a tiring night, and she couldn't blame her. She had inadvertently got off on the wrong foot and wasn't sure how to put it right. That first meeting with Gwen had been so fast, and there had been no time for the deputy to tell her any of this. She must have thought somebody else would inform her what had happened – but nobody had. Iris knew she had worked alone for too long to have recognised the gaping hole in her knowledge. Well, she knew now. She would have to work harder to fit in and put things right.

Mary frowned as she dragged her overtired aching body up the two flights of stairs. She would think about that conversation more rationally after she had slept, as she knew her brain was not making proper sense right now, but inside she was seething. All right, so Iris hadn't known about Ellen after all. But what a wooden response! Had the older woman no sense of fellow feeling? No doubt she'd been sheltered down in rural Devon, never knowing the risks everyone took day in, day out in the big cities. Her biggest danger would probably have been from a field of cows! Well, she had some shocks in store and no mistake.

She had been right to begin with. The new nurse was stand-offish. She was no replacement for Ellen and that was all there was to it.

CHAPTER NINE

There was to be no let-up in the doodlebug raids. While it was not as severe as the Blitz, when there had been very few unbroken nights for months on end, the buzz bombs fell regularly enough to keep everyone on edge. Not a week went by but somewhere in Hackney or the neighbouring streets took a direct hit and many people were at breaking point.

For Pauline's grandmother, there was a tried and tested way of calming the nerves. It was one she had spent a lifetime employing and just because there were two kiddies at home to look after, she didn't see why she should stop now. The girl was used to minding her younger brother, had been doing it since she was old enough to fetch him a cup of water. They would be all right on their own, she reckoned, while she herself had a few nips of gin in the pub.

As the weather was nice enough, she wandered a little further afield than her regular spot so that she could stretch her legs a bit. Exercise was good for you, that's what the government said, and her old pins had

92

been giving her gyp lately. So in fact she was doing herself a favour all round, a spot of exercise and soothing her worries about the never-ending war. There was a lovely little pub not far from the Hackney Empire, where they never asked questions when she stayed a bit later than she should. They'd even been known to extend her some credit, when cash was especially short.

The bar was warm and inviting although perhaps not the cleanest of establishments, but that didn't bother her. There was a vacant spot in the corner and once she had her glass in her hand, she settled herself onto the woodworm-riddled armchair, sighing with pleasure. Sunlight filtered through the greasy windows. The first sip slipped down easily. She took a few more. The barman fetched her another glass, and maybe another. The hour passed in a happy blur, with nearby conversations filling her ears with a comforting buzz, and she didn't need to join in, just soak it all up. Vaguely she became aware of another noise, higher than the voices, now growing louder. The barman disappeared in a hurry, but she couldn't bring herself to worry. What was the rush? The noise had stopped now, anyway. She was just about to take a final sip when the explosion happened.

Gwen was initially disapproving when Kenny came knocking early in the evening. She knew that he was walking out with Ruby and she had no objection to that as such, but it didn't do to turn up quite so blatantly. Then she realised he was in uniform and this was by way of an official visit.

'Sorry not to have rung ahead.' He polished his glasses with his handkerchief, which he often did when he was nervous. 'We got a bit of a problem and we could do with one of the nurses to help.'

Gwen relented a little, standing with her arms folded at the threshold of the home's front door. As ever, its navy paint was spotless in the slanted gold light. 'Let me guess, that nurse wouldn't happen to be Ruby, would it?'

Kenny polished even harder. 'Well, maybe. Yes. No, in fact they asked for Alice or if she can't come, then Belinda, 'cos they know the kiddies best, but after that the little girl trusts Ruby.'

Gwen raised an eyebrow. 'You'd best come in and explain.'

'There's no time, ma'am.' Kenny never knew what to call Gwen. He played it safe as she was, in effect, Ruby's boss. 'The kiddies are in the house with nobody but my colleague and to tell the truth he don't know what to say to children. He'll have them carted away to the children's home any moment now if we can't find someone what knows them better. I don't like to leave them.'

Gwen was a little taken aback. 'Why, what's happened?' She drew her thin fawn cardigan tight.

Kenny took a deep breath. 'That last explosion, you'll have heard it from here, it hit a pub down near Mare Street. The kiddies' gran was in it. She didn't make it out – the barman escaped and said she was in no state to walk by the time the bomb went off. He knows the family, said their ma died earlier in the year . . .'

'It's Pauline and her brother, isn't it?' Gwen knew exactly who he was speaking of. 'Right, Alice will indeed be the best person for this, as Pauline trusts her above all the others. Wait here, Kenny, and I'll fetch her.' She disappeared at her speediest walking pace along the downstairs corridor towards the common room. The young warden was left twiddling his thumbs and tapping his foot with impatience. He knew he was the least experienced of his team and that he should have been able to trust his more senior colleague, but something told him that he could not. He needed to get back to the little terraced house where the children lived as soon as he possibly could.

'Kenny! I didn't expect to see you tonight!' Ruby called out in delight as she came down the stairs from her room above and saw him waiting there. 'What a lovely surprise!'

His face fell. 'I'm so sorry, Ruby, I ain't here to see you. It's the bomb from earlier, I got to sort out someone to help the kids left on their own – Pauline and Larry. Gwen's gone to get Alice. I'll tell you all about it another time. It's proper sad, that's what it is.'

Ruby gasped. 'Oh, poor things. Can I do anything? Fetch them anything they need?'

Kenny couldn't help but smile. Ruby was so kind-hearted and it lit up her face.

'Maybe later,' he said, wishing they could have a few minutes to themselves. But standing at the front door was very public and he couldn't even hold her hand, much as he longed to.

Her expression told him she felt the same, and just as it looked as if she might give in to temptation and reach forward for him, there came a noise from behind her and she spun around. 'Oh, good – you were there, Alice,' Ruby breathed, a little flustered, and not only from the fading heat of the day.

'Kenny! What on earth has happened?' Alice was shrugging into her cream bolero as she spoke, juggling her handbag from arm to arm.

Kenny went back down the stone steps. 'I'll tell you on the way. There's not a moment to lose.'

Alice knew the route to Pauline's squalid house without having to think about it. 'You're certain it was her grandmother?' she pressed, hardly able to believe the children could lose their mother and then their gran in such a short space of time.

'Looks like it,' replied Kenny glumly. 'The barman told us straight. We went there right away to check on the kids and I left Mr Spencer there with them. By rights I'd as soon as sent him to fetch you but he's slower than I am and he don't know Gwen or Fiona. It was simpler for me to go. But he's not what you might call a natural with children so I hope he hasn't made them even more upset.'

Alice hurried along in the warden's wake, glad she was wearing her most sensible flat shoes, or she would never have kept up. Kenny was obviously anxious. What could be so bad about his fellow warden, Mr Spencer?

As they rounded the corner of the terrace and

approached the house, there was a movement of the filthy curtain, the door opened and Pauline shot out. For the first time that Alice could remember the girl ran to her and hugged her around the waist, sobs shaking her.

'Pauline, I'm so sorry.' Alice hugged her in return, rubbing the girl's scrawny shoulders. 'Don't worry, you'll be all right. We'll make sure of it.' Though quite how they were going to do that, she didn't precisely know.

Pauline sniffed loudly. 'Don't let him take us away, miss! We heard him say he would, but we ain't going to go. They'll try and split us up and they mustn't. I got to look after Larry, only I can do that.'

Alice gazed upwards for a brief moment. 'Don't take on so, Pauline. Nothing will have been decided yet and I'm here now.'

'Yes, miss, you got to tell him.' Pauline let go and her tear-stained face was mutinous. 'He ain't got no right to come in our house and say such things. You tell him.'

Alice nodded, wondering what the older warden had said to provoke such fury. Kenny waved her over to the open front door. 'Mr Spencer's in here,' he said. Alice moved to join him but Pauline stayed put outside.

The small front room was as dirty and untidy as ever, only this time a short man with rigidly upright bearing stood in the middle of it. His hair had a razor-sharp parting and his blue serge uniform still bore traces of neat creases, although he must have been wearing it on duty for some while. Alice's stomach sank; she'd met his type before. His hand shot out. 'Spencer. Henry Spencer. Are you the nurse who's going to work miracles with these miserable urchins?'

Alice reluctantly shook the chilly hand. 'Well, I've often attended the family and I'd say I had a good relationship with the children. I've already seen Pauline, but where's little Larry?' She cast her glance around but there was no sign of the child.

'He ran upstairs,' Mr Spencer said abruptly. 'Now, nurse, I need to know what the arrangements will be for these children with immediate effect. Obviously they are minors and apparently have no adult to care for them. The girl insists she can care for her brother but that is patently ridiculous.'

Alice cringed at the man's tone of voice and she could see from the corner of her eye that Kenny was trying to usher Pauline away from the open front door and out of earshot, but it was too late.

Pauline came rushing in, all guns blazing. 'I been looking after Larry ever since he was born! Nobody else can do it. I can cook and do the shopping and I got the ration books all sorted out. We don't need nobody poking their noses in our business!' She glared at the officious warden.

He took a step back in the face of such anger. 'Now then, little lady . . .' he began.

'Little lady yourself!' Pauline all but spat at him. 'I'll thank you to get out of my house. Nurse Lake will look after us, won't you, miss?' She turned to Alice in desperation.

Alice took a deep breath. 'I'm sure we can sort something out, certainly for the time being, while we consider more permanent options.' Dammit, she said to herself, she was beginning to sound like the warden, coming over all officious.

The man stood firm. 'It can't be your house as you're under twenty-one,' he argued pointlessly. 'We have to consider the legal position. And also the issue of hygiene,' he added with a sneer, his expression showing his contempt for the domestic arrangements.

Kenny came in to join them. 'For God's sake, her gran just died!' he exclaimed. 'She don't need a lecture, just a bed for the night for her and her brother.'

'That's as maybe,' Mr Spencer replied, 'and I'll thank you to remember my seniority here. I shall report your insubordination later. Meanwhile, we must follow the correct procedures.'

Alice went over to the foot of the stairs, which were just visible in the opposite corner of the room. 'Larry!' she called. 'It's me, Nurse Lake. You're safe to come down.'

There was no sound. Alice wondered if he had hidden himself away from the warden and couldn't really blame the boy. Her heart went out to him. He was a much quieter character than his big sister and had often been ill throughout his childhood. Then, just when he had seemed to turn a corner, first his mother had died and now his grandmother. No matter that it had been Pauline who had borne the brunt of caring for him, he would still miss his gran and Alice knew how much both of them were missing their mother. Whatever happened, she must keep the children together. 'Larry!' she tried again. 'Do come down so I can make sure you're all right.' Still no reaction from upstairs. Alice turned to Pauline. 'Perhaps I should go up and persuade him.'

'No, miss, don't do that,' Pauline instantly replied. 'It's not very nice. I do me best but . . . it's not very nice.' She squirmed and Alice felt desperately sorry for her. For years Pauline had had no idea that the conditions she lived in were so much worse even than many of her neighbours but now that she was that bit older she had begun to realise. Alice felt her shame with a dull pain of her own. None of this was the girl's fault and she had always tried so hard to make the most of the little she had.

'We should try to speak to him, all the same,' Alice explained. 'You go on up and see if you can bring him back down with you. How about that?'

'All right, miss. You won't go anywhere, will you?' Pauline's face showed how anxious she was not to be left with Mr Spencer.

'No, I'll stay here.' Alice gave Kenny a meaningful glance and he swiftly added, 'And so will I.'

They stood in silence as the sound of Pauline's footsteps echoed on the bare floorboards above. Mr Spencer made a point of looking at his watch. The footsteps moved from directly above them to what must be the back bedroom, and then returned to the front again. Then back to the other room. Then came the sound of running and Pauline clattered back down the stairs.

'What have you done with him?' she shouted at the older warden. 'He's not there, he's disappeared! What have you bleeding gone and done? Did you send him to a home already?'

The warden tutted. 'Don't be absurd, young lady – and mind your language. He'll be up there hiding, making a nuisance of himself. Probably trying for a bit of attention.'

Alice stepped in between them to intervene. 'What do you mean, he's not there?' she asked, cutting out Mr Spencer.

'He ain't, miss. I looked everywhere and there ain't that many places he could be. He's gone. How can he have gone?' she yelled at Spencer.

The warden showed the first sign of being flustered. 'Don't speak to me like that, young lady,' he snapped. 'You haven't looked properly, that's all.'

'I'd better have a try,' Alice suggested, but Pauline pulled on her arm in an agony of embarrassment even now.

'Why don't I go.' Kenny rubbed his hands together. 'I was a little boy once, I know what it's like to try and hide.'

Pauline looked dubious but then seemed to come to a decision. 'All right.' She turned away, unable to meet anyone's eyes, and her shoulders began to shake again.

'Come on, we'll go outside, we're not doing any good in here.' Alice put her arm once again around the girl's thin shoulders and guided her out into the street, into the low rays of the setting sun. The further

101

the girl was from Kenny's obnoxious superior, the better. He didn't seem to be able to open his mouth without upsetting her.

'He must have got all the way under a bed, or at the back of a cupboard or something like that,' Alice said consolingly, but Pauline was adamant.

'He can't get under the beds, they got boxes stuffed beneath them and there ain't no room. There's only one cupboard and it's not big enough to hide in. I checked all the same, but he's not there.' She shook her head. 'He heard that man say about putting us into a home and splitting us up. Larry couldn't stand that, I know he couldn't. It's all that man's fault.'

'There now, he was only trying to do his job,' Alice said automatically, but she knew in her heart that the girl had a point. She inwardly cursed the officious warden and his disregard for the children's feelings, in their hour of bereavement and need. Pauline sagged a little as if the effort of holding it together was all too much, and Alice let her lean against her as the dust rose from the warm pavements and the particles floated in the air.

After what felt like an eternity, Kenny emerged, shrugging apologetically.

'She's right – he's not there.'

'Are you sure?' Alice had been convinced against the odds that Kenny would magic the child from somewhere.

''Fraid so.' Kenny turned to the girl. 'Think, Pauline. How could he have got out? You were there all the time, weren't you?'

Pauline bit her lip hard. 'I was. The only time I came out was when I saw you coming down the street and run out to meet you.'

Alice sighed. 'Could he have left via the back door?' She knew it led into a communal yard, with several alleys off it.

Pauline screwed up her face. 'I don't see how . . . that nasty man was there all the time.'

Alice could imagine the scene all too clearly. Mr Spencer was probably staring out of the window, or at the wall, anything to avoid looking around the filthy room. As soon as his attention was diverted by Pauline rushing out of the front door, then Larry would have spied his chance and sneaked out the back.

'Right, let's assume that's what he did, right when we arrived and everyone was looking the other way for a minute. That wasn't long ago; he can't have gone far. Come on, we'll make a start and raise the alarm.'

Kenny looked grim. 'Nearest ARP post is a couple of streets away.'

Alice weighed up the distances in her mind. 'Why not ask Mr Spencer to go there and have him phone your headquarters? Meanwhile, we'll all go back to Victory Walk – it'll be almost as fast anyway, and it's got a telephone. We can ask the others to help look and they'll have the advantage as some of them know what Larry looks like. There, that's what we'll do. Kenny, you tell Mr Spencer, and Pauline, you pack a bag with whatever you need for tonight. Whatever happens, you're staying with us.'

Pauline gulped in relief and sped back into the house, returning a matter of minutes later with a few items wrapped up in a bundle of grubby material. 'You'll get him back, won't you, miss.' It wasn't a question.

Kenny waved Mr Spencer off as the senior warden strode purposefully to the ARP post and then nodded vigorously. 'We'll all get him back, Pauline. You just see if we don't.'

Heading back to Victory Walk, scanning the terraces for any sign of the missing boy, Alice reflected that Kenny might get his wish for a night with Ruby after all – just not exactly in the way he might have hoped for it.

CHAPTER TEN

Ruby was ready and waiting on the steps of the nurses' home, her light jacket on and shielded torch in her hand. 'I'll stay out until we find him,' she said at once, realising Larry was not with them. 'We'll all help, Pauline. You mustn't worry.'

Pauline only nodded, all words drained out of her.

'Shall you come with me and search, Ruby?' Kenny asked hopefully, but Ruby sadly shook her head.

'I want to, Kenny, you know I do, but it doesn't make sense. You know what he looks like and so do I. We'd better go separately.'

Lily emerged from the hall, fluffing her hands through her gorgeous blonde curls. 'I'll go with Ruby. I was just about to wash my hair but it can wait.'

Kenny raised his eyebrows, knowing that this was a major concession from Lily, but all he said was, 'Okey doke, then.'

Iris hurried out, also bringing a torch. 'I'd like to help too,' she said. 'I realise I don't know the little boy, but I've had . . . some experience of this. Searching

105

for missing personnel, that is.' She stood awkwardly on the top step.

Lily looked at her askance. 'What, in a little village?' she asked. 'I don't mean to be funny but wasn't that too small to lose anyone in?'

Iris shook her head. 'Not there. In – in Plymouth. Anyway, I'm ready and able,' she said decisively, turning the conversation swiftly away from whatever had happened. 'Just point me at wherever you think is best.'

Alice's ears pricked up at the new nurse's hesitation. Something had gone on that she didn't want to talk about and she made a mental note to check that all was well with her at a less pressured moment. 'Er, Kenny, I think you're in charge here,' she reminded him gently.

'Oh, Well, yes.' Kenny drew himself up to his full height, which was only a couple of inches taller than Alice. 'Right. Iris, you had best come with me, as you don't know the area so well, but I'll be glad of – of your experience.' He paused. 'Ruby, you and Lily go towards the high road and search the streets around the market. There'll be loads of places for a kiddy to hide down there.' He took a moment to smile at Ruby, as she gave him an admiring glance before setting off at once with Lily.

Alice thought swiftly. 'Pauline, we'll go in and get you a nice cup of cocoa,' she said. 'You've to stay here, in case Larry decides to come to the home as he knows it's a safe place. I'll take one of the others and how about I cross the high road and search around Jeeves Street and Butterfield Green?' She tried to give Kenny the impression it was his decision, but he was not fooled.

He nodded in relief. 'That's a good idea. Maybe you can send out anyone else who is able to help, and I'll wait here.'

'Of course. Pauline, come with me.' She led the exhausted child up the steps and into the welcoming evening light of the downstairs corridor. A few of the nurses were in the common room, and so Alice recruited Bridget to come with her, while Mary took charge of Pauline.

'You can have our spare bedroom,' she smiled, even though that was rather a grand name for it. In reality it was a converted understairs cupboard, but Ruby had slept there for her first couple of months when there hadn't been a proper room ready – and compared to what Pauline had come from it was a positive luxury.

'Why don't we see if there's anything on the wireless, Jack Benny or some music?' Mary suggested. 'Or, if there isn't, how about a tune or two on the piano?' Mary was the best pianist in the home, so this was no empty promise, but Pauline was too sad to appreciate it.

Alice swapped her light bolero for a summer jacket and then went out to rejoin Kenny, who was writing in his notebook. 'Got to keep track of who went where,' he explained. 'I don't want old misery-guts Spencer saying I wasn't doing things proper.'

'No, you're exactly right,' Alice assured him.

'Between us we'll cover every angle from here. If he's out there, one of us will find him.'

Kenny threw her a sharp look, and Alice thought how much he'd changed in the few years she'd known him, from a lad who liked to work hard and then play hard, to someone who took his responsibilities ever more seriously. 'We will, Kenny,' she reiterated. 'The police will have been informed by now, and the other ARP wardens.'

'Suppose so.' Kenny squared his shoulders. 'All right – we could be in for a long night.'

Iris was hesitant as she strode along beside the ARP warden. He seemed pleasant enough, which she was glad of as she had begun to realise just how fond Ruby was of this young man. However, to her mind he was a little wet behind the ears. Stop it, she told herself. You're older than he is – it's only natural that he appears that way. Besides, he obviously knew the area much better than she did.

It was a veritable warren of almost identical streets of terraced houses, the only difference being that some were two storeys high and others had an additional floor, some with a steep set of steps leading up to the front doors. She guessed these once had had iron handrails, but most of those had been removed when the government had needed all spare metal to go towards munitions. The front railings had been removed too, leaving metal stubs in the stone walls, like overlarge hooves.

Iris had to concentrate as the ground underfoot

was uneven, with rubble, broken glass and burnt pieces of wood littering the pavements and roads. 'Where are we going?' she asked, as Kenny was barely stopping to check behind fences or broken doors, all places she imagined a small boy would like to hide.

Kenny made a face. 'I just had this idea,' he admitted. 'I know where I'd go and that little nipper ain't so different to me, I reckon. I grew up not too far from here, a bit further towards Limehouse, and I know where I liked to play best.'

Iris narrowly avoided ricking her ankle on a fragment of old window frame. 'And where would that be?' she gasped, trying to catch her breath after her close shave.

Kenny didn't break his step. 'The canal. It's full of places to hide. I thought we could go there first and then if no joy, we'll work our way back.'

'It's also full of places to drown,' Iris said grimly.

Kenny dipped his head in acknowledgement. 'Yes, well, that's right enough. You been down there, have you?'

'I took a short cut along the towpath to one of my patients,' Iris told him. 'I wouldn't want to try that in the dark. So I suppose we'd better hurry.'

'We had. Follow me, I'll take us down the back way.' He sped up and Iris had to struggle to keep up.

The canal at dusk was a different creature to midday. Insects swarmed just above the surface, birds swooping in to catch their suppers, against the silhouette of factories belching smoke, running twenty-four hours a day to keep the government orders fulfilled.

Kenny wove in and out of various obstacles, mooring bollards and rings, pieces of junk, spots overgrown with brambles. He seemed to know the towpath well, and soon Iris began to suspect why. In the gloom she could discern another building, too low for a factory, but humming with the noise of conversation. 'What's that place?' she asked.

Kenny gave a little grunt. 'That's the Boatman's.'

Iris had to laugh. 'I take it you know it,' she ventured.

Kenny had to admit she was right. 'I don't know as I'd go there now 'cos it's a bit rough, to tell the truth. I used to drink there, back before I met Ruby. It's not what you might call salubrious. But,' and he came to a halt, 'everyone around here knows it's somewhere that nobody asks questions. You can disappear there, easy. There's a lot of stuff in storage, if you take my meaning. Even the kiddies know it.' He sighed, and Iris restrained herself from asking what manner of stuff he was referring to.

'You think Larry might be there?' she asked, keeping her voice low.

'I don't rightly know,' Kenny said, deadly serious now, 'but it's where I'd go. He's not a daft kid, just frightened. He won't have gone far 'cos he won't want to be a long way from his sister, but it's far enough not to be spotted at once. It's the obvious place.'

Iris nodded slowly. It made a strange kind of sense. 'In that case, you'd better go first as he knows you, and I'll keep back in case he tries to run. How many ways in and out are there?'

'One main door out front but he won't get in there, they won't let him. There's a yard round the back and it's got a gate where you can get in and out unseen. I'll try that. You watch out for him – he's got the knack of escaping fast, as we now know.'

'All right.' Iris readied her torch as Kenny strode off, making his obviously familiar way to the back entrance. She hoped he wouldn't be long. She didn't fancy encountering any of the clientele of what was plainly a dodgy establishment. She supposed she should be shocked that Kenny knew it so well, but he was a dock worker and they had to find their entertainment at all sorts of odd hours. It had been the same in Plymouth, but she wouldn't think about that now.

Waterbirds were settling in the plants along the canal's edge and she accidentally disturbed a furious parent, which quacked its annoyance at her. Well, there was her cover blown. If Larry had been crouching somewhere out of sight he'd know that somebody was on the towpath nearby. Then again, he might assume it was a punter – if he was thinking straight at all. How terrified he must have been, to run like that.

Kenny had disappeared, though she thought she could just hear him calling in a low voice. Meanwhile a couple of customers really did emerge from the gloomy path in the other direction and head for where the front door of the Boatman's must be. They must be doing reasonable business, she thought. Perhaps people from the nearby factories went there. She couldn't blame them after working a tough shift.

The light was really fading now and she had to be careful not to get too close to the water's edge. The path was narrow. She could swim well enough but didn't fancy a sudden dip. She shivered a little, wrapping her arms around herself. Perhaps she ought to feel wary of being alone like this in the near-dark, but she had spent so much time on her own, often with nobody else around for miles, day and night, that it barely occurred to her.

Then, up ahead, she could just make out a shadowy figure, Kenny's height, along with a smaller shape at his side. She caught her breath. Her immediate reaction was to run towards them but that would not do. She might frighten the boy, or she might end up in the canal. Neither would be any good. So she carefully picked her way along the tricky path, hoping that this was the missing Larry.

For a moment her attention was caught by a movement further away, just a brief flash of perhaps two adults, possibly in dark coats – but they were indistinct in the gathering gloom, and now Kenny was coming closer. She could see he had one arm around a little boy's shoulders. She could just make out the boy's pinched and frightened face.

The child came to a stop and gripped Kenny's hand. 'Who are you?' he demanded, his voice high but clear.

Iris dropped into a crouch. She reached to her throat

and drew out her Queen's Nurse badge that she had thought to transfer from her uniform collar, to prove her identity if needed. 'I'm Nurse Hawke,' she said quietly but steadily. 'Can you see this? It's just like the one Nurse Lake wears, isn't it? That means you can trust me. I work with her.'

The little boy cautiously reached forward and touched the metal, which glinted in the remaining light. He ran his fingers over it, carefully testing it. Then he nodded, apparently accepting it. He seemed to give it a few moments' more thought and then he pitched towards her, holding out his arms, a strangled sob coming from deep within him.

Iris steadied herself and hugged him, letting him cry, knowing he must have been holding in his tears for a very long time. Expertly she patted his back, her years of experience in comforting children letting her know what to do. It didn't matter that she had none of her own; she'd been midwife, health visitor and school nurse to all the youngsters in her old village and this poor little chap was exhausted and needed comforting. At last he stopped, and sniffed loudly. 'We'd best get you back,' she said. 'We're going to the nurses' home – would you like that? You've been there before, I know. Pauline's waiting for you there.'

He looked up at that. 'Me sister's there? We'll be together?'

'Yes, you will,' Iris said solemnly, hoping that somehow a plan had been put in place.

'Fancy a shoulder ride?' Kenny said, bending down to their level. 'You could climb up on that bollard. Nurse Hawke will help you.'

The tears had vanished. 'All right,' said Larry.

CHAPTER ELEVEN

Nobody had ever seen Mary pay so much attention to the news on the wireless. She had, up till now, shown interest only in concerts and comedy shows, and could call out 'Can I do you now, sir?' in a near-perfect impression of the actress Dorothy Summers, from ITMA. But now she was riveted by every new bulletin.

Alice was inclined to tease her, as she herself had been the butt of so many jokes ever since she'd arrived at Victory Walk, for preferring the news to going dancing. Yet she knew her friend had only one thing on her mind: where Charles might be and exactly what he was caught up in.

For once this made Mary the best-informed nurse in the building. 'The Free French have liberated Paris, along with the Americans,' she announced. 'They're handing out champagne in the streets, apparently.'

Gladys, who was trying to finish her day's work so that she could run home and feed her siblings before an evening on first-aid duty, came to a halt. 'Could you shift yourself for a moment?' she asked, trying not to sound exasperated. 'I need to clean that shelf right behind your head. I been waiting,' she added pointedly.

'Yes, of course, sorry.' Mary budged up along the old sofa nearest the wireless set so that Gladys could reach over her, but she did not move completely. 'Isn't it marvellous, though? You must admit that it is.'

Gladys rolled up her scrap of material she was using as a duster. 'Oh yes, marvellous. To think we been drinking champagne in the streets all this time and those poor people over there didn't have none.'

Mary rolled her eyes. 'That's not what I meant and you know it.'

Gladys relented. 'I know. But given the choice I'd have soon as have a big ham sandwich. Or a bit of chicken. Then wash it down with a drop of shandy. That would do me nicely. That's what I'd call a proper celebration.'

Mary laughed. 'Stop it! I can't remember the last time I had a real ham sandwich, I mean with normal bread and lots of ham, not that watery stuff we get now. As for the national loaf, ugh. I don't care that it's got added vitamins, it's too chewy and awful. And I haven't had champagne since . . . since . . . oh dear, sorry, Gladys. I'm not quite myself.'

Gladys nodded, knowing what the trouble was. 'Had some on your last night out with Captain Charles, did you? That must have been nice.'

Mary gave a long sigh and went back to her previous position on the sofa, from where she could control the dials on the wireless. 'Yes, that's what we did. It was lovely – and then he told me he was being sent away . . . Still.' She sat up straighter. 'Got to keep a brave face, haven't we. I don't know if he's anywhere near Paris. They said that British troops were near Rouen, so he might be there. Or anywhere, really,' she finally admitted. 'I just like to think of him in Paris.'

Gladys shoved her duster in her pocket. 'And why not, if it helps,' she said seriously. 'I don't know about champagne, 'cos I never had any and don't know if I'd like it if I tried it, but I bet if there's any where he is, then he'll find it, Mary. He's good at things like that. He'll be keeping everyone's spirits up.'

'He will, won't he?' Mary seemed comforted by the thought. Then she looked at her watch and gave a little gasp. 'Gladys – sorry, but if you don't mind, it's time for the next bulletin.'

Gladys raised her eyebrows. 'I was going anyway. I got to get the nippers fed. And not with no chicken and champagne neither.' She strode off to the kitchen, leaving Mary tuning in to the BBC news.

Alice was glad of her afternoon off. It had been another week of dealing with patients suffering from the bomb blasts, whether directly or indirectly, as well as the everyday illnesses and accidents that refused to go away just because there was a war on. Now that Ruby had raised the matter, she couldn't help noticing that the amount of stomach complaints had increased yet again. All of that, in addition to trying to sort out a permanent place for Pauline and Larry. The two children had been sharing the unofficial spare bedroom under the stairs, but that couldn't continue. Gwen had impressed upon her the irregularity of the situation, but Alice was determined to keep them together.

She had an unexpected ally in Iris who, while being naturally more reticent, could see quite well that here was a case for bending the rules in order ultimately to do the right thing. Alice found herself warming to the new nurse, whose air of unimpeachable capability clearly hid another side entirely. Alice resolved to get to know her further, when time allowed, but time was one thing they never seemed to have much of.

But now it was with some relief that she headed for the Banham household, her unofficial second home. However, when she got there, it was not quite a haven of peace.

'Me and my big mouth!' Edith muttered on her arrival.

'Why, what did you say?'

'Tell you later.' Edith drew her best friend into the big kitchen and out into the yard. 'Look who's come to see you!' she exclaimed and little Alan ran forward. He was getting sturdier every time she saw him, Alice thought as she bent to give him a hug. He proudly led her over to the pram where Teresa lay, temporarily quiet.

'You got to keep her out of the sun,' he said importantly.

'Ah, yes, I understand,' Alice assured him. He looked at her solemnly, as if to check that she really did understand, and then he ran off back inside, seeking somewhere cooler to play.

Edith slumped down into an old deck chair, and patted the one next to her, its canvas faded from its former bright colours to a uniform dull grey.

'What's wrong?' Alice settled herself on the chair and reached into her handbag. 'Look what I've got. Some of Gladys's special cordial.'

Edith smiled grimly. 'Thanks. It can be a peace offering.'

'Why do you need a peace offering?' Alice was puzzled.

Edith cast a surreptitious glance towards the open back door and then gave a long sigh. 'I've offended Mattie. I didn't mean to, but I did.'

Alice sat back in surprise. Mattie rarely took offence at anything. She was the most easy-going sister-in-law that Edith could have hoped for. 'I'm sure that can't be right,' she protested.

Edith shook her head. 'No, it is. The trouble is, it's been going on for so long, we all forget . . . it's all my fault. I was feeling a bit low and I said how I wished Harry could come home and see his baby. I really miss him . . .'

'Of course.'

'Well, he hasn't been back for ages, and I thought they might give him a spot of leave now he's a father, but no. I suppose all the train passes are needed for the troops still going out to France and all that. But I had a bit of a moan, wishing he'd come back, even for a little while, so he could see Teresa. He's missing all her early weeks and she's changed so much already.' Edith paused and bit her lip. 'Anyway, I just didn't think. Flo was sympathetic, of course, but then Mattie went all quiet and her face, well, it was completely white. We'd all been sitting around the kitchen table, sorting old clothes for Flo's Make Do and Mend class, and Mattie stood up and threw her pieces down on the floor. Said I had no idea of how lucky I was and then stormed out.'

Alice sighed as she realised why Mattie would have done such a thing. 'Of course. She'll have been thinking about Lennie in his prisoner-of-war camp. He hardly saw Gillian, let alone Alan.'

'He'll have had a picture of his kids in his Red Cross parcels if he's lucky,' Edith said sadly.

'It's been so long, it's what we're used to,' Alice added, 'but Mattie must feel it every day.' She glanced over to the pram in the shade. Teresa had never met her father Harry, her Uncle Lennie or her Uncle Joe. When the war was over, what a lot of people she would have to make a fuss of her, if all went well.

Mattie appeared at the doorway, leaning against the jamb, her hair awry as ever and her arms tightly folded.

'Hello, Alice,' she said. 'Sorry, Edith.'

Edith looked up. 'Don't be. I'm the one who should be sorry. I put my foot right in it. I wasn't thinking.'

Mattie came over and drew up one of the rickety old stools. 'I know, I didn't imagine you said it deliberately. It's just sometimes it feels as if he left only yesterday. It's been so long, I often worry I

120

won't recognise him or he won't recognise me. Or any of us.'

'Oh, Mattie!' Alice didn't bother to say that it couldn't be true. None of them knew. That was the terrible thing, the not knowing. 'Look, I'll go and get a jug of cold water and some glasses.' She stood and went inside.

'Sorry,' Mattie said again.

Edith put out her hand and grasped her sister-in-law's. In all the years they had known one another, they'd never had cross words until now. It was the strain, after so long. 'We've got some of Gladys's fruit cordial,' she said.

Mattie nodded, and sniffed a little. 'That's nice. That's kind.' She pushed her wayward hair out of her eyes and squinted in the bright sunshine. A line of freckles marched across her nose.

'Here we are.' Alice came back and started to pour the drinks, diluting the precious cordial. 'This'll make us feel better. Chin-chin.' She raised her glass and clinked it against the others.

'Thanks.' Mattie gulped half of hers in one go. 'I keep looking at the papers now it's all going well in France, wondering whereabouts he is, if he'll be freed soon. But he could be anywhere.'

'Still, it might come true,' Alice said, thinking it was as likely he was in France as somewhere else.

'It might.' Mattie sounded as if she was trying to be resolute, but not quite managing it.

'It just might take a while,' said Edith wearily, and fell silent.

They sat in the warm sun, sipping the rest of their cordial, three young women wishing and waiting.

Iris had thought about little else than the story behind her recruitment ever since she'd learned about Ellen's death, but there had been no chance to do anything about it. After the rescue of Larry, the little boy had attached himself to her and followed her around as much as he could. She had tried to dissuade him, because he wouldn't be able to stay in Victory Walk for long; how could he? She could tell some of the others thought she was being cool and standoffish again, but it couldn't be helped. The boy must not bond with her or he'd only suffer even more. All the same, she found herself backing Alice up whenever it was suggested the children should move somewhere more suitable. Even on such brief acquaintance she could see that they trusted the nurses, and that was no small thing, given what they'd been through.

And then their teacher had stepped in and come to the rescue. Iris approved of Janet Phipps. The woman was evidently very sensible, with her short-cropped brown curls, neat horn-rimmed glasses and straight cotton skirt. She and Alice had clearly been cooking up a plan, and Janet arrived at Victory Walk late one afternoon after school with a file of papers and a wide smile.

'Success!' she'd announced, striding into the common room. 'We've heard from them and they've said yes. There's a direct train several times a week, so they can both go on that.'

Alice jumped up at once. 'You're sure?'

'Who?' Iris asked, setting down the cup of substitute coffee that she had just made herself in the service room. Normally she would not have interrupted, but the fate of the children was at stake here.

Alice realised that nobody else would have a clue what she and the teacher were talking about. 'Sorry, Iris. I'll explain. Back at the very start of the war, all the children around here had the chance to be evacuated. Pauline and Larry weren't allowed to go – their grandmother didn't believe in such things. Pauline had a little friend and they were inseparable up until that day. Dotty Barnes and her mother left on the train along with most of the rest of the reception class, and I waved them off. It was a very sad day in many ways, and I'll never forget it.'

Janet cleared her throat. 'From my point of view, it made sense to try to keep track of as many evacuees as possible. Some took the risk and came back after a short while. Some then left again. It's been a nightmare predicting class sizes, I can tell you. Anyway, I kept in touch with Dotty's mother.'

'So we immediately wrote to Mrs Barnes when Pauline and Larry came here,' Alice went on. 'To see if she could help find somewhere for them, that is. And by the sounds of it, she has agreed.'

'That's right,' said Janet, seating herself at a table and making sure her file sat at right angles to the edge. 'From her letters, being evacuated has been the making of her. She was such a nervous soul when war broke out – such a contrast to little Dotty, who never knew the meaning of fear. Well, it sounds as if her mother has become a mainstay of the local Women's Institute, and they're staying in a big house with plenty of room. They'd be only too happy to welcome two more children. It's the perfect solution.'

Alice rubbed the bridge of her nose. 'I'm so relieved, I can't tell you. I felt as if we might be grasping at straws. Neither Pauline nor Larry ever showed any interest in leaving Dalston but I do know that Pauline has missed her best friend since the moment Dotty left.'

'That sounds ideal.' Iris felt keenly responsible for the little boy's wellbeing, remembering how he had inspected her nurse's insignia so solemnly. Something about him had touched her deeply, though she would not want to admit it out loud.

Alice nodded. 'I couldn't be happier. I know we shouldn't have favourites, but I'd never forgive myself if something happened to Pauline.' She turned back to her friend. 'Shall you tell them or shall I?'

Janet smiled, ticking a column in the top page of the file. 'You do it. It was your idea.'

Iris moved across to continue the conversation as Alice shrugged into her light cream cardigan and left to find the children. 'We haven't met,' she said awkwardly. 'Iris Hawke. I joined earlier this summer.'

Janet shook her hand. 'Pleased to meet you. You replaced Ellen, I take it? A bad business.'

'Yes.' Iris didn't want to talk about it, especially with someone she didn't know. 'Well, you must know all the nurses, then, if you teach around here.'

Janet nodded, carefully screwing the cap back on to her fountain pen. 'Just about. Our school isn't far away. St Benedict's is almost opposite Ridley Road market, except we've had to move out of the building and into temporary quarters now and again.' She grinned ruefully. 'I shouldn't complain. All of the teachers are in the same boat. It's why I like to keep seeing Alice – it reminds me that other professions don't exactly have it easy.'

'True enough.' Iris could feel herself warming to this plain-spoken woman.

'I must remember to tell her I've had a letter from our mutual friend, a doctor who worked around here briefly.' Janet smiled more broadly. 'I tell him he doesn't know how lucky he is, being based near the sea, but he claims he never has time to see it, as the operating theatre has no windows. What a wasted opportunity, I'd say.'

Iris swallowed a lump that had suddenly appeared in her throat. 'Yes.' She gulped again. 'I find I do miss the sea as it happens. Nothing to be done about it.' Before she could say more, or her abrupt difficulty be noticed, Pauline and Larry sped in, and Pauline hugged Janet Phipps. 'Thank you, miss. I knew you'd do something, I knew it!' She pulled away and nodded vehemently. 'Dotty will sort us out. She's good at that.'

Larry looked at Iris with a little confusion, as if unsure whether she would welcome any contact. Iris berated herself. She had kept away for the child's own good but surely one more hug wouldn't hurt. She opened her arms. 'Come here, Larry.' He rushed forward and she held him close. 'Good luck, and make sure you make the most of it. What an exciting adventure you're going to have.' She hoped it was true, but had to put her faith in Janet Phipps and Alice.

Larry nodded solemnly. 'I will, miss.'

CHAPTER TWELVE

'It's very strange,' Kenny admitted, as he and Ruby strolled along the Downs in the fading evening light. Gradually summer was ending and autumn beckoned, with the leaves beginning to crisp and change colour, a hint of a nip in the air. Ruby pulled down the sleeves of her blouse which she had rolled back as they started out for their walk, and Kenny took the cheeky opportunity to put his arm around her shoulders and draw her closer. 'Don't want you getting cold,' he explained, mock-innocently.

'Don't you get clever with me,' Ruby said smartly, but she didn't move away. 'But what do you mean, strange? What is it that's so strange?'

'Well, me being a new warden and all that, and yet they want me to look after one of the latest recruits.' Kenny lowered his head a little so that his cheek brushed the top of Ruby's dark hair. He loved her hair.

'Means they must think you're up to it,' she pointed out. 'They wouldn't ask otherwise.'

'That's as maybe. Or perhaps they think I'm the only one daft enough to say yes.' Kenny spoke in jest but secretly feared there was some truth to it.

'Don't be silly,' Ruby said at once. 'They wouldn't do that. They need all new recruits to be treated proper, you said as much yourself when you started at the beginning of summer.'

'That's as maybe,' Kenny said again. 'I dunno, Ruby, I don't want to get caught out of my depth or nothing.'

Ruby sighed and leant against his shoulder. 'You'll find you know more than you think you do. What's he like, then, this new bloke?'

'He's a bit younger than me.' Kenny chuckled. 'He's got dodgy eyesight and so he couldn't go in the army like what he wanted and his glasses are even thicker than mine. He's chuffed to bits to be a warden. He's called Cliff, he's from down Shoreditch way, and he seems nice enough.'

'Good,' said Ruby neutrally. 'Perhaps you should get him down the Duke's Arms one time, introduce him to everybody. Has he got many friends?'

Kenny thought about it. 'He don't mention many. I think he's a bit quiet. Tell you what he did ask, though. When he heard you were a nurse, that is.'

'Go on then,' said Ruby in a tone that showed she knew what was coming next. 'Surprise me.'

'He asked if you'd got any friends. Single friends, that is.'

'Of course he did,' said Ruby, and this time she did draw a little away from Kenny.

'Oh, don't be like that, Ruby. He didn't mean no

harm by it.' Kenny knew he had struck the jackpot with Ruby and couldn't blame the new man for trying. 'Like you say, we could introduce him to some of the others. Who knows, one of them might like him.'

'Hmmph.' Ruby was not impressed. 'What, like Lily, you mean? She'd eat him for breakfast.'

'Er, no, maybe not Lily.' Kenny could see that would not be a good idea.

'Everyone else will be older than him,' Ruby pointed out. 'I know some don't mind that, but I don't reckon any of the nurses will want to walk out with someone much younger unless he's older than his years, if you take my meaning. It's just that when you're a nurse you see everything, so you can't be a shrinking violet. You grow up fast, you have to.'

'No, I know that,' said Kenny, serious now. 'You don't need to tell me that, Ruby, I can see that for myself. We won't introduce him to, let's see, Iris for example.'

Ruby giggled. 'No, I don't think she'd be very interested. She's nice enough, don't get me wrong, but I can't see her letting her hair down.'

'Perhaps not.' Kenny thought of how the new nurse had been that night down by the canal. Not frightened in the slightest bit, which was saying something. Unexpectedly tender with the lost little boy. Somebody who could look after herself in a difficult situation. Unlikely to be on the lookout for a younger boyfriend, that was for sure. He pulled Ruby close again. 'And listen to the other news. This has really got Mr Spencer's goat. Oh, he don't know what to do with hisself about this. We got another new recruit – and it's a woman.'

'Good thing too,' said Ruby. 'Why shouldn't a woman be an ARP warden?'

Kenny laughed. 'No reason at all. I got nothing against her. But Mr Spencer, you'd have thought they'd asked him to go to the moon or dig a hole to Australia. Proper up in arms, he was. Said he wouldn't show her anything as she wouldn't be able to do it. They threatened him with a disciplinary and so he had to give in but he ain't happy, not one bit.'

'Poor woman,' said Ruby feelingly. 'I wouldn't want to get stuck with him, after everything you've said to me about the miserable old stick.'

Kenny agreed. 'I wouldn't want you to be stuck with him neither. But give her her due, Olive don't seem to mind. Gives as good as she gets, she does.'

'All the same, rather her than me.' Ruby shivered deliciously, as they stepped into the shadow of a big tree. 'Oooh, I am a bit cold now, Kenny.' She flashed her eyes at him.

'Can't have that,' he breathed, turning and pulling her as close as he decently could.

'Are you sure you want to do this?' Alice asked, buttoning her light jacket in the ground-floor hallway. 'You don't have to.'

Iris nodded seriously. 'I know. But I want to.' She fiddled with the collar of her blouse, unsure whether to leave the top button undone. The weather would soon be on the turn.

Alice gave a small smile. 'Then . . . thank you. I'm sure everything will go well, but it's good to have an extra pair of hands, just in case. Especially as Janet can't make it after all.'

Iris nodded again, glancing at the two small bags set at the foot of the stairs. 'Is this all they've got?' It didn't seem much, if this was the total of the children's belongings.

'They never had many clothes or toys,' Alice told her. 'We've been known to give them a few hand-me-downs over the years, or sometimes we've made them things. Actually, that's pretty well as much as most of the children on that first train of evacuees were allowed to take. They had this exact list of what they should pack, no more, no less. It was like a military operation.'

A faraway look came to Iris's eyes. 'I remember when some arrived, back in Dev—' she began, then a commotion from the door of the canteen halted her in her tracks. 'I'll tell you about it later.'

Alice flashed her a smile. 'I'd like that. Well, Pauline, Larry – all ready? Then off we go. Plenty of time to get to the station but we don't want to hang around much longer.'

Pauline was grinning from ear to ear. 'I never been on a train before, miss. Well, only the underground ones, but not often. Stank of smoke, they did. This one won't be like that, will it?'

Alice put her hand on the girl's shoulder in reassurance. 'It'll be daylight all the way.' She gently ushered her out through the big front door and down the steps, carrying one of the bags, while Iris did the same for Larry. As ever, the boy was more reluctant than his sister, but he clearly trusted Iris.

They caught the bus to Liverpool Street with no mishaps. Alice had privately worried that there would be a last-minute diversion, which happened frequently, but they were in luck. It was only as the four of them made their way to the platform, the noises of the trains and passengers echoing from the grand arches of the big roof, that Pauline hesitated.

'Miss . . .?'

'Yes, Pauline?' Alice still had to bend down to the girl's level, but not nearly as far as she used to. The child was growing up.

'We will be all right, won't we? Dotty's ma knows where to meet us?'

Alice knew that neither of the children had ever left London. She could hardly blame the girl for asking, in a rare moment of vulnerability. 'She does. Miss Phipps gave her exact instructions. You needn't worry.'

Pauline bit her lip. 'So . . . will I see you again, miss?'

Alice swallowed quickly. She hadn't realised quite how much she would miss this young girl, who had been a constant figure in her life ever since she'd come to Victory Walk. Then she smiled as brightly as she could. 'I bet you will. You know the address so you can write and tell us where you are and how you're doing. Then, when the war's over, it will be safe for you to come back, if that's what you want.'

'Is it going to be over soon, miss?' Pauline's voice sounded strained.

Alice didn't want to raise false hopes, but gave her considered opinion. 'Do you know what, Pauline, I think it will. Not like tomorrow, or even next month, but I do believe the end's in sight.'

Iris looked at her watch and cleared her throat. 'Time to get on board,' she said firmly.

Pauline cocked her head to one side and met Alice's gaze. Then she nodded decisively. 'Righto.' She took Larry by the hand. 'Ta-ta for now then, miss. And . . . thank you.' With that she picked up her bag and strode down the platform, Iris and Alice following with Larry's bag, as the two children who had bravely weathered all that fate had thrown at them set off for their new lives.

Alice stayed at the end of the platform as the train pulled out. She knew that they had done the right thing and yet she couldn't help wondering how the children would get on. Iris cast a glance her way, and seemed to pick up on her mood. 'Shall we go to find a cup of tea, now we're here?' she suggested.

Alice gave herself a mental shake. Here was a chance to get to know the newest nurse, something she had been meaning to do for weeks. 'What a good idea,' she agreed. 'There's a café around the corner – it'll be less busy than the nearest place.'

Iris brightened. 'Can't beat a bit of local knowledge,' she said, grinning, and let Alice lead the way.

The café was a five-minute walk away, off the main

road of Bishopsgate, tucked behind an old church. Its windows were polished and a cheery jug of flowers stood on the sill by the door in welcome. 'This is it.' Alice smiled at her colleague to see if it met with her approval.

Iris nodded. 'Much better than a station buffet.' They made their way inside, where there were few other customers at this time of day, a lull between the rush of customers who worked in nearby offices.

Settling at a table covered in a bright yellow cloth, cups and saucers with matching yellow rims and a generous teapot that could have served four people, the two women decided against teacakes or toast as well. Alice wondered how to broach the subject that had been bothering her: that Iris clearly had something in her background she had not shared with her new colleagues. As they traded stories of their backgrounds and how they had come to nursing, there seemed to be little in the way of an opening, until she happened to mention that Joe had been based at Devonport.

Iris looked up intently. 'I know Devonport docks well,' she said, and an expression passed across her face that Alice could not help but react to.

She cleared her throat a little. 'Do you want to tell me about it?' she offered. 'You needn't if you'd rather not – but I can be discreet.'

Iris met her eyes directly. 'I'm sure you can. It's not that . . . it's just . . . it's so long since I've spoken about it. I've come all this way from home but the truth is, what happened never goes away.' She swallowed hard and began, gazing out of the window now, as if remembering the scenes.

'I was working near Devonport for a while, not long after the war began . . .' She took a sip of tea, for courage. 'We nurses got to know the ARP wardens of course. Sometimes you received cases from them or had to exchange notes . . . things like that. Well, there was one warden I got to know in particular. H—he was called Peter.' She stopped, took a deep breath, put down her cup. 'He was about my age, and we had so much in common. He was an engineer and couldn't be called up, but he wanted to do his bit . . . He worked such long hours.' She sighed. 'Like those young men on the docks do now. I hear the other nurses talking, and I know those boys work all day and then several of them are wardens as well. It brings it all back.'

'What happened to Peter?' Alice asked quietly.

'It was down at the docks. He'd gone to attend a fire. You'll have heard what happened to the docks, to Plymouth, the bombings . . . it was terrible. The fires, the heat, the smell . . . we were rushed off our feet with the number of burns victims, I'll never forget it. But that night . . . well, Peter and another warden got to the fire and the emergency services were called, and it was terrible but no worse than other nights. Then one of the young dock workers cracked; he just couldn't take it any more. He'd somehow got hold of a revolver – they said it was his father's from the Great War, but I don't really know and it doesn't change what happened. He said he was going to kill himself, that he couldn't stand the constant bombings, the stress of it, not knowing when it would happen next. If he was going to die, then it would be at a time of his own choosing.

'Peter went to try and help him. The boy warned him not to, that he was serious. Peter carried on anyway.' She rubbed her hands together, in pain at the dreadful image.

'Go on.'

'The boy shot him and then himself,' Iris said bleakly. 'He killed Peter outright and then turned the gun on himself. Just killed my Peter, like he was shooting a rabbit or something. At least it was quick. It's the only good thing.' She stopped, took another sip of warm tea. 'We'd been engaged for three weeks. The best three weeks of my life. I thought I was going to die too, when they told me.'

Alice nodded again, sympathy in every line of her face. 'But you didn't.'

Eventually Iris managed to find her voice once more. 'I didn't. I had to leave Plymouth, though. I couldn't bear to be there any longer. All the places we used to go together . . . everything . . . it was all ruined. So I looked around for a rural position as a district nurse and moved to the village near my home town, so at least I could look after my mother. My father had died by then. People used to ask me was I sure; there would be so few young people to see, I'd have no friends my own age, but I didn't care. That was the last thing I wanted. To tell you the truth, being on my own was easier. I'd had the best – not for long, but I'd had it and known true happiness. I—I couldn't settle for less.' She came to a halt, her hands shaking a little as she set her cup on its saucer.

Alice reached out and briefly put her hand over her colleague's. 'I'm so sorry,' she said quietly. 'I can't imagine. It was bad enough when Joe's ship was attacked . . . but to lose someone, it's the worst thing.'

Iris nodded sadly. 'That's why my work means so much. I mean, it did before – but after Peter died, I had to pour my heart into something. That something was nursing.'

Alice nodded, knowing that she had done just that when Mark had broken her heart back in Liverpool. 'I'm glad you told me,' she breathed. 'We need nurses like you, Iris. Everyone says so. I just hope you can find happiness again.'

Iris poured the last of the tea. 'Maybe. It's not what I look for. Or rather, I get great satisfaction from a job well done.' She drained her cup and set it down. 'Thank you, Alice. You are a good listener – as a good nurse should be.' She broke into a small smile. 'Shall we get back?'

CHAPTER THIRTEEN

Everyone was keen to make the most of the beer garden at the back of the Duke's Arms before the summer came to an end. It was Friday, and even though plenty of people would have to work tomorrow, it was still an excuse to get together and enjoy the golden warmth of the sun.

The garden was not really much of a garden – it was more of a yard of stone slabs with a much-mended fence around it, but the landlord was determined to keep it cheerful so he had filled every available container with flowers and nasturtiums and geraniums spilled from all sides. Wooden benches and mismatched chairs were set around, and old beer barrels had been upended to use as makeshift tables. It was hardly smart, but it was welcoming and friendly and many of the nurses could think of nowhere better to unwind after a week of unremittingly tough shifts.

They knew there was a good chance that many of their other friends would be here as well and had first got to know the place when Harry had begun to take

Edith there, back at the start of the war. In those days the beer had been stronger, the lemonade not watered down, bar snacks varied and plentiful. Rationing and shortages had changed all of that, and yet they managed. There was always something to drink and usually to eat – just not what you might have thought you wanted. Harry's old school friends had always come here, as it was so close to where most of them still lived, and a group of them had gathered to enjoy the fine evening.

Gladys watched with pride as Ron expertly wound his way to the bar and returned with a tray of drinks, barely spilling a drop. 'Here we are.' He placed it on top of one of the upside-down barrels. 'Half a shandy for you, Glad.'

She smiled up at her young man, accepting her glass. 'Good job I'm not on duty,' she said.

'God knows you deserve a night off sometimes,' he replied. 'What with me so overworked down the docks and you never having a moment, it's been a week since I seen you. I'll start to think you're going off me at this rate.'

Gladys set her glass down, appalled at the very idea. 'Never, Ron! Don't you even say it in jest. Never in all my born days would I go off you.'

He grinned sheepishly. 'I didn't mean it. You know that very well.'

Gladys backed down. 'I know, I'm sorry. I'm a bit tired, that's all.'

'No wonder,' said Ron feelingly. He glanced around and spied a vacant chair. 'Here, have this, take the weight off your pins. You been running around all day, haven't you.'

Gladys nodded. It had been a busy day in the Victory Walk kitchen.

'Me too,' said Ron. 'Auntie Ida was took bad yesterday and we was up making sure she was all right. No, it was just something she ate,' he added in response to Gladys's anxious glance. 'She don't always store things right, her milk's always spoiling.'

'You know I told you she's got to cover it, and keep it on her slate shelf,' Gladys reminded him.

'I know, I know. I did tell her, but she don't listen,' he said glumly. 'Anyway, did I say that Kenny's bringing his new recruit along this evening? He thinks the lad needs to get out more, get a bit of company.'

Gladys smiled. 'Ruby mentioned it earlier. She and Lily will be along too. Sometimes I still have to pinch myself – who'd have thought it, Kenny going steady?'

'He's a changed man all right,' Ron agreed, raising his glass again. He'd known Kenny for as long as he could remember and they'd forged a strong friendship though working together, even though Ron had always been the steadier, more reliable of the pair. Until Ruby had come on the scene, that was.

Two men in civvies came through the back gate from behind Ron. 'Who's a changed man?' Kenny demanded, pushing his glasses up his nose.

Gladys batted him cheerfully on the elbow. 'You are. Ron's only saying what any of us would tell you to your face.'

140

'Oh, that.' Kenny beamed. 'You can tell me all you like. I shan't mind. Now, where are my manners – this here's Cliff, he's just joined our section as a warden. Cliff, say hello.' He indicated Gladys and Ron, and beyond them the wider group of old friends.

Cliff hovered shyly behind his mentor. He was slightly built, with a head of thick, dark blond hair, which stuck up as he ran his hand nervously through it. His glasses had sturdy brown frames and his shirt collar was open where it was missing a button.

'Hello,' he said, a little diffident. Then, more enthusiastically, 'Pleased to meet you.' Everyone nodded but could hear as he muttered to Kenny, 'Which one's Ruby?'

'I'll tell you everyone's names but you'll never remember them all in one go,' said Kenny hastily, and introduced the group of young people gathered around the beer barrel. 'We'll have a few more join us as the evening goes on,' he continued. 'Not everyone can get away so fast and some of the nurses are down the victory garden. That's where Ruby and her friend are.'

'Got to make the most of the daylight,' Gladys agreed. 'I usually go but it's my night off.'

Cliff nodded but looked somewhat overwhelmed. He played with his collar and ran his hand through his hair again. Kenny didn't blame him: not everybody wanted to be the life and soul of the party. He'd need a while to find his feet. He let Ron go on about the latest news from the docks, where there had been

141

the usual problems with stock going missing to the black market.

'Not that again,' Gladys groaned. 'Seems like as soon as you shut one lot down, more spring up.'

'That's about it,' said Ron, and Kenny nodded. 'Trouble is, we got all those goods and it draws them like bees around a honeypot. Anyway, we got new security precautions now. A right pain, they are, but we got to have them.'

'Oh, such as?' Cliff saw a way to join in the conversation for the first time.

'Not being funny but I'm not sure I should rightly say,' Ron replied, and Cliff looked crestfallen.

'Mum's the word.' Kenny nudged him. 'We wouldn't tell this lot where our training equipment came from or got stored, now would we?'

Cliff nodded reluctantly. 'Fair enough.' He looked around him and sighed. 'You don't half know a lot of people, Ken.'

'Well, you got to, in our position. It helps to know who's who and who knows who, in case you have to get hold of someone in an emergency,' Kenny pointed out. 'Look upon it as research, Cliff. Now you've met this lot, they'll tell everyone they know that there's a new warden and people will realise who you are. It all helps.' He took a swig of the beer Ron had thoughtfully got in for him, then his expression lit up. 'And here's Ruby, with her friend Lily. Ruby, this is Cliff, what I told you about.'

Cliff nodded shyly and then looked as if his eyes would pop out at the sight of Lily, done up to the nines, her bright blonde hair gleaming in the last of the sunshine.

'We had to go back and change, we were filthy from digging up the salad,' Ruby laughed. 'Pleased to meet you, Cliff.'

'Likewise.' The new warden gulped, barely able to meet the women's eyes.

Kenny noticed his reaction. The boy would learn. Meanwhile, he tapped him on the shoulder. 'Let's you and me go to the bar, get the drinks for the ladies and one for yourself,' he suggested. Cliff nodded gratefully.

'Are you really worried about thefts down the docks, Ron?' Gladys asked, after the young man was safely out of earshot.

He shrugged. 'It's always going on, just sometimes it's worse than others. It's not my job to stop it so it's annoying more than anything, unless it directly affects one of my cargoes. Makes me cross, though. There's us working all hours and risking our backs, and those thieving ba— sorry, so and so's – are getting something for nothing. It fair makes me spit.'

Gladys nodded sagely. 'Well, it would. You'll just have to keep a bit of an eye out, Ron.'

He pulled a face. 'At least I won't have to for a day or two. I got the weekend off for once. We're going up West, aren't we, Glad?'

'Oooh, aren't you fancy.' Lily laughed. 'You can keep your eyes open for bargains instead. Let me know if there's anything worth making the trip for.'

Gladys smiled, a little hesitantly, as Lily's taste was

143

far bolder than her own. 'I'll try,' she said. 'We're only going window shopping, really. Just for a bit of a change, you know.'

'I wish I could join you. It's been ages since I took my ma to Lyon's Corner House,' said Ruby, heartfelt. She smiled as Kenny approached, bearing more drinks. 'Oh, that's lovely and cold! Thanks. It's just what I need after the gardening.'

Cliff shifted from one foot to the other. 'Cheers,' he muttered, and gulped back half of his beer in one go.

Gladys grinned and was about to tease him, then decided against it. She wasn't sure how he'd take it and he'd only just met all of them; it wasn't fair to rib him on his first night out. She could remember being shy herself, overawed by many of the nurses with their qualifications and confidence born of years of study. Now, of course, she knew they were no more fearsome than anybody else. It hadn't felt like that, though, before she'd joined the Civil Nursing Reserve. Also, she had to admit, walking out with Ron had done wonders for her self-esteem. She was lucky, no doubt about it, so she would cut this new warden some slack.

'Are you from round here, then, Cliff?' she asked.

Cliff hastily wiped the foam from his top lip with the back of his hand. 'Not too far,' he said. 'I can get the bus home, towards Shoreditch. I never been to this pub though.'

'Nice, isn't it?' Gladys persisted.

'Oh yes. Yes, it's very nice. Very friendly.' The poor

fellow was doing his best. 'You, ah, you work with the nurses, do you?'

Gladys explained how she wasn't a district nurse and what the Civil Reserve entailed. 'We been busy at the first-aid post,' she told him. 'I expect you have to learn that too, don't you? Kenny said he had to practise on butcher's bones.'

Cliff cleared his throat. 'Well, yes, it's a bit gory. I know it's not like real bodies but it gave me a bit of a surprise, like.'

Gladys thought he'd be in for a few problems if he didn't like the sight of blood. Then again, he wouldn't be the first. In her experience, men were more liable to be afraid of blood than women were. She'd cleaned up her young brothers and sisters so often that she'd barely given it a thought, which had come in very handy, as things had turned out.

'I expect you'll get used to it,' she said encouragingly. No point in making the lad even more nervous than he was already. 'Some of the nurses tell stories about doctors they'd trained with, who could name all the parts of the body and tell you all the medicines in Latin or whatnot, but who would faint dead away at the sight of proper blood. One collapsed right in the middle of an operation he was meant to be observing. Just goes to show, you can have all the book learning in the world but it doesn't always count for much.'

'Blimey.' Cliff clutched his glass. 'Really? A doctor did that? A real doctor in a hospital?'

'So they said.'

'Do you know, Gladys, that makes me feel a whole lot better.' Cliff visibly perked up. 'I don't feel so daft now. I just got to practise till I get the hang of things, that's all.'

Gladys smiled inwardly. He wasn't so different to her brothers, and probably not that much older. 'That's the spirit,' she said.

CHAPTER FOURTEEN

'An accident, you say?'

Gwen nodded, having replaced the telephone receiver with some care. 'That's what they said.' She met the superintendent's steady gaze.

'Is there any reason to doubt it?' Fiona asked.

'On the face of it, no.' Gwen drummed her fingers on the back of the chair, where she stood to one side of Fiona's big desk, allowing the superintendent to come back into her office and deposit yet another armful of files onto the desk's surface. 'It's just something in the way they phrased it – well, you'll remember . . .'

Fiona pursed her lips. Both women were aware that some accidents were nothing of the kind. She had overheard enough of Gwen's side of the phone call to become suspicious.

Suicide, or attempted suicide, was one of the great unmentioned topics, and she automatically shifted a little further from the open window, while Gwen, without prompting, went to close the office door. It was all too easy for anyone passing in the corridor to overhear.

They had encountered the problem once or twice just after the Blitz, but the news had never got out. On those occasions it had featured servicemen returning home with their own firearms. For whatever reasons – and it was not within the nurses' remit to question why – that handful of young men had ended up turning the weapons on themselves. Rumours briefly flew – a love affair gone wrong, or the loss of everyone left at home, or sheer terror at returning to active duty – but those had been firmly quashed. It would be terrible for general morale if the incidents became widely known. Nobody involved was to talk about it.

Fiona was generally inclined to tell the truth and deal with the consequences, but she had understood the need for stern measures. As long as she didn't have to lie directly, she had agreed to remain silent. Only Gwen knew, as she had had to be party to some of the paperwork.

Now it looked as if they had another instance. What few details they had pointed to a self-inflicted wound and somehow they would have to ensure the news travelled no further. Officially, it was a case of a weapon misfiring and causing a shot to go wide. The young man in question had missed his heart by great good luck – or possibly not, depending on his current mental state.

'Who shall we assign to this?' Gwen wondered. 'Would it be better if I attended this patient myself?'

Fiona sighed and for a moment was tempted. There was no better nurse than her deputy: technically perfect, up to date on every aspect that could possibly be relevant, least likely to gossip. 'No.' She shook her head. 'The very fact of you going to a patient would attract attention and that's the very thing we do not want. In so many ways you would be the obvious choice but it cannot be. All it would take is one over-zealous neighbour to ask why and the cat would be out of the bag. They've worked hard to keep the details quiet while the young man was in hospital, but now he's been transferred home there's a risk that news will leak out.'

Gwen sighed in her turn. She loved the practical side of the job, not just the administration, or managing the team of nurses in their charge. She also knew how to keep her mouth shut. 'Sometimes I feel I've turned into nothing but a pen-pusher,' she breathed, safe in the knowledge that Fiona would not repeat such heresy. 'Such a complex case, we can't hand it over to just anybody. I begin to believe my skills are wasted. Sorry,' she said as she caught sight of her colleague's face, 'but you know what I mean.'

Fiona stacked and restacked the top pages of the pile of paper before her. 'That's as may be,' she said, 'but you know I'm right.'

Gwen shrugged, and sat on the chair she'd been leaning against. 'I can see your point,' she conceded reluctantly. 'It's such a shame though. That poor young man, and his family too – has he family?'

'I understand that he does. All the more reason for us to proceed with caution. Everyone will be on edge.' Fiona sat back, her arms behind her head, and gazed at the ceiling. A mark was beginning to appear in the corner, just under the pipes which led to the attic floor bathroom. She'd have to find a plumber somehow – but it would have to wait.

'We need to approach one of the nurses and quickly. We can't allow the patient's condition to worsen.'

'Very well. Who?' Gwen sat forward, clasping her hands together on the desktop. 'Of the younger ones, Ruby's proved that she's capable of discretion – look at the case of Pauline and Larry's mother.'

'That's true.' Fiona acknowledged it with a dip of her chin. 'Yet this might call for more . . . more life experience than she currently has. I don't doubt that her medical expertise is up to scratch, it's the emotional burden of it – the patient and those around him. It's not to be underestimated.'

'Alice?' Gwen had long admired the steadiness of this nurse.

'She's up to her neck in extra work with the school. I don't want to interrupt that. The poor woman has to sleep sometimes.'

'You don't,' Gwen remarked shortly.

'I'm paid not to. It comes with the territory,' Fiona responded briskly. 'Right, now let's see what you make of my suggestion. We don't know her as well as the others, but from our relatively brief acquaintance I would say that Nurse Hawke is well-qualified in every respect for this case. She will have had to handle every aspect of the job and on her own too, in her previous post. What do you say?'

Gwen unclasped her hands and dropped them into her lap. She cocked her head to one side as if in thought. 'That's a good idea,' she said decisively, after a moment. 'I sense that Iris is made of stern stuff. Shall I call her in?'

'Yes, no time like the present,' declared Fiona, swinging herself to her feet. For the new nurse to be described in such a way was praise indeed from her strict deputy.

The end-of-terrace house backed on to the railway lines leading to Liverpool Street, and was no more than a ten-minute walk from the nurses' home. Iris approached with trepidation, aware of what awaited her, and equally aware that she was not meant to know what was thought to have happened. In some ways it was not her business. The young man in question had a wound and, no matter how he had come by it, it needed treatment.

However, in other ways it was very much her business. Iris knew that some medical experts held the view that bodies were bodies and minds were minds, and what went on in one need not affect the other. She strongly disagreed. She might not have submitted learned papers to the doctors' journals but years of experience had reinforced her belief that mind and body were linked. Here was the most extreme case; but she knew that if the patient still harboured thoughts of suicide, his recovery would be slow, if he recovered at all.

It could go either way, she reasoned, noting the tidy front of the house: clean windows, curtains tied back, a pot of marigolds by the doorstep. He might feel resentful that he had not succeeded, and look upon her as being in league with those who had saved him. Or he might be relieved to have won another chance at life. The strong likelihood was that she would not discover which was true today, as he was probably still under heavy sedation. All the same, she must make acquaintance with his family.

Taking a deep breath, she knocked at the door with one hand, the other grasping the handle of her Gladstone bag.

A woman of perhaps fifty opened the door, and Iris's first thought was how respectable she looked: pale rose twinset, modest necklace of small, dark purple beads matching her clip earrings, her greying hair tidily combed back. Then she saw that the woman's face was almost as grey, with deep lines across her brow and heavy smudges under her eyes. 'Hello,' Iris said as cheerfully as she could, 'Mrs Chalmers? I'm Nurse Hawke.'

The woman looked at her, almost gazing straight through her. Then she seemed to come back to her senses. 'This way,' she said abruptly, and climbed the stairs, fitted with a well-brushed cherry-red carpet held in place with gleaming brass rods. Iris followed, noticing the framed portraits on the wall: a couple smiling rigidly for the camera, the same people with a baby held between them, a young boy in a romper suit, the boy in school uniform and then in that of the RAF. She realised that the woman in the pictures was the younger version of the careworn person in front of her. Iris took in a sharp breath at the contrast between the figure proudly holding her baby and how she was now.

'In here,' the woman said in a low voice, and pushed open a white-painted door to what must be the second bedroom. It held a double bed, in front of an old-fashioned tiled fireplace, and Iris detected the presence of a woman by the jars of cosmetics on top of the oak chest of drawers, the little pots of cold cream and a dish for jewellery.

The mother caught her looking. 'Connie's. My daughter-in-law's,' she said briefly, then indicated the bed. 'Here he is,' she said unnecessarily. 'This is Eddie. He won't speak. The doctor gave him something to make him sleep.'

'I see.' Iris moved around to the side of the bed, catching a glimpse of the train lines through the sparkling clean window. She bent down a little. The young man was deathly pale, made all the more startling by his jet-black hair. His eyes were shut, his breathing laboured. The sheet had been thrown back to reveal his tightly bandaged chest and shoulder.

Iris wondered if he would not have been better off remaining in hospital, but that was not her decision to make. 'Do you know when his dressing was last changed?' she asked.

The mother rubbed her forehead as if she had no energy to think about the answer.

'They brought him home earlier this morning,' she said at last. 'I think they did it just before he left the hospital. We wanted him home, you see. Got to keep a close eye on him. That's where we went wrong before,' she added bitterly, looking away.

Iris bent a little closer, all senses on full alert for a trace of a rotten smell, anything to indicate the wound was unclean. If the dressing was recent she would be better off leaving it in place and returning later. She would do her best to take his TPR, though. Gently, she adjusted the sheet and reached for his wrist.

The mother shot her a look then vanished through the bedroom door, and Iris could hear the muffled footsteps as she went back downstairs. In a way it was simpler; she could go about her business more freely if she wasn't being watched. This would be a preliminary visit and the real work would begin when the young man regained consciousness. She felt his forehead for signs of fever and was relieved to find none. She took his temperature by placing the thermometer under his armpit, the chilly glass barely disturbing him. He was, as she had expected, heavily sedated.

As she was packing away her equipment, the door opened again and a younger woman came in. Iris supposed this must be the owner of the items on the chest of drawers. 'Hello,' she began.

The woman looked as if she might cry, and then she jumped straight in with no social niceties. 'What have they told you?' she demanded, her voice shaky. 'You don't want to believe all of it, I can tell you.'

Iris wondered what had gone on downstairs while she had been tending her patient. 'I understand that Eddie's got a chest wound and has just been discharged from hospital, nothing more than that,' she said reassuringly. It really would do her patient no good to have his wife breaking down in the same room, no matter how sedated he was.

'Did they say why?' The woman's lower lip trembled and her eyes were red from crying. She dragged a lace-edged handkerchief from her dress pocket. 'They blame me, don't they?'

'Not at all.' Iris shut her Gladstone bag. She would rather have this conversation elsewhere, if she had to have it in the first place.

'It's lies,' hissed the woman – not much older than a girl, Iris could now see. Twenty at the most. 'They want to think the worst of me. All because I went out a few times while Eddie was away. I would never do anything to hurt him, never.'

'I'm sure you wouldn't.' Iris held her bag as if ready to go, hoping the woman would get the hint. Then she registered the way the girl stood, the arm around her stomach. There was a curve there, an unmistakable telltale bulge. The girl saw where her gaze had fallen.

'It's Eddie's,' she insisted at once. 'He came back on leave, only for one night but that was enough. He didn't believe me when I told her, then his mother said I'd been going out. She never liked me. I wish we never lived with her, I wish I never set eyes on the old bag!' She rammed the handkerchief against her mouth to stifle a sob. 'I swear, it's Eddie's! Only *she* wants to think the worst of me and it's not true.'

Iris sighed. So that was what lay behind this tragedy. Whatever the truth of it, the young man had taken his mother's word over his wife's. No wonder his mother looked so haggard and the young wife so distraught. What a mess.

'How far along are you?' Iris asked. The girl's dress was loose so it was hard to tell.

'I don't know, by rights. He was home in the spring. That was the only time we were together and I never been with anyone else, I wouldn't do that, I'm not that kind of girl. I don't know why she's so keen to believe it, and she had no right to tell Eddie. Now look what she's done! I'd never do anything to hurt him, I love him.'

'Shhh now.' Iris knew that nothing would be gained by allowing this distress to continue. 'We don't want to wake him. He needs his sleep. That's the best thing for him. He needs peace and quiet above everything else.'

The girl's face showed naked fear. 'He will be all right, won't he? I got to tell him that he got it wrong. He's got to be all right, for me and the baby. Otherwise . . . oh, it's not worth thinking about.'

'Then don't think about it,' said Iris firmly. 'You have to be strong, for his sake, and for your baby's. I shall come back later and check on him again.'

The girl's expression grew slightly more hopeful. 'You'll see that he's all right, won't you?' She reached forward and grasped Iris's free hand with both of hers. 'You got to help me. He's got to be all right.'

156

Iris took a deep breath. She didn't want to promise the impossible. 'I'll do my best,' she assured her, 'as long as you do yours. You must keep as calm as possible because panicking won't help. Do you see? You must be firm with yourself. No more giving way to tears. There are more important things to think about now.' She gently withdrew her hand. 'I must go and write up my report so that the doctor knows how his patient is doing and I'll be here twice a day until he tells me otherwise. But now, if you don't mind, I must take my leave.'

After her late-afternoon return visit to the household, Iris wanted nothing more than to creep into her bed and sleep for a week. She had carefully soaked the morning's dressing and removed it without causing any new bleeding, then managed to apply a new one without disturbing Eddie from his sedation – a feat for which she silently congratulated herself. He had groaned a little but not come round. She could now see the task she was up against; he must have been in hospital for longer than she'd thought, as the wound had begun to heal. That side of the case was a relief.

The hard work to come would be with his family. The atmosphere downstairs, where she'd gone to report on his progress, was thick with recriminations. Iris refused to get drawn in to the argument of any one side and kept matters as brief as possible, knowing she would be back here for many days to come. The mother and daughter-in-law could barely meet each

157

other's eyes, and the father sat silent in a corner, trying to hide behind his copy of the *Daily Express*.

Iris escaped as soon as she reasonably could and went to visit the doctor in question so that he could hear her news. She was beginning to have a great respect for Dr Patcham, who in other circumstances would surely have retired by now. His eyes twinkled as he asked if she had any goodies from the victory garden, and she was rather sad to report that she did not. He accepted her account of the patient's wound and seemed happy that she would be the nurse in charge. 'Glad to hear you've laid the groundwork there,' he said. 'The actual physical damage is going to be just the start, I'm afraid.'

'I know,' Iris said with feeling, packing away her notes and preparing to get back on her bike once more.

At least it was only a short distance back to Victory Walk and she hoped to be able to stack the old bike in its place in the rack and make her way to her attic room unnoticed. However that was not to be. Through the big window into the common room she could see a crowd of nurses gathering around Mary. Ruby looked out into the yard at that moment and waved her inside. Pasting on a smile, Iris could not easily decline the invitation.

'Look, Iris! Mary's finally had a proper letter from Charles.' Ruby and all the others were taking delight in Mary's cause for celebration.

'I have!' Mary waved it at Iris.

'Honestly, all that money his parents must have

spent on his schooling, you'd have thought they'd have taught him decent handwriting,' Belinda teased, leaning over her friend, who was ensconced on the biggest sofa.

'Stop it.' Mary batted her away. 'The poor darling probably doesn't have a decent light to see by. He'll have done this after a hard day's work, the poor lamb. He's allowed to be a little untidy.' Theatrically she held the sheets of paper to her chest. 'He's safe, he's not been hurt, they're taking ground all the time, he'll be in Paris soon! What did I tell you!'

'Of course,' smiled Alice, forbearing to mention all Mary's doubts and panics when the news appeared to suggest the Allied advance was not proceeding as fast as planned.

'That's lovely,' said Iris, trying to summon enthusiasm.

Ruby caught the exhaustion in her voice and tapped the cushion of the seat next to her own. 'Come and have a sit down, Iris. You're back very late. What have you been up to?'

Iris kept her smile in place but inside her spirits fell. She must not tell anyone the details of her case, apart from Gwen, Fiona and the doctor. Yet now, in the sanctuary of the big, homely common room, with everyone in such good mood, she felt the temptation to confess all, to share the sadness of that uptight house where the tragedy had occurred. What a relief it would be to compare this with other similar cases her colleagues might have known. Beforehand she had not had this luxury of being part of the team. But at the very moment she needed it most, she was under strict orders to keep her problems to herself. She could not even confide in Alice, with whom she had shared her most personal sorrow.

'Oh, I had to pop in to see Dr Patcham.' She struggled to keep it light.

'Oh, Dr Patcham, what a lovely man.' Mary loved everyone this evening.

'He's an old sweetie,' Belinda chimed in.

Ruby sat forward in her armchair. 'I'll never forget how kind he was to me that time I had to help out with an operation. You wouldn't believe it, Iris, this little boy had to have his tonsils out on the dining-room table because the hospitals were full. I never thought I could do it, but the doctor helped me manage. And we had the rudest, most miserable anaesthetist possible. I reckon if I did that, I could do anything, and all thanks to him.'

'Oh, that sounds hard.' Iris wasn't sure what to say. Where she'd come from, that was the norm. She'd held patients' hands through numerous home surgeries.

'He's very good like that.' Bridget joined in to sing the doctor's praises. 'Wish we could say the same for all of the others. Though we wouldn't mind if his old locum came back, would we?'

'Oh, he'd raise our spirits all right.'

'Raise temperatures all round, he would.'

'Pay them no mind, Iris, they always get carried away when they think of Dermot,' Alice said hurriedly. 'He's my friend from back home in Liverpool; we trained at the same hospital.'

'And he happens to be the best-looking doctor you're ever likely to see,' Bridget explained. 'He could be in the films. A proper tonic, he is, and no mistake.'

'Oh,' said Iris, unsure of what to make of this. She found it hard to care one way or the other that there was such a doctor out there somewhere. It was of no immediate use to her, burdened as she was by the case she and Dr Patcham now shared.

'Sorry, Iris, you've only just got in, and listen to us rabbiting on.' Ruby realised her colleague was worn out. 'Don't mind us, you go on up and change.'

'Well, I think I will.' Iris rose with relief. 'Glad you have had good news, Mary.' She picked up her bag and headed off.

Mary watched her go, a frown troubling her face. 'Bit of a killjoy, don't you think?'

Alice tutted. 'She's tired, and who can blame her? Look at the time. And she doesn't even *know* Charles. You can't expect her to dance for joy, Mary, but don't let it spoil the moment for you.' She kept to herself the knowledge that Iris had suffered such a personal loss.

Mary hugged the precious sheets of paper even more tightly. 'Oh, I shan't. This is a cause for celebration. What a shame there's no champagne. I might break out my special hot chocolate, though.'

CHAPTER FIFTEEN

Kenny shifted uneasily, and not only because his blue serge uniform was scratching his neck. He hated it when the wardens had to line up and listen to their superior lecturing them. He knew they had to respect his seniority, as discipline was paramount in their team, in order for them to do the work they needed to do. However, he was sure Mr Spencer was enjoying himself, exercising his power, relishing the chance to humiliate anybody he wanted.

Next to him stood one of the newest recruits, the only woman in their section. He knew Olive was older than him, and if he scrutinised her he thought he could make out the first grey hairs edging her temples, mixed in with her dark brown curls, now strictly swept back to meet Spencer's demand to appear smart. She had been happy to speak about her background, that she had two school-age children at home while her husband served away in the forces, and she relied on her mother a great deal for childcare. Kenny got the clear idea that Olive was not overly impressed with their superior. As he flicked his eyes sideways at her, she pulled the briefest of faces: one flicker and it was gone. Kenny bit his lip to prevent a chuckle escaping.

Too late. Spencer had noticed. 'Something amusing you, young man?' he snapped.

Kenny could tell he was starting to blush, which he hated. 'N—no, not at all,' he mumbled.

'Can't hear you. Speak up.' Spencer was right in front of him, and would practically have been spitting in his face, had Kenny not been several inches taller.

'Just trying not to cough,' Kenny explained.

'Just trying not to cough what?' Spencer had not moved.

'Trying not to cough, sir.' Kenny kept his expression as neutral as he could. Given the chance, his features would have twisted in disgust at this petty abuse of power.

Spencer then pivoted on his heel and swung back along the line, tutting. 'Coughing, well we can't have that, can we?' He spun around once more, glaring at Kenny from the end of the line. 'We need to keep our lungs in tip-top condition, don't we. We have to investigate fires, cope with smoke. Can't do that if we're prone to coughing, now can we?' His face displayed a nasty sneer. 'Of course there are some among us who don't care for such things. Don't have the bottle to do it, go into burning buildings and the like. People who are scared.' His beady little eyes bored into Kenny's.

Kenny gritted his teeth. How did Spencer know that he was afraid of just those situations? He'd passed that part of the training. Besides, after what Ruby told him about saving the old warden, it was natural to be frightened. The important thing was to do the job anyway. But he couldn't very well say that now.

'I'll be keeping a special eye on some of you – one in particular. That person knows who I mean.' Spencer stared at Kenny for so long that it was clear he intended everyone else to know who he meant as well. What a vicious little bully he was.

'At ease,' Spencer barked at last, and the line broke up.

Olive turned to face Kenny, her expression one of wry sympathy. 'If my kids tried something like that, they'd be on bread-and-water rations for a week,' she said. 'Doesn't exactly inspire confidence, does it? We're all adults – no need to speak to us like that.'

'Thanks.' Kenny pursed his lips, embarrassed. He knew Spencer was still resentful that the nurses had rescued Pauline and Larry, that Spencer himself hadn't been able to claim the credit for riding in like a knight in shining armour. Kenny had witnessed what the little man had come to regard as his loss of face, and that was unforgivable.

Olive cast her eyes to the corner of the draughty ARP hut, as the wind whistled through the gaps in the tin roof. 'What's he up to now?'

Spencer was talking to Cliff, and they could see the young man was basking in the attention. Clearly he wasn't being branded a coward in front of everybody. By the looks of it, he was being copiously praised.

'Let's go. I've got to clean my kitchen after my mother leaves – can't expect her to feed the kids and wash up after them,' Olive said. 'Bet you'll be glad to see the back of this place for the evening as well.'

'Too right.' Kenny straightened his itchy collar and made for the exit, holding the door open for his new colleague, who grinned at him as she stepped outside. Her frankness was such a contrast to the manipulative senior warden that he grinned broadly back.

Spencer's words drifted across the emptying hut. '. . . and I have to be off now, to see to some business. In fact, I might introduce you to my business partners one day – we're always on the lookout for sharp young men like you. Not a word to the others, mind.'

Kenny glanced back. A beaming Cliff was practically eating out of Spencer's hand.

Gladys checked the blackout blinds on the church hall windows. She had lost count of the number of times she had done this, but she couldn't let it become too automatic or she might miss something. She tugged the last corner into place and stood back, satisfied with a job well done. The echoey old hall would never feel cosy or homely but it served its purpose. There had been a first-aid post there for almost the entire duration of the war.

There were usually two first-aiders on duty at any one time. For ages she had been the junior, but now she was considered sufficiently experienced to have a newcomer in her charge. Gladys could not help but breathe a sigh of pleasure at this sign of recognition. Part of her still felt like that shy, put-upon young woman who dared not let anyone find out that she couldn't read. Those days were behind her, and in no small thanks to Alice and Edith, who had sat with her patiently in the early days of the blackout, teaching her at the nurses' home.

Now she had put that hard-fought-for learning to the best possible use. Her pride in joining the Civil Nursing Reserve knew no bounds. Perhaps, if it hadn't been for the war, it would not have happened, but she had grasped the opportunity as soon as it arose. She straightened her uniform. The evening was young but there was no telling what or who would come through the draughty old double doors.

'Would you like a cuppa, miss?' Queenie, the latest member of their first-aid team, called from the corner where the big shiny tea urn stood.

'Call me Gladys,' said Gladys at once. She didn't want the younger woman to stand on ceremony. They'd have to rub along without any of that sort of nonsense, so that they could work together in any crisis that might arise. 'And yes please.' Everyone said that you should never turn down a cup of tea when you didn't know when you might be able to snatch the next one.

Queenie pottered about, humming to herself, and Gladys tried not to find that annoying. The girl was only young, and full of beans. Let her have her fun.

All it would take would be one siren and she'd have to snap out of that soon enough.

Patients began to arrive in dribs and drabs. A new mother brought in her baby, anxious that there was something terribly wrong, but Gladys was able to show her how best to wind the child. Queenie's eyes were out on stalks as her superior expertly tapped on the tiny back and handed the baby back to its mother.

'Didn't know you had any kiddies?' she breathed.

'I got plenty of brothers and sisters and by the time I was your age I'd brought most of them up,' Gladys explained, then turned away as she ushered the mother out once more. 'Don't you go swinging the child around too soon after he's been fed, now. I know it's tempting to dandle him in the air but give his digestion time to do its job.' She waved them goodbye in the dusk.

'Smells funny in here, don't it,' Queenie observed, making herself useful by washing the teacups.

'It's the damp,' said Gladys. 'All church halls smell like that.' Not that she'd been in many, but so far it seemed to be true.

'Bet it's cold in winter,' Queenie went on.

'You'll have to knit yourself some fingerless mitts,' Gladys predicted. 'We do our best but sometimes you can see your breath in front of your face. Oh, look, here's our next customer. You see what you can do and I'll stay back here if you need me.' She watched as Queenie approached the new patient, who was an elderly hulk of a man, embarrassed at his bleeding finger.

'Thought I could still lift my toolbox,' she heard him

confess, and was pleased that Queenie reassured him and dressed his cut, despite being about half the man's size.

People continued to come in, in ones and twos, keeping them busy but not run off their feet, and Gladys was beginning to congratulate herself for a shift well completed. Her mind drifted to her next evening off, when she would see Ron, and she gave a little anticipatory shiver. He made her feel alive in ways she'd never dreamed possible, and she admired and trusted him as well. It was a combination she hadn't dared to hope for.

She was shaken out of her reverie by Queenie shutting the lid of the bandage box. 'Time to go home?' she asked, sounding tired now.

Gladys didn't blame her – it was hard to be on your feet most of the evening, especially if you'd worked all day, no matter if you had youth on your side. She knew that Queenie helped out in her auntie's shop and the girl had hardly had a break. All the same, it wasn't quite the end of their shift. 'Give it another few minutes, just to be sure,' Gladys said.

Queenie didn't question her, and Gladys felt a surge of pride at being shown respect.

Then came the sound of the outside doors cranking open, and a short man in ARP uniform half-dragged, half-carried another person inside. Gladys started up. This looked more serious than a cut finger or a baby with colic.

The ARP warden was not one of the ones she knew, but she recognised him from Kenny's description right away. There could not be two matching his comments: short, with grey hair sharply parted, and miserable as sin. All the nurses had heard about his over-eager threats to split up Pauline and Larry. Still, Gladys knew she should not pre-judge anyone. Perhaps he was just not used to children.

Her willingness to give him the benefit of the doubt did not last long.

'I require your assistance at once,' he barked, as Queenie rushed to shut the doors behind them. 'You, girl – fetch a chair.'

'What seems to be the problem?' asked Gladys, coming forward and giving a brief shake of her head to Queenie, who was pulling a face behind the man's back.

The warden wrinkled his nose. 'I should have thought that was obvious. This gentleman here is in need of immediate attention.'

Gladys nodded, grimly sympathising with Kenny and any of the others who had to work with this puffed-up little bantam. 'Well, let's sit you down, see what we can do,' she said as Queenie brought the chair across from where the spares were neatly stacked. 'What happened?'

The warden bristled. 'I was not present at the time of the incident,' he announced, and something about the way he spoke raised Gladys's suspicions. She'd had a lifetime of her siblings trying to put one over on her. Her sixth sense for falsehoods was finely developed as a result. 'Oh?' she replied neutrally.

The injured man groaned and slumped forward on the chair.

'No, I discovered this gentleman in the course of my evening duties,' the warden explained. 'He appeared to be in some pain and so I brought him here to have that pain alleviated.'

'And where did you find him?' Gladys probed.

The warden bristled. 'I do not see that it concerns you, nurse. The fact is, he is injured. It is immaterial where he came by that injury.'

Gladys sucked in her cheeks in annoyance. He was obviously hiding something and the more he protested, the more suspicious she became.

'Right, let's have a look at you. Queenie, you support this man's shoulders while I check his face . . . oh!' As Gladys carefully lifted the man's head she could see that somebody had beaten his features to a pulp. His lips were swollen, his mouth bleeding, his eyes purple and puffed up so much that they could not open, and his forehead and cheeks were shiny with bruising that seemed to emerge as she watched.

'Agh!' Queenie looked away fast.

'Do you know his name?' Gladys asked the warden.

The warden almost flinched. 'He was unable to tell me. You can see for yourself the condition of his mouth.'

As if that was a full answer, Gladys thought grimly. 'Well, we'll get you cleaned up,' she said, allowing Queenie to take the patient's weight as he rocked back against the chair. Gladys swiftly filled a bowl with warm water, found cotton wool, clean cloths and disinfectant. It would at least be a start. 'Now, try to stay still. This might sting a bit.' That was a grand understatement, she knew, but she couldn't tell if the man had even heard her.

'Well, as you seem to have everything in hand, I shall leave you to it,' the warden announced and hastily beat a retreat.

'Wait a moment,' Gladys called to his disappearing back, 'I need to—'

But he was gone. She bit her lip in frustration. He should have given her far more information. How was she meant to tell if there were further injuries when he hadn't even said if the man had been found standing up or lying in the street? She quickly assessed the state of the patient's clothing: a tear to his shirt sleeve, a rip in the shoulder. Scuffed shoes, more like boots, dusty but otherwise undamaged. Trousers splattered with blood, but perhaps from his facial injuries – not enough to suggest cuts to his legs. Nothing on the front of the shirt to indicate abdominal injury. She would have to presume the face was the main thing and proceed from there. It was far from ideal.

'Here we go. Queenie, hold him steady.' Gladys began her task of cleaning the man's face.

He groaned in pain as she gently dabbed at the wounds, writhing away but unable to escape. 'I know it's not nice but we have to get you clean,' Gladys said in her most reassuring voice. 'Don't want any infections, do we? We can't start to patch you up until we know what we're dealing with.' She realised she was saying this almost as much for Queenie as the patient himself, reinforcing all the training she would have had; it was so easy for all of that to slip your mind in the heat of the moment.

The hall was nearly dark now, just a spotlight of illumination from the bare bulb hanging directly above them. It swayed a little in the draught and Gladys had to squint to check what she was doing. She had to be accurate, not to miss anything, nor to overdo the pain unnecessarily. Carefully she felt along the man's jawline and he moaned in agony.

'Seems as if you could have lost a tooth there,' she said steadily, knowing full well it would be more than one. 'Better make a trip to the dentist as soon as you can.'

Queenie's expression was anxious. 'Will he be all right?' she mouthed.

Gladys nodded, dabbing again at the patient's eyes. 'That's better . . . that's better. Can you open your eyes at all? Try. That's right. How many fingers am I holding up?' She put her raised hand directly in front of his face.

He gulped and shifted his head a little. 'Or,' he slurred.

'Excellent! Yes, four fingers.' Gladys was relieved. He could see, if only a little, and he could understand and respond, in a fashion. 'Now let's see about your nose.' As she wiped away the dried blood she could tell that it was crooked, and it felt hot. 'Can you breathe properly? Be very careful of your nose, you might have a bit of a break there. Queenie, can you fetch a cold compress?' She judged the man was now able to sit still unaided.

Gradually she managed to clean his face and the blood that had dripped around his neck. Queenie returned with the compress and Gladys encouraged him to hold it over his nose. As he raised his hand she saw that his fingernails were broken and bloody, his knuckles purple and swollen. 'I'd better bathe your hands too,' she told him.

This man had been in a fight, then – not taken by surprise and beaten. By the state of his hands he had landed some blows. Someone, somewhere was suffering from this – maybe even in another first-aid post. What did the warden know but wasn't prepared to tell?

'What's your name?' she tried, but the man shook his head. 'Where did this happen? Do you know who did this to you?' He shied away from her questions, and if she hadn't known he could speak she would have assumed he was not able to form proper words. It was far from satisfactory.

'We can help you more if you explain what went on,' she urged. 'This is just the beginning.' She turned to reach for the bandage box, safe in the knowledge that Queenie had checked it was properly stocked. The younger woman took the bowl of water away to dispose of it and Gladys began to unroll a dressing of suitable size for the damaged hand. 'We'll do our best and then you should go to the hospital.'

At this, the man suddenly came to life, springing from his seat faster than either woman would have believed possible. He surged forward and ran, unevenly and making small groans as he did so, lurching into Queenie, still carrying her bowl of bloody water. She tripped and the water spilled over the wooden floor-boards, causing the man to slip, but still he carried on towards the main doors. With a crash, he wrenched them open and vanished into the night.

Gladys stood stock still, mouth open. What had just happened? The man was clearly in agony, but it seemed that the prospect of being seen in a hospital was more painful than coping with his injuries. And she knew she had only done the bare minimum compared to what he would ultimately need.

Then she reacted fast, turning to what she could do rather than what she could not. 'Queenie, are you all right? Did he hurt you?' She hurried to the front of the hall, sidestepping the wet boards, and hastily shut the doors again. The last thing she wanted was for anyone to complain about a light showing from the hall. Then she turned to her colleague.

'N—no.' Queenie's voice trembled. 'He just surprised me, that's all. I didn't think he could run, I didn't think he could move at all, not seeing what a state he was in when he got here.' She hugged herself, trying to stop the shaking that had overcome her.

Gladys took a deep breath. 'No, who'd have thought it.' She noticed his chair had tipped over from where he had shoved it to get away. 'He's going to be in pain with all those cuts and bruises, and as for his teeth! Well, we did our best.' She frowned. 'Something's not right about all this, Queenie. We'll clear up and it's time for us to go home, but first let's sit down and think.'

Queenie cautiously came across to the little table

where they wrote up their notes and kept paper and pens. She sank onto the little stool that was usually tidied under the table and Gladys didn't blame her. The girl looked white in the stark light from the swaying bulb.

Gladys picked up the overturned chair and came across, replacing the bandages box in its rightful position on the way. 'Right.' She drew a sheet of paper towards her. 'Let's put down what we know. I'm not sure why, but this all feels fishy to me. Let's see what we can remember. What time did the warden bring him here?'

Queenie had the instant answer. 'Ten minutes before we were due to go home.'

'And what did the man look like?'

'Well, he was covered in blood, and slumped forward, so it was hard to tell.'

'Exactly.' Gladys tapped her pencil against the table top. 'It's hard to picture him, isn't it? Try your best. Describe him, apart from his injuries.'

Queenie thought hard. 'Tall. Much taller than that little warden. He was bending over and he was still taller.'

Gladys nodded and wrote down a guess that he was at least six foot.

'Dark hair. Not just with all the blood in it. I was behind him and could tell it was nearly black, and no bald spots neither. Cut short at the sides but longer than if he was in the army or whatever.'

'Very good point.' Gladys wrote it all down. 'Strong build, would you say?'

'Queenie nodded. 'Well, yes. Now I think of it, when I was holding him upright, I could tell he had lots of muscle.'

Gladys gave a grim smile. 'Fighter's muscles, maybe.' She wrote that down as well. 'I'm not sure about his eye colour – I couldn't really see. Plain shirt, apart from the bloodstains. Dark trousers. Nothing out of the ordinary.' She sighed. 'It will have to do.'

Queenie stood up. 'So can I go now?'

'Yes, you go on, you've done more than enough. You were brave, Queenie. That might have got nasty.'

The young woman dipped her head. 'Well, we didn't know that at the time, not really. Anyway . . .' She took a breath to steady herself. 'What are you going to do with that?' She indicated the piece of paper.

Gladys stood, feeling for the big church hall keys in her pocket. 'I'm not sure.' She paused. 'Yet,' she murmured, as Queenie stepped through the big wooden doors.

CHAPTER SIXTEEN

Olive smiled broadly and told herself that she had done the right thing. The market was bustling and she'd had little sleep, but somehow she found the reserves of energy to hunt for what she wanted. Her mother had warned her that she would be mad to join the ARP, but Olive knew she had to do something. Now her children were a little older it was up to her to do her bit.

The best thing about being a warden was suddenly finding all these other women not much younger than her who worked for their living, and living for their jobs. Admittedly, there weren't any others in the ARP in her section, but that might change. The real bonus was meeting Kenny. He seemed such a nice young man, not at all deserving of their superior's spite, and keen to share what he knew – and through him she'd met his girlfriend. Then just yesterday she'd been introduced to the girlfriend's colleagues.

'Come down the Duke's Arms with us,' the one with the bright blonde hair had urged. 'You never can tell when it'll be useful to know the local district nurses.'

Olive had acknowledged she was right but had had to refuse. 'Got to get back to see to the children,' she'd explained. 'My mother has them for a few hours but she likes me to settle them when I'm not on duty. Perhaps another time.' Although she knew that was unlikely, as she had so few hours to spare.

Still, it was nice to be asked, and a real breath of fresh air. Olive pulled at the cheerful headscarf she'd hastily tied on before setting out, having had no time to wash or even brush her hair. That was the price you paid for having so much to do. But it was worth it.

There were plenty of apples for sale and she filled her basket. They could have apple pie tonight, which would soften the blow of her being back on shift. Then she could cook the rest into apple sauce and store it, or maybe make a chutney as that would last even longer. Apple chutney and a big piece of cheese . . . her mouth began to water, as she'd skipped breakfast so that the children could have more. She didn't like to send them to school without them having eaten properly.

Another stallholder had barley on offer, so she took as much of that as she could reasonably carry too. It would bulk out the stews and soups they tended to exist on during the colder months. Bracing herself against the heavy weight of her basket and her spare string bag, now fully loaded, she strode as fast as she could out of the crowded, noisy row of stalls and towards the big road that would lead her home.

'Need a hand?' A young woman in a dark cloak was pushing an ancient bicycle around the corner to meet the big road. 'Remember me? Ruby? I'm Kenny's girlfriend,' she added with a slight blush.

'Oh, Ruby! There's a coincidence. I was just thinking about your friend being kind enough to ask me to the pub.' Olive stopped in her tracks and nearly dropped the string bag. 'Look at me, what am I like, I'm not usually so clumsy.' She bent to retrieve it but the nurse was faster.

'I'm going the same way as you – I've got ten minutes spare before my next visit.' She went to take the string bag, to hoist it into her bike's basket. 'Blimey! What have you got in there?' Ruby knew she was no slouch, as all the nurses had to be reasonably fit to carry out their daily duties, but this weighed a ton.

'Just barley,' Olive said brightly, relieved to have offloaded the cereal. 'I might have overdone it, but he had so much on sale and you never know when there'll be more – I took advantage. Barley soup for us this evening.'

Ruby nodded. 'We have a lot of that as well. Good job I bumped into you when I did. How far are you down this road? I'll help.'

Olive would usually have said not to bother, but she really had bought more than she could happily carry, and also, if she was honest, she enjoyed the thought of the young woman's company. It had been so long since she had had any actual friends for herself. 'Not far. Third turn on the left,' she explained. 'Thanks, Ruby. You've been a godsend.'

Ruby finished her rounds later that day, replaying the conversation with Olive in her mind. She had been impressed with the way the older woman appeared to juggle so many calls on her time and energy. They had at least been able to share the frustrations of having to write up reports after their working hours had officially ended. 'Just when I'm ready to put my feet up for a well-deserved rest, I remember I've got to fill in those blasted forms,' Olive had said. Ruby had agreed wholeheartedly.

She tried to keep on top of such things, as they all did, but she hadn't gone into district nursing to compile lists. She knew that side of the job was necessary but it was far from her favourite part. So it was at the forefront of her mind as she went into the service room, intent on a hot drink to take upstairs where she would go through her notes to make sure she had left nothing out.

'You're in a hurry,' Gladys commented, as she carried through a pile of crockery.

'No, not really.' Ruby helped herself to a clean cup. 'Just wanted to get shot of my notes and then I don't have to think about them later.' She laughed. 'Turns out our new warden – you know, Olive? – feels the same.' She recounted their conversation as she boiled the kettle. 'Do you fancy a cuppa, Gladys? Do you have the time?'

Gladys looked tempted but shook her head. 'I haven't long had one. Better not.' Then a thought struck her. 'Of course, they have to keep records too. I wonder . . .'

'Something wrong?' Ruby caught the change in Gladys's expression.

'I don't know.' Gladys put the plates on their correct shelf. 'I was just thinking about something that happened at the first-aid post a couple of evenings ago. Do you reckon Kenny could check something for me? Nothing dodgy, or anything like that, just the name of a patient we didn't catch the right name of at the time.'

Ruby shrugged. 'I don't see why not. I'm seeing him tomorrow. I'll ask him then.'

Iris regarded herself in the mirror, turning first one way and then the other. Was her face getting thinner? Perhaps she had come to rely on all the little extras, back in her old district. There was never a shortage of eggs or good, fresh vegetables, and there was usually plenty of milk and cream to be had. Some patients would offer her a chicken or a cut of beef or pork, or even a rabbit. She had often felt reluctant to accept, suspecting they needed the food more than she did, but on occasions it would have been rude to refuse. Many had little spare cash and this was a way of paying their medical bills in kind.

She sucked in her cheeks and then stopped, noticing how it made the lines around her eyes seem deeper. Laughter lines, her mother had called them. Iris wasn't sure when she had last laughed, not properly. She'd got out of the habit. Sometimes, when she heard the younger nurses chuckling at the wireless in the common room, she felt as old as the hills. She couldn't see what was so funny about Will Hay and why anyone would want to call their teacher 'old crumpet'? She just could not understand the humour.

Her face was becoming paler, she was sure. It wasn't just that the hours of sunshine were diminishing. Out on the moors she'd acquired a tan, whether she'd wanted to or not, and her cheeks would glow rose-red from the copious amounts of fresh air. She was fading to a London pallor. Well, never mind. It wasn't as if there was anybody special to notice.

'Not exactly in the market for an admirer, are we, my girl?' she muttered to herself. She didn't usually spend much time in front of a mirror. As long as she was clean and tidy, her hair neatly restrained, she was usually content. All the same, she decided her figure wasn't so bad, with all the exercise keeping it trim, along with the filling and healthy diet – even if it was pretty monotonous.

Iris was not sure what had brought about this strange mood. Her usual aim was to keep busy for as long as possible and then to let tiredness overwhelm her. Then there was no chance for intro-spection. She didn't want to think too deeply. She wanted to do her job, be of use, perform the service for which she was trained. Thinking had never done her any good.

If she stopped to question it, she had to admit

that it was the new patient who had brought on this unusual moment of reflection. The young man who had shot himself was, on the face of it, beginning to heal. His wound had avoided infection, thanks in no small part to Iris's twice-daily visits, when she would check him thoroughly. Dr Patcham was still of a mind to keep him semi-sedated, and so Iris had had no conversations with him. Sometimes he would groan a little, or she would reassure him that all would be better as she went about her work, bathing and disinfecting and bandaging, apologising if it hurt.

She therefore had no insight into how he was feeling, if he still longed for death or if he was happy to have survived. It was a peculiar kind of limbo. Her clinical actions would have been the same in either case, but she knew there was so much more to it. If she knew what was going on in his brain she could encourage him or sympathise. Not knowing left her unable to help.

Iris did not like to talk to Fiona or Gwen about the case. If they asked then she would tell them, but they were so busy. She didn't like to interrupt their continual hard work in keeping the nurses' home running efficiently. She knew that this did not happen by magic; it took lots of effort, every day. That was far more important than her problems. A nurse of her experience should be able to sort them all by herself. The superintendent would not want her to come running every time something upset her. It couldn't be called an emergency. Iris acknowledged that she felt thoroughly out of sorts, but that was hardly a reason to take up Fiona or Gwen's valuable time. Besides, it would have to be done out of earshot of the other nurses, to guarantee the patient's confidentiality; not always easy with so many people around all the time.

'So, my girl, you'd better put up with it,' she admonished herself. Her image stared back. The daylight had almost gone and she knew she should fasten her blackout blind. The government had begun to relax the rules just a little, but this was London, not Dartmoor. She couldn't do anything that would place Victory Walk at risk.

As she made to turn towards the window, she caught a flash of herself from a different angle. For a moment it reminded her of how she had looked five years ago – and what a different person she had been then. That version of Iris had laughed heartily every day, had known how to let her hair down, and had paid far more attention to how she'd looked. In those days she had had good reason to.

Stop it right now, Iris told herself. Those days are over, and you were just a girl back then. You've had to grow up since. It's no use moping about what might have been. Put all those thoughts back in the box where they belong and lock down the lid for extra safety. It had been a risk to tell Alice what had happened and now she had to be on even more careful guard to stop those feelings leaching out and preventing her from working, from functioning at all.

Giving herself a firm talking-to had done the trick

for a long time now. Yet tonight it didn't quite. The image of that young man, ghostly pale with his shocking dark hair, lying on his bed while his family blamed each other and themselves, would not leave her alone.

'Getting a bit nippy for sitting outside,' said Kenny. He rubbed his hands together. 'Shall we see if there's a table in the bar instead?'

Gladys liked it better outside, as otherwise she spent most of her time indoors, but she had to admit it wasn't as warm as the last time a group of them had come to the Duke's Arms. Tonight it was just the four of them: Ruby and Kenny, herself and Ron. She didn't want to upset Kenny as he'd done her a favour.

So she picked up her half of shandy and followed the others through the door with its frosted panel, into the cosy bar. The barman met her eye and nodded towards the piano, but she shook her head. She wasn't going to stay for long as she had a big pile of mending to do back at home. She'd give them a song or two another day. Tonight she wanted to find out what Kenny had learned.

'Here we are.' Ron held out a chair for her, like the gentleman he was. She smiled up at him with appreciation. She could see by the way he moved that he was dog-tired but he'd still come out.

'So, Gladys, you sure you didn't get the wrong end of the stick?' Kenny was saying. ''Cos there ain't no sign of an incident that night. By rights it should have been written up but there's nothing like what you described.'

Gladys grimaced. 'I can't see how it was a mistake. It was your senior, and I didn't take to him one bit. He was all self-important and wouldn't answer my questions. Then the man he brought in did a runner. He wasn't in any state to look after himself. I worry for him because he had a broken nose and missing teeth and that's only what I could see on a quick inspection. He could have concussion. But I can't trace him without a name.'

Ron looked at her lovingly and patted her knee. 'Not your job to go worrying about him,' he pointed out. 'If you had to worry for every patient you treated, you wouldn't have no time left for yourself. You hardly do anyway. He sounds big enough and ugly enough to look after himself. You have to forget about it.'

Gladys twisted the beer mat in front of her. 'Yes, but it was odd. I didn't feel comfortable at all, looking back on it.'

Ruby bit her lip. 'You don't think he'll come back, do you?'

Ron's expression turned anxious. 'He better not try. I could come and sit with you, Glad, I'm not having anyone hurt you!'

'No, no.' Gladys realised she had caused trouble with what was meant to be a few quiet questions. 'I bet he won't want to come anywhere near me and Queenie. He'll be lying low somewhere. I was just curious, that's all.' She tried to make light of it.

'I could report old Spencer to Mr Banham,' Kenny said. 'Then he'd be for it.'

'You could, but then you might get in trouble yourself.' Gladys sighed. 'Best to leave it, Kenny, but thanks for checking. We'll have to assume Mr Spencer was in a hurry and didn't want to be quizzed by a couple of young women – and didn't know what sort of patient he'd brought in.' Although she didn't like the idea of giving the horrid warden the benefit of the doubt, she couldn't see an alternative. She'd done her best. She certainly didn't want to get Kenny into his superior's bad books.

'That's probably what it is,' said Ron. He yawned and hurriedly tried to cover it up.

'We keeping you out past your bedtime?' Ruby grinned.

Ron smiled but there was no denying he was not his usual lively self. 'Got a spot of bother at work,' he confessed. 'Ken, you missed it 'cos you was called over to Wapping before we finished up. Another load of cargo has gone missing and I had to run around trying to work out what. A right pain, it is. They can shout at me all they like, but I can't conjure up replacements out of thin air. Proper got my goat, it did.'

'Oh, and here am I waffling on about some ungrateful patient who doesn't deserve a second thought.' Gladys was guilty now, for causing Ron any extra fuss. 'Tell you what, let me get you another pint and how about a pickled egg? Did you miss your dinner with all of this going on? I bet you did.

Let me get you something to make up for it. Don't you go worrying about me. We got to look after you, you're the ones what keeps those docks ticking over.'

Ron was too tired to protest.

CHAPTER SEVENTEEN

There was a knack to riding these old bikes while wearing uniform, Iris observed as she pedalled along a potholed road, and she liked to think she'd mastered it by tucking up the long bit at the back and making sure the front was open only enough to cycle properly but not so much that the wind would make the sides flap like great unwieldy wings. She supposed everyone had their own technique, but she liked to think she had refined hers to cope with the London conditions. Back on Dartmoor it had been more a case of battening down the hatches as much as possible.

Dr Patcham had left her a message to come to his surgery at the end of her rounds, rather than them carry on leaving written notes for one another. It was all very well recording the exact figures for the patient's condition, but sometimes an informal chat was more useful. Iris liked what she knew of the old doctor and was looking forward to it, even if it cut in to her free time.

At least it was very close to Victory Walk. The

doctor's house stood out as it must have been one of the grandest on the street. Iris tried to imagine what it would have been like as a family home, with its tall bay windows and generous front porch. Above the bedroom windows were the smaller ones, which must have been for the servants' quarters. Of course that was what the attic floor of the nurses' home would have been too, but this place was larger and far more imposing.

Still, it was a family home no longer. Iris knew the basement was a refuge room, as Bridget had told her about being caught there in one of the early air raids and had had to help out with a diabetic clinic in the near-dark. Then Ruby and Lily had had to take shelter there much more recently. The ground floor was the doctor's surgery. She had been told he lived on the upper floors, always available to his patients. That must mean he had a comfortable flat, but by no means as impressive a place to live as when this had been lived in by just one family. From the outside it seemed as if it was neatly kept, as befitted a respected doctor.

Iris carefully propped her bike alongside the porch and lifted her Gladstone bag from the front basket. Her confidential notes were inside and she had no intention of tempting any passing thief by leaving her supplies on show, even if they were depleted after a full day's work. Some people would stop at nothing to steal a few bottles that might be worth something on the black market and she didn't want to encourage such loathsome behaviour.

She rapped on the bright brass knocker and a middle-aged woman answered, tying her headscarf as she spoke. 'He's just through there, in his study. That first door. Sorry, but I must be off to see to my mother.' The housekeeper smiled and rushed away, leaving Iris to find her way inside. There was the typical surgery smell of disinfectant, along with lavender polish and the faint aroma of cigarette smoke.

'Nurse Hawke! Come in, come in.' The elderly doctor rose at the sound of her footsteps and turned towards her as she entered the study. It was an old-fashioned room, leather armchairs clustered around a fireplace, a dark wooden desk with a maroon leather top taking up much of one wall. A small fire burned in the grate, in recognition of the changing season.

'Glad you could come. Thank you for humouring me.' Dr Patcham stood and smiled his welcoming smile, and Iris thought wryly that not many nurses would have refused his request. 'Set your bag down and have a seat over here where it's nice and warm.' The doctor indicated one of the leather chairs.

Iris was warm enough after having ridden the bike to get there but she was grateful for the comfort of the chair, which was sturdy and far less rickety than many of those in the common room. There was an embroidered cushion against the back and she wondered who had done the stitching, if there had ever been a Mrs Patcham. She was too tactful to ask.

'Will you take a drink, my dear? I usually have a glass of sherry at this time of day.' Dr Patcham moved across to a glass-fronted cabinet, through which Iris could see an array of bottles.

She hesitated. She rarely drank alcohol, not because she disapproved but because she was accustomed to having to be ready to go out on a call, day or night. It wouldn't have done to turn up at a birth late at night reeking of strong spirits. Then again, she was only a stone's throw from Victory Walk and there would be little risk of a callout later. She couldn't remember the last time she'd had sherry.

'Yes, thank you. That would be lovely,' she heard herself saying, before her sensible self could say no.

'Excellent.' He brought out two small glasses, beautifully etched with elaborate designs. 'To be frank, I rarely have a chance to share this pleasure. I'm very grateful to you, Nurse Hawke.'

Iris smiled. 'It's pretty rare that I'm offered such a thing.' She took a cautious sip, and the warm brown liquid made her mouth tingle. She'd forgotten how much she liked sherry, with its fragrant, woody flavour. 'It's delicious. Thank you.'

The doctor took his seat by the fire and raised his glass. 'Think nothing of it.' Then he set the little glass down on a small carved side table. 'Well, then. This tragic young man. What are we to make of the case?'

'Ah, I have the notes right here.' Iris twisted around and opened her bag, reaching in for the papers. 'Here you are, all up to date.'

'I'm sure they will be.' Dr Patcham took the file but did not attempt to read it. 'Tell me your impressions, first. Not your accurate measurements, I don't doubt those for a minute, but what you make of the whole set-up.'

Iris leant back and sighed. 'May I be honest?'

The kindly eyes looked back at her and he nodded.

'Well, then.' She hesitated, wondering if what she was about to say would make her sound unprofessional. 'I've found this one of the most disturbing cases that I can remember. I'm not sure why, exactly. It's a bad wound, but not nearly as bad as some I saw early in the war. It's thinking about what led up to him doing it . . . I try not to be fanciful, but he's so young, with all of his life before him, and his wife is distraught.'

The doctor nodded slowly. 'It is distressing, there's no doubt about it.'

'And there's so much going on in the family – the distrust, the blame.' She gave a deep sigh. 'I don't know the whys and wherefores and it's not my place to take sides, but I do wonder if he doesn't *want* to wake up. I mean, I know you're continuing to sedate him, but at much lighter levels now. Some people would be more alert – and he's otherwise young and fit. I have the impression that he's taken refuge in sleep so that he doesn't have to face what he's done and why he did it. I also wonder if he can hear more than he lets on.'

Dr Patcham took another sip of his drink.

'Does that sound far-fetched?'

'No, not at all.' He replaced the glass on the table. 'Sometimes it does us good to speculate, clear the air.

193

I don't imagine you have had any opportunity to do so back at the nurses' home?'

Iris shook her head. 'I thought it better not to.'

'Probably for the best.' He tipped his head so that he was looking at the ceiling. 'You are right to ask about what the patient can hear. It's said that many who are apparently in comas can hear more than we give them credit for. The sense of hearing could be studied so much more carefully. As could the mind. Ah, if I were younger and had my time over again . . .'

Iris got the impression that the doctor was enjoying himself, despite the subject matter, and it struck her that he too had few people to whom he could unburden himself.

'What do you suggest?' she asked. 'Do you have anything in mind? A new course of treatment, something like that?'

The doctor rose slowly and walked across to the big window with its heavy curtains in rich red velvet. Iris could just make out that their linings were a little moth-eaten and faded where they hung in habitual creases. 'I have made enquiries,' he said slowly, 'and there is a convalescent home which might be suitable.'

'On the coast?' Iris knew this was where many had been situated before war broke out but the area was now subject to bombing and now there was word of a new bomb, one even more terrifying than the doodlebug as there was no warning noise at all. She would be concerned if the young man was transferred there.

'No, in the Cotswolds. Inland, away from any urban centres,' Dr Patcham replied, cottoning on to her meaning. 'I don't know about you, but I feel that the domestic atmosphere in the family home is not conducive to his recovery. Contrary to most other cases,' he added.

Iris gave this some consideration. 'His wife will be dreadfully disappointed, but you might be right. His mother will be, too – she wants to take care of him, of course she does.'

'Only natural.' The doctor turned back towards the fireplace. 'Yet it is the very real tension between them that is one of my main sources of anxiety. Perhaps the young woman can lodge somewhere nearby . . . I don't know. That might not be practical. But as soon as there is a vacancy I am of a mind to recommend he is transferred.'

Iris took a final sip of her sherry. 'Well, I agree. He's not getting better fast enough where he is. I certainly believe his wife wants to help him recover as soon as possible – she's devastated by what has happened. Will there be doctors at this new place who specialise . . .'

'. . . in afflictions of the mind? Yes. Yes, there are a couple of very forward-thinking people there. It's one of the reasons I thought of it.' Dr Patcham drained his own glass. 'We overlook that aspect of our current situation far too readily. It's not generally known, but he's far from the only person to have made an attempt on his own life during the conflict. We hear so much about bravery, but there is a whole other side to the coin. Of course it's better for public morale to keep it under wraps, but it's there all the same.'

Iris refastened her bag. 'It's very sad, but I do understand. Also, if everyone around you is praising your bravery, or the bravery of everybody else and you feel as if you are telling them lies – well, I suppose it can make it worse. Then it takes only one more pressure to push you over the edge.'

'Very understanding of you, nurse,' said Dr Patcham. 'It's one of the elements of our job that rarely gets talked about. You might find it useful to discuss it with your superintendent or her assistant – when there's a suitable time. They are very well aware of the situation and have experience in such matters, all very discreet of course.'

Iris nodded, standing as she did so. 'Then I shall continue to treat him as usual but bear in mind your suggestion. I'll try to reassure his young wife and we'll get him to the stage where he is safe to travel.'

'That's the spirit.' Dr Patcham looked apologetic. 'I would offer you more sherry but the truth is that I am expecting another colleague. You probably haven't met him, he's an anaesthetist who occasionally helps me out in home operations.'

Iris looked quizzical. 'I can't say that I have.' She lifted her bag.

'Yes, Dr Leeson usually works at the hospital over in Homerton, but now and again they allow me to borrow him. Tomorrow's procedure won't involve any of the Victory Walk ladies as it falls within the remit of the Tottenham district.' He moved to usher her through the door, but before she could cross the room there came a rap at the front door.

Dr Patcham inclined his head in apology. 'I had better get that myself – you met my housekeeper on her way out, I think.' He left Iris standing in the middle of the room, her head slightly spinning from the unaccustomed sherry. What a good job there was another visitor; she would not have felt safe on the bike after any more, the short distance home notwithstanding.

She readied herself to be polite, thinking that Dr Patcham would probably invite only those he considered as friends at this hour, since it was getting late.

The man who must be Dr Leeson came in ahead of her elderly host. His face was drawn and gaunt, so heavily lined that she could not judge how old he might be. He moved like someone in perhaps early middle age but his expression was that of a Victorian schoolmaster.

'I didn't know you had other company,' he snapped, turning to Dr Patcham.

'Why, yes. Nurse Hawke was just leaving. We've had the most interesting chat,' Dr Patcham explained genially.

She held out her hand. 'Iris Hawke. Pleased to meet you.'

Incredibly, the man ignored her and turned on his heel to face the older man. 'I don't have long.'

Dr Patcham did not react to his rudeness, but waved his arm towards the door. 'I shall look forward to revisiting this topic, Nurse Hawke. In the meantime

197

we'll continue with the treatment plan as discussed,' he said, while the anaesthetist pointedly looked at his watch.

Well! Iris was not about to waste any more time where she was not wanted. What an abrupt end to what had been a pleasant discussion. Still, it was not Dr Patcham's fault. You couldn't pick your colleagues, and certainly not in times like these.

'Good evening, Doctor,' she said with dignity, then nodded coolly at the newcomer who continued to ignore her.

Placing her Gladstone bag back in the rack beneath the handlebars of her bike, Iris was intensely relieved that she hadn't had a second drink and didn't need to endure another second of the man's company. If she had ever doubted it, this was proof that Dr Patcham was a saint.

CHAPTER EIGHTEEN

'Brrrr!' Edith led the way to the warm fire burning in the grate. Now that November had taken hold, its blazing warmth was more necessary than ever. 'You must be freezing! Look at your hands, they're almost blue. Where are your gloves?'

Alice grinned. 'Are you practising for when you have to scold Teresa? They're in my pocket. My hands were so muddy I decided not to put them on.' It was Saturday morning and since she was not on shift, she'd made a beeline for the Banham household.

'You'd better wash them at the sink in the back kitchen,' Edith directed, and Alice meekly obliged, thinking that her friend had changed her ways. Once she had been the daring rebel, climbing into the common-room window when she'd broken curfew by staying out dancing. Now she stood over Alice while she scrubbed the soil from her nails.

'Oooh, how lovely. Mattie, come and see.' Flo had evidently caught sight of the fully laden trug of carrots from the nurses' victory garden, and liked what she saw. 'We can try that new pickling recipe you read about in the paper.'

Alice held up her hands for inspection, Edith approved, and they returned to the main kitchen where Flo stood, bending over the trug.

'Did you carry this all that way from the victory garden? It must have been very heavy.' Flo frowned even as she smiled in welcome.

'Strong arms,' said Alice. 'It's all that lifting patients that does it.'

'And controlling those blasted bikes,' Edith chipped in.

'That as well.'

Mattie came rushing in, keen to discover what her mother was talking about. 'Oh, what beauties!' she exclaimed. 'Thanks, Alice. Are you sure Gladys doesn't mind?' She picked up the trug and set it on a counter.

Alice shook her head. 'It was her idea.'

'Well, you can take some of our spinach in return. I know she can always make use of it,' Mattie offered. 'Meanwhile I'll get cracking with these. Ma's right, they said in the paper you can pickle carrots in brine and put in spices if you've got any. We've got pepper and perhaps some cloves.'

Flo wagged her finger. 'Don't you go taking all my cloves, I'll want them for Christmas.'

Edith went to the corner cupboard and started rooting around on the lowest shelf. 'Is this where we put the empty jars? I swear I saw them in here a few weeks ago.'

Alice sat down and let the pickling preparations go

on around her, knowing that the Banhams had this routine down to a T and she would only be in the way. No empty jar would ever have been wasted, but instead cleaned and set aside for moments such as this. Whatever Mattie grew in the back yard that couldn't be kept fresh was pickled or made into jam or chutney. What they did not eat themselves they gave away, and the nurses' home had benefited from any surplus over the past few years. Nobody ever refused the gift, as it was bound to be delicious thanks to Mattie and Flo's ingenuity; besides, it would have caused major offence.

Flo happily lined up the jars as Edith brought them out from the depths of the cupboard and handed them to her. 'Don't forget to keep some of those carrots fresh, just brush off the dirt,' she reminded Mattie, who tutted as if she hardly needed telling. 'Wouldn't it be lovely if Joe and Harry came home to eat them? I don't suppose you've heard anything, Alice?'

Alice glanced across at Mattie, to see if she reacted to Lennie being left out, but she didn't. Alice thought grimly that Mattie must know her husband's reappearance was least likely of all. 'No, not really,' she replied. 'He seems well, but I'm not sure where he is, and there's been no hint that he'll be home on leave.'

Flo pulled a face. 'No, I suppose not. I can't help wishing though.'

'I know,' Alice agreed, heartfelt. She remembered how he'd always enjoyed the big family occasions, when Flo would pull out all the stops to make sure everyone had more than enough to eat and drink, and enjoyed themselves thoroughly. As middle age began to take its toll on Flo, Mattie had stepped into her mother's shoes, and now Edith was joining in too. Christmas would be celebrated in style in this house on Jeeves Street, but without the young men of the household it would always feel as if there was something missing.

'I keep writing to Harry and asking him to request leave,' Edith added. 'Not sure what difference that makes but I don't want to give up trying.' She stuck her head inside the cupboard and all but disappeared. 'No, I think that's everything.' She re-emerged and sat back on her heels. 'Where's my hanky? I'm going to sneeze. It's a bit dusty at the back in there.'

Flo shook her head. 'Dust, in this house? That can't be right.'

Alice moved hastily to where she knew the rags were kept and passed one to Edith, who was blowing her nose. 'Here, wipe it down while there's room.'

Edith nodded her thanks and crawled back inside the cupboard.

'What's the news from Victory Walk?' asked Mattie, taking a handful of carrots and a vegetable brush to dislodge the earth from around them. 'Anything we don't know?'

Alice thought. 'You'll have heard most of it from your father – I know he still goes to those committee meetings with Fiona. Let's see . . . Oh, Mary's in a proper state because Charles is coming back from France. Sorry, Mattie,' as the young woman failed to hide her tiny flicker of despair, at so many returning when Lennie was not. 'We'll hear all the developments over there from the horse's mouth, anyway. Now that the Allied forces have taken most of France and advanced into Belgium, it seems he's needed back at HQ.'

'Lucky Mary,' said Mattie briefly. Then she squared her shoulders. 'You know what else we could put in the jars, Ma, how about some mustard seed and bay leaves. My little tree should have enough to go round.'

Flo nodded in approval. 'And how's Nurse Hawke getting on?'

Alice took a moment to consider, knowing she was unable to share what she knew of Iris's past. 'She's doing well – everyone speaks very highly of her. But she still prefers to keep herself to herself, much of the time.'

Edith came out of the cupboard once more, stood up and took the rag to the back door to shake. 'Stands to reason,' she said. 'If you've been working on your own for ages it must be a bit of a shock to be landed in the middle of a group of busy nurses who've all known each other for ages.'

'Oh, and the other news is, my old friend Dermot's paying a flying visit to London and is coming over to see us. He'll stay with Dr Patcham for a night or two. You can just imagine the excitement. It'll be as bad as when the king and queen visited the East End.'

Flo frowned as if this was sacrilege, but Edith laughed out loud. 'I bet everyone's suddenly keen to work the morning rounds and avoid evening first-aid lectures,' she predicted. 'Give him my best, won't you? It's not worth me coming over to see him. The evenings are getting so cold and I don't want to get a chill, not when Teresa's still so small.' She glanced across to the cot in the opposite corner to the cupboard, where her daughter was peacefully sleeping. Even the noise of moving the jars had failed to rouse her. 'Any more news? What happened to all those stomach complaints you were talking about over the summer? Just because I'm not nursing at the moment doesn't mean I forget these things.'

Alice grinned. 'I never thought that for a minute. It's odd, there was a time when we all saw several cases a week but now it seems to be calming down again. Nobody really knows why. Do you remember, there was a flare-up just after the Blitz ended and we were never sure what that meant either? Perhaps it's because we kept going through all of that because we had to, and then, when the worst of the danger was over, we had time to relax a bit. Then our bodies reacted, somehow. Just like when you have time off over Christmas and then you often get ill.'

'Suppose that makes sense. I certainly don't intend to get ill this Christmas though.' Edith opened a drawer and poked about in it. 'I'm after the scissors, Mattie – aren't they usually in here? I thought I could cut out some circles of material to make nice lids for the pickle jars we want as presents. You'll have some scraps I can use, won't you?'

'There'll be some in the Make-Do-and-Mend bag,'

Flo said with certainty. 'That's a nice thought, Edith. You can make them look festive like that. Use the bits that are too small for anything else.'

'Good idea.' Edith had found the scissors.

Alice sat back in the armchair, feeling for the hundredth time that she could happily stay here for hours. There was nowhere she felt more welcome. However, Saturday or not, she had tasks to complete. It was her turn to restock the district room with any stores that had been used up during the week, and that would not wait. Her life would not be worth living if a nurse went to refill her bag only to find something was missing. Reluctantly, she got to her feet. 'I'd best be off,' she said, a little sadly.

'Wait, I'll fetch you that spinach.' Mattie put down her vegetable brush and hastened outside, slamming the back door shut against the chilly draught.

Flo looked affectionately at Alice, reading her mind. 'He'll be back soon,' she predicted. 'I wish we could say exactly when, but soon. We have to believe it. It'll be all the better for the wait.'

Alice felt her lip give an uncharacteristic tremble. It would do no good to give in to the emotion that suddenly flooded through her. She had work to do. When Joe finally made it back home, that would be the time to show how she felt. Until then, she must bottle it up somehow.

'I know,' she said.

CHAPTER NINETEEN

November grew colder still as the month progressed and the nurses took full advantage of the big fire blazing in the common room after they finished their rounds. Despite the big windows, the room was always warm. 'I'm glad they mended those broken panes,' said Ruby, giving a theatrical shiver. 'You won't have seen what it was like, Iris. Earlier in the year there was a big bomb strike just a street away and all this glass shattered. We had to have it boarded up for ages and it was gloomy as could be. Imagine what it'd be like with that now.'

'Lots of people are making do with sacking or waxed cotton,' Iris pointed out.

'It's even better now that Gladys has adapted the curtains with thicker linings,' Belinda said. 'Still less chance of draughts getting through.'

Ruby was rebuttoning her chunkiest cardigan. 'You helped, didn't you? That's what she said.'

Belinda shrugged. 'She did the bulk of it. Are you getting ready to go out, Ruby?'

The young nurse stood up. 'That's right. Me and

Kenny are going to the pictures, down Mare Street. Several others are coming – do you fancy it, Belinda? You haven't been out for ages.'

The tallest nurse raised her eyebrows. 'What's on?'

'A Sherlock Holmes – *The Pearl of Death*. You like those, don't you?'

Belinda hesitated and then stood as well. 'You're right, I've been sitting in and moping. Perhaps I will come after all. I'll see you in the hallway, shall I?' She made for the door as Ruby nodded.

'How about a trip to the pictures, Iris? Would you like to come along too?'

Iris smiled at being invited, but had no desire to trek along like a last-minute addition. Ruby would be with her young man and they deserved time together; she knew from earlier comments that they hadn't seen one another for a week. Belinda would no doubt know whoever else was going so she herself would be a spare cog, and that would be awkward.

'Oh, that's kind of you to ask, but I have to catch up on my mending,' she said, hoping Ruby wouldn't mind the white lie.

Ruby laughed. 'Do it tomorrow,' she suggested.

'Oh, but you know how it piles up,' Iris protested, now forced to continue the fiction.

Ruby gave way. 'You're right, it does. If you're sure? You'd be welcome, really you would. Oh, all right, enjoy your evening, then – I'd better go and find Belinda.'

Iris was finally left on her own, watching the coals burning and remembering how she would gather firewood back in Devon, drying the wet logs in a little lean-to in her tiny yard, before making a neat pile in her scullery. It had been time-consuming but very satisfying, knowing she'd done the work to heat her own small house. On the other hand, it was nice to be somewhere where someone else took care of that side of things. Swings and roundabouts, she told herself. Think about the good things in this still-new place. Keep trying to do that.

There was something very comforting about a fire and she gazed into the flames, watching them flicker and then roar as the coals settled and shifted. Absent-mindedly she added a few more and watched as they changed colour in the heat. She had no idea of how much time might have gone by when she heard another voice behind her. It made her jump, as she hadn't noticed the door opening or any footsteps approaching. She had let down her guard for once.

'Iris! Just who I wanted to see.'

Gwen came and sat on the chair next to her, folding the narrow flares of her plain woollen skirt around her legs. 'Beautiful fire, isn't it? I do believe that we have Gladys to thank – she has magical powers of persuasion when it comes to obtaining fuel. I dare say she is on first-aid duty this evening, though.'

Iris gave a small smile but wondered what this was a prelude to. 'I'm not sure.' Perhaps Gladys and her young man – whatever was his name? – were part of the gang going to the cinema. It was none of her business.

'Well, it seems that for the moment we are without

other company,' Gwen went on. 'That being so, I wanted to discuss a case with you, if you don't mind. The young man with the wound from the misfiring weapon.' Even if there was nobody to hear, the assistant superintendent was scrupulous to avoid the word 'suicide'.

Iris nodded. After the visit to Dr Patcham, she had fully intended to seek out Gwen or Fiona to talk about the patient, as he had suggested, but for the few days afterwards there had never seemed to be a convenient moment. Then she had decided it would be better to wait to see how the young man progressed, if he would indeed recover enough to be fit for travel. Word had come yesterday that he had been accepted into the convalescent home and she had made what might have been her final visit to prepare him for the journey. She'd done her best to calm tensions in the household, reassuring Connie his wife, listening to her concerns, as well as downplaying his mother's accusations. She'd sat with the patient for a long while, telling him exactly what was planned for him. Yet in all that time, he had not said a word to her.

'Ah yes,' she said cautiously. 'I'd be glad of the chance to talk about that.' She felt slightly embarrassed, knowing how deeply her own feelings had become intertwined and uncertain how much of this to reveal to her superior. But before she could broach her complicated concerns, voices floated in from the corridor and she hastily clammed up while the conversation between Mary and Alice grew louder as the two nurses entered the common room.

'Oh, what a marvellous fire!' Mary hurried over, her hands spread before her. 'Alice, just come and warm yourself on this. You don't mind, do you?' She turned a little belatedly to Iris.

'Oh, not at all.' Iris backed away a little, aware that she was hogging the heat.

Gwen made to rise. 'Mary, Alice, excellent. I was just on the point of asking Nurse Hawke to check something in one of my files upstairs and it would be such a shame to waste this lovely blaze. You can have it all to yourselves.'

'Super!' exclaimed Mary in heedless delight, while Alice raised her eyebrows, catching a different meaning behind Gwen's words.

'Oh, yes. Certainly.' Iris rose as well, relieved that she hadn't been in the middle of saying something indiscreet. Truly, you had to have eyes in the back of your head in this place; there was no such thing as a confidential conversation unless you were very careful.

Gwen nodded in appreciation of the nurse cottoning on to what she meant. 'My room, then. Shall we?'

Iris wondered what Gwen's room would look like. She had an idea that it would be austere, with little in the way of personal items, and all the colours muted and restrained, to match the way the woman dressed when not in uniform. She could not have been more wrong.

Gwen's room was on the first floor, at the opposite end of the corridor to Fiona's office. The first thing Iris noticed was how large it was, and how pleasant, even though she could work out that if the blackout blind hadn't been in place the view would have been only of the back yard. There was a bed, chest of drawers and wardrobe on one side, and a small desk, but the other side was a generous living area, with an easy chair, a table with two chairs, and a big standard lamp in the corner, edged with a rose-gold fringe. Its glow made the whole space feel homely. There were plenty of shelves, and framed photographs were ranged along some of them.

Gwen took one of the hardback chairs for herself, indicating that her guest should have the more comfortable easy chair, which had an embroidered cushion. Iris sat down, glancing around the room as she did so. There was even a little wash basin in the corner, with a mirror above it. That was an unexpected luxury.

'Sherry?' Gwen asked, reaching into a cupboard for a bottle and two glasses without waiting for a reply.

'Thank you,' she said politely, accepting the little glass with its delicate stem.

'I keep this for special occasions,' Gwen added. 'It's not often that I have a visitor, and so I thought this would count.'

Iris nodded, trying not to show her surprise. This was a whole new side of Gwen. It made what she had to say less daunting. Perhaps that had been the idea. The deputy had many years of experience in nursing and that must mean she was well versed in all the quirks of human nature.

'So, tell me the latest news about that poor boy, Eddie Chalmers,' the deputy said.

'Well.' Iris blinked hard, and then gave a clinical update: the physical improvement, the move to the convalescent home. 'And therefore I won't need to attend the family any longer,' she finished.

'Hmmm.' Gwen rested her elbows on the table in front of her. 'That is, in many ways, better than we could have hoped for or predicted. There was a very real chance that he would die. However, you don't mention anything he's said to you.'

Iris shifted her position as she suddenly felt very uncomfortable, cushion or no cushion. 'That's because he hasn't – he never speaks. I don't think I'm the only one. His wife and parents say the same. It's as if he has completely withdrawn from the world. That was one big reason why the doctor wanted him moved away, so he'd be in a different atmosphere. The house is so full of tension that it can't be good for him.'

Gwen nodded seriously. 'Unspoken recriminations?'

'Something like that. The mother blames the young wife, doesn't believe the child she's carrying is her son's. The wife blames her mother-in-law for saying such a thing and making the young man distrust her. The boy's father hardly says a word. Normally you'd think that the patient would best be able to recover in his own home – but in this case the further he is away from it the better.'

'Indeed.' Gwen twirled the glass by its stem. 'And do you believe the young wife?'

Iris frowned. 'It's not my place to take sides. But

yes, I do. She's absolutely adamant, and desperate for Eddie to recover. And there's absolutely no evidence to the contrary.'

'And has she mentioned any arrangements for the birth of the child?'

'No, and it's not due until the spring; she wasn't very clear exactly when.'

Gwen took a tiny sip of sherry. 'If she trusts you, and feels that you believe her, then she might wish you to be her midwife,' she suggested.

'I'd be happy to,' Iris said at once. 'There's an idea that she might follow her husband if lodgings can be found near the convalescent home, but I don't know if that will be possible and, even if it is, how long that arrangement would last.'

Gwen nodded. 'Well, keep it in mind.' She looked steadily at the nurse. 'Iris, I hope I'm not speaking out of turn, but if you don't mind me saying, you seem a little . . . upset.'

Iris looked down to avoid Gwen's gaze. Here it comes, the moment she had avoided, had skirted around even in her own mind. 'Perhaps a little,' she admitted.

'Would you like to tell me why?'

Iris also sipped her sherry. It was sweet and warming, and made her think that maybe speaking the words would not be so bad. She'd managed to do it once, in that café, safely away from the walls of this house, after all.

'There was a similar thing that happened back in Devon,' she said slowly. 'Not in my village but down in Plymouth.'

'Go on,' Gwen said.

Iris took a deep breath to steady her nerves, and then came out with the whole sad tale: how Peter had stepped in, amidst all the horrors of the devastated docks, only to meet his end at the hands of a young man driven to distraction by fear. There was a moment's silence as she finished her story, in which she stared at her hands, gripping the little glass.

Then Gwen sighed, from the depths of her heart. 'So hard for you, my dear. I'm so sorry.'

Iris blinked furiously to ward off the tears that threatened to fall. 'Thank you. Yes, it was. Of course so many young men were dying – and old ones, and women and children. And yet it doesn't make it any easier.' She turned away, unable to look at her colleague's sympathetic expression. Her eyes fell on the photographs and for a few moments she stared at them vaguely, the unshed tears blurring their details. Then, as a few salty tears fell and she wiped them swiftly away, the focus grew sharper. Slowly she took in what she was seeing.

The photograph of the young man on his own had a slight impression of fingerprints on the glass, as if it was frequently picked up. He wore an old-fashioned captain's uniform, and he had a proud, confident bearing, his eyes lively. Dreading the answer, Iris turned back to Gwen with an unspoken question on her face.

The deputy superintendent nodded. 'That was Wilfred,' she said softly. 'He didn't make it back in 1918. All those years ago, and yet I've never forgotten him. There could never be anyone to take his place.'

For a moment neither woman spoke. Distant noises from the far-off streets filtered through the thick blind, as muffled sounds came from downstairs, doors closing, voices from the nurses who had not gone to the cinema. Someone was playing a wireless upstairs on the attic floor. A faint tune by the Glenn Miller Orchestra was just about recognisable.

Iris felt utterly drained and yet curiously lighter too. It had been bad enough telling Alice, although on her better days she recognised it had been a good thing to do, to begin to share this sorrow. But now she saw that she was not alone. Someone here understood what she had gone through. The case of Eddie had brought it all flooding back, but ultimately death was death, the manner of it just a detail when set against the unmovable horror of the loss.

'That's important, isn't it,' Iris found herself saying. 'Not to forget. It means they didn't die in vain.'

'I'm glad you understand,' Gwen breathed. 'I hesitate to tell people who have not experienced a similar loss.'

'They all said he was a hero.' Iris tried to keep the bitterness from her voice. 'Well, maybe, yes, but he was doing his job, and he'd have done what he did anyway, for anybody. I hate that word. I don't care if I never hear "hero" again for the rest of my life.'

Gwen took a final sip of her sherry. 'Sometimes I know what you mean.' She gave a small smile. 'It doesn't bring them back, does it? Nothing does. I do take comfort in the knowledge that he was doing his job, just as your young man was. He'd have had it no other way. The alternative, doing nothing, was unthinkable.'

Iris finished her sherry as well. She felt a little less shaky now.

'That goes for all of us,' she said. 'I don't want to die any more. But I don't want to be a hero. I just want to do my job.'

Gwen rose. 'And you do it very well, my dear,' she said.

CHAPTER TWENTY

Ruby had come downstairs to sort out her Gladstone bag good and early, as it was a free Saturday for her and she was going to meet up with her mother for a treat in Lyons Corner House in the West End. She knew it might take several buses to get there depending on how many diversions there were in place, and so had allowed plenty of time.

Unusually for a Saturday when she wasn't on duty, Mary was already up. Normally she would take the chance of a lie-in, mornings being her least favourite time of the day. But here she was, staring at a small package wrapped in brown paper, cradling it carefully in her hands.

Ruby glanced towards the service room, from where Gladys could be heard singing 'We're Going to Hang Out the Washing on the Siegfried Line'. Clearly she was getting chores out of the way as well.

'Everyone's up with the lark this morning,' Ruby observed.

'Oh, I didn't feel like slouching around today,' Mary said and shrugged, attempting to sound casual.

Ruby caught the undertone in her colleague's voice. 'What's in your parcel, if you don't mind me asking?'

Mary's face broke into a huge smile. 'It came this morning. It's a present from Charles.'

'Goodness, all the way from France?'

'Yes, imagine that.' Mary held it tightly to her. 'He was out there in the middle of everything that was going on and he still thought of me. I'm so happy, I can't tell you.'

'What is it? Have you opened it yet?' Ruby was curious now.

'Yes, I couldn't resist it,' Mary said, 'but I wrapped it up again to keep it safe. It's a miracle it didn't break. It's a little bottle of perfume, really tiny, but very special all the same. Apparently there was an old lady and she was so delighted that the Allies had routed the Germans that she wanted to give him a present. He wrote to say that people were offering them bottles of wine, or chickens, or anything they had. He felt he couldn't take food or drink, as there's so little of it over there. But this . . .' She blinked slowly. 'She asked him if he had anyone waiting at home for him and he said yes. So she said she had the very thing for him, and gave him this – insisted on it. She'd been given it by her husband and he'd died during the occupation and she said she couldn't bear to wear it any more but it deserved to go to someone who'd put it on and go out on the town and celebrate. Isn't that lovely? It almost made me cry, to think of it.'

'Goodness.' Ruby didn't know what to say.

'I know.' Mary gulped as if she was at a loss for words too. 'I haven't dared try it yet. I want to keep it for a special occasion.'

Ruby nodded. 'Maybe when he comes home?'

'Yes, that's what I thought too,' Mary said and there was just a small catch in her voice. 'I know it sounds silly, but if I don't open it yet, then it means he'll come home to me safely.'

She put the little parcel carefully into the pocket of her generously flared skirt, one that she'd managed to keep in wearable condition since before the war began, though now the waistband was rather loose.

Ruby nodded. 'He'll come back to you, Mary,' she said as reassuringly as she could. 'It won't be long now – and then you can wear his perfume. It's a lovely idea.'

Iris was also up early this Saturday morning, in order to lend Fiona a hand. The superintendent never revealed just how tired she was for much of the time, but Iris could spot the signs. When Fiona mentioned over breakfast that she needed to visit the Hackney Hospital down in Homerton to deliver some paperwork and to check their preferred method of first aid for burns victims, Iris volunteered to go in her stead. Fiona had gratefully accepted without too much protest, which in itself was an indication of how exhausted she was.

'You can put your feet up and listen to the wireless for a couple of hours,' Iris prescribed. 'That's my professional recommendation and therefore you have to do it.'

Fiona smiled. 'Do you know what? I just might.'

Which explained why Iris found herself cycling along Homerton High Street on a chilly morning when she might reasonably have expected to be snug and warm in her attic bedroom or the common room, perhaps catching up on her letter writing or reading the paper. All around people were beginning to show signs of preparing for Christmas, as a few wreaths had appeared on front doors, decorated with whatever was at hand. Before the war she might have thought them scrappy and badly made but now she recognised the effort that must have gone into them.

She had set out in her civilian coat and knitted scarf, one she had made herself during the long dark nights in her lonely cottage on the edge of Dartmoor. She had done a lot of knitting back then. It was a thick, soft scarf, in cheerful emerald green, but she'd made sure to wear her Queen's Nurse badge underneath it, in case anyone should question her authority.

Briskly leaping from her bike before it had quite stopped, she propped it under the entrance archway to the hospital and set off for the office in the main red-brick building, which she knew was on the ground floor. The whole place carried the familiar smell of disinfectant, but had an air of busy efficiency, which she approved of. This part of the hospital had been completed only a few years before the war started, and she appreciated its modern touches, big Crittall windows and a dedicated switchboard room. It was in many ways the opposite of Victory Walk, she thought, which, while warm and homely, could not be called new.

A sister was waiting, expecting Fiona, but she soon realised that Iris knew what she was talking about and they quickly sorted out what needed to be done. Iris turned down the offer to visit their upstairs clinical room dedicated to dressings, even though she was tempted, because she knew Fiona would be keen to hear how things had gone. So she reluctantly bade farewell to the sister, who had struck her as extremely organised, and retied her green scarf firmly around her neck, ready for the journey back.

As she rounded the corner of the porter's lodge she was almost knocked sideways by a man hurrying in the opposite direction.

'Well, excu—' Iris began but she was cut off.

'What do you think you're doing? This is a hospital,' the man snapped, irritated and abrupt all in one go.

Iris drew herself up to her full height of five foot five and a half. 'I am perfectly aware of that, and that is why I am here,' she said, firmly but coolly. 'And I dare say the same goes for you, Dr Leeson.' It was the appallingly rude anaesthetist from Dr Patcham's surgery. Evidently that evening had not been a one-off. The fellow was habitually bad-tempered and she was heartily glad she didn't have to work with him.

His eyes bored into hers. 'Do I know you?' No pleasantries, no apology.

'You do.' She loosened her scarf so that he could

see her insignia. 'Iris Hawke. District nurse. From Dr Patcham's,' she added, as he was still glaring at her.

'Hawke.' He said it flatly, not as a question.

'Yes, that's right.' She held out her hand, and stood her ground. She was going to force him to acknowledge her if it was the last thing she did.

'I see.' He cleared his throat. Then he relented a little and hurriedly shook her hand, dropping it as soon as he could. 'Well, goodbye, Nurse Hawke.' He spun on his heel and went on his way, not deigning to look back.

Iris exhaled loudly. How some people ever qualified, she could not imagine. What must his bedside manner be like? She pitied his patients, but at least as he was an anaesthetist they'd be asleep for most of the time. At this sudden thought, she had to cover her mouth before she laughed out loud.

'All right, miss?' asked the porter from his lodge.

Iris gave herself a shake. He must think she was upset, and that would not do. 'Yes, thank you, quite all right,' she said with her brightest smile. She tied her scarf about her neck once more.

'Only he's always like that, don't you go minding him, though I say it as shouldn't,' the kindly grey-haired man went on conspiratorially. 'His bark's worse than his bite, believe it or not, but it takes years to see it. Anyhow, your bike's all safe, just where you left it.'

'Thank you. I'll be on my way,' Iris assured him, eager now to leave the premises before she broke into a fit of giggles. She didn't know what had come over her. She never giggled, never laughed any more, but the encounter with the dreadful doctor had for some unaccountable reason filled her with high spirits. 'You'd better calm down, my girl,' she told herself as she pedalled back along Homerton High Street, heading west. All the same, she could hardly stifle her chuckles as she headed home to Victory Walk.

CHAPTER TWENTY-ONE

'I can't help it, I got my hopes up and that was silly,'
Flo said as she carried her heavy basket back along
Jeeves Street towards her house. She had collected her
rations from the different shops and now her shoulders
were aching. She could have done it in two trips, but
she was so used to getting it all out of the way in
one go. Old habits died hard.

'Well, that's only natural,' said her neighbour, who'd
been out doing the exact same thing. 'You want your
family all around you at Christmas, don't you, like
everyone else. I'd love for my lot to come home. Even
Jeannie's abroad now. She went on the ambulances
and we think she's in Italy.'

'Brave girl,' said Flo, hitching the basket into the
crook of her elbow.

'She is.' The neighbour reached her door in the row
of houses. The street ran at an angle away from the
main high road and had little through traffic at the best
of times, and so they had always been able to stand

in the middle of the road to say their hellos and farewells. Now that road was often littered with rubble from nearby damaged houses, although there had been no raid for some weeks. 'Right, I'd best be off indoors.' She turned to her house, drawing her big key from her coat pocket.

Flo realised she would have to put her basket down before searching for her own key. She didn't know what she was like these days, unable to remember which pocket she had tucked it into. Sighing, she balanced the brimming basket on her low front wall, patting each pocket until she found what she was looking for. The cold breeze blew and she felt it sharp as needles around her chilly hands.

'Mrs Banham!' someone called from the far end of the street and Flo turned automatically, nearly knocking the cheese out of the top of the pile of shopping. Muttering under her breath, she caught it just in time.

'Thought that was you,' said the young postman.

Flo nodded at him, knowing he was doing his best. The old postman had finally retired, his knees having had enough. Walking the pavements day after day, especially these uneven ones, had taken its toll. His replacement was pleasant enough, and from his jam-jar glasses clearly had eyesight too bad to enlist, but she just couldn't take to him.

'Now I can give these to you directly,' said the postman – little more than a boy, really, Flo thought. He fished in his large satchel and brought out a couple of envelopes. 'Here you go, one for you and one for Mrs Harry Banham – that's your daughter-in-law, isn't it?'

Nosy parker, thought Flo. Still, she smiled as she took the letters.

'From someone in the forces, if I'm not much mistaken,' he went on, blatantly fishing for gossip.

'You're probably right,' said Flo. 'Well, I must get on.' She was itching to rip open her envelope but was damned if she would do it in the street and give him the satisfaction.

'Yes, of course. Bye, missus.' He slung the satchel further around his skinny body and strode off to where he'd broken his rounds to catch up with her.

Flo told herself not to be churlish and hurriedly got her front door open. For once the place was quiet: Mattie was on shift at the gas mask factory, Gillian was at school and little Alan was round playing at a friend's house. Edith had mentioned something about taking baby Teresa for a check-up, which had amused her greatly. 'Nice to be on the receiving end of health advice for once,' she'd grinned.

Flo heaved the basket up one last time, groaning as her back gave a twinge. That was what age did for you. Time was when she would have lifted twice this weight and thought nothing of it. She set it on the kitchen counter, placed Edith's envelope on the big table, propped against the pepper pot, and then sank down into the armchair by the still-warm embers of the fire.

Eagerly she drew out her own envelope and carefully slit it open. Nobody wasted any scrap of paper any more. She recognised the writing, of course, but wanted to savour the anticipation. She tried not to imagine what the letter might say. Any news was good news, something to be savoured.

Even so, once she had read the single sheet, she held it to her chest, shut her eyes and sighed in relief. Her eyes would have watered if she'd have let them. It was from Harry, and he'd kept his message short and sweet. He'd managed to obtain leave. He would be home for Christmas. He'd meet his baby daughter at last. Her wish had come true. Edith's wish as well. Perhaps this was a good omen, showing things were changing at last. Perhaps it was a testament to the eternal power of wishing, when it came straight from the heart.

For a moment Flo sat there, happiness seeping through her. She could also now allow herself to admit that she'd secretly feared this day would never come, that some further disaster would befall him before he could see Teresa. Ever since Dunkirk, when they all thought he'd died, she could not take his survival for granted.

Then the thought struck her that he would expect all his favourite food. They'd have something to celebrate, that was for sure. Drawing the empty envelope towards her once more, she grabbed a pencil from a jar on the mantelpiece. She'd have to make a list immediately – there was not a moment to lose.

'Honestly, Charles, if you'd have given me a bit more warning, I'd have had time to get ready.' Mary threw herself into his arms, longing and relief and excitement filling her in equal measure. Then she stepped back after a long moment, torn between delight at finally seeing him again after his being in France for so long, and quiet horror that she was far from at her best. She'd had a hectic day on the district, had gone straight to a first-aid lecture that she was helping with, and had arrived back at Victory Walk with one aim in mind: to have a bath and wash her hair. She knew he loved her hair and she was rightly proud of it: her crowning glory, thick and wavy and vivid chestnut in colour. Sadly, now it was dank and dusty and pinned up any old how to keep it out of her eyes as she cycled home.

'Sorry, old girl. I had a couple of hours free and I just couldn't wait any longer.' He grinned at her, and Mary realised all over again how handsome he was, in his army captain's uniform, his blue eyes sparkling, his blond hair freshly cut to regulation length. 'Look, I've brought the motor. Hop in and we'll go for a little spin.'

Mary gasped. 'Surely you shouldn't have?' Petrol was more precious than gold these days.

'Probably not. But they're not going to say anything, not when I've been away all that time. Thought I'd take advantage before they got sick and tired of my face.' Mary thought that she would never get tired of that face.

'Gosh. All right.' She hastily ran to lock up her bike in the rack. 'Where have you parked?'

'Just at the end of the road.' He pointed, but it was

too dark to see much. He slung an arm around her shoulders and she knew that if she couldn't see the car, then nobody peeping from any nearby windows would see them either. Not that she would mind much if they did – Charles was back and the rest of them could be damned for all she cared.

'Sorry I was snappy,' she said quietly. 'I didn't mean it. I was so surprised to see you. I thought you were coming over on Sunday.'

'I am.' Charles opened the passenger side door to the car. 'It was just that this afternoon's meeting ended unexpectedly early and not a moment too soon. I can't tell you how boring those briefings can be – and I thought to hell with it, I was going to see you, come what may. I missed you so much, Mary, you can't imagine.'

'Oh, I can.' Mary turned to face him as he reached to start the engine. 'I thought about you every minute you were away. I felt as if a whole part of me was missing. It was like an ache, every single day.'

'Yes, that was exactly what it felt like.' Charles seemed a little jumpy, when she'd have thought he'd be relieved at being back safe and sound. It wasn't like him. He was the most unflustered man she'd ever met. 'I'm so glad to have made it home to you, Mary, I . . . I can't tell you how glad.'

They drove slowly down the road, guided by the shielded headlights, which cast a narrow pale band on the uneven surface. 'Was it very bad out there?' Mary asked cautiously.

'Well . . .' Charles hesitated to begin.

'I'm a nurse, remember. I'm not one of your melting Minnies,' she reminded him.

'And thank God for that,' he said at once. 'I won't lie to you, Mary. I saw some pretty awful things. Stuff nobody should ever have to see.'

'Worse than the Blitz? And those early doodlebugs?'

He sighed. 'I know they were rather awful. Let's just say, different to that. Whole villages, towns, cities even, where they hadn't had enough to eat for months, years maybe. I know they've had it rough around here, but this . . . some of the stories . . .' He cleared his throat. 'Yet they were so glad to see us, they made us so welcome, it was humbling, really. How generous people who had virtually nothing could be. I tell you, there are some over here, and I include my colleagues at HQ, who could learn a lesson or two from those people.' He exhaled loudly and she stroked his hand as they came to a stop opposite the Downs. She could just about make out the shadowy forms of the big trees, lit from the beams of the anti-aircraft lights.

'You said in your letter about the old lady who gave you the perfume.' Mary automatically fluffed her hair a little, even though it was still in its makeshift bun. 'I was going to wear it on Sunday night – I haven't opened it yet, I was saving it for when you came home. I mean, I still will wear it, of course.' She giggled. 'I thought I'd dress up and remind you of what you'd been missing.'

He flashed her a look that she could not quite read. 'You don't have to dress up to do that, Mary. You look wonderful no matter what you wear.' He cleared his throat again. 'Perhaps I should have waited . . . no, I couldn't have borne to. You see, she was quite something, that old lady. She had all sorts of tales to tell. She welcomed a few of us into her home, what was left of it, and even fed us – some sort of potato soup, but being French she'd made it taste special even with so little. We got chatting, me with my rusty French. Well, like I said, she asked me if I had anyone at home waiting for me, and when I told her yes, she wanted to know all about you.'

'Gosh,' said Mary, not quite able to read his mood. He was usually so straightforward. A small murmur of cold fear brushed her mind. He wasn't ill or anything, was he? Perhaps something truly dreadful had happened and he was about to confess.

'I showed her your photo. Did I tell you I took one with me? Well, I did. I kept it on me all the time – it was my good-luck charm, you could say.' He laughed and looked straight ahead. 'It was one we took last summer over in Regent's Park – you had that frock on that I like with the – what do you call it, that curvy neckline?'

'Sweetheart neckline, darling. That's what you mean.' Mary was glad, because she knew she looked good in that frock. It made the most of her curves – or what curves remained, after years of rationing.

'She said you were elegant. That's a big compliment, coming from a Frenchwoman.'

'Oh, I know. That's lovely. Elegant, me! Well, she wouldn't say that if she could see me now.' Mary brushed her uniform frock with her hand, knowing how crinkled it was, how unglamorous she must appear. Still, Charles had said he didn't mind.

'Then she gave me that perfume. I can't wait for you to wear it. I know it will suit you.' Charles turned to her with a new intensity in his eyes, or was she imagining it as the light was so bad? He was feeling for something in his jacket pocket.

'She gave me something else too. She made me promise . . . well, I wanted to say it anyway but to have this . . .' His voice fluctuated again, with a note she didn't recognise.

'Charles, whatever is it? Spit it out. You're making me worried. You didn't get injured, did you? You can tell me, you know. There's nothing too bad that you can't tell me.'

He shook his head. 'That's why I love you so much, Mary. I know that's true. But don't worry, I'm not injured, I'm just not very good at this.' He finally managed to draw out what he'd been searching for. 'Here, she gave me this. It was hers, her husband bought it for her when . . . when he proposed to her. Fifty years ago.' He drew in a swift breath. 'She said I should use it for the same reason, so here goes. Mary, will you marry me? Open the box, see if it fits. Say you will, Mary.'

'Oh!' Mary clapped her hand across her mouth. She was totally unprepared. Of course she had dreamt of this happening, of Charles popping the question, and it was always somewhere terribly romantic – one of the big hotels, maybe, in those beautifully lit restaurants, all the glasses glinting and the silverware shining.

Or in the country on a rare day out. Even after one of the concerts they used to go to, coming out into the dark streets all buoyed up by the exhilarating music from the orchestra. Never in her wildest dreams was it by the side of the road in the car borrowed from HQ when her hair needed a wash.

'Mary?' He sounded uncertain.

She gave a little shiver. 'Charles, of course. I'll marry you like a shot. This is the most amazing thing ever. To think you helped liberate her town and she gave you this . . . well, it's worth all the jewellery in the West End.' She stopped, suddenly overcome with the urge to cry.

'Do you like it? Does it fit?' Now she had said yes, his voice was returning to normal.

She laughed at that and the tears receded. 'I don't know, I can't really see it.'

'Hold on, there's a torch in the glove compartment. One moment, righto, there it is.' He leant across and retrieved it. Carefully he shone it downwards, its shielded beam casting a woeful ray of light. It was enough, though. The little ring slipped onto her finger and its single stone shone back at them, twinkling. 'It's a bit big,' she admitted, 'but we can get it altered.'

'But do you like it?'

Mary gulped. 'I love it. It's just what I would have chosen. It's simple but elegant and it'll go with anything.'

'She said it was a diamond,' Charles said. 'It certainly looks like one, in the daylight. We'll get it checked at somewhere reputable if you like. So glad you like it, old girl.'

'Of course I do.' She leant towards him and they kissed properly at last, the months of separation fading away. Then she broke free. 'Better turn that torch off, or the ARP will tell us off and that wouldn't do,' she giggled.

'Sorry. And I know this isn't very comfortable.' Charles laughed and his voice was now warm, back to its old cheerful and confident self. 'We'll go somewhere special on Sunday, I promise. I just couldn't wait.'

Mary looked up at him and drew his beloved face to her one more time. 'I'm so glad you didn't,' she breathed. 'I'm so glad you're home.'

CHAPTER TWENTY-TWO

Iris looked around her at the bustling street, struck by how many people there were in a small area. Even after all these months she still wasn't quite used to it. The noise was even louder than usual, with stallholders crying their wares in a last-ditch attempt to persuade customers to buy something before Christmas. The festive season was very nearly upon them.

'Do you like it here? It's a bit different, isn't it?' Ruby had suggested that they try another market for a change, even though they wouldn't know anyone here and might not know where the best bargains were to be had. Iris didn't really mind one way or the other, as she had not struck up any particular friendships over at Ridley Road, and Ruby wanted to give Roman Road a go. As it was further away, it meant taking their bikes, but it was Saturday morning and they were in no hurry.

'It's certainly very popular,' Iris replied, holding her bag tight as shoppers pushed past her. 'Were you looking for anything special?'

Ruby shrugged. 'I thought I'd see what there was for sale. No point setting your heart on something and then finding there's none to be had.'

'That's very true,' Iris agreed. These days you had to make do with what there was, rather than what you especially wanted. She smiled wryly. She would have loved a new pair of boots, pretty ones, with a little heel, and delicate buttons or buckles, but that would not be practical. Even if there were any boots, she knew she would have to choose sensible ones, no heel and with non-slip soles, that could easily be undone if she got them dirty. The thought of it did not bring her joy.

'I'll keep an eye out for something for my mother,' Ruby went on, 'and I suppose for my sister as well.' She pulled a face. 'We don't really get on but she means well. It'll make Ma happy if I buy Beryl something, even if she won't like it.'

Iris frowned. 'Why wouldn't she like it?'

Ruby grimaced. 'Because I bought it. I can't do anything right for my sister – it's just the way it is. Do you have brothers and sisters back home in Devon?'

Iris shook her head. 'No, I was the only child. My father died a while ago, and then my mother earlier this year, so there's nobody to go back for.' She thought there was no point in mentioning the memory of Peter. If he had lived then she would never have come here to start with.

'What about friends?' Ruby pressed.

'No, not really.' Iris didn't expand, but knew that the truth was she had lost contact with most of her friends after Peter had died, certainly all the ones of her own age. She couldn't bear to be seen as the one left behind, the broken half of a couple after one was missing. They had been part of a big group, nurses and wardens and other emergency staff, all with a common purpose and shared ideas. That had been blown apart when he was shot. She'd rather be on her own.

Ruby did not pursue her line of questioning, sensing that she was getting nowhere. Instead she turned her gaze towards the colourful stalls, keen to spot something her mother would like. 'Now that's interesting,' she said, squinting into the distance. 'I reckon that one on the corner has some scarves. I might go and have a closer look.'

Iris craned her neck but could not quite work out where Ruby meant. Besides, she had no huge desire for new scarves. 'You go on, I'll have a walk down this way,' she said.

'See that pie shop? Meet you outside there at half past,' said Ruby, pointing at a shop front tucked behind the main drag. It seemed to be doing good business even though it was only mid-morning.

Iris nodded and made her way to a cluster of nearby stalls from which emanated tempting smells of roasting chestnuts and something spicy. She was drawn to see, though she'd had a good breakfast not long before, piling up the toast. Still, cycling in cold air made you hungry. It wouldn't hurt to see what there was for sale.

An elderly man was arranging glass bottles full of

a warm amber liquid, while calling out, 'Apple juice, apples all the way from Kent, get your apple juice here.' It looked as if he had a big copper pot full of juice and from the aroma he had added cinnamon and cloves. 'Warm up the cockles of yer heart with a drop of spicy apple juice. Bring yer own mug.'

Iris shook her head sadly. She'd have to buy a mug, and she didn't really need one. Still, it was entertaining to watch people coming and going, and the smell put her in mind of her mother's kitchen, making baked apples or spicy biscuits, in times when the ingredients had been more easily available.

Reluctantly she turned away and wandered across to where another stallholder was displaying an array of cut branches and berries, to be used to make wreaths or other Christmas decorations. Iris watched as a few children tried to persuade their mother to buy some but the woman was having none of it. 'We'll find things like this down on the canal path,' she insisted. 'You can't eat branches. We're saving the money for potatoes – you like those.'

Iris grinned to herself, knowing that the children would not see the sense in that argument. They'd have potatoes all year round and there wasn't much that was exciting about them. She couldn't blame them for trying.

Turning to the next stall along, she caught sight of a face she remembered. It was a patient, surely. She wracked her brains to recall exactly who it was and how she knew them. Then it came to her: the woman with stomach pains, from a few months ago – the one with the horrible husband. A swift glance revealed no sign of him, fortunately.

The woman clearly recognised her too. 'Nurse! Hello – it is you, isn't it? You came to treat me, I'm Mrs Spencer.' The woman came to a stop, worried that she had got the wrong person.

'Yes, yes of course.' Iris snapped into professional gear. 'I do remember. You live not so far from the canal, isn't that right? How are you? Did your condition improve?' She thought that Mrs Spencer looked very thin, but did not say so.

Mrs Spencer was huddled in a thick coat, a big scarf wrapped around her neck. Despite its cheery brick-red colour she was pale. 'Y—yes, it did, well, a bit anyway,' she said, more hesitant now. 'I did what you said, had very plain food, made sure I had my milk ration, that kind of thing.'

Iris nodded. 'That sounds very sensible. Have you bought anything special today?' She deliberately steered the subject away from treatment, thinking that the poor woman didn't need to be thinking of such things when she was out and about.

The woman shook her head nervously. 'I'm keeping an eye out for something for my husband, but he's not an easy man to buy for.'

Iris stopped herself from replying. She could imagine only too well how difficult that would be.

'Yes, he's very particular,' Mrs Spencer went on. 'It has to be just so. I can't simply pick any old thing from a stall or shop. He likes his quality, does my Henry. He wears ever such nice things. He'd be mortified if I brought home something cheap or nasty, or in a colour that doesn't suit.'

Iris cringed inwardly but kept her expression bright. 'Well, we all like to wear our favourite colours, don't we? I noticed your lovely scarf. Such a warm colour.' She didn't add that it contrasted with the poor woman's gaunt face. Her cheeks were the polar opposite of rosy. Still, this comment brought a smile in return.

'Oh, do you think so? I got it in last year's sales. He said it was too young for me, mutton dressed as lamb I think were his very words, though I shouldn't repeat that; he wouldn't like for you to know. I like it, cheers me up, it does.'

'Exactly, and why shouldn't you wear it if you like it?' Iris said lightly, privately appalled that the officious little warden should say such a thing.

Before she could add anything more, the man himself strode along the centre aisle between the stalls and came to a precise halt by his wife. Even on a day off, his hair was immaculate, the parting absolutely straight. 'There you are!' he snapped. 'What frivolous nonsense have you managed to find today?'

The woman visibly quailed. 'Nothing yet,' she said. 'I've just been looking.' Then, more boldly, 'You remember Nurse Hawke, don't you? From the summer.'

The man glared at her rudely and then appeared to recall who she was. 'Yes, of course,' he said, with slightly more respect in his voice. 'I'm sorry, you were in uniform before.'

Iris nodded, forbearing to add that even nurses were entitled to a day off now and again.

'You mustn't mind my wife,' he said, as if the woman wasn't right there beside him. 'She entertains the most fantastical ideas. There's nothing wrong with her, not in that way at least. All in the mind, you know, all in the mind.' He nodded sagaciously, as if he were the medical professional in this conversation.

Iris raised her eyebrows. To contradict him might cause problems later on for his wife; but not to challenge him at all would be to concede to him, to imply that she agreed with his preposterous point. 'We find, in general, that the mind and body are closely linked,' she said steadily. 'It's increasingly old-fashioned to believe that they are two separate entities. Humans are more complicated than they might appear.'

The man glared at her as if she was speaking a completely foreign language. 'Indeed,' he said dismissively. 'Well, you must believe what you like, nurse, but I speak as I find. Come along,' he roughly took hold of his wife's arm, 'it'll soon be time for my dinner and I'm on shift this afternoon.'

Iris pursed her lips. 'Well, don't let me detain you,' she said frostily, and then turned to his wife. 'Nice to see you, Mrs Spencer. I do hope you continue to improve.' She watched as the couple walked swiftly away. The man was not exactly dragging his wife but it was very clear who was setting their speed of departure.

'Blimey.' Ruby had appeared out of the crowd, clutching a big paper bag. 'Is that who I think it is? Misery-guts Spencer? The one Kenny has to put up with?'

Iris nodded. 'I'm afraid you're right.'

'What did he want?'

'I was talking to his wife, who was my patient back in the summer, but apparently it's time for her to make his dinner and so she had to go,' Iris replied wryly. 'What have you got there, Ruby? You've been busy, that's for certain.'

Ruby beamed. 'I have. I'll show you somewhere that's less busy. It's nearly time for something to eat – do you fancy pie and mash? I bet you've never been to one of those places.'

'No, that's true.' Iris reflected that they didn't have such things in Devon. It would be warm inside besides, and welcoming.

'Oh, it's lovely, you get liquor and everything. That's like a parsley sauce, it's tasty as can be and it'll set us up for the day,' said Ruby eagerly. 'Then you can tell me all about that blooming man. Kenny doesn't have a good word to say about him and you know how kind *he* is usually. Then we can forget all about him. This way.'

Iris allowed herself to be escorted down the pavement behind the stalls, dodging boys running errands, stepping over cardboard boxes and wooden crates piled out of the way, ready to refill the displays. As they neared Kelly's pie and mash shop she could have found her way blindfold – the mouthwatering smell crept through the cold air, drawing her towards the bright door, with its signs to either side promising jellied eels and meat pies.

'Never mind what that mean old codger said,' Ruby

told her. 'This will set you right, you see if it doesn't. Put a bit of Christmas spirit inside you.'

'You awake?'

'Mmmmmm. Just about.' Edith snuggled against Harry's side, too content to move or even to reply properly. She was also too full. It was Christmas night and Flo had pulled out all the stops to welcome home one of her beloved boys. Harry's presence had guaranteed a fully laden table, for the Banhams and their guests.

Alice had come over, of course, her face shining with happiness because she'd received a long letter from Joe, along with a card and a small parcel. It had contained a beautifully carved pair of wooden bookends. Edith had raised her eyebrows when her friend had described them. Privately she would have preferred something to wear or a pretty piece of jewellery, but she knew it made Alice happy to receive such things and Joe happy to give them. She had to accept that this was an aspect of life on which they would have to agree to disagree. She never had time to pick up a book anyway, unless it was the treasured collection of recipes that Flo had inherited from her own mother, to which Mattie and Edith were now adding bit by bit.

While Flo roasted a turkey to perfection, Mattie and Edith had prepared a mound of vegetables, including more carrots from the victory garden, and whatever could be taken from the back yard with all its makeshift ingenious planters. The result was a meal fit for a king, or indeed an entire royal family.

243

Marrowfat peas filled a large tureen. Swedes had been mashed with precious butter and there was an enormous pudding, the fruit for which had been saved for months. Edith had improvised Christmas crackers by rolling up thin pieces of cardboard, filling them with silly trinkets, and Gillian had helped. Then the two of them had wrapped the tubes in newspaper and drawn on cheerful patterns in green and red crayon, before carefully twirling the edges closed. They might not have gone off with an explosive bang but they were a big success nonetheless.

Neither Flo nor Mattie would take no for an answer when it came to the offer of second helpings, the upshot of which was that Edith could not remember when she had eaten so much. She stifled a giggle. It wasn't even last Christmas; on that occasion she had been feeling horribly sick as she was expecting Teresa and hadn't told anyone. Come to think of it, it was a year ago that Harry had been home and she'd broken the news to him first of all.

'Penny for 'em,' said Harry, sounding sleepy himself. No wonder, thought Edith. Stan had been free with his supply of drinks, bringing out bottles of beer for the men and sherry for the ladies, those who wanted it. Edith was still feeding Teresa some of the time and had turned down the offer.

Edith reached up to stroke her husband's face. He would always bear the scars from where he had been so badly burned at Dunkirk and she could feel the uneven skin under her fingers. The strange thing was, she had become used to it and it was all part of what made him who he was now. True, he had been quite outstandingly handsome when they'd met – and he had known it, too. But she thought all the more of him for having suffered so much and come out the other side, as lovely to her as ever.

'Oh, nothing.' She smiled in the dark. There wasn't much room in the bed. It was Harry's old bed from when he'd been a boy and not built to hold two people, but she didn't take up much space. She had turned off the old Tilley lamp, catching a last glimpse of the shelf on which stood the framed photo of Harry, Joe and Mattie when they were young. Beside it now stood another picture, a print of which Edith had sent to Harry at his army base in the north: Teresa, in her best smocked frock, showing how she could sit up when held on her mother's lap.

There was even less space in the bedroom these days as Teresa slept in a Moses basket tucked up against the footboard. Little snuffles coming from that direction suggested all was well. Edith wondered if her little one was dreaming.

She gave a quiet chuckle. 'I forgot to tell you the news from Victory Walk. Mary is engaged.'

Harry rolled over slightly. 'What, to Charles?'

'Of course to Charles! Who else?'

Harry blew out a short breath. 'Well, you never know. I didn't want to put my foot in it. Good for them. Are they getting married straight away?'

'Don't think so. He's too busy at HQ from what I heard. Isn't it lovely? They've known each other almost as long as we have.'

Harry made a noise which she took for agreement, even though she knew he was less interested in such things. He liked the couple very much but he was only asking for details to please her. 'Bet they'll have a big posh wedding when it does happen,' she went on.

'Probably.' Harry enjoyed a good party as much as anybody. His breath smelt very slightly of whisky. One of Stan's grateful neighbours had given him a bottle in thanks for getting him out of a collapsed building after a raid and Stan had, of course, shared it around after dinner.

'Maybe Teresa will be old enough to get dressed up to go.' Edith moved a little, thinking of how the baby would look. 'She's got your hair, Harry. Lovely oak brown.'

He laughed, and then muffled it in order not to wake his daughter. 'She's got her mother's face though. She'll be a looker, sure enough.'

'I hope she doesn't have her mother's height,' Edith muttered. She had never liked being so small and slight. 'I wonder who she'll take after when she starts to talk? You mother sits with her and tells her stories, just as if she could understand what's going on. Perhaps she'll start early.'

Harry groaned. 'What, like Gillian? One of those in the family is enough. She answers back to everything. The frightening thing is, she makes sense. She'd not rude. She's just good at arguing. Thank God I'm not her teacher.'

'Well, there's never a dull moment when she's around, that's for certain.' She half sat up. 'Oh, Harry,

I'm so happy you made it home at last. I so wanted you to see our daughter when she was little. She's such an easy baby to look after, we're very lucky. All right, she cries a bit now and then but nothing to complain of really. I can't believe she's here, even after all these months.'

Harry squeezed her tightly. 'You two are the most precious things in the world and don't you forget it. I love you both more than life itself. In fact, there's only one thing that would make me happier.'

'What's that?'

He breathed in her ear, warm and familiar. 'Well, we don't want her to be an only child, do we? So if she was to have a little brother or sister . . .'

'Harry! You know how thin these walls are.' Edith pretended indignation but knew she wasn't doing very well, as he gave her a little tickle around the waist.

'Then we'll just have to wait until everyone is asleep,' he said happily.

CHAPTER TWENTY-THREE

The winter light was bright in the common room, flooding through the big windows and even the battered old bikes in their racks gleamed with the frost. Alice stood staring out at them, her mind elsewhere as she warmed her hands around a mug of strong tea. The voices on the wireless had been cheerful, and she could not help but wonder if 1945 really would be the year when all the fighting would end. She remembered her conversation with young Pauline all those months ago. Surely it would be so? All the signs were pointing in that direction but it felt so painfully slow.

She had been deeply disappointed that Joe had not made it home for Christmas or New Year, but knew that it would not have been for lack of trying. He was simply needed more urgently elsewhere. Sometimes she could hardly believe that was possible as she longed for him so strongly, feeling his absence like a wound. It was no good. She had to hang on to the hope that soon it would all be over and then they could plan their future together. She had lovingly arranged her precious bookends on her shelf, filling them with titles she knew he had read as well as her. He was thinking of her, just as she was thinking of him. How she wished for the day when they could do more than think, when she could hold him as tightly as she had that evening before he'd had to leave so suddenly.

Meanwhile it would be churlish to begrudge her friends their happiness. Edith had been delighted beyond words to have Harry back, if only for a few days. Mary had been on top of the world ever since Charles had returned from France and had made sure they all saw her new ring. Alice had to admit it was very tasteful; in fact, it was just the sort of thing she would want for herself. She gripped her mug a little more tightly. No point in getting carried away. That would be a long way off yet.

She had stayed at Victory Walk throughout the holiday season, knowing it would take too long to get home to Liverpool and back, and it had given her the chance to get to know Iris better. After sharing the sad story of her past, there had been an underlying understanding between the two of them, which Alice sensed gave the newest nurse some much-needed comfort. Besides, Iris had no intention of battling all the way down to Devon, where she had nobody close left to visit anyway. Fiona and Gwen had remained at their posts, and Bridget had laughed at the very idea that she would try to get home to Ireland. They had all rallied round her, to help her through the first

Christmas without her best friend Ellen. Alice sighed aloud. They all missed Ellen; time might have made the loss less sharp but they remembered her every day, any tiny detail of life at Victory Walk serving as a reminder.

Alice could tell that her replacement was very like Gwen in some ways: the vein of professionalism ran deep and could seem hard to penetrate, until you knew her better. They had shared several evenings chatting by the fire, enjoying the extra tasty cocoa that Alice's mother had sent. Iris had taken the chance to describe the village where she last lived with such vividness that Alice could imagine how it would be to stand there on top of the moors, the wind buffeting the rocks. She shivered at the notion.

'Come away from the window if you're cold!' Gladys scolded, coming in from the kitchen to check that all was ready for the breakfast rush. 'You're up early. Couldn't you sleep?'

Alice turned away from the big windows. 'No, it wasn't that so much as waking up and then thinking I might as well get going,' she said.

Gladys rearranged a couple of chairs to make more room at one of the tables. 'Wish I could have had a lie in,' she said. 'We was run off our feet at last night. There wasn't any particular reason, just one of those sessions where everything seems to happen at once. I got to hand it to young Queenie, she kept going without no fuss. Calmed down one of the nippers what had twisted his ankle, playing football where he shouldn't. His poor mother was in a right state.'

Alice smiled in sympathy. 'That's your young trainee, isn't it?'

Gladys nodded. 'She's almost done her first six months, and she's coming on in leaps and bounds. Bit of a relief, that is, 'cos I can't do everything. Bad enough having to do that at home,' she added almost under her breath.

Alice just about caught the end of her remarks and knew that it was true. Gladys rarely complained but she had precious few moments for herself with so many calls upon her time. 'How's Ron?' she asked, thinking it might cheer her up.

Gladys pushed the chairs neatly under the table. 'I hardly saw him last week,' she said. 'He's working hard as well, doing late shifts so that Kenny can get away for his ARP duties. If he can't be a warden himself he likes to make sure the others get away on time. Then he wonders why he's tired.' She gave the table top a quick wipe with a duster she whipped out from her apron pocket. 'He says Kenny's none too happy, having to put up with difficult colleagues. His supervisor is convinced he's in charge of the whole of Hackney and that young one he's meant to be supervising thinks he knows it all. Blimey. What are things coming to when Kenny's the sensible one?'

Alice laughed. 'Who'd have thought it?' She put down her mug, now empty. 'Have you made any New Year resolutions, then, Gladys?'

Gladys gave the chair back a quick wipe as well. 'To make sure Queenie is properly trained and then maybe I can start taking things easy a bit more,' she said, surprising even herself at such an idea. 'Honestly, Alice, I think I been run ragged for the past few years. I don't want to fizzle out.'

'I know what you mean.' Sometimes Alice thought she too was tired of being tired. It came with the territory. She had to remind herself it had been worse in the Blitz, when none of them had had a proper night's sleep for months on end. 'Still, did you catch the news while you were in the kitchen? That fighting they're calling the Battle of the Bulge is going our way now. I don't think the Nazis can hold out much longer on the Western Front if they've failed to break through in the Ardennes.'

'If you say so,' said Gladys. 'That's good, then, is it?'

Alice nodded decisively. 'Yes, I'd say it is. We just have to keep faith and hold our nerve, Gladys. We could be looking at the beginning of the end.'

'I don't see why we have to do this,' Cliff complained, kicking the heels of his boots against the kerb. 'The fire service will be here soon. It's their job.'

Kenny bit back a rude answer. 'Because we're here and they aren't,' he replied succinctly. 'Until they get here, it's up to us. What if a kiddy got hurt because we couldn't be bothered to help? How would you feel then?'

Cliff tutted and stuck out his chin in defiance. 'It's not even a proper fire. Not from a raid, I mean. They just haven't cleaned their chimney properly. It's not worth the bother.'

'Cliff,' said Kenny, trying not to let his exasperation

show, 'just get in that neighbour's house and count off the number of children who usually live next door. We got to establish everybody's safe. I'm going to the neighbours on the other side to see if they've taken anyone in. Someone said there's a dog to account for as well, so ask about that.' It was hard to remember what the young man had been like when he was a new recruit – that eagerness had long gone, to be replaced by a mistaken air of superiority. It was all down to Spencer, who'd continued to favour the lad, visibly drawing him aside at the end of inspections, generally making him believe he was something he was not. True to form, Cliff had to bring him up even now.

The lad pulled a face. 'Mr Spencer says we shouldn't waste our time checking on pets.'

'Mr Spencer don't know his arse from his elbow,' Kenny muttered, safe in the knowledge that the noise from the chimney fire would drown out his words. Aloud, he said, 'Mr Spencer isn't here to decide and I am. So get yourself in through that door and do your job.'

Cliff sloped off up the short garden path, looking sulky, and Kenny knocked on the other front door to the right of the damaged house. He was relieved to find a friendly welcome, in marked contrast to his young colleague's attitude. He was also relieved to be jumped upon by a lively brown dog, some kind of mongrel, who seemed none the worse for his experience. Kenny supposed that if the mutt had lived through the raids then this was nothing. 'Good boy, good boy,' he said, ruffling the creature's ears.

'Like dogs, do you?' asked the elderly man who'd opened the door. 'Got one yerself, have you?'

Kenny shook his head regretfully. 'I don't have the time to look after one,' he said. 'Maybe when all this is over, I'll see. He's a right rascal, isn't he?'

The man looked fondly at the dog. 'He is, all right. I can't manage one myself but I always says to them next door, if you need anyone to mind him, I'm happy to oblige.'

Kenny smiled and made a scribble in his notebook. 'I'd best be going, but thank you. Now we know this little fellow's safe.' For a moment, out of nowhere, he felt a lump forming in his throat. An image came to him of Ruby and him, together with a little dog like this. They'd be like a family, and they could take him for walks . . . but this was pure fantasy. Come to think of it, he didn't even know if she liked dogs.

'Goodbye now,' he called, and went back outside, to find Cliff waiting. 'Well? Are they all accounted for?'

'Suppose so,' Cliff said sulkily. 'All apart from that bloomin' dog.'

'He's all right, he's with the other neighbour.' Kenny wondered if this was the time and place to have a go at the young warden about his demeanour, but then came the sound of an approaching fire engine. 'Righto, better let them know what's happening,' he said, setting off at a run as the vehicle drew up at the kerbside. Cliff made no move to join him. Honestly, what was wrong with the boy? His closeness to Spencer wasn't doing him any good at all.

Quickly Kenny told the firefighters what they needed to know. It was all pretty straightforward; no lives appeared to be in danger, the household was safe and there was little chance of the fire spreading now that the experts had arrived. Kenny finished his hasty report and turned back to the terrace of redbrick houses, two-up, two-downs, not prosperous but respectable-looking all the same. The kind of street where people looked after one another, where you could sit around your neighbour's table and bring your family if you were in trouble. Nothing special; just ordinary people behaving with dignity and compassion. Sometimes he felt proud to be a Londoner.

The door to the left of the burning house opened and a middle-aged woman came out, neat in a grey skirt and knitted twinset. She waved him over. 'Are you the young warden's superior?' she asked.

Kenny pursed his lips. 'Sort of,' he said. 'Is there a problem, madam?'

The woman looked worried. 'I don't want to cause trouble, but we thought you should know. He wasn't very polite, you see. In fact he quite upset the youngest children. It's bad enough they had to be taken from their nice warm beds and sat around our table instead.'

Kenny groaned inwardly. 'I'm sorry to hear that. What did he say exactly?'

In the light of the chimney fire he could have sworn he saw the woman blush. 'It was more the way he spoke. They're frightened, they need sympathy, not to be spoken to like they're pieces of rubbish. Well, I suppose he's too young to have children of his own.

But he didn't seem to want to give us the time of day. Made us feel like we were causing a nuisance, like we were putting it on, but the kiddies are scared witless.'

Kenny nodded. 'I do apologise on his behalf,' he said formally. 'I'll have a word. I'm sorry the children are frightened.'

The woman nodded. 'I should be getting back to them. Thank you.' She disappeared back inside.

Kenny sighed long and hard as he made his way over to where Cliff was having a puff of his cigarette. This young man was becoming a liability. On the other hand, looking on the bright side, those kids were safe with a caring neighbour. It took all sorts.

CHAPTER TWENTY-FOUR

Iris tried to tell herself not to be so mean. She should be cheerful. It was a new year and that usually raised her spirits. Birds seemed to sing more loudly, even if around here it was mainly sparrows and pigeons. The beginnings of buds were just about showing on the trees, tiny spots of fresh green against the brown twigs. She walked along the outermost path of the Downs, avoiding patches of mud, acknowledging that this was a pleasant open space, even if it would always be a poor substitute for the moors.

She had been grateful of the chance to throw herself into her work over the Christmas holidays and it had given her the chance to become better acquainted with the nurses she admired most, Fiona, Gwen and Alice. It was good to be able to talk to them when the pressure of everyday rounds was reduced a little. Alice had obviously been disappointed that her young man had not made it home for the festive season, but she hadn't gone on and on about it.

Iris had to admit that she found it harder to warm

to Mary, who simply reminded her too much of some of the nurses she had trained with so long ago – ones who had no trouble finding the money for their equipment, who didn't have to worry about the chill of the ancient nurses' quarters as their well-off families would buy them beautiful wraps and elegant slippers. It wasn't Mary's fault that she spoke in the same cut-glass accent. Yet the showing-off of the new engagement ring had set Iris off all over again. Evidently Mary's fiancé was a popular figure among the nurses, and from a photo she had brought out one day in the canteen, he was a handsome fellow, especially in his army captain's uniform, somebody to be proud of without a doubt. Why then did it rankle with her so much?

You're jealous, my girl, she told herself, stepping neatly over a particularly wet patch of ground. Ruby had her young man, the warden, and Gladys was walking out with his best friend. She didn't know about the other nurses, but so many of the ones she had most to do with seemed happy with their menfolk and, try as she might to deny it, it brought it all back. How did Gwen stand it, to be reminded over and over again what she had been deprived of when her own young man was killed? Iris gritted her teeth and strode on more quickly.

It wasn't just missing Peter, although that was bad enough. It was the sense of being part of a couple, which in turn was part of a group, with shared interests and a common purpose. Yes, she had that with the other nurses, especially the senior ones. But it wasn't the same. She could not quite allow herself to be part of this close-knit group. She was always at one remove, yet they had shown her nothing but kindness. No, it was no good. While the others could chat and interact and enjoy one another's company, once again she sensed she was behind a barrier.

'You didn't use to be like this,' she told herself, staring at the neatly laid out vegetable beds, some heaped with mulch in readiness for the planting season. Gladys would approve. Perhaps she should make more of an effort to become involved with the victory garden; she'd grown fruit and vegetables before, although the conditions in Devon were different. It seemed a small thing, though, when set against the overpowering sense of loneliness. Even in this massive city she felt the ache day in, day out.

For a brief moment she thought that she would give way and cry. Nobody would see, here under the trees. However, that would not do. It would be to give in and that wasn't how she had been brought up. There was always somebody worse off, her mother had told her, and she knew full well that there were many, many people in a far worse position than herself these days. She had a job she loved, she had excellent accommodation and was well-respected. It should be enough. It would damn well *have* to be enough. Chin up, she muttered.

The good spirits of new year lasted all the way through January, as slowly the dawn broke earlier and the evenings grew imperceptibly longer. Mary's happiness had infected her colleagues and nobody begrudged her the joy of wearing her ring, even if she carefully took it off before doing her rounds. The news from the continent continued to give everyone cause for hope. The feeling was growing day by day that there really might be an end to the fighting, that peace was not too far beyond their grasp.

But it was too much to ask that it would last, that the path to peace would be smooth and pain-free for them all.

Belinda had arrived back at the annexe flat with her dark hair windblown and her cheeks red from the cold, but her eyes gleaming.

'You look as if you've had a good morning,' Bridget said, pausing from arranging her handwashing over the wooden rack in front of the little living-room fire. 'Don't tell me you let Geraldine persuade you to ride on the back of that motorbike again? You said you'd never go near it for the rest of your life after the last time. Please say you haven't forgotten?'

Belinda laughed and undid the collar of her bulky tweed coat. 'No, not likely. Once was enough, that thing is lethal. Anyway, she can't get the petrol at the moment. We just went to the market, got a few odds and ends.' She began to unload her bag.

Bridget sat back, satisfied that she'd arranged everything in such a way as to minimise any ironing. 'Shall I put on the kettle?'

'I'll do it, I'm closer,' Belinda offered, hanging up the big coat on a peg next to the door. She was checking that she'd tucked both of her gloves into her patch pockets when somebody rapped on the letterbox. 'Hold on, I'd better see who that is.' She disappeared and Bridget wandered over to the tap to fill the kettle after all. With half an ear she registered the front door opening, a murmured exchange and then a sharp gasp.

Belinda came back into the room, all her cheerful colour gone, followed by Gwen, who was holding a telegram. Bridget stared at it in recognition, a feeling of dread growing in her, catching her breath. Before she could say anything, Gwen spoke.

'I'm afraid to say that Belinda has just had some bad news,' she said, not beating about the bush. 'Take a seat, there.' She guided the tall nurse to a chair by the window, though now Belinda had hunched in upon herself, almost as if she was shielding from the impact of a blow.

Bridget's hand flew to her mouth. There was one person her flatmate was always worried about, who continually put himself in danger. Of course it could be anybody – her parents, her parents' close friends, even Geraldine . . . but no. This was the news that Belinda had dreaded for so long. It could only be her brother.

'David?' Bridget gulped, and Gwen gave a brief nod.

With a sharp pang Bridget realised it was similar to how things had been last June – except then Belinda had rushed to look after her, when the news had come about Ellen. Two loved ones in the space of just over half a year. It was too much to comprehend.

Gwen set down the telegram on the little dining table, barely big enough for two people to sit at. 'The only good thing is, he won't have suffered, it was so quick,' she said. 'He was shot down over Germany and a fellow pilot from his squadron witnessed the crash. It was fast and nobody survived, is what he reports.'

Bridget shut her eyes tightly for a moment. As Gwen had said, at least it was quick, but she didn't want to imagine it, the flames, the noise, the smell of fuel . . .

Belinda was hugging herself hard, the sinews in her lower arms tight as ropes. Her lips were trembling and she began to shiver.

Gwen sat down at the little table, maintaining her calm. 'I won't insult you by saying how brave he was,' she said quietly. 'You've always known that. He never wavered. He knew what the risks were but never hesitated to do his duty. He lived his life knowing it could end in this way, in fact, knowing that it probably would, and yet he went back time and time again. He was remarkable, but you don't need me to tell you that.'

Belinda made no comment, just gripped her arms across her chest, staring straight ahead.

Bright winter sunshine poured through the window which overlooked the pavement that ran along the front gates of Victory Walk. Sounds of voices filtered up from the nurses' home; some of the young women must be standing on the front steps on the way in or out. Soon they would learn the news, that another of their colleagues had been bereaved.

'Shall I fetch someone?' Bridget offered. 'Someone from next door? Or Geraldine?'

Belinda's eyes came back into focus but she gave a quick shake of her head.

Gwen turned to look at her. 'Maybe later,' she suggested. 'Let's leave it for a little while. They'll have to know, of course, but there's no rush.'

'Of course not.' Bridget struggled to remember the procedure for dealing with shock, which normally came to her as easily as breathing. Yet somehow it was different when it was somebody you were close to, not a patient. Yes, she should offer Belinda some sugary tea . . . She made the tea, placed a cup by Belinda's hand, then stayed still and quiet and the minutes ticked by, the sun warming the small room, with all the bits and pieces the nurses had added to make it cosy. Ellen's cake tin still sat on a top shelf, from the days when she had persuaded her family to send over the ingredients. It felt like a lifetime ago.

Bridget looked down at her feet, trying very hard not to think about Ellen right at this point, yet the shock of bereavement was too fresh and the loss of her dear friend flooded through her all over again. She bit her lip hard. Now was not the time to give way to that sorrow, which had always bubbled just beneath the surface since that dreadful day last June.

At last Belinda gave a long, slow exhalation and cleared her throat. 'I can't believe it,' she choked out. 'I've expected this since the day he joined up and

I—I thought I was prepared, but it turns out I was wrong.' She dropped her hands to her lap and wrung them together. 'You can't prepare, not for the reality of it. There'd always been a chance he'd be one of the lucky ones, that he'd make it through.'

'Of course.' Gwen patted her shoulder gently.

'He's lasted longer than most of the ones he trained with,' Belinda continued grimly. 'Many of them didn't even survive their first year. Boys, they were, just boys. Not old enough to vote, even.' She cleared her throat. 'At least he loved what he was doing – he really, really loved flying. Always said he'd take me up for a spin, but he never did.'

'It would be worse than being on the back of that motorbike,' Bridget put in, trying to help with humour.

'Maybe.' Belinda shrugged. 'I shan't know, now. I don't want to go up in a plane ever. He loved it, though. Seeing the ground from above, the towns and the fields. He'd write home long letters about it – finding your way by following the rivers, what it was like to cross the Channel, dodging the enemy aircraft, doing aerobatics.'

'He packed more in to his short life than many people twice, three times his age,' Gwen pointed out.

'Perhaps.' Belinda finally took a sip of tea. 'He was never half-hearted about anything. It was all or nothing, with him. Always was. He never let being afraid stop him. Even when we were little, he'd always climb higher, run faster. My mother used to say it was because he understood, somehow, what she'd escaped, that he knew he mustn't waste a minute, that we'd been given a second chance.'

Bridget nodded, knowing this was something that was beyond her immediate comprehension. Belinda and David's parents had fled mainland Europe many years ago, already aware of what their fate as Jews was likely to be if they stayed.

Belinda set her cup down suddenly, with a crash. 'Do you know what? I'm glad he went quickly. It's a thousand times better than if he'd survived and been taken prisoner.'

Bridget raised her eyebrows. 'Because he'd have been in pain . . .'

'No,' Belinda said firmly. 'Well, yes, but that's not it. They'd have tortured him, singled him out because of our faith. We all know what happens to Jews in Germany. It's worse than death, what they do, it's inhuman. At least he was spared that. It's what he wanted, he told me the last time he saw me. He said he'd never go quietly if he thought they were about to take him prisoner. At least . . . at least he didn't have to make that choice. He knew what the odds were. He hasn't had to go through that. This is bad enough, but if he'd been taken prisoner . . .' She could not go on. Full realisation hit her and she let out a sob, bending forward and rocking, the grief overwhelming her.

Gwen pulled her own chair forward a little and began to rub her colleague's back, murmuring words of comfort. 'That's right. You have a good cry. He was a wonderful brother and he loved you very much.'

Bridget looked away, the sadness too much to witness. Yet the truth of what Belinda had just said filtered through; death was terrible but the alternative might have been worse. It was a cruel comfort to hang on to, but a comfort, nevertheless.

CHAPTER TWENTY-FIVE

Ruby hefted the handles of the big canvas bag further up her arm to see if it would be any easier to carry that way. It was an improvement, but only just. Not only was it heavy, but it was cumbersome too, much worse than a Gladstone bag. She didn't know how Belinda usually managed it, but of course there was a big difference in their height. Maybe that made it easier for her friend. Be that as it may, Ruby was now stuck with getting the bag containing all the equipment back to the nurses' home. She had volunteered to take her colleague's place at the regular hygiene lessons at St Benedict's school, at least for the time being because Belinda had gone to spend a week with her parents, who lived in North London, and all the other nurses had rallied round to fill in where necessary.

Ruby paused to rest the huge bag on top of a low wall, gathering her breath and her resolution for the next few minutes. It wasn't far; surely she could manage? She was no weakling. She resisted the thought that she might have bitten off more than she could chew; returning to the school was not an option, as Janet Phipps had locked up as she left. There was nothing for it but to try again.

With a gasp, she started off once more, but almost overbalanced. Reddening, she righted herself, not wanting anyone to see her in uniform and think she couldn't cope. She didn't want to let the side down.

'Hello, Ruby!'

Ruby would have spun round but the heavy weight prevented that. Instead she tottered a little as she carefully turned in the direction of the voice. Someone was waving at her.

'Looks as if you've got a lot in there!' the voice went on cheerfully. The sunlight was behind her and for a moment Ruby couldn't work out who it was. Then the angle changed and it became clear.

'Olive!' she exclaimed. 'Haven't seen you for ages. How are you?'

The ARP warden nodded brightly. 'Busy as ever. I'm just on my way home to collect the children from their gran. Would you like a hand?'

Ruby hesitated for an instant, not wanting to appear incapable of carrying a bag. Then she relented – after all, she'd performed the exact same favour for the woman standing in front of her. 'That might be a good idea,' she admitted. 'I didn't realise the schoolkids used so many things. Then there's all the posters we put up as displays and the easels to hang them on. They all have to come back to the nurses' home because we can't leave them at St Benedict's from week to week, so I was a bit stuck.'

Olive nodded. 'Stands to reason. Tell you what, I've got a couple of spare string bags on me – let's transfer whatever we can into those and then it'll be more evenly spread.'

Ruby agreed readily and they swiftly unpacked and repacked the items, leaving her with something that she could lift far more easily. 'That's better,' she breathed. Now she could walk along the pavement without nearly falling over. 'You've saved my bacon, Olive.'

Olive smiled and nodded. 'One good turn deserves another. I don't suppose you'll be seeing Kenny later, then? He's on duty – that's why I can look after the children, I'm off for a few nights now.'

Ruby pulled a face. 'It's true, I don't see him as often as I'd like, but we've got a visit to the pub planned for Friday. So that's something to look forward to. I don't suppose you can come?' she added.

Olive shook her head ruefully. 'No, I'll be back on duty then. Do you mean the Duke's Arms, like you said before? Not the Boatman's?'

Ruby laughed. 'Ooh, no, I don't want to go there. It's further away from us than the Duke's for a start. And from what everyone says I'm not at all sure I'd like it.'

Olive nodded sagely. 'Best keep it that way.'

Something in her tone made Ruby glance at her companion's face. It sounded as if she meant more than a general disapproval of what was known to be a less than salubrious watering hole. 'What do you mean, Olive? Has something happened, something in particular?'

Olive carried on walking to the next corner and then paused. 'Not exactly,' she said, swapping over her two string bags. 'There's something that's not quite right there, though. I wouldn't want to think of you getting your hopes up for a night out and ending up there.'

Ruby hitched the canvas bag more firmly into her elbow joint. 'Kenny only takes me to the Duke's Arms – we'll most likely see our other friends there too. He's never so much as suggested trying the Boatman's. I don't think he likes it any more either.'

Olive resumed walking, a little more slowly now. She looked slightly uncertain. 'I don't really know how to put this, but has Kenny ever said anything about it? Other than he doesn't want to go out for an evening there?'

Ruby was doubtful. 'Not that I can think of. What do you mean?'

Olive glanced at her and sighed. 'I don't exactly know. It's just that Kenny's usual patch to patrol is down that way, and so is mine, and yet Henry Spencer often gets us to help out at neighbouring stations – not that it's unusual, we all go to where we're needed most. All the same, it seems to be happening more and more often. He's never wanted to work with me – we all know he can't cope with a female colleague – but to begin with he was perfectly happy to let Kenny show Cliff what to do, to teach him the ropes. Now he seems to want to work with Cliff most of the time.'

Ruby mulled this over. 'Kenny did say something about not seeing so much of Cliff but I didn't take much notice. To be honest, I wondered if Spencer just used Kenny to teach Cliff the basics, take him under his wing and whatnot, because he was too damn lazy to do so himself. Now that the lad's trained up, he's happy to work with him. Wouldn't that be just like him?'

Olive sucked in her cheeks. 'Maybe that's what it is. He's a lazy sod underneath all his swagger. Likes to be seen to be in charge but not to do any of the actual hard graft. But we know he's up to something, as he keeps having private chats with Cliff and claiming it's important business if anyone asks. It's not me imagining it, Kenny's caught their discussions as well, but they clam up as soon as anyone gets near. Don't suppose he's mentioned anything to you?'

'Not really, but if Kenny says anything more then I'll be sure to remember it,' said Ruby.

'Enough about him, it's my day off and I don't want to think about him any more,' Olive declared. 'We're nearly back, but before we say goodbye, tell me what you were doing with the schoolchildren?'

'Hygiene lessons,' Ruby replied. 'All the simple stuff but some of them just haven't been taught. How to clean their teeth, how to comb their hair, how to check for nits.'

Olive broke into a broad smile. 'Excellent – then you can pass on any tips! I'd love to know how to persuade my little darlings to do some of that. The time it could save me! Please spill the beans, Ruby.'

Iris was hurrying back to the nurses' home part way through her rounds because she'd mislaid her soap.

271

She was meticulous about the contents of her nurse's bag and never let supplies run down. The soap was always kept in a special box in the outside section of the bag and she strongly suspected it had been taken by somebody in one of the houses she had already visited this morning, but could not say for certain who.

She sighed heavily. It was a nuisance, but she could always get more, even though it might mean she was a little late for her next patient. She knew some families struggled to buy soap, and from the conversations she'd overheard between her colleagues who took the children's hygiene classes, some of the youngsters were barely acquainted with the stuff. So in some ways she could not blame whoever it was. She tried to think charitably. Perhaps their need was greater than hers – but it had a knock-on effect. Now her morning schedule would be disturbed and she hated that.

So she was not in the best of tempers when a figure waved at her from the pavement along Cricketfield Road and she squinted as she quickly applied the brakes.

It took her a moment to realise who the heavily pregnant young woman standing before her was: Connie, the wife of the poor young man who had attempted suicide. Iris had assumed she was still safe in the countryside, trying to help her husband recover.

'Hello,' she said, dismounting as neatly as she could. The woman swayed shyly. 'Hello, nurse.'

Iris set aside her impatience to get back to the district room to restock. Here was somebody she had

272

never stopped thinking about, but had not heard of for months. 'Well, how nice to see you. How are you getting along?'

The woman shrugged. 'Oh, well, you know. Not so bad.'

Iris's sharp eyes took in the state of her clothing. Before, she had been quite smart – or respectable, at least. Now her shoes were scuffed, the cuffs and collar of her thin coat frayed, and her face looked pinched. She could not be described as blooming.

'That's good,' said Iris encouragingly. 'Are you living around here now? I thought you had gone down to the Cotswolds.'

The young woman grimaced. 'I did, when Eddie first got sent to that special home. I had a room with a family but we didn't get on. They looked down their noses at me, I could tell, though they never said anything. Bad as Eddie's folks, they were.'

Alarm bells began to ring gently but insistently at the back of Iris's mind. 'I'm sorry to hear that,' she said. 'And what about Eddie? How is he?'

Connie shrugged. 'I don't know as I can say. He still hasn't spoken to me. Nor to anyone, as far as I know. He woke up and everything, but he didn't want to know, not me, not about the baby, not anything at all. He just stares out of the window all day. I wasn't doing any good there and I think I was actually making him worse. I couldn't bear the idea of that, so I came back.'

'Didn't you like it there? Wouldn't it be better to have stayed?' Iris had never been to the Cotswolds but the thought of being out in the clean air, of rolling hills, appealed to her greatly. It wouldn't be as wild as Dartmoor, but it would at least be countryside.

The woman shivered. 'If I wasn't sitting with Eddie, and him just staring into space, there was nothing to do. Everyone knew everyone else's business, all farms and animals. It was all anyone talked about. So I thought I might as well come home to Dalston.'

Iris hastily pulled her bike out of the way of a passing van. When the engine noise had faded, she asked, 'So, are you living with Eddie's parents again?'

'Not on your life!' Connie said. 'They still blame me for everything, when it was all their fault to start with. Meddling old bag, his mother is. No, I got a little place of my own.'

Iris looked at her dubiously. 'What sort of place?' Accommodation was in short supply, thanks to the raids destroying so many houses.

The woman hesitated for an instant and then tilted her chin. 'It's all right. It's got four walls and a roof, just about.'

'Is it warm enough?' Iris pressed. 'You have to take care, you know. You must be quite near your time. When did you say your baby was due?'

Again Connie hesitated and Iris made sure to maintain eye contact. From the state of the girl, it had to be soon.

'Oh, I'm not sure,' she said lightly, but Iris could pick up on the anxiety behind the bravado. 'Babies come along when they feel like it, don't they?'

'Sometimes,' Iris agreed. 'All the same, it's best to

be prepared. Have you been in touch with Dr Patcham? Have you got a midwife in mind?'

Connie would not meet her gaze now, but turned away as if suddenly intrigued by a couple of sparrows bickering on a nearby branch of privet hedging. 'Not yet,' she admitted. Iris tutted and the young woman turned back to her. 'Wait, are you a midwife? You could do it, couldn't you?'

Iris smiled carefully. 'Not all district nurses are midwives as well, but as it happens I am. I'd be happy to help, but you must register your new address and speak to Dr Patcham, unless you want to go to a different practice.'

Connie shook her head. 'I don't know anyone else. Do I have to? What if he tells me off for not staying with Eddie? I know it was him what sorted it all out, the home and that.' She was growing ever more distressed.

'He won't,' Iris assured her.

'He might.'

Iris could tell the girl was doing her best not to break down, her show of confidence just a fiction to hide her precarious position. 'All right,' she said. 'It's not exactly going by the rules, but I'll have a word with him. Why don't you write your address down,' and she fished out a notebook and pencil from her pocket, 'and you keep a note of my name. Nurse Hawke, Iris Hawke. From the Victory Walk home.' Connie quickly scribbled her address, and Iris tore a sheet from the notebook and wrote her own. 'And that's the telephone number, just in case,' she added.

The young woman nodded, all fight gone. 'All right. Thank you,' she said, quietly but sincerely.

Iris nodded. 'I must be off. I'll speak to the doctor and tell him of our arrangements and I'll try to visit you, to give you a proper check-up and see if we can't be a little more accurate about baby's arrival. Promise me you'll get in touch if anything happens in the meantime?'

The girl nodded again, more slowly this time. 'I promise,' she said.

Iris cycled off, now later than ever, but glad she had stopped, nonetheless. Every instinct told her that Connie was in trouble. What she was doing for money, she had no idea, but she dreaded to think what sort of room she had managed to find. She could only hope that she kept her promise.

CHAPTER TWENTY-SIX

Gladys was first to the pile of post, which was bigger than usual. It was part of her job to help sort the mail when she had a spare moment from working in the kitchen. This gave her the chance to scan the envelopes, some official and some not, wondering if there would be anything for her. To her joy, there was, right at the bottom of the heap, written in a scrawl she had come to know. She smiled; his writing was far more untidy than hers. Perhaps that was what came of learning to write so late; you made sure that everything was as clean and neat as could be. Ron's hand was probably not so very different to what he'd produced as a schoolboy.

She patted it with affection and tucked it into her apron pocket, before tidying the rest of the post onto the shelf in the hallway. She would bet that she had a pretty good idea of what some of it was and who it came from.

Gladys would have liked to have found an excuse to hang around in the hallway to see who came along next and if they had an envelope as well, but duty called her back to the kitchen to help prepare lunch. All the same, she left the doors open to the common room so that she could hear anything that went on.

When Cook took her tea break at eleven, Gladys seized the moment to open the envelope, cautiously so that it could be re-used, even though she was so eager to see what it contained. Ron had chosen a very traditional Valentine's Day card, with a picture of a red rose and an elaborate ribbon tied beneath it. Inside, he had not signed his name but had written 'Be my Valentine!' in his distinctive scrappy hand-writing, and so there was little mystery to it. Gladys didn't mind. She wasn't looking for mystery. Having the love of a straightforward man like Ron was worth a thousand times more than any shallow silly games, she reckoned.

By lunchtime, all the envelopes had been claimed, and Gladys smiled as she brought in a stack of side plates to the canteen area. Mary was making no secret of her delight in what Charles had sent her. It was very obviously from one of the fancier West End shops, with real velvet edging and elegant gold lettering. 'Oooh, that's very classy,' Gladys said as she went over to Mary's table. 'Just look at that card. That's quality, all right.'

Mary beamed. 'Isn't he a poppet? I know it's a bit of fun, but give him his due, he's got good taste.'

Iris was passing by as she said this, and nodded distractedly. Mary nodded back but a flash of annoy-ance passed across her face as she turned to Gladys.

She clearly wanted and expected everyone to join in her happiness, but Gladys could see the older nurse had something else on her mind. 'Shall you see him this evening?' she asked, to distract her colleague and not ruin the mood.

Mary shook her head. 'No, sadly not. He's got more meetings. It's all he ever does, poor lamb, sit around in committees. We'll have Friday instead, which is better anyway.' She sighed, putting the heavy card back on the table. 'I sent him one as well, one of those cartoons with everyone in uniform. I suppose he'll get teased, but too late now.'

'They'll be jealous and quite right too,' Gladys predicted. She turned to welcome Ruby. 'Look what Mary's got. Did you get any post this morning?' Gladys knew full well that something had arrived with Ruby's name on the front.

Ruby raised her eyebrows and smiled. 'I might have.'

Mary tutted. 'Go on, Ruby, you can tell us.'

Ruby laughed as Gladys attempted a poker face and failed. 'You took the post in, Gladys, I know you did, so you saw it all anyway. You know what Kenny's writing is like – almost as terrible as Ron's. But yes, he did send me something. He only went and made it himself,' she added shyly.

'Oooh, let's see.' Mary sat forward on her ladder-back chair.

Ruby felt in her pocket, a little self-consciously. Then she drew out a sheet of paper folded over into quarters to make it stiff. Images from magazines had been carefully cut out and glued to the front: a bunch of flowers, a bird of some kind, and a box of chocolates.

'He did that?' Gladys was taken aback. 'It must have taken him ages. I never thought he had it in him.'

Ruby nodded and blushed. 'He did. He never has much money or time to go to the shops but he must have done this on one of his evenings off. All right, that bird is more like a pigeon than a dove, but I never thought he'd go to such trouble. I'm at a loss for words, really.'

Gladys looked at her friend, all shy and proud at the same time. 'I reckon he must really think a lot of you, Ruby. To go to all that trouble and everything, when he never usually does anything like that.'

Ruby's eyes shone. 'Yes, I suppose so.' Then, more boldly, 'Yes, yes, I think he does. Imagine! I'm very lucky and I know it.'

Mary beamed back, happy for her friend. The two cards could not have been more different but what they meant amounted to the same thing. Despite all the disruptions and hardships of war, these two young women had won the love of men who appreciated them, and it was no small achievement.

From across the common room, Iris watched the short scene play out. She didn't begrudge her younger colleagues their fun. Ruby was positively glowing with happiness, and Iris was generous enough to admit that her friend more than deserved it. Her young man seemed a decent sort too, not one of those who'd

280

make easy promises and then disappear. Well, good for them.

She had more than enough on her plate. Belinda was due back tomorrow but Iris had been covering many of her patients in the meantime, combining them with her own, and so she was bone tired. All she wanted was something hot to eat and drink, and she didn't really care what it was – at this stage, it was simply fuel to get her through the rigours of the coming afternoon. It was an extra effort, as Belinda's patients seemed to expect their nurse to be light-hearted and to ease their pain with humour. Iris had never taken that approach. Never mind, as long as they got the treatment they needed, they could enjoy the return of their regular nurse all the more. Although she might not be as light-hearted once she got back from her parents'.

Iris mentally gave herself a shake. 'Chin up,' she murmured, heading towards the big soup tureen. There was no time for self-pity. A bowl of root vegetable and barley stew would set her right, and then it would be back on the battered old bike and the demanding afternoon rounds.

What could you do? An exhausted Iris collapsed onto her bed some hours later. It was only natural if a patient, worried for his family, asked her for 'just a little favour'. Now that she was in the house, she wouldn't mind looking at his grandson, would she? So, having seen all of her own cases, most of Belinda's and now this final one, she had little choice but to agree to see the child as well. It wasn't strictly in the rules, but what if the child was genuinely very sick and it took ages to go through the approved channels? Iris had said yes, albeit reluctantly.

As it turned out, the child had a nasty case of flu but she was pretty sure nothing more serious. She had delivered her usual lecture on scrupulous hygiene but the child, although old enough, was too fractious to take it in. 'Clean hankies, and then wash your hands,' Iris said for the twentieth time, letting herself out of the sweltering bedroom where a fire blazed in the small fireplace. She had instructed the grandparents to leave the window open, but it had been hard to do as the wooden frame was warped and rotten; she would put good money on them shutting it as soon as she left.

Now she stared at the ceiling of her own bedroom, shadows swaying across it in the light from her dim bulb. She would have to summon the energy to go downstairs for the evening meal. Every muscle screamed for rest – or better still, a warm if shallow bath, and then rest. Maybe later, she promised herself.

A sharp knock on the door made her hurriedly sit up. 'Iris, you in there?' It was Ruby's voice.

'Yes, yes, come in.' Iris hastily smoothed her skirt and patted her hair, then made her way the short distance to the door as Ruby opened it.

'Sorry to disturb you – I know you only just got in.' The young nurse was all apologies. 'But there's a phone call, they asked for you in particular.'

'I see.' Iris automatically picked up her Gladstone

bag. 'I'd better find out what it is. Do you have any details?' she asked, as the pair of them walked swiftly along the attic corridor.

'Not really. They're still on the line and you can use Fiona's office,' Ruby explained, leaving her colleague to find out more. She closed the door with a soft thunk, as you never knew how confidential any conversation might need to be.

'Hello?' A rough voice was on the other end as Iris picked up the Bakelite receiver. 'Is that the nurse what she wanted? You took your time.'

'Nurse Hawke speaking.' Iris would not let herself be riled.

'Yes, that's the one. Your patient's in trouble.' It was a woman, elderly by the sounds of it, husky from many years of heavy smoking if Iris was any judge.

'I see. Which patient?' she asked, picking up a pencil from Fiona's desk and preparing to make a note of the address.

'The one what's having a baby. Connie, she said she was. She's screaming the place down,' the woman told her. 'I can't stay here all evening, I'm in the iron-monger's across the road what's got a telephone but he needs it back. I'm doing this out of the goodness of me heart because she's me downstairs neighbour and raising hell, she is. You got to come and sort her out.' The line went dead.

Connie! Iris groaned aloud remembering how she had intended to go round for an ante-natal visit, but because of the extra workload she had not found the time. She hoped it wasn't too late. At least she had the address. Swiftly she scribbled a note for Fiona to let her know what had happened. That bath and rest would have to wait.

Ten minutes later, Iris was at the front door of a narrow, four-storey terraced house, shining the beam from her shielded torch to check the number. Paint blistered and peeled from around the crooked brass figures. It was a far cry from the front door of the girl's in-laws' house. Cautiously she pushed it and it opened. 'Hello?' she called.

A gas light sputtered in the hallway and a bent figure emerged from a doorway. 'You the nurse? She's in the basement.' The voice was familiar from the recent phone call. 'You'll know which room is hers, just follow the noise.' The door slammed again before Iris could ask anything further. Right, my girl, you're on your own, she told herself, shining her torch in front of her and carefully beginning to descend the stairs. The treads were worn smooth with years of use and were uneven in places, which made going down to the lower level trickier still.

The old neighbour had been right about one thing though: there was no doubt that she was in the right place – screams were echoing around the cold stairway. Iris hurried as much as she could, hefting the heavy bag, which contained not only its usual general supplies but now all the additional ones required of a midwife. The place smelled of damp.

Now she was on the bottom landing and the screams were even louder. She tracked them to one of two doors. 'Connie? May I come in? It's Nurse Hawke.' The only reply was another scream, so she tried the handle and it turned.

It was just the one room, narrow and cold. The only light came from a Tilley lamp, with a cracked glass shade, balanced on a rickety shelf above a cupboard which was missing a drawer front. Most of the space was taken up by a low bed, on which lay the distressed young woman, who did not stop screaming when Iris bent over her.

'Connie, it's me. Nurse Hawke. Can you talk to me?' Iris tried to impose some order on the situation but the patient was beyond that. She took in the overall state of the place and then focused on Connie, who was pale and sweating despite the freezing temperature. There was no sign of a tap or any means of heating water. Iris attempted to take the girl's pulse but was thrown off, noticing that the bedding was wet and not only with sweat. So the waters had broken. The baby's arrival was in motion, but she needed a clearer idea of how matters were progressing.

Deliberately keeping her voice calm, she began to murmur words of comfort and reassurance, keeping her eyes on the girl's face, waiting to see if her presence had an effect. After what seemed an age, the screams grew less and the patient registered that Iris was there. Finally she could begin an examination and form a clearer picture of just what stage the labour had reached. Connie even managed to gasp a few brief answers, as Iris pieced together as much as she could. When she had learned as much as possible, from observation, examination and what the girl had said, or even what she had not said, Iris shuddered. Not from the glacial temperature though.

Iris was confident in her abilities as a midwife. She had delivered babies in small moorland cottages miles from anywhere, with only her own skills and instincts to rely on. If a case was within a midwife's capabilities then she could cope as good as any. The key thing was to know when extra help was required.

Iris looked at Connie, who stared back at her with dark, terrified eyes. She did her best not to reflect the terror. This was one of those rare instances beyond her level of expertise. To her mind, the girl needed a Caesarean operation as soon as possible. There was not a moment to lose, and she, Iris Hawke, was not permitted to perform such a thing. She would have to get help – somehow.

CHAPTER TWENTY-SEVEN

'Bleedin' hell, do you think I'm some kind of first-aid post,' the ironmonger complained when Iris rapped on his door to ask to use his telephone. He was old, his grey hair shiny with brillantine in an effort to look respectable. He was still in his brown work overalls. 'It's through there – and don't stay long. You can tell 'er over the road she's not to make a habit of it.'

'It's an emergency,' Iris assured him.

The elderly man stuck out his lower lip. 'Is that so?' He sounded as if he still thought he was being taken advantage of.

'Life or death,' Iris stressed, willing him to show her the telephone and step out of the way.

'In that case . . .' he said sourly, and allowed her to go through the aisle of shelves with their meagre spread of dusty goods.

Swiftly she asked to be put through to Dr Patcham. On her way here she had calculated the odds. To get an ambulance and then have it take Connie to the nearest hospital with room – the Hackney at Homerton was closest, but she already knew how full that was, so it might be a more distant one – would take longer than calling in the doctor and letting him decide the next steps. At least he would know the patient because Iris had spoken to him recently to bring him up to date with the girl's unfortunate circumstances.

Unflappable as ever, he did not sound remotely surprised when he answered. 'I was afraid something like this would happen,' he said sadly. 'Very well. You say the baby is in totally the wrong position and she's been labouring on her own for too long? She's not a big girl, is she? Very slender, if I recall. I'll be there in a jiffy. Luckily I have a colleague with me at the moment who will assist.' He rang off and Iris turned to meet the disagreeable face of the ironmonger.

'Have yer done?' he demanded.

'Yes,' Iris snapped, but then had a thought. 'But first, can you let me have the largest bottle of Dettol that you have, and on the way through I saw you had a camp stove in stock. I'll take that and a big bottle of methylated spirit. Here's the money – and keep the change.'

He stood open-mouthed for the briefest of moments and then hurried off, finally pleased as he was making a vast profit on the goods. He shoved them into a box and Iris grabbed them, hurrying back over the road. At least she had found a back entrance to the basement corridor, separate from the front door, so she would not have to run the gauntlet of the neighbour's disapproval.

While her Gladstone bag contained the regular bottles of Dettol and meths, she suspected far more would be required. While she waited for Dr Patcham, she set up a makeshift nursing station in the damp corridor. She had noticed a big saucepan in the corner of Connie's room and now she balanced it on the meths-fuelled camp stove, having filled it with water from a tap in the garden wall. It was far from perfect but would have to do, if it came to the worst.

At the sound of a vehicle pulling to a stop, she ran out to the front steps. There was the doctor, getting out rather stiffly from the passenger door of a dark saloon. 'Round here,' she called, keen that he shouldn't waste time taking the route through the house. 'Follow me.' She didn't wait to see who the driver was.

Careful not to knock over the saucepan of water, she showed him into the grim little room, where Connie lay groaning, clutching her distended abdomen, kicking back the sodden sheets.

The doctor repeated Iris's initial examinations, murmuring similar words of comfort as he did so. 'You remember me, Connie? I'm here to help you.' After a couple of minutes he nodded to Iris, indicating that she should step outside into the foul-smelling corridor. She automatically turned off the stove and then faced him.

'You did well to call me,' he said, speaking quickly. 'The only possible way to save her – and with luck the baby – is to perform a Caesarean. I can see you've started to make preparations but even with your undoubtable skill, we will never make this place suitable for such an extreme measure. It's manifestly too unhygienic. She could die of an infection from any number of sources. We'll have to move her.'

Iris's face fell. Somehow she had hoped that the doctor would see a way of delivering the baby without surgery, using some arcane method of turning it that she had yet to learn. It had been clutching at straws, she realised. 'But how . . .'

Dr Patcham addressed the wall behind her. 'Between us we shall transport the patient back to my surgery, where my housekeeper is preparing the refuge room. My colleague here has agreed to help. You've met Dr Leeson . . .'

Iris turned to see the gaunt face of the unfriendly anaesthetist, glowering in the shadows.

Looking back on that evening, Iris would find that much of what followed was a blur. She had no time to speculate why the grim doctor had appeared, learning later that he had dropped round to Dr Patcham's surgery to discuss a procedure they were due to perform the following day and, even more fortuitously, bringing his equipment with him as his own storage had been damaged in a recent raid.

Iris's entire attention had been focused on the patient, as she sat with Connie's head on her lap in the back seat of the spacious saloon. It was no distance at all to Dr Patcham's, and the main difficulty had been lifting the girl from her filthy room into the vehicle, and then manoeuvring her out and into the prepared room at the other end. Connie, by now, was almost beyond pain but at least that look of sheer terror had faded. It was as if she knew that whatever happened now, she would not be alone.

'Far from ideal,' Dr Leeson had muttered as he set about preparing his equipment, his disapproving face offset by the efficiency of his movements. Iris set about her own preparations. She had been present at Caesareans in the hospital where she trained, rare though the procedure was, and she had been sure to retrieve her bag from Connie's basement room and so had her overall, cap, mask and rubber gloves to hand. Sighing in desperate hope, she lifted out the foetal stethoscope and baby scales that the big bag could accommodate, in the hope that she would have cause to use them.

Then it was over to the two doctors to lead the way towards the big examination table, surrounded by the newspapers on the floor that the housekeeper had thoughtfully set out. Iris could only guess at the risks such a hasty anaesthetic might bring, but she held on to the knowledge that Connie was young and, before all this, reasonably healthy. The room was as clean as a domestic setting could hope to be.

The men worked in tandem, used to one another's methods, and Iris responded to their brief requests or, in Dr Leeson's case, brusque commands, with everything to hand. She could see that this would have been impossible in the patient's own room, and shuddered to think what germs lurked there. Apart from operating in the hospital, this was as safe as it was likely to be. The girl could not have survived much longer on her own: the baby had been lodged in an impossible position and would not have come out unaided. Iris bit her lip. She had to trust the men's skills and their medical knowledge now.

She drew on all of her professional demeanour when Dr Patcham made his incision into the girl's abdomen, painted yellow with iodine. It was a large cut and less-experienced onlookers might have recoiled in horror but Iris knew that she must not.

Then, in what seemed like no time, he was lifting out a red bundle and handing it to her. 'Clamp, please,' he said calmly, and she exchanged it for this new creature, holding it gently and curiously, waiting with bated breath to see if it moved. Time froze. Then, faintly at first, the bundle made a gurgling noise and then a wail. The baby had survived its harsh arrival into the world.

Now Iris moved swiftly, cleaning it, rubbing its back, reaching for the clean towels the housekeeper had known to leave out, laying one in the cold pan of the scales so as not to shock the child with the chilly metal. Iris focused on the numbers. The baby, a boy, was small but not dangerously so. Nearly five pounds in fact – respectable, if he was, as she suspected, premature.

A sharp noise made her look up. 'Damn it,' said Dr Patcham, the strongest curse she had ever heard him employ. 'Beg your pardon, nurse, but I slipped on this newspaper and I fear I've twisted my wrist trying not to fall. Give me a moment and I'll resume.'

Iris glanced at him in consternation. There wasn't a moment to be spared. He had injured himself at a crucial time, closing the incision in the patient's abdomen. They could not wait for his wrist to recover, or to be suitably bandaged.

She turned to Dr Leeson, but he was concentrating on his side of things, monitoring Connie's sedation. 'Dr Leeson,' she said, perhaps more sharply than necessary, 'can you take over?'

He looked at her, his eyes dispassionate as ever. 'I am needed here,' he said simply. 'Besides, I can't remember the last time I used sutures.'

The man was impossible. Iris wanted to scream. He was so much more qualified than her, on paper at least, must have had full medical training before specialising. Of course he could make a clean job of suturing the wound! Couldn't he?

She glanced towards Dr Patcham, who was uncharacteristically silent. He had paled a little. Damn it indeed – he had really hurt himself but was doing his best not to show how much pain he was in. Iris took a deep breath. What would she have done back home in Devon? While she had not actually performed this procedure, she had certainly been forced to give plenty of patients stitches. Not all of those cases had been straightforward. At least here the patient was still, the place was clean and well lit.

There was no time to lose. 'Sit down, Dr Patcham,' Iris said, trying to make it sound polite but really giving her superior no choice. 'Here, you take the baby in your good arm. I'll carry on where you left off.'

She carefully placed the little boy, now wrapped in a clean towel, in the crook of the doctor's arm as he subsided onto one of the soft chairs he kept for waiting patients. Then, ignoring the cold glare of the anaesthetist, she changed into a fresh set of gloves and set to work. She did not allow herself to think of what an unorthodox situation this was, just forced herself to concentrate on stitching the incision as cleanly as possible. There would no doubt be a scar but she aimed to minimise it, carefully positioning the skin, matching the sides, making the neatest stitches that she could.

Finally she was satisfied. Standing straight, flexing her arms, she realised she was aching all over. She blinked, almost in disbelief that she had managed to salvage the operation. Connie was breathing steadily under the anaesthetist's care and the baby was making little noises as Dr Patcham attempted to soothe it while keeping his injured arm safely out of the way. Iris sat on the wooden chair beside him.

'We did it,' she said softly. 'They both came through. I . . . I had my moments when I thought they might not.'

Dr Patcham's colour had returned now that he was resting. 'No, you did it, Nurse Hawke. I don't mind telling you, I could not have carried on there. You can't do stitches with one hand, and I fear my left one is out of commission for a while. I'll take something for it once we've finished up here.'

In the background, Dr Leeson was now moving around, making his arrangements to revive the girl.

'What's best to do next?' Iris wondered. 'You can't look after her here and she'll need careful monitoring after a general anaesthetic.'

Dr Patcham nodded. 'I was going to suggest moving her in any case. After what she has been through, she needs to be in hospital. The urgency is not so great now; we can call them and arrange an ambulance. If you take the child, I'll go upstairs to my office and make the call. No offence but they'll act faster if it comes from me.'

'Very well, if you're sure.' The doctor huffed as he stood, but that was the only sign of discomfort he made. Iris took the little boy, who avidly sucked on her finger once she had removed her glove. 'We'll have to find you something to drink,' she murmured, wondering if the good doctor had any stores of powdered baby milk. 'There, there. Won't be long. Your mummy will wake up soon and be so pleased to see you.' She walked slowly around the side of the room, keeping out of Dr Leeson's way, gently rocking the baby so that he would not be too shocked at his abrupt transition to this outside world of new noises and bright lights.

Now that the danger was over she had an immense desire to lie down and go to sleep, but that was a luxury she could not yet allow herself. She might have to accompany Connie and the baby to the hospital; Dr Patcham would be unable now, and no doubt Dr Leeson was too grand. She cast her glance around for a dressing to help the old doctor's wrist. She would have some in her bag, in any case. She could examine him as soon as he returned, if she had two free hands.

Iris turned to the anaesthetist, who had ceased his movements and was now keeping an eye on the sedation level. 'I don't suppose you would mind holding the baby, while I find a suitable dressing for Dr Patcham's injury?' she asked.

Dr Leeson glared at her as if she'd suggested killing his grandmother. 'Absolutely not,' he hissed. 'You must be aware the mother still requires all my attention.'

Iris mentally cursed him but had no reasonable argument in response. He was the superior in this situation. Anyway, she could prop the baby in the soft armchair, with the aid of a few cushions. He would be warm, comfy and safe there, while she dug out the right sort of bandage. Damn the anaesthetist for standing on ceremony, but her years of solitary working had given her plenty of practice at doing several things at once. She didn't need his help.

She did her best to ignore him as she found what she needed in her bag and laid it out in readiness. When Dr Patcham reappeared she swiftly sat him down and checked his wrist, pressing the by now inflamed area with her cool fingertips. Then she treated it just as if he was one of her regular patients. 'Why, Nurse Hawke, I do believe you have done this before,' he commented, back to his cheery self, and Iris said a silent prayer of relief. Here was one case she wouldn't have to worry about for much longer. 'The ambulance will be here soon. I've told them the full circumstances, and they'll bring a nurse with them, so you won't have to make the additional trip to the hospital. You've done more than enough.'

Iris smiled, in appreciation and relief. 'As long as you're comfortable, I'll set about clearing up, in that case.' She began to go through the familiar routines of tidying the room after a home operation, removing all used dressings and swabs, ensuring they were ready for burning, setting aside utensils to be disinfected, and finally taking off her overalls and cap. She would replace them with new ones tomorrow. Dr Patcham returned upstairs to await the ambulance, so they need not ring the bell and wake the baby.

All the while she could sense Dr Leeson's critical eyes on her. What was he thinking? Perhaps he blamed her for the older doctor's accident. Was the newspaper not put down properly? Even if it was the housekeeper who'd laid it out, it was Iris's job to ensure it stayed in its place throughout the operation. Yet she couldn't have prevented him slipping, even if she'd had the time to check the paper every five minutes, which she hadn't. She'd had the new baby to tend, checking his airway, temperature and weight. That had been the most important thing. If Dr Leeson tried to make her responsible, she knew what she would say in return.

Sounds of footsteps above them heralded the arrival of the ambulance and soon Connie and her small boy were being carefully loaded into the vehicle. Iris checked that the nurse had been briefed and was reassured at once. 'Dr Patcham has told me everything,' the woman said, her pleasant expression conveying her years of experience. 'They'll be in the best of hands now. They'll want for nothing. You can set your mind at rest.'

'Good.' Iris exhaled heartily and then made one final trip downstairs to collect all her possessions. Exhausted, she packed what she could back into her bag, cramming it in any old how, vowing to sort it out first thing in the morning. Still the anaesthetist stared at her, while he wound one of his many rubber tubes into a neat coil. She supposed he too would have much to do in the morning.

Just as she was about to depart for the nurses' home, he cleared his throat and she looked up. His expression had changed – it was less guarded, although not what she would have called friendly. 'Ah, one moment, nurse.'

Here it comes, she thought. He'll say the accident was my fault. Or even threaten to report me for performing a procedure beyond my qualifications.

'You did well, Nurse Hawke,' he said awkwardly. 'You, ah, must have done something similar before. You were very, um, professional.'

Iris clasped her hands together in sudden fury. She supposed she should be grateful, but she felt anything but. What did he know of how a nurse coped on her own, far from any colleagues? What did he know of all the times she'd stitched wounds in the cold and dark, in cramped cottages and even in farm outbuildings? How dare he be surprised that she had known what to do.

She felt like shouting all of this into his gaunt, drawn face but she controlled herself just in time.

'Yes,' she said instead. 'Yes. I was. I know.' Then she swept out, before she said something she could not take back, revealing herself to be anything but professional.

CHAPTER TWENTY-EIGHT

You'd never believe the state of the room I'm in now. I'm bunking with the messiest man in the world. Good job he gets plenty of extra rations from his family and is prepared to share them, otherwise I don't think I'd be answerable for my actions. You'll be pleased to find I'm a man transformed, I'll be a paragon of domestic tidiness . . . that is, when we finally see each other again. When we're together like we are meant to be. Oh, Alice, that moment cannot come soon enough. I don't know if this will reach you in time for Valentine's Day or even by the end of February, but please know that I'm thinking of you every minute of every day . . .

Alice shut her eyes so that she could imagine the scene. She didn't mind about not receiving a Valentine's card, now that she had something far more precious, a long letter from Joe. She could relish the chance to hear him speak through his words, to pretend he was there in the room with her, describing his days, his ideas, and increasingly his hopes. She could sense his longing for the fighting to be over, so that he could come home at last and be with her. Yet there was no word of when he could get leave.

Sometimes she imagined every detail of what their life could be like when they were finally together, even if she had no clear thought where they might end up. Perhaps they would stay in London. They might move to Liverpool so that she could be closer to her parents. Maybe they would be somewhere altogether different . . . Then she would abandon such fanciful notions, in order to avoid the inevitable disappointment when he still didn't mention a date when he would return. The news from the continent continued to improve, although she was uncomfortably uneasy about the destruction of Dresden. But surely it all pointed to an end to the war. There were times when she didn't know for how much longer she could go on, living in limbo like this. He had to come home soon. Every part of her ached for him.

With a deep breath, she refolded the sheets of paper covered in his writing and tucked them into her drawer, where she had kept all of his letters. Perhaps one day they would sit together and laugh at their contents, reliving this tumultuous time, but that was still a long way off.

Meanwhile she had another letter, with very different writing on it. She laughed as she recognised the carbon copy of the hand that Janet Phipps attempted to instil in all her pupils. Pauline had been a keener student than she had let on. Despite her many absences, she had managed to adopt a decent style and Alice could easily read her news.

Pauline and her brother had settled in well. Pauline shared a room with Dotty, her schoolfriend from so many years ago, and it was the best thing ever. 'I never had a sister before but I got one now,' Pauline wrote, and Alice smiled at the words. The young girl deserved some happiness and the chance to act like a child at last, freed from the need to look after her brother. By the sounds of it they even called Dotty's mother 'auntie'. Now that was something that would never have happened before the war. 'Please give my kindest regards to Miss Phipps,' Pauline finished, which made Alice laugh again. She couldn't quite imagine the girl saying those words; perhaps Auntie had suggested them. Whatever was behind the formal flourish, she would certainly pass on the good wishes the next time she saw Janet.

Alice decided to take the letter down to the canteen so that anybody who'd been involved in that frantic search for Larry could share the news. Iris would certainly want to know that the children were doing so well. She paused at her attic window, looking out in search of any fresh signs of spring. It was coming up to the first anniversary of Edith moving out, but much had changed in that year. Alice could only wish that as much would change in the year to come.

'Go on, try a teacake.' Ruby was keen for Olive to enjoy a rare trip out to the café together. She'd asked her many times now but there had always been a reason why the older woman couldn't come, usually because the children needed her. This Saturday, though, they'd gone with some friends from their Sunday School for a walk along the Walthamstow Marshes. Olive knew they'd come home muddy as anything but they liked their Sunday School teacher and it would do them good to get out for a day.

The café was just opposite Ridley Road market and they'd been able to combine a good nose around for bargains with the prospect of a warm brew and something to eat that they hadn't had to bake themselves. Gladys had come along too. She was particularly pleased with a couple of old jumpers she'd found which could be unravelled and then re-knitted into something for her younger siblings.

Olive liked Gladys. She liked her even more once she'd heard her story, how she'd had to learn to read and write years after being forced to leave school to look after her family. Then she'd had the determination to train as a Civil Reserve nurse, all while working full time at Victory Walk. That was the sort of young woman she could admire. She knew some people thought all nurses were la-di-da and had life handed them on a plate, but it wasn't true. Ruby wasn't like that either.

Olive cheerfully accepted the offer of a teacake and splashed some more milk into her cup. The little café was bustling, the windows steaming up because outside it was still chilly. Inside it was toasty warm, as shoppers bundled around the rickety tables and the owner skilfully twisted in and out of the customers, balancing trays of hot drinks without spilling a drop. 'I'm glad you talked me into coming out. Look at these lovely bright carrots I got. I can make a cake for the kiddies with these.'

'Help them see in the dark,' Ruby said with a grin.

'Heavens, no, don't say that. It's hard enough to get them to sleep as it is. Proper bundles of energy, they are.' Olive sighed in mock-annoyance but the nurses could see that she loved her family.

'Takes me back, that does,' Gladys mused. 'My brothers and sisters are growing up a bit now so at least they don't need tucking in at night. All the same, that means even the younger ones are getting ideas of their own – you know, that difficult age.'

Olive nodded sagely. 'I know what you mean.'

Ruby cocked her head. 'How's that, then? Your kiddies aren't anywhere near their teens yet.' She buttered her own teacake, having let it reach the ideal temperature: warm enough that the butter would still melt, but not so hot that it all turned to liquid and ran off onto the plate.

Olive stirred her tea and then set down the spoon in the saucer. She rested her elbows on the striped tablecloth and pulled a face. 'This will sound daft, but you know that young man in the ARP, Cliff? The one who began around the same time as I did. Everyone says that joining one of the voluntary services teaches you new things, makes you more mature. Well, I dunno but it seems to me with him it's the opposite. He just gets worse. Ruby, you know what I mean, he was bad enough the last time I told you about him.'

'That's odd,' Gladys said. 'I thought he was all right when we met him but mind you I only seen him a couple of times down the Duke's Arms. Seemed nice enough, harmless anyway.'

Olive fiddled with the spoon some more. 'He was, to start with. Keen to learn and respectful of his elders and what not. Now he's impossible, thinks he knows it all. Gives me lip when I'm daft enough to point out his mistakes – and he makes heaps. I pointed out how he mixed up his bandages, that you need a big triangular one to make a support sling for an injured arm. He almost bit my head off. Made up that he was just testing me, to see if I was up to standard. Me! And he doesn't record things properly, just scribbles the bare minimum if at all.'

Gladys sat up straighter at the mention of bad record-keeping. Such sloppiness offended her, for one thing. She and Cook could never run the domestic side of Victory Walk without impeccable planning and accounting. Also, she had never got to the bottom of that strange incident at the first-aid post, the injured man that Henry Spencer had abandoned to their care and who had scarpered at the mention of the word hospital. He had not been seen again and she and Queenie had gradually felt safer in their work, but Gladys had not forgotten all the same.

'I don't like the sound of that,' she said succinctly.

'Imagine if we didn't write up out notes!' Ruby exclaimed. 'Fiona and Gwen would have our guts for garters. Quite right too.' She took a bite of the teacake, savouring the buttery warmth.

Olive nodded vigorously. 'You've got to, of course. Lives are at stake, after all. It's the same with us only a bit different. We've got to know who lives where, who might be missing if there's a raid, at what time ambulances or the police are called, all of these things. It can seem like one extra duty when you've been out late or there's a bad bombing, but it's got to be done. It might not be the most exciting part of the job, but you can't get round it. Cliff seems to think that if he ignores it, it'll go away.'

Ruby pursed her lips at that. 'And I bet Spencer lets him get away with it. His blue-eyed boy. Kenny said the same as you, that the two of them are always in a huddle together, and Cliff follows him around like a puppy.'

'Spencer's the worst of all, even though he pretends he's so particular,' groaned Olive. 'I have as little to do with him as possible these days. If I need to speak to someone senior, I go straight to Stan Banham. He's not strictly on my patch but he knows everybody. He won't brush off my concerns or spout a load of old hogwash.'

Gladys nodded approvingly. 'You can't get better than Mr Banham.'

The three of them sipped their tea, in total agreement.

'I dread my children growing up like Cliff,' Olive confessed. 'Of course sometimes they're naughty and don't do what I or their granny tell them but to think of them turning out like that, rude and workshy? Well, it fills me with dread.'

'They won't,' Ruby said at once. 'You set them the right example, they'll know what's what. Perhaps Cliff never had that.'

Olive shrugged. 'I couldn't say, and I'm not about to ask him, that's for sure.'

Ruby finished off her teacake and licked her lips for the last rich taste of butter. 'There's all sorts in the ARP, isn't there. Cliff came in as green as could be and now he's fallen under the influence of the wrong person, when he could have chosen Kenny or you or Mr Banham to look up to and learn from.'

Olive turned around and waved at the café owner, who was standing in the corner by the counter, drying plates with a red-checked tea towel. 'I've had enough of thinking about Spencer and Cliff. Let's each have another teacake, my treat. No, don't argue. I've waited ages to make new friends and now I've found them the least I can do is buy them a teacake. I'll take offence if you refuse.'

Ruby grinned and the tension was broken.

CHAPTER TWENTY-NINE

'Are you sure you're going to manage to eat all of that?'

Mary was full of the joys of spring and that included a blossoming of her extremely healthy appetite. She loved nothing more than to begin the day with the largest possible breakfast, but in Victory Walk the choice was limited. Alice raised her eyebrows as she put one hand over her last piece of toast, before Mary could purloin it.

'You're miles away,' Mary pointed out, 'so I didn't think you'd miss it.'

Alice snapped out of her daydreams and quickly finished the rather dry toast. 'Sorry,' she grinned. Her mind had been occupied by thoughts of the evening before.

She'd gone to meet Janet Phipps for a quick drink after work, still feeling rather daring as she'd approached the familiar and welcoming doors of the Duke's Arms. Janet had never cared about such things, happily sitting on her own nursing a whisky as she ploughed through a pile of marking. Alice had fetched herself a half of shandy and they'd begun comparing their working weeks.

Alice had remembered Pauline's letter, which delighted Janet. She propped her sensible glasses on top of her cropped brown hair and smiled broadly. 'I'm so glad it's going to plan,' she said. 'Surely something has to go right for those two children after all they've gone through?' Alice nodded. 'I mentioned what happened to Dermot the last time I wrote,' Janet went on. 'He said he'd like to be kept informed – he knows how hard we've worked over the past few years to look after them.' She said this very casually and Alice didn't react, but on the way back to Victory Walk she pondered the significance of the remark.

Maybe there was none, she reasoned, digging her cold hands into her coat pockets. Dermot, her old friend and colleague from Liverpool, and Janet had known one another for a few years now, and had always got along well, with a common interest in children's health. They wrote to each other, just as she and Dermot had always corresponded. Yet he hadn't said anything about Pauline and Larry in his latest letter, even though Alice had told him about their departure. Well, he'd most likely forgotten. He'd been working flat out in his position as a doctor on one of the south-coast army bases.

Unless he had a particular reason for wanting Janet's happiness. Approaching the corner to Victory Walk, Alice gave herself a good shake. All this missing Joe so badly was making her sentimental. It didn't mean she had to go pairing off all her friends. She was going soft, there was no doubt about it.

Iris had to give credit where it was due. Dr Patcham might have been tempted to put his feet up while he recovered from his accident but he had done no such thing. Being unable to conduct some of his usual surgeries, he had instead taken an active interest in the welfare of his former patients. He'd been on the phone almost constantly to the almoner at the hospital where Connie had been admitted, eager for news first of her own recovery and the baby's progress, and then to learn what the in-house doctors thought should be the next step.

Iris had used several of her afternoons off to visit the new mother and her baby, catching the bus north from Dalston to the unfamiliar hospital. She never stayed long, not wanting to tire either of them, and wary at first of reminding Connie of the circumstances of the birth. She needn't have worried. By the second visit, Connie was alert and proud to show off the tiny boy. 'Come a bit closer,' she said, drawing back the woollen blanket so that Iris could see him properly. Staring back at her was the spitting image of Eddie Chalmers' own face, a clear sign that Connie had been telling the truth and that her mother-in-law had tragically got the wrong end of the stick.

Iris remembered the red-faced crying bundle she had delivered, and breathed out in relief that he was doing so well. 'He's a beauty and no mistake,' she chuckled, stroking him gently on the forehead. 'What are you going to call him?'

'I wanted him to be named after his daddy but not as a first name, or we'll all get confused,' the young woman explained. 'Then I asked what Dr Patcham's name was, being as what he's been so good to me and Eddie. So our son is going to be Jonathan Edward. Isn't that nice?'

'Very nice,' said Iris, who hadn't known what Dr Patcham's first name was, just that he signed himself J. Patcham. The doctor would be delighted. 'I won't keep you up any longer now, Connie, but I'll be back soon. As long as you continue to improve.'

'Oh, I will now, Nurse Hawke,' Connie said at once. 'I have to, for this little one's sake. And for Eddie's,' she added sadly. 'I do wish he could see his son. It might make all the difference.'

Yes, it might, thought Iris as she boarded the busy bus for the journey back. Well, she would see what she could do. Or, if it was a little beyond her sphere of influence, then she knew a man who could pull some strings. As the bus wound its way southward back down the main road towards Dalston, she formed her plan . . .

It was perfectly natural that she would call on Dr Patcham after his surgery had finished, to check if his wrist was mending properly. He was pleased to see her, demonstrating how he could flex and rotate the joint, assuring her that her prompt treatment had made all the difference.

'I'm pleased to hear it,' she said, 'although I hear

tales of you examining patients already. You're meant to be taking it easy, you know.'

Dr Patcham waved off her concerns. 'Care for a sherry, Nurse Hawke?' he asked amiably. 'You'll have to help yourself if you're so worried about my wrist – you know where it is. And you might be so good as to bring me one as well.'

Iris did as she was asked. 'Did you let me in purely to pour your sherry?' she demanded.

'Not a bit,' he smiled. 'I imagine you have something on your mind. You have that particular expression which suggests that is the case.' He was enjoying this, Iris could see. She set down the delicate little glass on a highly polished oak table beside his favourite chair and took her place opposite him.

'As a matter of fact, yes. Dr Patcham, I need your help once again.' And she launched into her idea: that Connie should return to the Cotswolds, and little Jonathan too, and so they would need accommodation near the nursing home where Eddie was, and that his doctors would have to be in agreement. 'I'm sure it will be for the best, for all concerned,' she finished.

Dr Patcham nodded approvingly as Iris sipped carefully from the elegant little glass. 'You don't need to convince me,' he said. 'I trust your judgement, in this case as in many others. You have succeeded in bonding with that young woman and her prospects are all the better for it. Now we must see if we can do more for her poor husband.' He raised his glass. 'Leave it with me. Your very good health, Nurse Hawke.'

*   *   *

312

It did not take Dr Patcham long to put their plan into action. The only problem they encountered was how Connie and her son were to make the journey to the little town, which was deep in the countryside. There was no mainline train station, and it would require a very complicated series of buses, any one element of which might be subject to disruption and risk leaving her stranded in the middle of nowhere.

'Not to worry,' Dr Patcham beamed. 'We both know somebody who has a saloon car, and as this case is by way of a medical necessity there will be no problem with petrol.'

Iris stared at him, with a sinking feeling she knew what was coming next.

'Obviously everything will go far more smoothly if you can accompany the patient and baby. Since you do have that special bond.' He smiled even more broadly. 'My colleague is happy to agree to my request, and even feels as if he has a special interest in the case, since he was present at the birth. He'll be responsible for the transport, you for the mother and child. I've already spoken to Fiona. We're all ready to finalise the arrangements.'

'You mean, I have to travel there and back with Dr Leeson?' Iris said in disbelief. Of all the people she had encountered since moving to London, he was the one she least wanted to spend any more time with. Let alone for such a long journey.

Dr Patcham brushed aside her objections. Dr Leeson respected Iris's abilities and after all, it was for only one trip. How lucky they were that he had a suitable vehicle and was kind enough to volunteer his help, going so far out of his own way. It was the best possible solution and would be for the undoubted benefit of Connie, Jonathan and, with luck, for Eddie as well.

Iris knew she was being backed into a corner. She would just have to overcome her own feelings and approach the idea with professional neutrality. Dr Patcham was right – it was for a comparatively short period of time. How bad could that really be? The man was unpleasant but she had dealt with worse. 'All right. I'll do it,' she said reluctantly.

CHAPTER THIRTY

So it was that, as soon as Connie was deemed fit to travel, Iris found herself once more in the dark saloon with Dr Leeson at the wheel. They had set off bright and early, in the hope of getting there and back in one day. That would depend on there being no raids, or damage to the roads. Iris settled Connie and the baby in the back seat, in great contrast to the previous journey. Now Connie was happy and smiling rather than groaning in agony.

Iris sat in the passenger seat and made conversation, turning round to the patient, while Dr Leeson was content simply to drive, deftly avoiding the many potholes, ignoring the pair of them.

The roads opened out once they left the farthest reaches of the capital's suburbs, and Iris sat back to enjoy the unfolding countryside. Most of the other cars on the road were military vehicles of one sort or another, and they were blessed with good driving conditions, with no rain and few diversions. If the driver himself was silent, Connie had enough to say for both of them, and now that she was safe, with a healthy child, there was no stopping her. Iris recognised she was also probably covering her nervousness at the forthcoming encounter with chatter. She was even determined to make a fresh start in the little town she had previously hated. 'I'm doing it for Jonathan,' she said.

Iris had only to nod in approval and make encouraging noises, and Connie did the rest. Jonathan slept for most of the time, rocked by the movement of the car. Iris had to admit that Dr Leeson was a smooth driver, unflustered by the occasional poor surface or, in one case, cows crossing the road. Despite the lack of road signs he seemed to know his way and she hadn't needed to consult the maps she'd remembered to bring.

He didn't seem to be worried by the circumstances in which he found himself, but Iris couldn't help but wonder. Yesterday evening, Ruby had knocked on her door as she was packing a light bag for the trip.

'I heard what you're going to be doing tomorrow,' she'd said, rather hesitantly.

'Come in, come in. I'm nearly done, so let me move this bag and you can sit on the bed.' Iris had made space for her guest, and sat down herself on the one chair. The lampshade cast a rosy colour to the light in the room.

Ruby twisted her hands awkwardly. 'I'm not sure how to say this and maybe you already know . . .'

Iris's head went up in surprise. 'Know what?

Whatever can it be? Has something dreadful happened, Ruby?'

The younger nurse bit her lip. 'No. Yes. Well, sort of. That is to say, it must have been dreadful at the time but it was years ago, back at the start of the war.'

Iris was both puzzled and concerned. 'I really don't know what you mean, Ruby. Please, tell me what it is?'

Ruby cleared her throat and dropped her gaze to her slippered feet. 'It's about Dr Leeson. You know I did that operation with him and Dr Patcham last year?'

Iris nodded. 'I heard, yes.'

'Well, after it was over, Dr Patcham took me to one side and said not to mind about Dr Leeson being a bit . . . well . . . you know, rude. That he had his reasons.'

Iris was confused now. 'And they were?' She wasn't sure if she wanted to know but she could not turn Ruby away.

'There was a raid.' Ruby's words tumbled out all in one go. 'He had a wife and child and they were being evacuated, meant to be heading for safety and . . . and a lone bomber dropped its load right over this village, out in East Anglia I think. They died.' She stopped abruptly. 'So he's never been the same since.'

Iris let out a breath she hadn't realised she'd been holding. 'I see,' she said, though she hadn't yet begun to take on what this might mean. 'That's a terrible story.'

Ruby nodded. 'And now you'll be in a car with him, and you'll be taking a mother and baby to safety . . .'

Iris nodded, and shut her eyes briefly. She couldn't imagine what quiet torment that might mean for the doctor. Or, on the other hand, he might be so immured in his sorrow that it might not mean anything. Yet he had volunteered. He must be prepared. Now, at least, so was she.

'Thank you for telling me,' she'd said, frowning, wondering what she should do with this new information.

'I'll let you get ready for bed now.' Ruby had risen and made for the door. 'I just wanted you to know. In case it makes a difference.'

Iris had kept all of this to herself as the morning went on, the doctor as inscrutable as ever sitting at her side. While she pitied him, her focus had to be on her patient and her son. All in all it was a relief to arrive at the convalescent home and to have the excuse to get out of the car. 'I'll show Connie and the baby inside and take the chance to see Eddie,' she said, keeping her voice bright. 'I'm sure there's somewhere in the building where you can get a cup of tea, maybe a sandwich?'

The anaesthetist looked away. 'I'll make my own arrangements and meet you in this exact spot in an hour,' he told her, speeding off as soon as Iris had lifted Connie's big suitcase from the boot.

'Come along, then. Let's not mind him,' Iris said,

determinedly cheerful, ignoring the sound of departing tyres on gravel.

As Iris stood waiting for her lift home to arrive, she reflected on the miracle she had just witnessed. It wasn't an exaggeration to describe it like that. She had kept to the doorway when Connie had brought baby Jonathan to see his father, not wanting to interfere, but to be close enough if things went wrong. She had no idea how this might go; Eddie could react in many ways or, possibly worse, in none at all.

Connie grew nervous right at the last moment but walked straight ahead anyway, into a room painted a calming shade of pale golden yellow, with a view over well-tended gardens. Eddie sat in a wing-back chair, his posture indicating to Iris's eyes that he was much improved physically, at least, but his expression was dead.

Little by little he turned and then seemed to back away when he realised who it was. Connie did not falter but went straight to him, holding out the precious bundle that was their son. For a moment Iris was afraid that Eddie would recoil, rejecting the child, but then Connie drew back the delicate, lace-edged blanket so that he could see Jonathan's face. 'He's the image of you,' she heard Connie murmur.

Eddie gasped, almost in disbelief, and then said, 'It's true! He is.' His voice was rasping and hesitant from disuse but he had spoken nonetheless. Iris felt it best to withdraw, to leave them to it. They would have much to say and now that she was satisfied he wasn't going to turn his back on his wife and child, she could happily step away.

It was the best possible outcome, one that she hadn't dared to hope for. Eddie had spoken and accepted his child. That meant he believed his wife and they could begin to mend everything that the lack of trust had broken. There would be a long way to go, but the main step had been taken. Iris could not have wished for more – and could do no more. It was all up to Eddie and Connie now.

Iris brushed a crumb from her jacket as the saloon rounded the far corner of the street. She had taken the chance to have a ham sandwich in the convalescent home's tea area, and very welcome it was too. She sighed to herself. They were in farming country – the very thing that Connie hated, but where she felt completely at home. The butter had been spread thickly and the ham was a generous slice, all served with home-made piccalilli. She had been tempted to buy an extra one to wrap and take with her in the car, but that would have been greedy. The patients were all there to be built up, to recover. Their need was greater.

Dr Leeson pulled into the neat gravel driveway and Iris got back into the passenger seat. She was not looking forward to the return leg but perhaps it would be as smooth and problem-free as the outward one. 'It went well,' she said as she straightened her collar, then placed her bag at her feet. He hadn't asked, but she assumed he would be interested.

Instead he nodded briefly and turned out of the gate, the last few houses of the town soon giving way to the gorgeous open country. Iris exhaled slowly. She didn't need conversation. She would make the most of being out in the rural surroundings, beginning to come to life now spring was actually here.

The hedgerows were full of new buds and flowers, primroses peeping between the clumps of grass at the verges. Birds were singing, which made her smile. It was good to hear different types of birdsong again, aside from the sparrows and pigeons that lived on Victory Walk. Her thoughts drifted, remembering how her mother had been able to identify so many birds by their songs and calls. She'd tried to pass on this knowledge to her daughter but Iris had never been able to tell the difference . . .

The next thing she knew she was jolted awake by the chill of the side-window glass against her face. Hurriedly she sat upright, appalled that she could have drifted off. How could that have happened? She'd fallen into a doze, and in the presence of this forbidding doctor. How unprofessional – what must he be thinking?

'Ah, awake, are we?' Dr Leeson noticed her discomfort and cast a quick look in her direction before returning his gaze to the road ahead.

Iris cleared her throat. 'As you can see. I do apologise.'

'No need,' he said smoothly, and Iris cast a glance

over to him in turn. If she hadn't known him better, she could have mistaken that for a friendly comment. She might even have thought he was smiling. That couldn't be right. Even now, knowing what she did about him, she still clung to the thought that he was by nature a cold and unfeeling man, which was how he had always been around her. Except, a little memory murmured, he had tried to compliment her in his own awkward way, that unforgettable evening when Jonathan had been born.

'We've been delayed,' he went on, 'and you missed the excitement. A butcher's van had run into a ditch but luckily nobody was hurt or we'd have had to pull over and offer our services.' He cast her another look. 'Happily I didn't have to disturb your beauty sleep.'

Iris was deeply affronted. 'It was no such thing! Anyway I would have been pleased to help.'

'I know.' His eyes flashed with what might almost have been amusement as he indicated for a turn onto a main road. They drove along for a few minutes in silence once more, but Iris was aware it was a new kind of silence. There was none of that studied indifference of earlier. 'It shouldn't be too long now.'

She nodded back at him, unable to return the silent treatment. If he wanted to talk it was only good manners to join in.

'Oh. Good. That's to say, I'm sure you're tired as well, with all that driving.' Damn, that wasn't what she'd meant to say at all. 'I could take over for a spell if you like,' she offered. 'I haven't always travelled

322

around riding those old bikes. Where I was before, I had use of my mother's car for a while.'

He nodded. 'I am perfectly all right,' he said, and Iris thought she should never have made the suggestion. But he wrongfooted her. 'Thank you for mentioning it,' he continued. 'Why am I not surprised? You are a woman of many talents, Nurse Hawke, and of course I should have guessed that driving was one of them.'

He was definitely making fun of her now. Iris's cheeks flamed and she hoped he hadn't noticed. 'It was necessary, out on Dartmoor,' she said shortly.

He nodded again. 'Dartmoor. Beautiful part of the world. How lucky you were to work there.'

If it had been someone else, she would have loved to talk more about her beloved home, asked him which areas he knew, if he'd gone there on holiday, if he'd walked on the magnificent moorland. Yet she didn't feel she could trust him not to mock and couldn't bear the thought of his sarcasm. 'Yes, I was,' she said.

Now she could make out the faint skyline of London in the early evening light. They would be back soon, as he'd predicted. They couldn't get there soon enough as far as she was concerned. She was confused by Dr Leeson. She could not understand what had brought about this sudden thaw in hostilities, although she understood well enough that the hostility wasn't reserved for her alone but directed at the world in general. And no wonder, really, after what he'd suffered. Perhaps she should cut him some more slack.

It had been bad enough losing Peter, but if they'd had a child . . .

Their brief foray into conversation lapsed and Iris began daydreaming once more, snapping out of it when she became aware of a soft noise. For a moment she wondered if she was imagining things. No, her mind was not playing tricks. Dr Leeson was humming a tune. He was doing it extremely quietly but there was no doubt about it, the man was humming. Something by Glenn Miller, if she wasn't much mistaken – a tune that Mary had taken to playing on the piano in the common room when the wireless wasn't on. Iris could hardly have been more amazed if he'd pulled the car over, got out and started dancing.

'Sorry, am I disturbing you?' he asked, eyes flashing as they'd done before. Now she was sure it was with amusement, not antipathy.

'No, no, not at all.' Iris clasped her hands in her lap.

He looked back at the road once more, the traffic growing busier now, and resumed his tune, at such a level that she could hardly hear it. This was far and away the strangest journey she had ever been on. She just wanted it over and done with.

By and by they came into London proper. Iris willed them to get back before her stomach started to rumble. Perhaps she should have taken that extra ham sandwich. If they made it back within the hour she might catch the end of the evening meal. Maybe Gladys or one of the others would have saved her something anyway. Ruby would have thought of it, she was sure.

Suddenly the car swerved and for a moment she was flung against Dr Leeson, catching the scent of his tweed jacket as her face made contact with his lapel. She was too stunned to say anything. A jolt of electricity had shot through her. It must be the shock.

'Are you hurt?' he demanded urgently. 'That stupid cyclist suddenly turned left without so much as a by-your-leave. I only just missed him. He's fine, I checked in the rear-view mirror. But are you all right?'

There was nothing mocking about his tone now. It had a deep sincerity to it that Iris could not take in or make sense of. 'Yes, yes, just a little shaken,' she assured him. 'That'll teach me not to pay attention. My mind was elsewhere.'

'As long as you're sure?' He certainly sounded as if he meant it.

Iris laughed off her embarrassment. 'I am, don't worry. I'd know if I was injured. All that nursing training, you know.'

He gave a brief chuckle. 'Ah, of course. Well then, you'd know better than most.'

'I most definitely would.' Iris almost pinched herself. This was almost like a normal conversation. Wait till she told Ruby. Her friend would never believe it.

The change in mood lasted until the car finally reached Victory Walk, now guided by its shielded headlights. Darkness had fallen and she really hoped that Ruby had set aside some of tonight's meal.

'Thank you for driving us,' Iris said formally as she got out.

'No, thank you, nurse,' the doctor said, his face now indistinct in the low light, but once again she registered that sincere tone, so utterly different from how he'd spoken before.

As she made her way up to the big front door, she couldn't get it out of her head – that, and the sensation of being thrown against him.

CHAPTER THIRTY-ONE

Mattie waved at her daughter as the little girl ran across the school playground to join her classmates. Gillian had taken to school as naturally as breathing and never hesitated at the gates. Mattie was thankful. That was at least one thing she didn't have to worry about. Gillian was taking off her coat already, prior to hanging it inside on the special peg with her name beneath it. The spring sunshine was warm and Mattie loosened her scarf as she watched the crocodile of six-year-olds wend its way into the school building, Janet Phipps guiding them, reassuring the shyer ones.

Mattie had worked the night shift at the factory but had been determined to stay awake long enough to bring Gillian to school, which she didn't manage often enough. Frequently her mother Flo did it, or Edith. Indeed, there was never a shortage of willing adults, and Mattie knew that this was good for Gillian, helping her to move beyond her mother and see a wide range of adults as safe and reliable. All the same, sometimes she liked the routine, the feeling that she was being a good parent to her beloved daughter. She gave a long sigh.

In her coat pocket was an envelope, tattered from its delayed journey from France to Jeeves Street. Perhaps she should have waited to open it until she'd dropped off Gillian, but she hadn't been able to resist it. She'd read it while the little girl did up her shoelaces after breakfast, a new skill that she was very proud of. Mattie had just about held herself together to say 'well done' but it had been a close-run thing. She'd kept the mask of calmness all the way from home to the school, but now she could drop the pretence.

It had been a very short letter from Lennie, forwarded by the Red Cross. Admittedly, all his letters were short – even the ones from before he had been taken prisoner, back in 1940. He wasn't a great writer, never had been. Even by his standards, this had been brief, though, and his handwriting had been shaky, some words barely legible. It basically said he was alive, he loved her and to give his love to the children. Then to her it seemed as if he'd stopped in exhaustion.

Mattie stepped into a deep doorway and dashed her hand across her eyes. She didn't want to be seen crying in public. Somehow, in all that time since his capture, she'd kept going, telling herself that he would be all right. She was no fool. She could guess what the conditions were like in prisoner-of-war camps, knew he would have been moved around, with less and less to eat as the months went by. It was almost as if she could sense him fading, and these few sentences were all he could summon from the last of his energy. He would be weak and therefore prone to all manner of infections, and she reckoned that there would be plenty to choose from in the POW camps.

Come on, she told herself, you're tired, you've been up all night. She had to carry on, no matter what. Gillian and Alan needed her, but how she longed for their father to come home. It was a bitter irony that while everyone was quietly hopeful now that the end of the fighting was in sight, she knew that time might be running out for Lennie.

Kenny was pleased to find himself partnered with Olive on the midweek, mid-evening shift. He'd said as much to Ruby when they'd grabbed a few minutes at the café near Ridley Road after work. He'd had enough of babysitting the stroppy teenager, which was how he now thought of Cliff. A cup of tea with Ruby had been just what he needed, as she bolstered his confidence and made him feel that he had someone warm to come back to. She'd looked especially lovely today, for some reason. Perhaps she had washed her hair. It had been gorgeous and wavy and she'd put on a little necklace he'd given her, with a shiny metal bird on a chain. It wasn't silver or anything, but it had caught his eye and he knew she appreciated it, because her hand kept going to her throat as they'd talked.

The evenings were growing longer. Now that Easter was over, they could almost think of summer being on the way. Weeds poked from the bomb sites as they walked along the pavements, but there had not been any bombing raids in the area for weeks. Kenny didn't want to tempt fate but that background tension of always wondering when the next V2 missile would fall was slowly lessening. He could feel that his shoulders weren't as hunched, his neck not as stiff. All the same, he didn't want to get too over-confident. You still had to be ready for anything, every time you put on the blue serge uniform of a warden.

Even so, he couldn't help but wish that tonight would be a straightforward, uneventful shift. He'd had more than his share of excitement since becoming a warden. He wasn't like some of them he knew, who actively enjoyed the thrill of a dangerous incident. There were a few colleagues who were at their happiest in burning buildings or at crashes, their eyes bright with excitement, revelling in the knowledge that they were heroes. That wasn't his way at all.

Nor was it Olive's, as he had come to realise over the months that they had worked together. She was far too down to earth. She wanted nothing more than to survive the night and get home to her children. She sometimes commented that they were enough excitement for anybody, and she came on shift for a nice rest.

With the longer evenings, there was a far smaller risk of people putting lights on and not drawing their curtains or blinds. There just weren't the hours of darkness in which it was a problem. Kenny liked that. Everyone thought that ARP wardens spent most of their time rushing around shouting 'put that light out', but that was another thing he could do without. Later on, some families might become sloppy and argue that it didn't matter any more, now the raids had stopped, but he knew he couldn't allow that; yet it was only a tiny minority who behaved that way. By and large, everyone had simply got into the habit of pulling the curtains before switching on the light.

'Quiet one tonight, Olive,' he said amiably as they wandered along, the streets emptying as most workers were already home unless they were on late shifts. A few older children were hanging around their front doors, a couple of lads playing football in a half-hearted way. It was still warm and flies buzzed about in the evening sunshine. The ball rolled in their direction and Kenny neatly kicked it back, causing Olive to raise her eyebrows at him.

'Look at you, they'll sign you up for the Arsenal if you keep on like that.'

Kenny grinned back. It was a source of amusement or annoyance that Arsenal's ground had been taken over as an ARP centre, depending on if you supported the team or not. 'Not likely. My family would kill me. We all support West Ham 'cos me uncle had a trial for them once.' He waved at the boys. 'We have a bit of a game down the docks now and again. I'm not as good as others, to be honest, what with having to wear glasses. You should see Ron, he's like lightning – you wouldn't think it to meet him, but it's true.'

Olive laughed. 'I'll make sure to mention it next time I see him. Does Gladys know?'

'Oh yes, you can't hide a talent like Ron's.' Kenny

made a silly face and Olive laughed, making the boys turn around to see what the joke was.

They carried on walking towards the sun hanging low in the sky, the edges of the clouds beginning to turn pink. It would be a fine day tomorrow by the looks of it.

Before they could reach the small grocer's shop, now shuttered up on the corner of the road, a young man in police uniform caught up with them. 'Need your help, if you'd be so good.' He was slightly breathless from running. 'A spot of bother in a house a couple of streets away. We could do with an extra pair of hands. Probably just a domestic accident. We think a chip pan's gone up.'

Kenny and Olive looked at one another. 'Well, lead the way.' Olive nodded at the young man, even younger than Cliff. 'That's what we're here for.'

Gladys finished writing her list and tore the sheet of paper from her notebook. 'Here you are. Now don't forget to use the hoe on the new weeds,' she instructed as she passed the list to Ruby. 'They're much easier to get rid of before they're established.'

Ruby nodded meekly. She'd volunteered to spend tomorrow, her day off, at the victory garden, and was now receiving her orders. 'Lily can help me,' she said. 'Well, as long as she has time to get smartened up afterwards. I think she's going to the cinema with one of her admirers.'

'I can't keep up,' Gladys confessed. 'I suppose she'll tell us if one of them is serious. Good luck to her, it makes me feel tired just thinking about it.' She hung up her apron on the door between the kitchen and the service room. 'Have a nice evening, Ruby.'

'I will. I'm going to take it easy,' said Ruby, helping herself to a cup of cocoa as her friend left for the night.

She wandered back in to the common room and turned on the wireless. Wilfred Pickles was reading the news, with details of more Allied successes on the continent. Mary came through the big double doors from the hall and set down her sheet music beside the piano. 'Are you listening to that? I've got a few new tunes I'd like to try. Would you like that?'

Ruby nodded. 'I wasn't really paying much attention, not once I'd heard the headlines. You go right ahead.'

'I know it's mean but I can't take anything he says seriously, not with that Yorkshire accent,' Mary replied breezily, opening the lid to the old upright which was pushed against the long wall. 'Doesn't he sound dreadful? You must admit it.'

Ruby shrugged. 'I don't mind. You'd better not say that in front of Lily – she'll think you don't like anyone from the north. Or Alice, come to think of it.'

'Oh, nonsense.' Mary backtracked hurriedly. 'I wasn't thinking. Of course I don't mean them. Anyway, the Liverpool accent is nicer; it's completely different to that Pickles man.' She spread out the music, picked a song and attempted the opening chord. 'Ugh, that's not right. Let me try again.' She had another go and this time was happier with the result. 'Recognise it?'

Ruby huffed. 'What, with just those notes? Don't be daft. Let's hear some more.'

'All right.' Mary played the opening line all the way through. 'Now do you know it?'

Ruby turned as Iris arrived from upstairs, knitting in her hands. 'I think I've got it now. Iris, did you recognise that song?'

Iris shrugged apologetically. 'I'm afraid not. I don't really keep up with these things.'

'Carmen Miranda!' Ruby proclaimed. 'I'm right, aren't I, Mary?'

'You are. It's "Chica Chica Boom Chic", straight out of *That Night in Rio*.' Mary played some more, got a few bars wrong, tried them again. 'This is trickier than I thought. You'll have to forgive me, Iris, it isn't meant to come out like that. I got carried away. Imagine wearing those big hats made out of fruit! Like in *The Gang's All Here*! That would make you the centre of attention all right.'

Ruby sighed. 'Imagine having all that fruit, full stop. I wouldn't waste it on a hat. I'd eat the lot.'

Iris nodded amiably, not really knowing what they were talking about but not wanting to seem rude. 'I've almost forgotten what some of it tastes like,' she said wistfully.

Mary gave the whole song another go, putting her heart and soul into it, and it was hard to feel low-spirited in the face of such a tune. Even Iris was tapping her foot to it when Gwen came in, looking serious. She did not seem in the mood for film music.

'Lovely to hear you playing again, Mary,' she said,

with a nod, 'and sorry to interrupt. We have an incident requiring our services. Nothing too terrible but swift treatment is needed, nonetheless. Apparently the only free ambulance has just been called out to Clapton and that's in the other direction. Can I ask one of you to attend? You'll need to cycle there, it'll take too long to walk.'

Mary looked a little crestfallen, having had to stop just when she was getting the hang of it. Still, she began to gather her music into a pile, ready to set off.

'No, no,' Iris said at once. 'You carry on playing. You've only just started. I'll go. After all, it's not fair to ask Ruby as I know full well it's your day off tomorrow and you don't want to have a late night tonight and miss half of it.'

'Oh, I shouldn't think you'll be out very late,' Gwen assured her. 'It's a domestic fire, by the sounds of it. You're perfect, Iris, as you discussed the latest burns treatments with the sister at the Homerton hospital, didn't you? Thank you, my dear. I'll pass you the address. You'll probably be back before Mary reaches her grand finale.'

Iris approached the row of small houses, knowing that the message Gwen had received might be entirely accurate, or merely the tip of the iceberg. With her restocked Gladstone bag, she felt as ready as she could be for whatever lay in wait. When she reached number 35, although there was a smell of acrid smoke, there seemed to be little other damage, and she could see two familiar people sitting on the outside wall with a third, who was cradling her arm. The ARP had got there first and she was pleased to see it was two of the most trusted wardens.

Olive looked up. 'Here comes the cavalry!' she laughed. 'Over here. It's Nurse Hawke, isn't it? You can prop your bike against the gatepost. Just one patient for you, and we've done what we could.'

The patient was a woman of about sixty, who appeared more embarrassed than hurt. 'I don't know what I was thinking of,' she said crossly. 'I know you mustn't turn your back on a chip pan but then I started to do the crossword and lost track of time. All me own fault. I'm sorry to put you to the trouble.'

'Not at all,' Iris said briskly. 'Now let me see where the damage is. Ah, you've had some first aid already from my colleagues here.'

The woman nodded. 'They covered the pan with a wet towel then made me put me arm under cold running water – we got a tap out the back.'

'Excellent.' Iris could tell she would have little problem here. The burn was not a bad one and she couldn't have done much more herself to begin with. She might have guessed that Olive would have known what to do; Ruby had told her that she had a young family and women with young children usually had first-hand first-aid experience. Iris set about treating the injury as carefully as she could, having disinfected her own hands first; it seemed unlikely that they could go back inside the building until it was confirmed as safe.

'Will you have anywhere to go, to sit quietly and get over the shock?' she asked.

The woman nodded, her greying hair bobbing as she did so. 'Me daughter lives round the corner. Give me a right earful, she will, but no more than I deserve.'

'Don't be so hard on yourself, it's easily done.' Olive tried to comfort their patient but she was having none of it.

'No, I'm the one as is to blame. I shall just have to grin and bear it. She's a good girl, though, she'll look after me.' The woman sighed and shrugged her shoulders in her thin cardigan. 'Good job you got my handbag, sir; I don't like to leave my ration books around for any Tom, Dick or Harry.'

Kenny reddened a little at being called 'sir'. 'All part of the service,' he said. 'Shall we see you to your daughter's?'

'No, no, it's not far.' The woman clearly didn't want any more fuss.

'Well, you give us her address and we can make sure someone checks your dressing,' Iris said kindly but firmly. 'It doesn't look as if it will cause permanent damage but we don't want any complications.'

The woman gave in to her authoritative tone and Iris wrote the information on the back of her piece of paper, putting it carefully in her pocket. The woman thanked them and headed off, carefully protecting her arm as she did so.

'Looks as if there's not much more for us to do,' Olive observed.

Kenny agreed. 'Better resume our patrol, then. We're

all behind. We'd better set off towards the canal and do the streets down there.'

Iris went to her bike and secured her bag in the front basket. 'Would you mind if I came along with you?' she asked. 'I could do with a stroll and it's one of the first proper warm evenings. I do like the canal.'

Suddenly the idea of sitting knitting back in the common room wasn't as appealing. Besides, she felt like a wet blanket when Mary played her tunes. It wasn't that she didn't enjoy them, but if you hadn't seen the film then it didn't mean as much. She didn't want Ruby to have to keep explaining everything. Much better that she stayed out of the way for a while. The knitting could wait.

'Yes, why not?' said Kenny easily. 'The more the merrier.'

CHAPTER THIRTY-TWO

As she pushed her bike, Iris fell into the rhythm of the noise of the pedals turning, the bumping of the tyres on the rough path. Her thoughts meandered from their usual concerns of patients needing help, forms to be filled in, notes to be sent to the various doctors, local organisations and voluntary organisations, all of whom had a role in the wider welfare of her charges. You could spend twenty-four hours a day at the task and still not complete everything, which sometimes preyed on her mind. It was good to let her thoughts wander, as Olive and Kenny walked a little way ahead, checking off the streets on their section.

The last time she'd had the chance to do such a thing had been during that journey back from the Cotswolds. She felt her face flush at the memory. She had not had any contact with Dr Leeson since, but that did not mean she hadn't thought of him. Really, she didn't know why, she told herself crossly. Nearly every time she'd met the man, he'd been difficult to say the least.

Iris hadn't told Ruby about the events of the return journey after all. Perhaps 'events' was too grand a term; not much had happened, she insisted to herself. She'd exchanged some pleasanter-than-usual words with the anaesthetist and there'd been a moment where she'd been thrown against him as the car swerved.

Yet she sensed that something fundamental had changed and she could not quite work out what. His face kept flashing before her eyes, the hard, uncaring one she had endured on all previous encounters and the one he'd shown her at the end of the trip, totally different. She gave a small shiver. Which was the real one? Was she seeing something that wasn't there? Had she been mistaken and misread the situation?

'Careful of that bramble!' Olive called, and Iris's reverie was broken. She ducked out of the way of the prickly branch, emerging from an empty shell of a house looking as if it had been damaged beyond repair some years ago. The houses on either side clung on, managing to stay upright. If Gladys had been here, she'd have tried to use that space to grow food, Iris thought.

The sound of running footsteps made her turn around, careful not to knock her bike over. A young man in a policeman's uniform rushed towards them. Iris was about to ask if she could help when she realised that the wardens knew him already.

'Fancy seeing you again so soon!' Olive called cheerfully. 'Well, you won't have to worry about keep fit classes after this evening. They've got you running all over tonight!'

The policeman gasped for breath, bending forwards, his arms braced against his knees.

'What's the trouble?' asked Kenny.

'Sorry.' The young man gulped in air, trying to get his message out. 'We need your help again. Something a bit more serious than a chip-pan fire this time.' He wheezed painfully, and Iris wondered if he'd tried to join up and not passed the medical.

'All right. Better tell us where,' Kenny suggested.

The policeman hauled himself back up to his full height. 'It's that pub along the canal path. You might know it. We aren't sure what's happened, but you can see the smoke from here.' He pointed in the direction of the waterway. 'Maybe it's their empty barrels, or whatever they keep out the back – it's gone up in a right old blaze. We don't know who's inside.'

Kenny and Olive looked at one another and then at Iris. 'The Boatman's,' Kenny groaned. 'Might have known it.'

Olive gripped her tin hat. 'We should hurry, then.'

Iris cleared her throat. 'I'd better come too. You never know when you'll need a nurse.' She tried to sound cheerful but her heart sank. According to everything she'd heard, that pub drew trouble like moths to a flame.

Mary finally put down the lid of the piano. 'That's enough,' she said reluctantly. 'I don't think I can play another note. Still, we got through most of these.' She shuffled the sheets of music into a neater pile and glanced around for somewhere to leave them. 'Oh, look. Iris has forgotten her knitting.'

'So she has.' Ruby reached for the needles and wool, which seemed to be the beginnings of a cardigan in deep purple, almost blackcurrant in shade. 'This is nice – it hasn't been unravelled from something else, that's for sure.'

Mary raised her eyebrows. 'Makes a change.' She paused for a moment. 'Do you think Iris took that job this evening to avoid us, Ruby? I never know with her. I still don't feel that she's one of us, somehow.'

Ruby shook her head at once. 'No, no I don't. I think she stepped forward because she could see you were enjoying yourself and she knew I wouldn't want a late night so I could make the most of my day off.'

'Oh.' Mary was slightly taken aback by her colleague's vehemence. 'But she's never been very friendly, has she? Keeps herself to herself most of the time. I do try not to be offended, but all the same . . .'

Ruby set down the knitting once more. 'You got to give her a chance,' she said, feeling slightly daring even now to be challenging one of the senior nurses. 'You got to remember, she was working on her own for ages. She's not used to being part of a team, 'specially not one that's been together for a long time. It wasn't her fault that she was brought in to replace Ellen. Nobody could do that, be exactly like her.'

'Well, that's certainly true.' Mary's voice revealed she was uneasy about being taken to task.

'And she's a bit older than most of us and her

interests are different as well. Doesn't make her a bad person,' Ruby said stoutly.

Mary retreated a little. 'No, well, I never thought that . . .'

'Of course not.' Ruby gave her some ground.

Mary sank down onto one of the battered but comfortable easy chairs. 'I'm just not used to somebody like that, perhaps that's all. I'll have to make more of an effort, that's what you're trying to say. I trust your judgement, Ruby. And after all she did endure an entire day with that grim Dr Leeson – I tell you, my blood ran cold at the thought of it.'

Ruby nodded. 'I wouldn't have wanted to do that. It had to be her, though, 'cos the patient didn't trust anyone else. Poor Iris, stuck with that miserable old so-and-so.' Although she wondered if he'd spent the whole day thinking about a similar journey at the beginning of the war, when his wife and child had fled to so-called safely and been killed on the way. Had he been ruder than ever and taken it out on Iris? Iris hadn't said anything about it, but that was just the sort of thing she would have kept to herself, accustomed to absorbing all the slings and arrows that came her way. If it had gone badly, she probably would have clammed up so as not to hurt Ruby, guessing that Ruby would have blamed herself for saying something in the first place.

'Surely she should have been back by now?' she said.

Mary shrugged. 'She's probably gone off for a ride on that old bike, missing the moors like she does.'

Clearly she wasn't prepared to start making an effort just yet, then.

'Oh, crikey!' Olive stared at the scene before them, the flames rising high into the air, showing bright gold against the fading sky at dusk. The smell had grown stronger the closer they had come and now they could see why. The Boatman's Arms was caught in a conflagration.

'Do you know who might be inside, Kenny?' Iris asked, aware that they were standing near the very spot where she'd waited for him to rescue little Larry, all those months ago.

'I haven't been down here for ages, or not what you might call socially,' he replied, pushing his glasses up his nose. 'Not since I started walking out with Ruby, in fact. It's not a proper place to bring someone like her. I heard the landlord's brother had shown his face again, the one what had to do a runner a while back when he got in trouble with the police. But I don't know if it's true, or if he'd be there every night anyhow.'

The policeman squinted in the dim light, trying to write it all down in his notebook.

'Thing is, with the Boatman's,' Kenny went on, 'it used to be busy right after most folk finished work, when they'd drop in for a pint before their tea. Then it would get busy again after dark. Around this sort of time there wouldn't be many customers.'

Iris nodded. That made sense.

'It's not to say there won't be any,' he went on, 'but

it's less likely. Also, I know for a fact there's more than one way in and out of there. We'd best go and check, but I don't imagine there'll be a crowd of people stuck inside.'

'Good,' said the young policeman, sounding very out of his depth.

Iris shot him a glance. 'All the same, like the warden says, we'd better go and check,' she prompted.

The young man cleared his throat and squared his shoulders. 'Of course. Ah, yes, we should do that.' His reluctance was palpable.

'Very well, I'll go.' Olive could wait no longer and strode out, swiftly followed by Kenny. Iris waited for a moment, knowing that it was their job to do this, not hers. She'd only come along for a quiet walk. But the policeman didn't look to be much use in a crisis. She couldn't blame him – he still had spots, for goodness' sake. He was probably used to running messages, nothing much more than that. She couldn't stand by and watch, doing nothing.

'Take my bike,' she said firmly, lifting her bag from the front basket. 'Ride it as fast as you can and bring help from the fire brigade and your superiors. Then bring it back – I'll be in deep trouble if it goes missing. And watch the back brake, it's a devil. Right, off you go.' If he wasn't going to help on the scene, the least he could do was find reinforcements.

'Tell us what's what around here, Kenny.' Olive's eyes were streaming in the smoke. 'It's hard to see.'

Kenny cast his eyes around the building in which

he'd spent more hours than he cared to admit. It had been the place to come to in his wayward youth, especially once he'd started on the docks and begun to earn a wage packet. You could while away the time very nicely if you didn't have high standards, with no questions asked.

'The main entrance is over there, facing the canal path,' he explained, pointing. 'Looks like that's no good to us now. It takes you into the bar. Then around the side you got a storage area. You can get to it from the back door of the bar and it's got an exit on the other side as well. Some of the storage place is kind of under cover, like in a big lean-to, and some of it is just a yard, but they always kept all manner of stuff there. It has high walls so nobody passing by can look in. I don't even want to guess what's been there, over the years.'

Olive studied the place as well as she could. 'Right, so we don't even try to go in the front. We'd better go around to the back – looks as if we can get there down the side. Iris, you'd better stay here just in case anyone comes out of the front, or we need to bring anybody to you. You'll be all right on your own, won't you?'

'Of course I shall,' Iris said promptly. That was the least of her worries. She reached into her pocket for a cotton handkerchief to press against her nose and mouth, to help her breathe.

Kenny was relieved to find that the direction of the wind was guiding the worst of the flames away from the side of the building that led to the yard. They would be able to edge carefully along the little alley and approach in relative safety. It was hot, but he could just about bear it. He'd been in worse spots, he told himself. He found comfort in the knowledge that Olive was right behind him. He could rely on her. She wouldn't flinch away at the first sign of danger.

Here was the outside wall to the lean-to section of the back yard. He groaned. No, here was where the wall should have been. It had collapsed, or at least much of it had. He couldn't see why, but that wasn't his concern right now. Olive exclaimed aloud. 'What's happened here? Was it always like this?'

Kenny coughed as he inhaled a mouthful of smuts. 'No, it must have just happened. Perhaps the heat done it.' He felt cautiously along what was left of the wall. 'It'll make it harder for us to give it the once-over though.'

Olive stopped in her tracks. 'Can you hear anything? I thought I caught something then.'

'Like what?'

'I don't know. Never mind.' Olive urged him forward.

Kenny stepped over the wall at a point where it was now below waist height. 'This'll do as a way in,' he muttered. 'Mind your feet, Olive, it's all rubble and whatnot. Don't want you ricking your ankle.'

'No, that wouldn't do,' she agreed, her figure outlined in the strange light. 'There it is again – are you sure you didn't hear it?'

Kenny shook his head. 'Maybe me hat's too far over me ears,' he suggested. 'Do you want to go and see if you can find what it is, while I check out the old storage shed? It's not too bad round here, is it? We'll manage somehow.'

Olive stood up straighter. 'Of course we will. Yes, if you don't mind, I think it's coming from over there – would that be the back way into the pub proper? It might be nothing, or it could be a trapped animal. It didn't sound quite human but you can't be certain.'

'You best go and look,' Kenny said, though he felt a sudden reluctance to lose her by his side. Still, he was the senior here; he had better buck his ideas up. He cautiously crept around what he thought would have been the border of the lean-to, but the collapsed wall had brought down its roof, which blocked the way into the far corners of the yard. Then again, he reasoned, if anybody had been in the open half of the yard they would have got out into the back lane. He knew of several characters on the run from the law who'd made their escape that way.

No, the only place that anybody could be trapped was under this pile of rubble and roof. It wasn't likely. He was just considering whether he would be more use going to help Olive, or even returning to the front path to confer with Iris, when he saw something.

His heart hammering, he edged closer. A boot, shining in the blaze-bright light. Now bile rose in his mouth. The boot was not lying on its own. Its owner was still wearing it. Closer still, he could make out that here was a pair of legs, the rest of the body buried in the rubble, the remaining wall looming above. It was his worst nightmare come true.

He had to try to rescue whoever it was. They might be crushed to death already but he mustn't assume that. If there was a life to be saved, it was up to him to do it – but that wall might fall. 'Remember your training,' he muttered, pulling his tin hat still further down on his head. 'You've done this before. You did it then and you can do it now.'

He hoped he wasn't going to be sick. He'd never liked enclosed spaces. He hadn't liked it that time when he'd searched for Larry in the upstairs rooms of his house, having to poke his head into the dark little cupboard and under the beds. He took a deep breath. This was outside, though. The fire was mostly on the other side of the pub. He'd be able to breathe as long as he didn't panic.

Slowly, bit by bit, he began to lift the rubble out of the way, trying not to dislodge any more of it. He didn't want the rest of the wall to fall in on him. 'Then you'd be a goner for sure, and what would Ruby do then?' he murmured. When he got out of here, he was going to have a proper think about their future, he decided. Being in a spot like this made you consider what mattered and Ruby would top any list, he knew that. First, though, he had to make sure he *had* a future, and that meant avoiding any dodgy bricks. Several had crumbled from the loose sections where the roof should have been. One hit his hand and he cried out.

His other hand came into contact with the trouser

leg of the prone body. Strange . . . it felt familiar. Kenny tried not to think about what it meant as it was hardly a priority in the rescue mission, but it nagged away at him as he doggedly lifted away lump after lump of wall. He groaned when he realised. It was serge – it was a uniform. Perhaps a warden's uniform just like his own.

Faster now, he scrabbled to free the body, to reach the head. It was bad enough to think that this was a stranger, but what if it was someone he knew? He had to find out. He teased away the stones that had jammed around the upper torso, the neck, an outstretched arm and finally the face.

In the frenzy of shadow and flame Kenny found himself looking into the open, staring eyes of Henry Spencer.

'Oh no.' Kenny rocked back on his heels, aghast at the sight. He couldn't think straight. How had this happened – what was his high-and-mighty superior doing in such a place? Had he come here to investigate criminal behaviour, perhaps? He couldn't leave him here – but he couldn't move him either, not without help of some kind. Slowly he backed away, out of the tunnel of rubble he had excavated. 'Olive!' he shouted. 'Iris!'

Now he was far enough along to stand up and he shouted again as he did so. Before he could turn to look for either of the women there was a grating, rushing sound and the rest of the wall gave way, covering the body once more, leaving just the arm and the legs visible. Kenny had to stop himself exclaiming in fright. He'd got out just in time. A few seconds later, and he'd have been—

'Kenny, what's happened?' It was Iris, running at his call, now coming to a dead halt in front of the heap of stones and brick.

Kenny explained, gulping back the bile that rose in his gullet, his voice shaking now that the immediate danger had passed. Iris took in the dire situation and approached the mound of debris, squatting next to the arm. She reached down and placed her hands around the wrist, shaking her head as Kenny came closer. 'One moment.' She set the wrist back down again. 'Stand back, Kenny, you can't do any more. He's gone. Been gone for a while, I should say.'

'Really? Are you sure? Shouldn't we try . . . try . . .' He tailed off, the enormity of it all hitting him. Fair enough, he hadn't liked Spencer, but he wouldn't have wished this on him.

'No point,' said Iris briskly. 'I realise that only a doctor can declare death, but believe me, Kenny, that poor man has breathed his last. You can't help him. Let the fire brigade get him out of there when it's safe to do so. We'd better concentrate on the living. Where's Olive?'

Kenny remembered with a shudder that Olive had set off on her own, towards the flames. 'She went to investigate a noise. She thought an animal might have been trapped.'

Iris looked at him. 'An animal?'

'Or – or maybe not. Maybe nothing. But we'd better find out.'

Iris set off in the direction in which he'd pointed and Kenny followed, filled with new dread at what fresh horrors the blazing Boatman's might have in store.

CHAPTER THIRTY-THREE

It grew even hotter as they reached the back entrance to the pub. Kenny knew it as the way out that some customers had used for their various assignations – buying or selling the stolen goods often stored in the lean-to; romantic encounters in the courtyard, although that was maybe too fancy a way to describe them. There'd been at least one attempted murder. This doorway had seen it all.

'We can't go in there, it's lethal.' Iris had to shout above the roar of the flames. 'Is there any other way?'

Kenny racked his brains. 'Perhaps one of the big windows around the far side?' he suggested. 'Or along the front, 'cos that would be out of the worst of the fire as it is now.'

They retraced their steps and ended up back on the footpath. Iris hoped the young policeman had alerted the fire brigade. The grass and weeds around the pub were dry after days of no rain – she could just imagine how they would catch and then the flames would spread. She'd seen such things take hold on the moors

353

and they could burn for days if unchecked. That couldn't be allowed to happen here.

Then she could hear voices – a woman, and one that was less easy to identify. It was high and sounded panicked. In contrast, the woman's was low and measured. Olive. Iris had no idea who she might be with, but beyond the pub, through the smoke, she began to make out two silhouettes. 'Over there, further along the path.' She nudged Kenny, who started to go forward.

Iris strained to hear what was being said. 'Careful,' she murmured. 'Something's not right. She's trying to calm somebody . . .'

Kenny nodded but carried on, and they edged around the worst of the heat. The voices were interrupted by the loud crashes of the roof caving in and glass shattering. The whole building was collapsing. If anyone had been trapped inside they would stand no chance.

He halted a few yards away from the couple. He could make out Olive now, facing him, holding up one hand to stop him going any further. The other person, a man from his height and build, had his back to them, and Olive was concentrating hard on his face, Kenny could tell. The man spoke. 'You don't understand! I got no choice.'

It was Cliff, but his voice sounded much higher than usual and it trembled with fear.

'You do, Cliff. You've always got a choice,' Olive insisted. 'Don't do anything rash, now.'

'What's that, who have you seen?' Cliff swung

around to face Kenny and Iris, and to their horror they could see that he was holding a gun.

Kenny gasped in shock. 'Cliff! What are you doing with that? You shouldn't be waving it around, someone might get hurt.'

Cliff's expression was desperate, made worse by the flickers of flame that lit it. 'Don't come any closer. You aren't meant to be here. Don't try to take it off me. I'll pull the trigger, I'm not afraid to.' He swung his arm and Kenny took a step back, gripping Iris around her elbow.

'Get away, raise the alarm, he's gone crazy,' he muttered, but not quietly enough.

'Don't call me crazy! I'm not crazy. You're not going anywhere,' he snarled, still waving the gun at them.

Iris took in the situation with a sickening sense of inevitability. History was repeating itself, hundreds of miles away from where Peter, her Peter, had faced this same dilemma. Well, he had not run from the threat. Now it was her turn.

She weighed up the costs. Olive had two young children, who needed her. She couldn't afford to be hurt, far less killed. Kenny was the light of Ruby's life. Iris remembered that early conversation with the junior nurse in the little attic bedroom, when she confessed how she was growing to like this man, and how she feared for him. Iris knew things had grown far more serious between them, that love had blossomed and endured despite what they had seen and gone through over the past year.

Whereas she, Iris Hawke, would not be missed in

anything like the same way. Her death would cause no one to despair. People might mourn the loss of her medical experience but others could provide that level of expertise. It wasn't the same as the devastatingly personal bereavement like the one she had suffered when Peter was killed, or even at her parents' death.

She tried to recall what the witness had said when Peter was shot. His killer had panicked, was out of control. He had felt he had no choice – just what Cliff was claiming now. Somehow she had to diffuse the situation.

'Let me talk to him,' she whispered to Kenny. 'Don't try to be a hero. I've . . . I've got some experience in this area.'

Kenny stiffened. 'Don't be daft, it's my job.'

Iris knew he would be affronted but also that she stood a better chance in this case. Kenny had been wonderful with Larry but that emergency was nothing like this one. 'Trust me, he'll respond better to a woman. I'll be less of a threat. Even less than Olive as I'm not in a warden's uniform.'

She could tell that Kenny was about to object but Cliff cut him off. 'What are you saying? Are you talking about me? You can stop that right now.'

Iris took a step towards him, catching, out of the corner of her eye, that Kenny was signalling to Olive to get out of the way. 'You don't know me, Cliff, but you have met my colleagues,' Iris began. 'I'm a nurse. So you see, I can't hurt you. You can put that gun down.'

He shook his head, wildly. 'No, no. I can't do that. I need it.'

Iris cautiously took another step along the canal path. It really was very hot but she dared not move her hands to loosen her collar. 'You don't really, Cliff. You only need it if you're going to hurt someone and you don't have to hurt me.'

He would not give in. 'You don't understand! It's all gone wrong . . .' For a moment Iris thought he was going to cry but he swallowed hard and continued. 'There's nothing left for me.'

She took one more step. 'Why do you think that, Cliff? You're a respected warden. People look up to you.'

He wrapped his spare arm around his stomach as if he was in pain. 'They wouldn't if they knew. I see that now but I didn't to start with, you got to believe me.'

'I do believe you, of course I do. Tell me exactly what you mean.'

'No! It's a trick.'

'It's not a trick, I promise.' Iris had almost reached him now. Carefully she crouched down. 'Come and tell me what you mean. You put that gun down on this grass and come down here and explain why you're saying such things.'

She thought he was going to object but suddenly he knelt on the sharp stones of the path, seemingly oblivious to them, still clutching the gun. He was shaking all over.

'Go on, I'm listening, and I'm not going to hurt

you.' She met his gaze and held it. 'Trust me, Cliff, you can tell me.'

With a deep cry he gave way, recounting the whole sorry tale. How his superior, Henry Spencer, had lured him in, praising him and making him believe he was special and the other wardens weren't worth bothering with. How they had their little secret, black-market goods being run out of the pub. How easy it was because the landlord's brother was in charge. He had to keep a low profile because he was a wanted man, but nobody would suspect a pillar of the community like Mr Spencer. He could do whatever he liked and had amassed a small fortune over the past year or so. He wasn't flash; nobody would have guessed.

Cliff had been recruited partly because things had started to go wrong. Iris recalled the incident months ago at the first-aid station when Gladys had felt threatened. The character Cliff described matched her mysterious patient, somebody the landlord's brother had had a fight with and broken his nose. The man had done a runner but left a gap in the organisation. The remaining members of the gang had begun to turn on one another, vying for bigger shares of the profits. Spencer and the brother had become deadly enemies but were still bound together by their shared interests. Tonight things had come to a head and the brother had picked a fight. He was taller, younger, fitter; there was only ever going to be one winner. Cliff, terrified, had hidden behind the bar and made his escape when he'd seen the brother carrying the inert form of his boss out of the back door. He could only guess that the man had set the fire to cover his tracks. He had dropped the gun at some point and Cliff had grabbed it in case the man came after him.

'So you can put it down now,' Iris urged, keeping her voice level, very aware that the fire brigade must arrive at any moment and that they might panic him all over again.

'I can't. I've spoilt everything.' Suddenly Cliff moved and turned the gun on himself, pressing it against his heart. 'There's no future for me. Everyone will say I was a thief. But I didn't know for ages, honest. He said it was private business to start with. I just did what I was told; I had to, he was my boss.'

Iris wasn't sure if this story would wash or not but she could believe all too readily how Spencer would have made use of Cliff's vulnerability. He would have flattered him, drawing him in until it was too late to back out.

'He said he thought of me as his son,' Cliff wailed. 'I was the boy he never had, he told me. That's how he treated me. I couldn't say no.'

Iris sighed deeply. What a cruel little manipulator Spencer had been. It wasn't unlike the way he behaved with his wife: demeaning her, bullying her, but keeping her tied to him. Letting her know how much he despised weakness.

'He was using you, Cliff, you know that, don't you?' Iris said gently but insistently. 'It wasn't your idea. He picked on you and he should never have done that. Don't throw your life away before it's barely begun.'

'I *have* no life!' shouted Cliff. 'It's all ruined! Everybody will hate me. I'd rather die!'

'Cliff, no.' Iris didn't know if she was imagining an increase in the background noise, signalling the arrival of reinforcements. The dying crashes of the disintegrating Boatman's were drowning out nearly everything. There must be little time left before Cliff realised what was happening. She couldn't let him do what Eddie had tried. She knew first-hand how much pain that had caused to all who loved him. 'You're still young and we all know what Mr Spencer was like. Believe me, we know. You won't be the only person he's damaged. Look at me, I'm telling you the truth.' She sensed him wavering at last, even as he continued to press the barrel against his chest. At some point he had thrown off his serge jacket and now wore just his white shirt, which glowed almost luminous in the bright orange light of the fire. 'Help us do our job. Was there anyone else in the pub?'

Cliff shook his head.

'There, you're thinking like a warden again,' Iris reassured him. 'You can put that gun down now. You don't need to hurt yourself or anyone else. You'll be safe, Cliff. That's your job, to keep people safe. So start by keeping yourself safe.'

'No . . .' But he was less decisive now.

'Put it down, Cliff. Put it here on the grass, then you'll be safe.' Iris was unbearably hot now, the scorching air from the fire blowing towards them, but she could not break concentration. Still she held his gaze. 'It can't hurt anyone if it's on the grass. Let it go, Cliff, set it down right here.' She patted the dry grass between them.

She could sense renewed activity now from somewhere behind her. All would be lost if the young man noticed anything. 'Now, Cliff.' She did her best not to let the urgency show. 'Just here. Then you'll be safe.' She nodded reassuringly and then, from nowhere, he dropped the gun and folded forward in on himself, holding his stomach with both arms. Iris immediately grabbed the weapon and flung it away in case he changed his mind. Behind her the fire brigade surged forward, too late to save the pub and Henry Spencer, but she ignored them, as she leant in to hug Cliff, weeping inconsolably now, like the young boy that in reality he still was.

CHAPTER THIRTY-FOUR

While the common room was full of all the nurses wanting to congratulate Iris the next day, Alice was first to the pile of post. The morning delivery had just arrived and, as usual, Gladys had stacked all the envelopes on the special shelf. Then she had gone to join the crowd.

It was a brisk, bright spring day and Alice decided to sit on the front steps to read her letter. For once she ripped it open, not waiting until she could find a paperknife. She was too impatient to see what it said. Some keen instinct told her that this might be the news she had waited for. Usually she dismissed superstition but for whatever reason, her instinct this time was right.

Joe's writing flowed across the single sheet.

I don't have time to write more than a short note but it doesn't matter. I can tell you all the news in person. I've got leave, Alice – at last, I'll be home for a few days. It will be in early May. I'll let you know as soon as I have the precise dates. I'll finish now because I want to write to Ma to tell her as well. See you soon. You have no idea how long I've wanted to say that. All my love.

Alice stared up at the sky where white clouds scudded along. A blackbird was singing nearby, guarding his patch. The step was uncomfortable and chilly but she didn't care. Joe was coming home.

Her heart was hammering. Finally she would be able to tell him in person all the things she'd wanted to when he'd had to leave so urgently. It was one thing to write them down; she imagined him reading and rereading her letter, as she did to all of his. But to tell him face to face, to assure him that she had waited for him, that she had never been more certain of anything in her life, that would be another matter entirely. Her arms ached to hold him, as she should have done that morning last June. How good it would be to fall into his arms and hear his beloved voice. . .

Then she came back to earth as the door opened behind her and Belinda stepped out, ready to begin her rounds on foot, as all of her current patients lived close by. Alice glanced up at her friend. Her face had acquired fine lines since the news of David's death, and her cheekbones were more prominent because she'd lost weight. Alice remembered what Belinda had been like when she'd first joined the nurses' home, full of joie de vivre and keen to go dancing with Canadian servicemen. That young woman had gone for good. However, she still swung her bag as she came down the steps and smiled at Alice.

'Aren't you having breakfast?'

'I'll go in in a minute,' Alice said, refolding the single sheet.

'See you later.' Belinda wasn't being rude, Alice knew; it was more that she wasn't inclined to make small talk any more.

Alice nodded, smiling but not trying to prolong the conversation. Belinda was coping as best she could. She herself could not fix her mind on the day to come – it was already racing ahead to when Joe would return. Somehow she had to rein in her dreams, to get through the following days. He was so close now, it was almost as if he was here with her already.

She stood up, giving herself a mental shake. Time to go back inside, to try to resume a normal routine, as if this were just a normal day. Yet deep inside she felt as if it was anything but. Joe was coming home. It was all that mattered.

Iris was overwhelmed with the outpouring of congratulations over breakfast. She hadn't said anything but word had got around. She was totally unused to being the centre of attention like this and didn't quite know which way to turn. Then Ruby worked her way through the other nurses to come and stand beside her, which steadied her.

'It wasn't just me,' Iris insisted to her colleagues. 'Kenny and Olive were there as well. They went into the grounds of the burning pub – they were terribly brave.'

Ruby nudged her gently. 'Yes, but they're trained for that, and anyway, Kenny said you did the really difficult bit, getting Cliff to put that gun down. Don't deny it, it's true. I wanted to thank you for that in particular. I couldn't have borne it if anything happened to Kenny.'

Iris gave a reluctant smile. 'Well, it didn't. You should have seen him trying to rescue Mr Spencer, lifting those big lumps of rubble. If ever I'm in an accident, I'd want Kenny to be the one to find me, I don't mind telling you.'

Ruby blushed with pleasure. 'He doesn't like to give up,' she said. 'If there had been a way to save him I'm sure he would have found it.'

Iris shook her head. 'But there wasn't. We were too late for that.'

For once Fiona had come to the common room at rush hour rather than taking her early breakfast upstairs in the office. She came forward now. 'We can't save everyone, as well we know,' she said forcefully. 'However, Iris, you clearly went to remarkable efforts to try. We're all proud of you. Are you sure you don't want to take the morning off? You'd be very welcome to, you know.'

Iris shook her head again, as Ruby jumped in. 'I'll do your rounds if you like. I'm free all day, I can step in.'

'No, I won't hear of it.' Iris was her businesslike self once more. 'I know very well that it's your day off and I wouldn't dream of stopping you enjoying that. You've been looking forward to it. Anyway, I don't want to take any extra time off. I'd like to do my rounds as usual – I enjoy them.'

'If you're sure.' Fiona grinned broadly. 'I have to say, Nurse Hawke, that I would have expected nothing less. The offer still stands, if you find that you're more tired than usual. I won't prevent you from going ahead with your regular morning, though. I know exactly what you mean; sometimes it's the best possible way of spending your time.' With that she took a plate of toast and departed.

The group began to break up, some nurses collecting their own breakfasts, others who had eaten already heading off to their work. Alice came in, having made sure the coast was clear. She was in no mood for an excited gaggle of friends. 'Well done, Iris,' she said quietly, now the fuss was over.

Iris looked her in the eye and nodded. She knew Alice understood. 'I only did what any of us would have done,' she said.

Gladys was polishing the banister running from the ground floor to the first before going home. It was a task she felt she never got around to often enough, as the scent of the polish made the whole hallway smell fresh and welcoming. She rubbed hard at the last section and stood back in satisfaction.

Now she could put away the rag and carefully hoarded tin of beeswax, before considering what to wear to the cinema later. Ron was taking her out to a film with Arthur Askey in it – he knew she liked the comedian. She could do with a bit of light entertainment after hearing what had happened to Iris, Kenny and Olive – or, what had been plaguing her imagination, what might so easily have happened. She wondered if the dockworkers had made a fuss of Kenny in the way the nurses had of Iris. If Ron had anything to do with it, she expected that they would have.

When the flap of the letterbox sounded, she was a little annoyed. The nurses rarely got anything in the late post and she had not factored in the extra few minutes needed to sort a new pile of envelopes. Looking around, she saw with relief that there was only one – in a handwriting she didn't recognise and it was for Iris. Perhaps someone outside the home had heard about last night and was sending more congratulations. Swiftly she put it onto the shelf and then made for the cleaning cupboard to put her things away.

Iris was surprised to see that she had some post. She occasionally heard from old friends or neighbours back in Devon but never very often, and she knew all their handwriting. This envelope was a mystery and she waited until she was in her bedroom to open it. She didn't hurry. It was still only early evening but she had already allowed herself the luxury of a warm bath for the second day running; last night she had been too tired after all the events to enjoy one properly. She had scrubbed her skin as hard as she could to try to get rid of the clinging smell of smoke, but tonight she had drawn the water to the regulation depth and indulged herself with a handful of bath salts.

The rosy fragrance had helped to banish what remained of the smoky traces and she'd wrapped her hair in a towel and her body in her old dressing gown. Now she felt a little more like normal. She was glad she had not given in to temptation to take time off today; doing her rounds had stopped her dwelling on what, in retrospect, had been a deeply frightening episode. However, Fiona had been right in one way – now she was as tired as she could ever remember being.

Opening her letter woke her up fully once more. For a moment she thought she must be imagining it. The most unlikely person had written to her. Then, a little voice whispered, had she not wondered if this might happen? It was not exactly a letter; it was more of a note.

Dr Leeson had heard about the events at the Boatman's. He would like to congratulate her in person. Of course he understood if she was busy, particularly after those events, but if she was not, would she do him the honour of meeting him, if only very briefly? He would be waiting at the end of Victory Walk, on the side road that led to the high street. It all sounded rather formal, but Iris could recognise the effort that had gone into overcoming his natural awkwardness and reticence. Well, she should know all about that.

She glanced at her watch, which she had left on her bedside table before taking her bath. Goodness, he would be there in ten minutes! Should she go? On the one hand, it was so tempting now that she was warm and cosy to simply throw back the covers and climb into bed, to sleep off the exertions of the past forty-eight hours.

And yet . . . and yet. She recalled all too vividly that sensation of brushing against his jacket, that look in his eyes. So she had not invented it. He thought there was something there too. She'd put aside any hopes of romance after Peter had been killed. Nobody could take his place and nobody had ever come close, not even remotely. That side of her life was over and done with, wasn't it? And yet . . .

Iris shook her hair free and vigorously towelled it dry, rubbing at the roots and then the ends until her arms ached. Then she teased her fingers through it to loosen any tangles, before picking up her hairbrush and turning to her mirror, which was set on her bedside table.

She spent hardly any time looking at herself. Usually it was a quick glance to make sure that she was tidy, and that was that. Now, for what felt like the first time in ages, she studied the image before her. Her cheeks were rosy with warmth from the bath and the effort of drying her hair, her eyes were bright, her hair now soft and wavy, shining in the lamplight. Perhaps she didn't look so bad.

Iris had become accustomed to being the eldest of the group, with the exception of her superiors, and not really part of the team. However, this morning, even though she'd been wary of all the attention, her colleagues had genuinely welcomed her success of the evening before. They'd made it clear that she was one of them now, if there had ever been any doubt about it. Almost without her realising it, she had changed. She'd enjoyed knowing that they valued her, that they were worried she might have been hurt. She was not a separate unit, shut away in her attic. She was one of the Victory Walk family.

Iris remembered her thoughts of last night, that nobody would miss her. Perhaps that was not true. The nurses would not only have missed her for her knowledge of the job, but for herself. They really cared. It was a revelation.

Shaken, Iris stood and began to pace across her room, her cosy slippers slapping against the floorboards. If she had altered so much, then maybe it was not out of the question that she could allow herself to feel again. She had kept her emotions on a tight leash because it had been the only way to deal with all the loss and heartache and after a while she had convinced herself that it was too late to do otherwise.

She didn't know if she dared to try once more. It would take courage. She hadn't thought that way before, when she was younger, starting out in her career, confident that she loved and was loved. That was before she'd learnt how heartbreakingly painful it was to lose it all. Now she knew what it was like to be in the depths of despair, of loneliness and she didn't want to go through that ever again.

All the same, the image of those eyes looking at her at the end of the journey home refused to fade.

There was something in them that told her he was sincere, that this was no joke – that she should gather her courage and take the risk. Life was there for the living and she was finally being given another chance.

She glanced at her watch again. Two minutes to go. Decision time. She threw off her old dressing gown, threw on the clothes she had set out for the morning, and raced down the stairs.

Once the colder evening air hit her, Iris wondered again about the wisdom of what she was doing, but she'd got this far and it would be ridiculous to bow out now. If he was waiting at the end of the walk, he would have seen her. To retreat would be to invite ridicule. Besides, she *wanted* to see him.

He was there, leaning against the bonnet of the big saloon. 'You came,' he said simply. 'I didn't know if you would. Forgive me . . . I didn't know how else to contact you.'

Iris paused a little way from him. 'I . . . that's all right.' She was suddenly tongue-tied.

He hesitated for a moment and then rushed on. 'I heard about your bravery. It was remarkable. You . . . you are a remarkable woman, Nurse Hawke. Iris. I hope you don't mind me saying.'

She was about to protest but then saw those eyes looking at her, those eyes that she had thought about ever since the end of the car journey. She hadn't mistaken it. She knew what that look meant. 'No, I

He nodded, taking in the meaning behind those

few short words. 'Then allow me . . .' He reached into the driver's seat and drew out a bunch of flowers. 'These are for you. To . . . commend your bravery. And as a token of my appreciation.' He stopped, as if he realised how formal he still sounded. 'I have to say, when I heard what you did, I understood . . . I understood that I would not have liked you to have been hurt, Iris. I . . . would have been very . . . distressed if anything had happened to you.'

Iris reached out and took the flowers. They were simple and unshowy, as she might have expected, plain white blossoms of some kind against dark green leaves, but the effort that must have gone into finding them spoke for itself. And she'd never been one for blowsy pink roses. 'They are lovely,' she said sincerely. She looked up at him again.

The daylight had nearly gone. Shadows were beginning to enfold them. 'I'm glad you liked them.' He reached out again and this time touched her arm, letting his hand rest there. 'Iris, may I ask you . . . would you consider . . . seeing me again? Maybe coming out for a drink or something?'

Iris took a breath. On the face of it, this was a simple question, but deep inside she knew it was anything but. Boldly she put her hand over his. 'Yes,' she said. 'That would be lovely too.'

'Thank you.' His face was almost unrecognisable from the taut, gaunt one he usually presented to the world and she realised he was not much older than she was. What years of hell he must have been through! Then he leant forward and kissed her cheek, very gently and swiftly, before standing back. 'I won't keep you any longer. Goodnight, Iris.'

'Goodnight,' she said, standing on the same spot as he drove off. She hugged the small bouquet close to her, the subtle floral scent rising from it in the darkening air as she was flooded with the realisation that she had taken a momentous step. There was no going back. She had done it.

CHAPTER THIRTY-FIVE

It had been the strangest week. Right at the end of April came the news that Mussolini was dead, hanged by partisans, and shortly afterwards the Germans surrendered in Italy. Ruby was beside herself; her brother-in-law had been over there for ages, having joined up with a group of other young men from West London, many of whom she knew, and to think of them all suddenly safe was overwhelming. 'It's like I can breathe out again and I didn't even know I was holding my breath,' she tried to explain.

Everyone who had doubted that the end was in sight, now began to hope that these really were the final days of the war. The whole nurses' home was on tenterhooks. They tried to carry on as normal but they were torn between anticipation and confusion. The weather joined in; it snowed, when only days before it had been a typical late spring. Surely it would all be over soon?

Then two days after Mussolini's death came the even more startling news that Hitler had committed suicide in his bunker. The end was surely coming any minute now. The wireless was permanently left on in the common room from breakfast until last thing at night, so that they would not miss the announcement when it came. Yet still they had to wait.

Alice was waiting for other news: confirmation from Joe when he was due to arrive. She had shared her agony with nobody else, as they could do nothing about it. If Edith had been there, that would have been different. On one occasion Stan Banham had visited Victory Walk to go over some committee minutes with Fiona, and Alice had taken the chance to ask him if he had heard anything. 'No, in fact I was going to ask you,' he said, and so they were both in the same boat.

Meanwhile, Alice worked every shift that she could and even some extras, volunteering for the weekend rounds so that she would have the maximum spare time when Joe eventually turned up. Mary raised her eyebrows at this and commented that Alice was getting a bit keen, but Alice did not allow herself to take the bait.

At last, he sent word that he would be back by 8 May, and Alice could properly prepare. She made sure her best clothes were washed and ironed and persuaded Lily to trim her hair. Lily, suspecting that something was up beyond the general festivities waiting to break out, offered a free choice of all her accumulated nail polishes and lipsticks, but Alice declined. Lily's taste ran to strong crimsons and cherry reds, not what she would choose at all. Besides, it didn't really matter. Joe had seen her in her best and at her worst; he wouldn't mind.

Gladys brought out her scraps bag and recruited anyone who had a spare five minutes to help her pick out any material in red, white or blue in order to make bunting. 'They're starting to sell it down the market, ready for the big day,' Ruby told her, but Gladys carried on anyway. 'It's better when you've made it yourself,' she insisted. 'Help me cut out some triangles, now you're here.'

On Sunday, two days before Joe was due, Alice set out to see to the patients who could not manage without a daily visit while some of the others went to church. Bridget made her solitary journey to mass, as she was the only Catholic left at the home, with no Edith or Ellen. Belinda, who often did the Sunday rounds, was glad of a chance of a lie-in. 'Then I'll go over to see Geraldine at the ambulance station, keep myself busy,' she said. 'I've done more than my share of bunting-sewing.'

The afternoon and evening dragged on with no change in the news. Mary lost patience with the Home Service when it announced a play by Anthony Trollope. 'How about some songs from the shows?' she offered. 'I can't listen to this, sorry.' Nobody disagreed, not even the few who liked such high-minded entertainment. Mary put back the lid of the piano and began to play the Carmen Miranda tunes that she'd now perfected, doing her best to take their minds off what must be happening among the world leaders and military chiefs. It was in their hands now.

* * *

Monday's rounds seemed to last for ever. Alice moved as if in a daze, cycling slowly from house to house, checking each patient carefully but struggling to bring all her attention to the work. Every cell in her body was primed for the moment when she would see Joe again, hear him speak, feel the touch of his hands. Every minute was now like torture. She couldn't show it, though. Somehow she made it to the end of the afternoon, the longest working day she could ever recall.

Approaching Victory Walk, it looked as if mayhem had broken out. A big dark car stood at the end of the pavement, with Union Jack flags attached to its roof. People were gathered on the front steps. 'You're back at last!' called Mary, whirling round while catching hold of Charles's arm. 'Look who's here. He's come to drive us into town, anyone who wants to come. It's official, the ceasefire starts tonight! It's really over!'

Lily had managed to get changed from her uniform, into her silkiest, slinkiest dress, and apply full make-up in what must have been record time. 'Come on, Alice! Get your glad rags on!'

Alice shook her head, laughing. 'I don't think so. But is it true? It's finally been announced?'

Charles grinned at her, all attempts at maintaining his solemn officer front now set aside. 'It really is, Alice. Take it from the horse's mouth. We did it. We've won. Now we can celebrate. So if you'd like to hop inside the car, I'll drive in to Piccadilly Circus and we can see what's what.'

Alice was tempted for a moment – this would go down in history. But she wanted to look her best for tomorrow. She'd need her beauty sleep and she knew what the younger nurses were like when they started celebrating – there'd be little chance of an early night.

'No, you go on,' she said. 'I've had a busy round. I'll join in tomorrow.'

Bridget and Belinda came through the front door. 'I'm dragging this one with me!' Bridget called, pulling on Belinda's arm. 'We've got to celebrate, even though we've lost our loved ones. They'd have done the same if things had been the other way round.'

Belinda looked a little strained but she was gamely doing her best to be happy. 'They would,' she agreed. 'We'll cheer twice as hard, since we're doing so on their behalf as well.'

Alice threw her a quick glance, to check that she was really sure, but Belinda held her head up, determined to be part of the festivities even though she would mourn her brother for every minute.

'Come on, then. I bet we won't be the only ones on the road.' Charles led the group of young women towards the car, opening the doors for them with a grand gesture. Alice smiled at them. He was such a gentleman; he'd make sure no harm came to anybody, and he could bask in their attention while he did so. He'd been working flat out since the war started; he deserved to let his hair down, as much as the rest of them.

Ruby and Gladys were pulling on their light jackets in the hall as Alice walked inside. 'We're going down the Duke's Arms,' Ruby explained. 'Ron and Kenny are meeting us there. Why don't you come? The girls from the gas-mask factory are bound to be there. You'll know heaps of people.'

Alice didn't doubt it but she shook her head. 'No, you go on. I'll see them another time.'

'Are you sure?' Ruby didn't like to leave anyone on their own at such a moment.

'Of course. I'm just a bit tired, that's all.' Alice waved them off, glad they had the prospect of the evening with their young men. She wouldn't get in their way. She felt she wouldn't be good company, with her mind elsewhere.

The big house felt unusually empty as she moved around, from the hall all the way up to her room, to the bathroom to freshen up, to her room again to change into something cooler, back down to the canteen for her evening meal. She thought she could hear floorboards creaking in Iris's room but there was no other sign that she was in. Alice decided she had probably chosen a quiet night reading. She didn't blame her. She'd probably do the same once she'd heard the news on the wireless.

Cook had stayed late to clear up, so that Gladys could go to meet Ron. She so rarely asked for any extra time off that Cook felt she couldn't begrudge her the request. 'You're the last, Nurse Lake,' she said, passing Alice a plate of Woolton pie. 'I've put some of this aside to keep on the cold shelf for tomorrow. Them young nurses took off without eating a thing. They'll regret it in the morning, gadding off like that.'

'Maybe they will,' Alice said amiably. It meant she got a bigger helping, at any rate. 'I'll wash this up after I've finished – you don't have to stay.'

Cook grunted in gratitude and collected her bag and coat, setting off into the fading twilight.

Alice ate her pie then went into the big kitchen to wash and dry up. She rarely ventured this far; it was Cook and Gladys's domain. Large pots and pans were stacked neatly on shelves, big boxes of vegetables arranged along the back wall. Everything was in its place. Alice made sure to put her few items away carefully and returned to the common room in time for the news on the hour. She sighed long and hard as the announcer described scenes in the streets: crowds thronging together to share the good news, the relief that after six years the war was about to end.

Perhaps if she went to stand on the front steps she would be able to hear the sound of people cheering. She'd give it a try, before heading up to her room and her latest book. It would be good to feel part of something bigger, the joy of belonging, even if part of her was reluctant to celebrate so wholeheartedly. There had been losses for everyone and although her immediate family had survived, there was poor Ellen, Belinda's brother David, Pauline's grandmother, Iris's fiancé. Not to mention the injuries Harry had suffered, the scars he would bear forever, and Lennie imprisoned who knew where. Along with the many patients who had died, or been bereaved, or injured, or frightened out of their wits day in, day out.

As she approached the big door, there was a knock on the other side. Alice took a sharp breath. Please don't let it be the police or a warden with bad news, she thought. Her heart squeezed. How cruel it would be if an accident had befallen one of their team at this eleventh hour. What if Charles's car . . .? No, it was pointless to imagine. She'd better get on with it and open up, facing whatever needed to be faced. Willing her hand to be steady, she turned the door handle.

It was a man in uniform, but not that of the police or the ARP. It was a naval uniform. Alice gasped. It couldn't be. Today was still the seventh.

'Hello, Alice,' said Joe. 'I couldn't wait. I've come a day early.'

CHAPTER THIRTY-SIX

The twilight had deepened and they walked with arms entwined around one another, safe in the knowledge that not many people would be able to see, and not really minding if they did. It was the eve of the war's end. Everyone had bigger things to care about.

Their feet led them along the pavement from Victory Walk along to the big park between the nurses' home and the ambulance station, its many victory garden vegetable beds now quiet for the night, its big trees in new leaf. It was strange to be here without keeping one ear alert for the air-raid siren. The air was heavy with a thunderstorm brewing, and yet it did not feel threatening. It seemed right, as if such a momentous occasion deserved the drama.

As they came to a halt near the trees, Alice turned and looked up at Joe. She searched his face for any indication that his earlier injuries had changed him, or if whatever sights and sounds he had witnessed since D-day had affected him in any way. But he just looked like Joe – her wonderful, beloved Joe, the best man in the world, the one who held her heart in his hands.

He laughed down at her. 'You're examining me like a nurse again, I can just tell.'

She shrugged and laughed back. 'It's habit. Anyway, I can look at you, can't I? I've waited long enough.'

'So have I.' He tilted her chin up to him and leant to kiss her, and she kissed him back as she had longed to do for the whole year in between their sudden parting. There was no reason to stop. Now they had all the time in the world. They had gone from famine to feast and it was the best feeling ever. She was here, with Joe, he was safe and they could be together. If he hadn't been holding her so tightly she could have almost fainted at the joy of it. The fact that her deepest longings had finally come true made her giddy.

Slowly he released her. 'Alice,' he said and hugged her to him, so that she could breathe in that unique smell of him, which she would have recognised anywhere. Joe, her Joe. He had come back to her at last, as he had always said he would, but now he was here she could admit to herself how badly she'd dreaded that he would not make it. She gasped at the idea and he kissed her again, to put everything right.

The birds had grown quiet now that dusk had turned to night and there was little light left. From far away came sounds of celebration, families and friends gathering, but Alice knew that she was with the most important person in the world. Tomorrow, she'd join in with the communal fun, enjoy the company of others, maybe manage to call her parents on their new telephone, but this evening was for Joe.

All her remaining doubts fell away, those lingering fears that he would change his mind or she'd misunderstood what he wanted from her when he'd asked her to wait for him. Now he was here in person, that was all revealed as silly anxiety, with no basis other than the sickening horror that she'd missed him when he was suddenly called back on duty. In the months of uncertainty that followed, the deepest instincts of her heart had been right. They were made to be together and finally that was going to happen.

They stood holding tightly to one another until the temperature dropped so low that it grew uncomfortable. 'Better get you back,' Joe breathed. 'I don't want to let you go but it's only for a few hours. Ma said to invite you all over for a party in Jeeves Street. They're planning it tonight. Bring the rest of the nurses, your other friends, whoever would like to come – and any contributions, come to think of it.'

'Really?' Alice was impressed but not surprised. Flo would be in her element, throwing together a huge celebration and wanting to include as many people as she could.

'Of course,' laughed Joe, 'and you know as well as I do that she'll be mortified if you don't turn up. Come for teatime, then she'll have had time to put out the flags and everything. Tell the rest of Victory Walk, once they're back from Piccadilly Circus or wherever they end up.'

'We'll dig out our Sunday best,' Alice promised,

mindful of her favourite good clothes hanging ready for Joe's return – and here she was, in a washed-out and mended old cotton frock, its original colour long faded, a mismatched button on one cap sleeve. As she had guessed, he hadn't cared.

'You'll look perfect whatever you wear,' he promised, and hugged her again to show he meant it. 'I might even dig out my civvies. It's been a long time since I wore those. They'll be stuffed at the back of the wardrobe behind Edith and Harry's things.'

'I don't suppose he'll be back?' asked Alice, more in hope than expectation.

'I wouldn't have thought so. He had leave at Christmas, didn't he? Not much chance he'll swing this, then, as even my baby brother with all his persuasive charms can't lessen the distance between his base up north and Dalston.' Joe chuckled. 'Though I dare say he'll have a go.'

'I expect he will.' They had reached the start of the Victory Walk pavement. Alice tipped her head up to Joe for one last kiss. This time when they told each other 'see you tomorrow', it would actually happen. She could sleep safely knowing that Joe was finally home.

Iris sat on her narrow bed and considered what she now knew about Dr Leeson. They had met up on Saturday and she'd chosen somewhere on the far edge of Islington so that nobody would see them. She wasn't sure how she would explain this meeting to any of her fellow nurses.

She had daringly asked for a small sherry in the very respectable lounge bar of a small pub. He had smiled as if he had seen that little glass on Dr Patcham's table, when he'd been so rude all those months ago. Now she understood that he had probably been unbearably pressed for time, on top of his natural diffidence.

There was less and less sign of that now. He had sipped on his pint of pale ale, and she had felt emboldened to mention that she knew something of his background. For a moment his face had clouded over, but then he gained the confidence to share the sorry details, and she could see as he spoke that it was a relief to talk about it, knowing his pain would not be ignored.

Iris had nodded. She understood. Taking a deep breath, she had dived in and recounted the tale of her own loss. So there it was, out in the open; they had both known the worst kind of bereavement. It had altered the tracks of their lives and there was no denying it.

He had listened without interrupting and then, once she had fallen silent, had reached out and taken her hand, where it rested by her sherry. 'Thank you,' he said simply. 'I understand.'

She looked into his eyes, those mesmeric eyes. 'I know,' she said. Silence fell between them, but of a comfortable sort. It was a dreadful thing to have in common but made it easier for them in some ways. Anybody who had not endured such a torment would not have been able to connect with that dark place that always lurked just below the surface. In the quiet hubbub of the bar, Iris had an idea of how the future just might be, and let her hand rest there, where she sensed it belonged.

Now she reached for her hairbrush and began to get ready for bed, wondering what tomorrow would bring. She was going to meet him again. Against all the regulations, he had telephoned her this evening, correctly assuming that many of her colleagues would be out celebrating and that nobody would mind. She had no desire to join in with whatever big parties might happen. She could look forward to more intense conversation, slowly letting the light back in to all those gloomy, shadowy places she had hidden away, begin to truly feel again. Part of her could not believe this was happening. But she was starting to see a different side to him now, and to understand all too readily why he too had hidden it away so thoroughly. That was more enticing than anything.

For the first time since packing her case, she brought out the treasured cream frock that had belonged to her mother. Carefully she hung it on the back of her door, so that the creases could drop out before the morning.

CHAPTER THIRTY-SEVEN

Gladys was already regretting that second glass of shandy she'd had the night before. It wasn't fair to blame Ron; she'd happily accepted, wanting to mark the occasion, the end of the everlasting war. Now she was paying the price. Breakfast was over and she was preparing whatever could be spared to take over to Flo's party later that day, and her head ached every time her knife hit the chopping board. She made herself drink another mug of water. It would wear off eventually, she supposed.

The kitchen door swung open and Ruby came in, a large shopping bag bursting with goods in her arms. 'Ooof, let me put this down.' She sighed in relief as she set it on the counter. 'Right, I think I got most things on your list. If it was in the market, I bought it. Lily's gone over to the victory garden to see if there's any early veg ready for picking as well.'

Gladys looked at her askance. 'Are you sure she'll know what's ripe?' she asked. She still didn't fully trust Lily to dirty her carefully manicured hands.

'Stop worrying, she'll be all right,' Ruby assured her, beginning to unload her shopping. 'Look, extra fish paste! They just got some in. Better still, I got dried lentils and can make some little rissoles. They won't taste too bad if I put Bisto in them.'

Gladys nodded. 'You recovered from last night, then?' she said. 'Must be going out in the fresh air. I could go back to bed for two pins.'

Ruby chuckled as she unpacked and put away more items from her bag. 'I feel on top of the world,' she said. 'I can't remember the last time I had such a good evening – I reckon it was because we didn't have to keep one ear alert for those blasted sirens. It was like being sixteen again – only I'm glad I'm not or I don't suppose I'd have been there with Kenny.' She giggled at the memory.

'What?' Gladys demanded, her headache making her unusually tetchy.

'Oh, nothing. Not really.' Ruby clasped her hands and swayed around a little. 'It's just that Kenny started asking me did I like dogs. I'm not sure what he was on about, but he didn't half sound soppy. It was almost like he was thinking about setting up home. Him, me and a little dog.'

'Blimey!' Gladys dropped her knife and then winced at the clatter. 'Didn't know he wanted a dog. You don't see many around any more, costs too much to feed them.'

Ruby laughed again. 'I didn't either. Turns out he does. Anyway, I said I quite liked them and I'd have to think about it. He'd had more than one pint by

389

then so perhaps he don't mean nothing by it.' She hastily changed the subject. 'Guess who I saw down Ridley Road?'

Gladys shrugged, not really in the mood for guessing games.

'Only Mrs Spencer. You know, whose horrible old man got killed in that fire?'

'Didn't realise you knew her.' Gladys began chopping her vegetables once more.

'Well, I don't, not really, but I'd met her with Iris, and she knew who I was. She made a point of stopping and saying hello.' Ruby had recalled Iris telling her about the poor woman's sickness and general sorry demeanour. 'She was like a different person, wanted me to pass on her regards to Iris. I can't wait to tell her. She had on this lovely shirtwaist dress, bright blue, it was, and when I said how it suited her she said she'd made it. Said her husband would have hated it but now he wasn't here to stop her, she was going to wear what she liked.'

'Quite right.' Gladys approved. 'I bet that'll make Kenny feel better too, knowing she's all right.'

'It will; he's had a lot on his mind,' Ruby acknowledged. 'He was worried about Cliff for ages. I said, "that boy made his own bed and must lie in it", but Kenny, he's more kindhearted than me. He was proper glad when they decided they wouldn't prosecute him or nothing. I think Mr Banham put in a good word, said he'd been manipulated by that Spencer and it wasn't really his fault.'

'But they won't let him be a warden again, surely?'

Gladys was all for forgiving people but this felt like a step too far.

'No, he's got to be with a close team so he can be supervised all the time. As he's been first-aid trained, he'll be transferred to volunteer ambulance duties, something like that.' Ruby sighed. 'Anyway, with the Boatman's destroyed and gone for good, maybe all that black market business will stop.'

Gladys harrumphed. 'More likely they'll start up somewhere else,' she prophesied. 'At least in the meantime Ron and Ken don't have to have eyes in the back of their heads with all the goods down the docks. Those missing cargoes have mysteriously stopped.'

'Long may it last.' Ruby began setting out what she needed for her rissoles. 'Budge up, Gladys. I got to get these done and then have time to get dolled up before the Prime Minister's speech this afternoon. You're coming to the party, aren't you? Your headache'll be better by then?'

Gladys pitched up her sleeves. 'Just you try and stop me.'

'Well, we haven't got any more tables.' Flo was stating a fact. 'I can't bring out what we don't have. We'll have to think of something else.'

Mattie harrumphed in frustration, knowing that what they had laid out so far in the street outside their front door would not be enough to accommodate all the guests.

'Could we use something else? Anything flat?'

'Alan, come away and play with Gillian,' Flo urged,

ushering the toddler inside, where he could follow his big sister around. 'Like what? Oh, maybe I have an idea. Stan! Stan!' She called through the doorway so that her voice would reach the kitchen where her husband was having an unexpected day off. Even more unusually he had had a proper night's sleep, with no ARP duties. She hated to disturb him, but needs must. If they were going to have a party then they would do it properly.

Stan Banham emerged into the light, rubbing his eyes. Even last night's thunder and lightning hadn't woken him. Now the pressure of wartime duty was suddenly removed, he felt as if he could sleep for a week, though that would not come close to replacing all the hours of rest he had lost over the past six years. 'Yes?' he said, adjusting his grey elastic braces. 'Can I help?'

Flo beamed at her husband, standing there in his shirtsleeves. 'The doors, Stan. Do you remember, we had those spare doors, when we thought we might build a chicken coop? What have we done with them?'

Mattie's head went up. 'Oh yes, the doors! They're in the back yard, covered in a tarpaulin. Behind the potato bins. We could prop them on something . . . I know, those small barrels I'm going to use as planters come the summer. Let's roll them out here.'

Stan frowned. 'You will do nothing of the kind, Mattie. That's just the sort of job your brother has come home for. I'll give him a hand.' He disappeared back inside.

'Well, then I'll find some spare tablecloths to cover

392

them,' Mattie said, 'or sheets – we might have run out of tablecloths. There's bound to be something.'

'Check the oven while you're in there,' called Flo, surveying the progress they had made so far. The bunting was up, the flags she'd saved from a carnival many years ago were draped over the window, there were piles of plates, platters and saucers at the ready and neighbours had promised to bring more. She had been up since dawn, chopping, boiling, frying and roasting whatever she could find, to turn into a variety of snacks for whoever might come. She rested her aching hands on her hips, absentmindedly registering that the edges of her old apron were even more frayed. The storm of the night had passed, and the day was set to be fine. All being well, the party would go with a bang.

Joe emerged with one small barrel and set it down where directed by Mattie, following with a pile of fabric in her arms. He hurried back to fetch the next one while she set about unfolding the material, shaking it to make sure there was no dust, assessing how much of it they might need. She was concentrating so hard that she didn't notice the approach of the young postman. She started up in surprise when she realised he was directly in front of her, handing her a letter. Automatically she thanked him and then, as she took in the envelope, her heart sank. Swiftly she glanced around. Her mother was counting cups and Joe and their father were inside, as were all the children. She needed a moment in private to deal with whatever the contents might bring.

It was from the Red Cross and it could be the news she'd been dreading since Dunkirk. Lennie's last letter had sounded so desperate beneath the surface that she had tried to prepare herself for the inevitable, but now that moment might be upon her she felt as vulnerable as ever. She had to do this alone. Abruptly she turned from the party preparations and ran inside the house, up the stairs and into her cluttered bedroom, where scattered children's toys and clothes lay pooling on the floor.

The sun was shining through the window and suddenly she couldn't bear it, so tugged the curtain half across the panes. She took a deep breath and bit hard on her lower lip to stop it trembling. There was no point in giving way now. There would be little chance for time shut away in private once the gathering got started. Best to get this over and done with.

Her hands shook a little as she ripped open the envelope and shook out the contents, scanning the sheet for details of his death. She hoped it had been peaceful, not painful, but didn't want to think about what it would really be like to die of starvation. The Lennie she had known had always been stocky, and it was too hard to imagine him skeletally thin.

She was trying so hard to banish that image that for a moment she misread the words that were staring up at her. Then she cried out, immediately pressing one hand to her mouth so as not to frighten the children. He was not dead! He was alive. Better yet, he was in England. Taking another deep breath, she forced herself to concentrate. He was gravely ill but now expected to survive, being cared for in hospital, somewhere near Southampton. She wasn't entirely sure where that was, but it didn't matter. She could visit, somehow. She could post him food, clothes, anything to help his recovery, and not fear that whatever she sent would be stolen by prison guards. He was safe, he was alive. It was too much to take in.

She thought she might be sick. She wanted to scream and also to laugh, to shout the news from the rooftops. She didn't know what to do. Lennie was alive, he was alive; he hadn't starved in a camp behind a barbed-wire fence. She'd seen those pictures, had tried not to look, but she'd seen enough. She'd been having nightmares about them for as long as she could remember and hadn't been able to tell anyone. Speaking would have made it come true.

She was reading the letter through once more when there came a knock at the door and Edith poked her head around it. 'You all right?' she asked quietly. 'Only I thought I heard . . .'

Mattie shook her head, which loosened her hastily assembled bun, pins spilling over the counterpane. 'He's alive, Edie,' she breathed, her eyes glistening. 'It's news of Lennie at last. He's going to be all right.' Then she could hold in her sobs no longer, the dissolving of many years of tension rocking her to her core, as Edith held her and rubbed her back. The country was celebrating a public victory but nowhere would there be more delight and relief than in this small, private bedroom.

*   *   *

'Ready?' Joe smiled at his mother.

'Almost.' Flo straightened her best apron, stiff with starch, tied over her favourite skirt, with its generous pleats. The family were gathered in the big kitchen, where the last few sandwiches had been cut and arranged under a damp tea towel to stop their edges curling. The guests would be arriving shortly but now, coming up to three o'clock, the family had clustered around the wireless, ready for the prime minister's speech.

'When can we start eating . . .' Gillian began, but her grandmother shushed her.

'Not now, we're going to listen to Mr Churchill,' Flo said, bending down to hug her.

Stan fiddled with the volume so that they could all hear it and stood back, taking in the opening fanfare and then the speech that followed. 'We may allow ourselves a brief period of rejoicing . . .' said the instantly recognisable voice, as Edie muttered, 'I should think so too.' Little Teresa lurched against her, having recently worked out how to stand up on her own, but not quite how to walk.

Edie glanced at Mattie and could tell she was not really taking in the words. Not that it mattered. They would hear them again and again on news broadcasts for the rest of the day and beyond.

Once it was over, the final frantic preparations were made, bottles of beer brought from the cold shelf, cordials mixed, the kettle boiled afresh, and then they all poured out into the street, ready to welcome the guests. Jeeves Street bore its scars proudly, all the terraced houses still standing, but pockmarked by flying debris, some windows boarded up, many tiles missing, and the road and pavement uneven from countless blasts. Flo nodded in acknowledgement. This was her house, her haven, and the Nazis had not destroyed it, despite their best efforts.

A group of the nurses were first to arrive, Alice immediately going to Joe's side, to receive a hug before setting down a big cheese flan. 'We pooled our egg ration and Cook made it this morning,' she explained.

Gladys had brought a tin of biscuits that she and Ruby had decorated themselves, as well as the rissoles, while Mary had a spicy gingerbread loaf to add to the table. 'Charles is going to join us later,' she said. 'He's got to work for a bit, seeing as he had a few hours off yesterday to take some of us lucky ones into town. It was a hoot, we had the best time! Sorry you missed it, Alice.'

Alice smiled back. 'I think I had a better time,' she said softly, catching Joe's eye.

Mary was no longer listening, instead waving at the new arrivals from the docks. Ron and Kenny had come straight from work, with no time to dress up in their best, but nobody cared. Kenny was still the man of the moment after his dramatic bravery on the night of the fire, having to go through it all again for Joe's benefit. Ron took a moment to observe Gladys handing around a tray of sandwiches, even if it wasn't her party to host. He knew she could not pass up the chance to help out, no matter what the circumstances.

Alice was hearing all about Lennie's miraculous

survival and nodded eagerly as Mattie explained as much as she knew. 'He's near Southampton,' she told Alice, Edie nodding encouragingly at her shoulder, while eating a fish-paste bridge roll. 'I want to send him a new picture of Gillian and Alan. I bought a proper frame but I don't want it to break. It should be better if it's only got to go a short distance though. I'll wrap it up in lots of layers of cardboard.'

'Southampton – well, that's very near Dermot,' Alice said, almost laughing because she'd never been so free to divulge his location before.

'Maybe he could take it back, if he's up this way again,' Edith suggested, catching her friend's meaning. 'Is he likely to be, Alice, do you know?'

'Hmm, not sure. But I can tell you an even quicker way,' Alice said, aware that she was about to drop a bombshell. 'When I was out this morning buying the newspaper, I bumped into Janet. She's going down to visit him next weekend. I'm sure she'd be happy to take the picture.'

For a moment Mattie didn't realise what Alice had just revealed. It took Lily, who'd overheard the conversation, to get the full story. 'I'm sorry, did you just say that Janet is going to visit Dermot? Janet? As in Miss Phipps? What's going on? How long have you known about this, Alice? Are you sure?'

Alice began to laugh, while Edith muttered that she didn't think the teacher was going all that way just to discuss the school hygiene lessons.

'But Janet . . . well, she . . .' Lily didn't know what to say without sounding rude.

'She's nothing much to look at, you mean,' said Edith, pinpointing what Lily was thinking but reluctant to spell out.

'I—I . . . well, yes. I'd have thought that he'd want someone drop-dead gorgeous and glamorous, what with his film-star looks,' Lily stuttered, her entire world-view being stood on its head.

Alice shrugged. 'I think that's the attraction. Every woman he meets throws herself at his feet. Janet's the only one who's never been interested like that. Also, she can drink him under the table when it comes to whisky. He's never come across anyone like her, and she gives him a run for his money in every subject under the sun.' Alice raised her eyebrows. 'Takes all sorts – and they both seem really happy. So you can make the most of it, Mattie, as Janet's so relieved she doesn't have to keep it a secret any longer.'

'Blimey.' Lily was for once at a loss for words.

Alice looked across the gathering and rested her eyes on Joe, as he lifted a bottle of beer to his lips. She still had to pinch herself that he was here, in the flesh, not a dream. He wore an old green shirt that she recognised as Harry's, the sleeves rolled up, his brown forearms catching the spring sunshine. Whatever happened next she would not be far from his side. Then she looked down as a speeding blur hurtled past her, followed by another: Alan and one of the neighbours' children chasing each other in between the grown-ups.

'Don't worry,' said Gillian grandly, striding after them. 'I'll tell them to stop and then give them some sandwiches to keep them quiet.' She disappeared in their wake, through the crowd and into the house.

'Well, look at that.' Stan was heading that way as well, to replace the two empty bottles of beer he had in his hands. 'Gillian's got us all organised.'

'She has. She told me I ought to go in and tidy myself up,' Mattie laughed. 'There's no doubt who's in charge around here. She'll be prime minister one day, the way she's going.'

Stan laughed easily. 'I don't know about that. A woman prime minister! We won't see such a thing in my lifetime, and I don't expect in yours either, Mattie.'

Alice looked up at him with a quizzical expression. 'I wouldn't be so sure, Mr Banham. The world's changing fast. Look at all the things women have done in the war that we were told we could never even try before. The sky's the limit.'

Stan dipped his head in acknowledgement. 'We'll have to wait and see. Anyway, I'd vote for her.' He went on his way to fetch the beer.

On the other side of the front door, Mary was leaning against the brickwork, while Ruby watched Kenny basking in the attention and congratulations. 'He did well, didn't he,' Mary said. 'You must be so relieved about the war ending, Ruby. He won't have to do that any more.'

Ruby shuddered. 'You can say that again. When I imagine what it must have been like, and how he hates closed-in spaces . . . doesn't bear thinking about.'

'Then don't,' said Mary firmly. Then she turned to face her friend. 'I have to admit it, Ruby, I was wrong

400

and you were right about Iris. I know she's got her funny ways but boy, she must have nerves of steel. I'm sorry she's not here to apologise to. She's not working, is she? I thought Fiona and Gwen said they'd cover the rounds for once?'

Ruby shifted her stance a little. She knew what Iris was doing but it wasn't her news to tell. She'd been completely taken aback when her colleague confessed she was meeting the anaesthetist, and not for work reasons. Then again, Iris was old enough to know what she was doing. If this was her path to happiness, so be it. Ruby was glad she herself had such an uncomplicated boyfriend, who was now a hero too. 'I don't think so,' she said. 'She probably didn't want to face the crowds, you know what she's like.'

'Oh, all right.' Mary wasn't going to make a point of it. 'I say, Ruby, you'll be around in August, won't you? You're not rushing off anywhere, are you, not being whisked away by Kenny or anything like that?'

Ruby stared at her. 'Don't be daft, Mary. I'll be working, of course. People won't stop getting sick just 'cos the war is over.'

Mary nodded. 'Well, make sure you don't. Charles and I will be setting the date as soon as we can get our parents to agree when's best for them and we want all our friends at the wedding. You'll come, won't you?'

Ruby gasped. 'Really? Are you certain? Of course I'd love to come, you've waited so long for him. But your families . . . won't they expect your friends to be posh? Won't they mind if we're not?'

Mary tsked loudly. 'No, they won't. They'd jolly well better not. That's not why we want you all at our wedding. It's because we've been through everything together – that's what counts. Doesn't matter what you sound like, where you come from, or anything like that. We've stuck together regardless of what the war threw at us, haven't we? Heavens, I'll even ask Iris, if we can winkle her out. She's one of us now, after all.'

'She is, isn't she?' said Ruby happily, glad that Mary had finally seen the light. And now she'd have a few months to plan a new frock. They could maybe all go to the market together.

A stirring in the crowd at the far end of the street turned out to be the most unexpected arrival of Fiona and Gwen, doing the unthinkable and leaving Victory Walk unsupervised. 'We couldn't resist the invitation after all!' cried Fiona, dressed in a bright poppy-red frock that none of them knew she possessed. It should have clashed with her auburn hair but somehow it didn't, and it matched her infectious energy to a tee. 'Come along, then! I can hear music on the wireless. Who's for a conga? If ever there's a time for dancing, then it's today.'

'Blimey!' exclaimed Ruby, her jaw dropping open. It was almost more than she could take in – the two embodiments of propriety setting aside their responsibilities and preparing to kick up their heels.

'Well, come on then.' Mary grabbed her before she could object. And there was Lily, coming from the other side of the street, and Edie, protesting but laughing, even Alice, and her young man, and Gladys, forgetting she had the remnants of a hangover, dragging Ron to join in as well. Bringing up the end of the line were Belinda and Bridget, managing to smile despite everything.

'You'd better step in and take your place,' Ruby laughed as the serpent of dancers swept past Kenny. She swung out of line so that he could fit in behind her and catch her around the waist.

'Don't mind if I do,' he laughed in her ear. 'You and me fit well together, don't we, Ruby? You, me and maybe a little dog . . . Do you take my meaning? What do you say?'

'You pick your moments, Kenny!'

'Well, think about it,' he breathed, and then someone turned the music up and their words were lost to the air.

Towards dusk, Stan and Joe, having had a few bottles of beer each, decided that it would be a good idea to have a speech and then sing the national anthem. Gladys was ushered to the front, as she had by far the best voice, to lead the singing.

Alice watched Joe with loving amusement, how he politely deferred to Stan, who was so widely respected it almost went without saying. She raised her glass of shandy to toast the king, and Edith at her side did the same, though she was drinking lemonade.

'Remember when we first came to Dalston?' she began. 'That hot day in June before the war had even started, lugging those big cases? Sometimes I wonder how we ever did it.'

'Then we had to get them all the way up the stairs to the attic floor at Victory Walk. Gladys let us in and she would hardly say boo to a goose.' Edith chuckled. 'Look at her now.'

'And then you meeting Harry like that.'

Edith laughed more loudly. 'He was wearing that green shirt! Joe's borrowed it because all of his needed washing; they'd gone musty while he was away so long. I reckon he looks all right in it but Harry looked better.' She sighed, and Alice thought of what the younger Banham brother had been like before his injuries, at ease with his good looks, accepting attention as his due.

'Oh, I don't know, I think it suits Joe very well.'

'Yes, but you would say that.' Edith grinned up at her much taller friend. 'Do you know what your plans are yet, Al? Joe is going to be part of them whatever happens, isn't he?'

'He is,' Alice answered at once. 'It's too soon to say, really, but he thinks they'll want to keep him on in the navy, to develop what he's doing now – even if the war's over, it's still hush-hush so he can't say exactly what it is. At least it seems as if he'll be based just north of London so that I can stay put and see him often. What about you?'

Edith shrugged. 'I suppose Harry carries on as he is for the moment, but with more leave, and quicker transport to and fro. Imagine, a train running on schedule! Then we'll want to find somewhere of our own to live – but near to Flo and Stan too. That might take some time, what with all the houses being bombed.'

'Of course.' Alice turned around to glance at the full street, the laden tables, the milling crowd of neighbours, nurses, friends, and at the heart of it all, the various Banhams, still passing around food and drink. There was a good reason why Edith would not want to be too far away from here.

Suddenly she found there was a lump in her throat. 'We did all right, didn't we?' she whispered. 'We couldn't have guessed what we were in for. If we had, we might have turned tail and run back where we'd come from.'

'No we wouldn't,' said Edith like a shot. 'We'd have done exactly what we ended up doing. Nursing the patients as well as we could. No doubt about it.' She slipped her arm through Alice's and pulled her closer. 'That's what we trained to do. Like you say, we did all right.'

Alice smiled at her and then at the crowd, rejoicing that the war was over at last. 'We did, didn't we?' she said.

If you enjoyed *The District Nurses Make a Wish* by Annie Groves, turn the page to discover some of her other wonderful titles.

Why not dive into **more** of Annie Groves' engrossing stories?

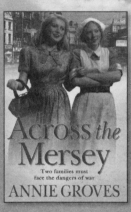

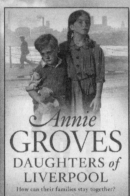

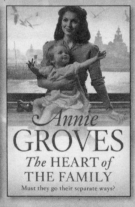

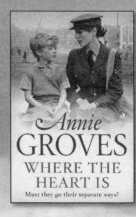

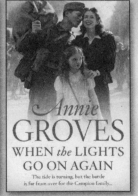

'**Heartwrenching** and **uplifting**
in equal measure'

Take a Break